sweet collide

AVA HARRISON

Sweet Collide
Cover Design: Anna Silka
Editor: Robin Covington, Editing4Indies
Content Editor: Readers Together
Sensitivity Editor: @books_jill_reads
Proofreader: Hawkeyes Proofing

author note

This book deals with sensitive mental health issues that were inspired by personal experiences. A sensitivity reader was used to be sure these issues were handled with care, but please be reminded that this is a work of fiction and is in no way meant to inform the treatment/care of mental health issues in reality.

For a full list of triggers, please head to https://shor.by/SWTriggers

"That which does not kill us makes us stronger."
—Friedrich Nietzsche

sweet
collide

chapter one

Cassidy
Twelve Years Old…

FAIRYTALES ARE FOR SUCKERS.

I used to live for the happily ever afters. Dreamed about what my perfect life would be like.

Now I know it's all bullshit.

A twelve-year-old isn't supposed to know these things. Isn't supposed to be so jaded. But I'm not your typical twelve-year-old who gets to daydream and wish upon a star. Nope. Not this girl. Life has it out for me. It's prepared to kick a girl while she's down. I can see another gut punch coming from a mile away.

I can feel it in the air. The thick scent of doom. As our beat-up car rolls to a stop, life as I know it is about to change. And by the looks of it—not for the better.

Peering out the window from the backseat, I stare at the small trailer we've pulled up to. It's old. Almost as fossilized as the tooth Dad lost in a parking lot bar fight, wedged so deep into the hood of his car, a pair of pliers couldn't yank it out. Stripes of paint peel away from the siding. What was once white has now rusted over.

Corroded. Water-stained.

The roof is probably saving its collapse for the moment I step foot in the place. That's life for me. One big punishment, occasionally punctuated by an odd serving of oatmeal or buttered toast.

I smooth out a hole in the backseat bench, fussing over loose threads, doing everything I can to avoid leaving this car. My mind shifts through a series of inconsequential thoughts.

Who was the last owner?

Is it abandoned?

And if so, for how many years?

Probably since the last world war.

It definitely looks like a casualty of one. I sigh, blowing a strand of hair out of my eyes.

The trailer sits on a snatch of grass, overgrown with weeds that scale up the sides like something out of a horror movie. It's scary.

We sit here for so long that I convince myself that Dad's thinking the same thing as me and we'll ditch this place soon. But that hope quickly vanishes.

Reality is where dreams go to die.

Dad turns off the engine and steps out of the car. I watch as he walks toward my side. A part of me wonders if he's coming for me. If he'll open the back door and try to convince me it isn't so bad.

He walks past me to the trunk. I knew it was wishful thinking. My dad barely acknowledges my existence.

My heart hammers, but I make no move to get out. He must realize I have no plans to exit because he storms to my window. His jaw clenches so tight it might snap.

"Come on." He stomps his foot on the paved sidewalk, acting like more of a child than I am. "I don't have all day."

Normally, I wouldn't want to piss him off. An angry Dad is a dangerous Dad. But right now, his impatience is the least of my problems. My lack of response must tip him off to the fact.

He yanks the car door open, glaring down at me. A stream of cold air blasts past him and smacks me right in the face. Goosebumps pebble over my arms.

I should get out. I should face my future head-on, but the uncertainty of what awaits me in this new dump I'm supposed to call home has me glued to my seat.

If I sit here a little longer, I can pretend this isn't happening. Maybe Dad will grow a conscience. Maybe he'll see how unfair this is and have mercy on me.

And maybe I'll win the lottery and move to Maui.

It's useless to hope. I know this. I've known it all my life. And still, I clutch my worn-down pink bag tight to my chest and hope.

Dad said I couldn't bring anything. That we didn't have room. Judging by the speck of a trailer, I can see why I had to leave my things.

I glance back down at my bag and force a smile, trying for positivity, but it's short-lived.

This is all you have left in the world, Pippa.

That fact stings worse than the cold bite of air.

He slams a palm on the car frame, eliciting a flinch. "Get out."

Dad must have more pressing issues than me and my turmoil. He always does. Everybody does.

Is it booze? Drugs? Probably gambling. It could be any of them—and more than likely all three. I imagine the time and attention he gives *those* three rival what a real parent would give their child. Not that I would know.

What I *do* know is we're in this shithole thanks to these vices. It's tempting to find some of my own. Anything to escape this hell seems good about now.

My heart rattles in my chest as I step out of the car on shaky legs. The door slamming shut behind me sends a shiver sprinting down my spine.

Dad pinches my crusty sleeve, almost disintegrating it. "Why'd I give you money for a new coat if you don't even wear it?"

I turn in time to catch his vicious snarl. He scrapes his gaze up and down my practically see-through frame, sneering as though I'm dirt stuck to the bottom of his shoes.

I *am* wearing a coat. Just not a new one.

Turns out, Dad forgot we had no groceries. So, instead of warmth, I chose to eat.

I don't say any of that because it would do no good. He'd grumble something, likely yell some nonsense excuse, and then stomp off, leaving me to wonder if I made a mistake

It's always my fault.

I glance down at the white-striped, navy jacket. The coat has seen better days. Ripped and tattered, it's practically useless. But the truth is, that's not why I shake.

I'm scared.

I hate change.

And this is more than change. My whole life is about to be uprooted.

Nothing will ever be the same again.

I swallow down the lump in my throat and rub at my chest. I won't be able to survive unless I fortify my walls. A skill I mastered at the tender age of ten, when everything went to shit, Dad lost his job, and I was forced to grow up.

This is your life, Pippa. You have no choice but to survive.

I find a new sense of purpose and stride up the path that leads to the weathered metal door. As soon as I'm in front of it, hand lifted to turn the knob, the squeak of rusty hinges sends me jumping backward. My spine goes ramrod straight as it swings open.

An older woman glowers down at me. Deep lines pepper her forehead, short gray hair sprouting from her scalp.

"Pippa," my dad barks. "Get back here."

The stranger narrows her eyes at me, running a hand down her pinstriped pants, her nose turned up. I blink several times until one bushy eyebrow lifts, and I realize my dad ordered me back to him.

Turning around, I try to navigate the rickety steps with tears welling in my eyes. I stand at the bottom, silently waiting for my father to approach. The muscles in my back tense as he strides past without a word, making his way toward the nasty woman.

"It's about time you got here." She motions him in, turns without waiting, and stalks farther into the trailer. "We have some things to go over."

I follow behind, giving my dad some space. Crowding him only makes him angrier. The two of them start talking about things I don't understand. I lose interest very fast. It doesn't matter. It doesn't pertain to me. Even if it did, I wouldn't be allowed a say, anyway. I'm used to being invisible and easily dismissed. It comes naturally.

I take a step deeper into the small trailer, deciding I might as well look around. It's much smaller than the last place we lived, which is oddly comforting. Dad might act like he'll run the place, but I'm the one who will have to clean and care for this space. Small is a blessing.

Every inch of the trailer can be viewed from my spot by the door. Chunks of wood peek out of holes in the carpet. Dents pepper the walls, along with mysterious stains. Could be worse.

It's a roof.

And walls.

That's a plus.

In my nightmares, I envisioned this place. The reality is much better than the fears that plagued me before I arrived.

I catch bits and pieces of words the woman barks out.

Rent.

Utilities.

Maybe I should be at this meeting. These are all things Dad forgets to do when he's drinking. I've never had the luxury of being a kid. My father is an alcoholic, barely around, leaving me alone to raise myself. When he's not working, which is always seeing as he gets fired more often than he changes his clothes, he's drunk.

And Mom…

She's dead.

What does this mean for me? If we want to eat, I have to buy it. It also means that it's my responsibility to cook the food. There will be no dinner if I don't. If I want a clean space, free of beer cans and booze bottles, I pick it up. If I want to keep the roof over my head, I ensure the bills are paid.

If this woman wants the rent on time, she'd be better off telling me where to drop off the check, because my dad might appear sober right now, but this is temporary. By tonight, he'll be passed out on the couch, not even realizing where we are.

Glancing at the woman, I know it would be pointless to insert myself. She wouldn't listen to a thing I say. She's bad-tempered and dismissive.

"Dad, can I look around?" I ask, wanting to get away. To explore my new living arrangement.

That's what this is.

It's not a home. It's temporary.

One day, I'll be old enough to escape. To have my own place. Somewhere I'll feel safe. When that day comes, I won't walk away.

I'll run.

Dad gives me a nod, and I don't wait for any more words before rushing off.

I have no desire to hear anything else that woman has to say. It's clear she owns this trailer park. She's only said it at least ten times in the last two minutes. Now she's rambling on about rules. The lady should save her breath.

He'll break them, anyway.

Seems pointless to waste her breath when she'll need to explain them another forty times before we're on to the next temporary situation.

Once, a few years back, before everything went bad and Dad lost his steady job, we had a home. A real one.

Now, I'm happy to not be living in Dad's car.

That was our situation right after we got evicted. Then he started gambling and had a short run of luck, which allowed us to hop around to places that at least had beds and heat.

The farther I move into the trailer, the colder and draftier it gets.

It's not hard to figure out why. The windows have broken seals, which explains the chill. I'll have to forge a note from Dad to that woman in the next week to figure something out about the window situation. We're renting. Surely, that's something she must do.

My head tilts as I take in the living space. It's a tiny area, large enough for the single couch facing the tiny, gloomy yard. The taupe material is worn and barren, even from the back. As if someone spent a lot of time here, gazing out into the glum world beyond the wall of windows.

How depressing.

There isn't much going on in here. We could probably fit a TV stand and maybe a recliner. It'll be tight, but possible.

I take several steps toward the filmy window to check out the view through the milky white residue built up on the glass. Some trees and a patch of grass. That's it.

Beggars can't be choosers.

Some of my reservations fade as I continue my tour.

Just a few steps down a narrow hall is a door. A door that's hopefully the key to my privacy. Somewhere that I can make my own. Somewhere I can attempt to make my safe space.

I throw it open and know instantly that I was correct. There's a tiny twin bed pushed up against the singular window that provides a sliver of light to stream in.

It's the same sad view from the living room.

It's more like a prison than a safe space. The dash of hope is gone. Suddenly, I feel claustrophobic. Like the walls are closing in around me.

Before I can stop myself, I run from the room, rushing toward the door to freedom. When I make it down the steps, the breath bursts from my chest. Cold air hits my face, but it's not enough. I need to get far away from here. Away from my dad. Away from that awful woman and her grimy trailer.

I need to get away from my life.

I look from left to right, trying to figure out where I can go.

My gaze locks on a trailer a few feet away, and an elderly woman catches my sight. She's at least in her eighties with sparse white hair and a wrinkled face. She lifts her hand and waves, a large inviting smile welcoming me. At least there seems to be one nice neighbor. That can come in handy in the future.

I raise my own hand and wave back. Normally I'd say hi, but right now, I'm too emotional to talk to her.

Instead, I take off in the opposite direction.

Picking up my pace, I head toward the trees I saw from the window. That'll be the sole reason our utilities will be astronomical. The cold air will have our heater working overtime, and still, I'll likely freeze at night, considering my one and only blanket is also threadbare and pathetic.

My feet carry me without a destination. My mind doesn't care where I go. A dense path materializes beyond the trees. Maybe it will pull me into an alternate world. One with centaurs, and cozy homes with windows that work, and a bed as soft as clouds.

I follow the path, daring to explore. Hoping that maybe I'll find some semblance of solitude from a world determined to tear me down.

My feet stop. I pitch forward. My hands slap my knees as I suck in deep breaths, desperately trying to stave off the attack that threatens to pull me under.

Inhale.

Exhale.

I continue to focus on my breaths, pulling in a lungful of air until my heartbeat slows and the panic slowly retreats. A trick I learned from the social worker at school.

I've been standing here for several minutes, giving myself time, when the sound of crinkling leaves alerts me that I'm not alone.

"Are you lost, kid?"

I twist at the throaty voice. When my eyes land on its owner, I freeze. The boy standing in front of me is tall. Way taller than me. I inspect the crest on the left side of the blazer he's wearing.

I have no idea what it's for. Maybe a school logo. Maybe not. It looks like the kind of logo you'd see on a fancy school uniform, but that makes no sense since he's here. Unless he's visiting someone.

I tilt my head as I take in the design, determined to figure this out. It looks a bit like a triangle, but not one I recognize. It's silver, standing out starkly against the solid black of the rest of the jacket.

Realizing I'm not going to figure this out, I crane my neck, looking up into his face.

His features are hard to make out because the trees are blocking what little sun shines through the clouds overhead. He's cloaked in shadows, and it's a bit disconcerting.

I take a step back, and he takes a step forward into a space where more light filters through the trees. My breath hitches, and my mouth drops open.

He looks like a fallen angel. Dark and ominous. With chocolate-brown hair and piercing blue eyes. Eyes I can't turn away from. They have me captive. His irises remind me of the water in the Pacific Ocean I once saw on a TV show. The edges, ringed in black like a violent storm. Looking at them feels like looking into a dark sky and waiting for lightning to flash.

"Hey, kid," he says. "You alright?"

I shake my head and furrow my brows. Is he talking to me?

"Who are you calling a kid?" I straighten my shoulders, trying to appear taller as I glower up at him. I'm practically a teen, or at least I will be in six months. He looks like he's one, too, so who is he to talk? It's not like he's an adult. Four, maybe five years older. Max.

He smirks down at me, and my stomach tumbles. I hate that feeling. The only time I've ever experienced that sensation was swinging on the swings at the park close to our last place. I'd lean back as I swung toward the sky, trying to contain the giggle that threatened to burst from me. I felt alive. Free.

This stranger doesn't get to make me feel that way.

"Pippa," I say, crossing my arms over my chest.

His eyes narrow as he looks down at me. "What?"

"It's Pippa." I move my hands to my hips. "Not kid. And I'm almost thirteen if you must know," I fire back.

I start to turn and walk away when the guy speaks again.

"You looked like you were about to lose it. You good?"

I blink several times, not sure why I'm feeling warm all over and annoyed at the same time. "I'm fine," I scoff, turning my back on him.

"Whatever you say, Pip."

Looking over my shoulder, I level him with a glare. "As I said before, it's Pippa. My name is Pippa. But since you clearly…"

"I like Pip. It suits you." He shrugs. "Pippa sounds pretentious."

I roll my eyes. "Big word."

"Is it?" He grins. "What can I say? I guess my education is working."

My face screws up. "Whatever."

I turn on my heels, ready to run back to my trailer, and bump into a hard wall.

Not a hard wall. Another boy.

This one gives off a bad vibe that has me on edge immediately. I'm met with tapered eyes and a scowl. Trouble with a capital "T" if I've ever seen it.

"Watch it, you little shit." His arms dart out, and before I know what's happening, I'm pushed.

Things escalate quickly after that.

I fall backward, my eyes close, and I brace for impact. It doesn't happen. Instead, large arms wrap around me, holding me in place.

"What the fuck, Ace?" the lesser of the two evils grits through his teeth, not looking down at me as he barks at the new guy.

He lifts me up, holding me in place until I'm steady on my feet. When he's sure I'm okay, he moves away from me and steps into the asshole who tried to push me down.

"What the hell do you care, Slate? She was in my way. I was simply removing her from my path."

Slate.

The name suits him.

Slate is eye to eye with the jerk, who doesn't move an inch. "You don't touch her. You don't fucking look at her." He straightens his back, effectively making himself taller than the douche. "Pip is off limits."

I don't have to see his eyes to know they've darkened to deep pools. A hurricane building as he levels the shorter guy with a look that promises violence.

The guy sneers, baring his teeth. "Pip? You've got to be kidding me," he jeers, looking toward me. "Fitting. Fucking pipsqueak."

"Cut the shit."

"Or what?" Ace puffs out his chest, trying to look tough, but failing in comparison to the dark-haired god.

"Or I'll kick your ass. It's as simple as that."

"Careful," Asshat tsks. "Start a fight again, and the cops will come. Doubt your fancy school will keep you on, let alone let you skate…"

The threat hangs in the air. I look back and forth between the two, wondering what that's all about. Finally, Slate steps forward, anyway. The space between the two is almost gone, and the bully's back hits the tree.

"If you ever so much as touch her, I don't care what anyone says, I'll kick your fucking ass. Pippa is off limits." Slate's hand wraps around the guy's throat, strangling him. "She's under my protection. You hear me?"

Ace's face begins to turn blue, and fear courses through me. I can't make out the words he says, but it's obvious Slate does, because he removes his hand, stepping away. The kid doesn't waste time. He dashes off.

What a coward.

I have no idea what that was all about, but I do know that Slate just gave me a gift.

A place to feel safe.

And that place is him.

chapter two

Cassidy

Eight months later...

W HERE IS HE?
    I knocked multiple times on his trailer door, but no-
body answered. I even peeked into the window to check for him.
Nothing. No matter where I search, I can't find Slate, and that
shouldn't have me panicking like it does.

In the past eight months, he's made life bearable.

He's treated me like I was his little sister. Acted like he was
my protector.

He made this awful place feel like home.

I slouch onto the worn couch, dust flying into the air and
circling me. Huffing, I make a mental note to vacuum this room
and pay special attention to this area. I blow out air to move the
particles away. My gaze skates across the room and lands on the
window.

It's a nasty day out.

The sky is a dark shade of gray, with clouds forming in the

shape of black pillows. I'm just waiting for the clouds to open and the rain to drench the earth. The only downside to that is I'll be stuck inside, sitting among the dirt.

Something moves in the distance, but it's probably just a branch swaying with the wind. When it moves again, I narrow my eyes and lean forward, trying to focus on whatever's out there.

The longer I stare, the more I question whether it's a tree or a person. The object moves again, and I get a glimpse of a profile.

Someone is walking to the lake.

It's got to be him.

Aiden Slate is a creature of habit.

Of course. The path that leads to that place. It should have been the first place I looked.

It's his refuge. His escape. Now that it's summer, he'd be heading to his tree.

So, that's where I go.

I head outside toward the tree that faces the small lake that lies right beyond the outskirts of the trailer park we live in. A small piece of land that allows us both to pretend we don't live here with parents who don't care about us.

In the winter, the water freezes, and I love to watch Aiden skate. In the warm months, once the frost is gone, he likes to stare out into the horizon, I like too also.

Sometimes, I like to pretend we live in another town far from here. Hell, I'd even be okay living one trailer over with the Matthews. They might be old, but at least I'd know someone cares about me.

A crack of thunder halts my steps for a second. I wait for the sky to open again, but I trudge on when no more rain falls.

I thought the weather would stop him, so I didn't bother going down the path and out the little hole in the fence that led to where he likes to spend his days. Instead, I wasted time knocking on his door, moving into Peeping Tom territory.

It was a mistake. A big mistake.

When he's fixated on something, it wouldn't matter if it were raining; he'd still be in his spot.

That's how he is. I don't know why, and after everything he's done for me, I don't ask questions. He needs structure, and he needs things to go a certain way.

Those two things I learned early on about him. It was strangely comforting to know that one thing will remain the same in a world full of constant changes.

Aiden is my North Star.

Which is how I know the shadow in the distance is him.

As I continue my trek, I'm hit by the smell of rain that lingers in the air. The ground is still damp from the earlier downpour, and the pungent stink of earthworms is harsh. I don't let it stop me.

My heart pounds the closer I get to him. It's always like this. My breath quickens, hands get clammy, and my legs become a bit weak. Today, my reaction is for a different reason.

I heard from one of the other kids who lives in a trailer a few down from his that he was upset. That's so unlike Aiden, and it has me jittery. I put the kid through an inquisition but got nowhere. He didn't have any answers for me. It's what led me to search for Aiden.

Now, fear and worry course through my veins as I imagine what could have happened. Aside from Aiden's penchant for things to be a certain way, he's a fortress. One not easily shook.

Taking a few steps, the wind hits my face as droplets of water start to fall from the sky. The farther I get, the harder the rain falls. I'll be drenched—like a drowned rat—in no time.

Wonderful.

I'm almost there, close enough to make out a body leaning against the trunk of the tree. The branches of the large oak give little coverage from the water belting down from the sky.

It's Aiden.

His face is buried in his hands.

Shit.

I rush toward him.

My dampened clothes cling to my body, but I don't care. All that matters is finding out what happened and doing what I can to help. Just like he'd do for me. Like he's done a million times in the past eight months.

Since the very first day that I got here, he's protected me. Taken care of me. It's my turn to reciprocate. To ensure he's okay.

It's obvious right off the bat that something terrible has happened. The pain etched on his face makes my chest ache, and my feet slow to a stop. I'm careful not to disrupt him. I'll be here if he needs me, but I won't press him right now.

Cautiously, I take a seat on the dirt ground next to him.

He doesn't react. He doesn't say a word and doesn't look my way.

We sit in silence for a few painstaking minutes. My hands twist around each other as I try to remain quiet. When Aiden scoots a little closer to me, I interpret it as a sign that he's prepared to talk.

I suck in a deep breath. "Aiden, what's wrong? Why are you out here alone"—I lift my hand, and a raindrop hits it—"in the rain?"

Aiden turns toward me, his eyes red and filled with tears. It feels like someone punched their hand through my chest and grabbed my heart. At this moment, I know the thing I hate most in the world is the way Aiden looks right now. Broken.

He wipes away the tears hastily and lets out a heavy sigh. "Pip, I…" He stops mid-sentence, letting the unsaid words hang in the air between us.

I reach out and gently touch his arm. "You can tell me anything."

He looks into my eyes and holds my stare. "I need to get out of here."

I nod, feeling the bile rise in the back of my throat. "I know."

This day was always going to happen. It's what I've feared since getting to know him. The realization that Aiden Slate has so much to offer this world, and that one day, someone would recognize it, swoop in, and take him away.

"Things will be different. Our lives will change forever." My own eyes start to well with unshed tears. "I don't know what the future will hold." His voice shakes.

"What do you want, Aiden?" It comes out in barely a whisper. The fear of what he'll say eats me alive.

"You know my mom wouldn't let me apply to college," he says.

It's her way of keeping him stuck here so she can drain him.

He can provide for her. He can pay the bills.

She's a leech and Aiden's her host.

"There's this hockey game coming up, Pip. And well, this is it for me. This is my chance to break out of here. It's my best shot at getting scouted by professional teams."

I swallow the lump stuck in my throat. My body shivers at the thought of losing him.

"It's the opportunity I've been dreaming of, but…" He hesitates for a moment, struggling to find the words. "She took all my money. I can't afford the ticket to get there."

"What?" I shriek, sitting up straight and forgetting about the rain and everything else he said, choosing to focus on the part about his awful mother stealing from him again.

"You know she—she doesn't want me to succeed. She wants me stuck here for good." He groans, head tilting back. "I feel like my dream is slipping away because of her. Because of money. It's always money."

My fingers grip the hem of my shirt. A nervous habit I've had for as long as I can remember. As I twist the material, I start to think.

I've always known he loved to play hockey and is incredible

at it. I just never understood until now that it's his way out. It's his only way to gain freedom from her.

I have to do something.

I have to help him.

My mind concocts a whole list of ideas, some more ridiculous than others. Then, like a lightning bolt striking down to the earth, it hits me.

"I have money, Aiden," I whisper as though someone else will hear.

Aiden's eyes widen in surprise, but he shakes his head. "No. I can't. Absolutely not, Pip."

I crawl up on my knees, facing him. "I want to give it to you."

"There's no way I can take it."

"Sure, you can. It's no big deal." My hand cups his knee. "It's only money."

"Pip. It *is* a big deal. You need it."

For kids like us, any amount of money is a really big deal. It's the difference between surviving or ending up on the streets when our time comes to escape our current situation.

"It's not a lot. But it should be enough to get you to the game," I say, mentally counting how much I have saved up.

His stormy eyes land on mine. *"Pip."*

I scoot closer toward him so we're eye to eye.

"No. Don't 'Pip' me. I want to give you this." My eyes stay trained on him. "Consider it an investment."

A side of his lips quirks up. "An investment?"

I bob my head once. "A business arrangement," I suggest.

"So it's just business?" The heaviness from moments ago lifts slightly, and a grin spreads across his handsome face.

"Yep. And one day, you will pay me back." I wink.

As the rain pours down and thunder rumbles in the distance, Aiden looks at me with a mix of disbelief and hope. He reaches out and takes my hand in his. "Just business?"

"Just business." I smile up at him. "But you have to promise me one thing."

He takes a deep breath, exhaling as he says, "Anything."

I inhale, readying myself to be more vulnerable than I'm typically comfortable with. Even with Aiden.

"Promise you will never forget me."

His head tilts to the side, his eyes still holding mine captive. The dark ring surrounding his irises moves toward the center, turning the deep blue even darker. Something…more.

"I'll never forget you."

I stick my pinky out. "Pinky promise on your puck."

He links our fingers together with a smirk. "I promise."

chapter three

Aiden

Ten Years Later…

I SLUMP DOWN ONTO THE COUCH IN MY HOTEL SUITE ACROSS FROM my agent, feeling the weight of stress pressing down on my shoulders.

Despite everything, round one looms over my head like a dark cloud, and I can't shake the feeling of unease that gnaws at my insides.

Tomorrow is game one.

We're facing off against the Detroit Renegades. As a five seed facing off against a four seed, I should have my head on straight. Hell, this is the best team we've had in well over five years, but being back in Michigan is fucking with me.

Which is not something I have time for right now.

Ever since getting my big break all those years ago, I've prided myself on having full control over my life and, in turn, the game. I've been focused and dedicated, but the moment I crossed the state line, it seems like my mind is a mess.

Everything rides on this.

I can't fuck it up.

This is our best shot for the Cup. Something I've dreamed about my entire life. Since that day all those years ago, when the coach of the prestigious academy saw something in me and changed the trajectory of my life. Had I not gotten the scholarship to the private school for my academics, I never would have started playing hockey.

Hockey isn't exactly a typical sport a poor kid from the trailers falls into.

Every sacrifice I've made has gotten me to this point, and I won't let myself or my team down.

But instead of having my head in the game, it's everywhere else, like usual.

My agent, Mike, leans forward in his chair, his brow furrowed with concern. "What's going on, man?"

Mike is one of a kind. A good, loyal man. He's supported me throughout my career, guiding me through the highs and lows of playing professional hockey.

"Nothing," I lie, not in the mood to discuss my inner turmoil.

He sits back on a huff. "Cut the shit, Aiden. I know you."

He does, and I know there's no skating around the talk he's determined to have.

I let out a breath. "I'm stressed."

"Okay, and..." He motions toward me. "Aren't you always stressed?"

"Not like this." I ball my hands into fists at my side.

"I thought your routines helped with—"

I wave him off. "They do. But this is different. I'm on edge, and it doesn't matter if everything is perfect, it still feels like..." I shake my head, closing my eyes and clenching my teeth. "Just forget it."

"No. Explain." His voice is harsher than it's been toward me in a while, and I don't blame him. I'm acting like a child, but when you've lived the life that I have, you're just waiting for the floor to give out underneath you and for all that you've built to crumble into ruin.

"It still feels like my life is utter chaos," I admit, giving him that much.

"It's being back here, right?"

"Yep," I respond. There's no reason to deny it. Mike has known me for a long time. He knows what being back *here* means to me. It doesn't matter that Birmingham, Michigan, is technically two hours from where I grew up. It still feels too close.

"You're always edgy when you play here, but I assume it's worse this time because so much rides on this game." He sucks air through his teeth and taps his chin, eventually lifting one finger into the air. "You know what you need?"

Nothing good ever comes from those five words from Mike. His answer to everything is a pair of well-sculpted legs and two perfect double D's.

"Something tells me you're going to tell me."

He smiles, leaning forward. "You need to get laid."

I bark a laugh because I called it. "Easy for you to say…you can just fuck with no consequences."

His head shakes back and forth while his lips purse. "Not true, but I hear what you're saying. Puck bunnies are getting better at hiding in plain sight."

I bite my lower lip, trying to refrain from laughing.

"Maybe it will take the edge off." He shifts in his seat. "It could be the solution for you—a way to help you relax and get back in the game."

"Yeah, but at what cost?" I bite out, knowing full well there are many problems with his plan.

"No cost. I know of a girl…"

"This is how all good intentions start. You remember I'm notoriously evasive with who I take into my bed. One wrong move and I'll become Hudson." My teammate is one of the best guys I know, but he can't go anywhere without women throwing themselves at him. They know they have a shot because he's a player, and I have no interest in having that happen to me.

My private life is my own. It needs to stay that way. "Also, since I'm so selective with who I spend my time with, the local press will be all over me, and for good reason. They'll do anything for a glimpse into my life. A night in the sack with the wrong girl, and they'll get that story and wreck my reputation in the process."

Hockey players might not be followed around by the paparazzi like football stars, but the local news…they love a good story.

"Can you let me finish?" He crosses his arms over his chest. "You're always so damn pessimistic."

"Fine," I huff. "Proceed."

A faint smile tugs at the corners of his mouth. "A while back, a client of mine had the same problem as you." I raise an eyebrow. "Okay, not exactly the same problems, but he needed to blow off some steam, and he told me about this girl."

"Is she a professional? Because I can't have that shit on record. The press would eat it up if they found out I paid—"

"Not a professional, per se. There is no money exchanged."

My lips form a thin line before my mouth drops open in utter confusion. "I'm not following."

"This is her thing. She enjoys helping players loosen up. She's like a good luck charm. From what I hear from my client, he's never lost after he's seen her."

"So, what you're saying is she's a puck bunny? That sounds like the beginning of a horror story."

"She's solid," he says so nonchalantly, you'd think we were talking about a dog. "She just likes to be *useful*, if you catch my drift."

I lean forward in my seat and lift my brow at him. "And what does she get out of it?"

"A mutually beneficial fuck. How the hell should I know? But she's discreet. And we can have her sign an NDA." He lifts one shoulder and widens his eyes. "It's a win-win. She's kinky as all fuck too. She'll let you do anything to her."

I don't respond. Instead, I mull over what he's said. Normally, I'm able to handle my stress better, but right now, it's like pushing a large boulder up a hill. Nearly impossible.

"I know it might sound unconventional," Mike continues, his tone softening. "But sometimes, that's the only answer. Your mental state is all I care about right now. This is your shot at the Cup. Maybe this distraction is what you need to get your head back in the game."

"It sounds dirty."

"It sounds fun." He grins. "This girl understands the pressures you're facing, and if it doesn't work, where's the harm?"

The idea of sex holds merit. Most of my teammates claim they require sex before every game to help them loosen up. The difference is that they're all matched up with girls they care about, or they're the kind of guys who don't give two fucks about what's written about them.

It's been far too long since I've been with anyone.

With how closed off I am, getting laid is a luxury I often have to go without. I can't risk my personal life getting out. It's not just about sex. Obviously, I don't want that leaked, but it's my past too. My family. My quirks…

I can still hear my mother's voice. The things she used to say to me.

You ruined my life.

You're useless.

You can't get anything right.

Stop being so weird. I would have loved you if you were normal.

That one hurt the most.

No. I can't let anyone in. Walls are just bricks of memories laid by the people who've hurt you.

The solution?

Keep everyone at arm's length. Letting someone in is a recipe for disaster.

One I can see coming a mile away and need to stop before the collision does irreparable damage.

"I see those cogs turning, and I know you think it's a bad idea. But I'm telling you, you're wrong. This is a solid plan. A woman who knows what she's getting into. I'll repeat…is discreet. And best of all? Kinky, yet clean."

Maybe he's right. Maybe I am refusing to see reason. I can temporarily escape the relentless pressure on my shoulders and not have to worry that anyone will find out more about me than I want them to. This could work.

Perhaps it can even be the solution I need to find my focus again.

I sigh, my exhaustion evident. "You know what? Why the fuck not?"

A small glimmer of relief flashes in his eyes. "I'll call my client and get her number. I'll arrange everything."

This is either the best idea ever or the worst.

chapter four

Cassidy

THE CHILLED GOLDEN LIQUID SLOSHES IN MY GLASS AS I TAKE another sip of tequila. Its smooth burn travels down my throat, instantly loosening my nerves.

Today has sucked.

As did the day before and the day before that. My life has been a series of unfortunate events lately, and I don't see a silver lining in sight.

I've been crashing on my friend Emma's couch ever since I got evicted from my apartment. It's your classic case of rent going up at the same time my salary went down. And by down, I mean it's nonexistent. Zero. I'm unemployed.

Since I graduated from college, one thing has become clear... jobs do not come easy, despite what you're led to believe.

I've been looking, but without experience, nothing comes through. The problem is, I can't get experience if no one will hire me. Which brings me back to the here and now. Jobless. Homeless. Just...less.

The familiar taste of salt and lime brings me back to my college days. For a time, my life was easy. Or easier than normal.

With a full-ride scholarship, I made do. And that is the one silver lining if I have to find one. At least I didn't come out of school with a lifetime's worth of debt.

But now that I'm no longer living on the school's dime and have no job, paying rent on the tiny apartment I had in Detroit turned out to be impossible. I'll need to find something to make ends meet—and fast. As much as I appreciate Emma's hospitality, I can't make her couch my home.

It's Friday night, and at least I have a roof over my head. For now, I'll focus on that…and the booze gripped between my hands. Truth is, after what I've been through, I can live through anything.

My grip tightens as memories push through my mind.

You won't always have someone there to protect you …

No. I can't go back there. I can't dwell on the past.

You can't reread a chapter in a book you hate.

Closing my eyes, I remember my therapist's prompts, then open them.

Something I can see: My drink.

Something I can smell: Also, my drink.

Something I can taste: That one makes me laugh.

All the previous thoughts and anxiety fade away.

Close call. If there is one thing I don't want, it's my past ruining my future.

I survived, and that's all that matters.

The smell of popcorn fills the air as Emma walks over to join me, carrying a huge bowl of the buttery goodness in hand. She lifts an eyebrow as I bring the glass of liquor to my lips to drink my sorrows away.

"Mind if I join you?"

I place the glass on the coffee table, grab the bottle of tequila, and sweep a hand out, motioning for her to help herself to *her* couch.

The muted noise from the television draws my attention, but

the cushion sinks as she takes a seat next to me. Both of our eyes are glued ahead. She begins flipping through the channels, which could go on for hours.

This is typical. Neither of us is good at choosing what to watch. She'll likely still be scrolling in ten minutes. Meanwhile, I'll be zoning out.

She channel surfs so quickly that the images fly by in a whirl. As they flash across the screen, a familiar profile captures my attention.

Everything around me stills.

I white-knuckle the bottle. "Stop."

She turns toward me with wide eyes. "You wanna watch this?" She's landed on some gorefest, but I can't even focus on it to determine which one.

"Go back," I tell her, motioning to the flat screen. My heart tightens in my chest. It feels like a hand is holding onto my heart and squeezing me.

Is this what it feels like when you're dying?

"To the rom-com or the horror movie?" Her voice pitches with the latter, cutting through my morbid thoughts. "I'm so not in the mood to watch someone being hacked to pieces, but if that's what you need to get out of this—"

What the hell is Emma going on about? I know she's speaking, but suddenly there's a ringing in my head that comes out of nowhere. *Breathe, goddammit.* You will not have a panic attack.

"Neither." I finally spit out, pouring more booze into my glass, and then placing the bottle down. "Go back to the local news."

From the corner of my eye, I can see she's looking at me like I've sprouted another head. "Just do it, Em. Please."

Emma is a stickler for manners even though hers could use some work. Ask nicely, and she's far more malleable.

Her fingers on the remote echo through the small space as I hold my breath, nervous to see if it's who I think it is. The blood pumps in my ears so hard it almost drowns out the sound of the TV.

A clip from a past hockey game dances across the screen. The newscaster is speculating if our local team has a shot at winning. My eyes scan over the opposing players as they fly down the ice.

"Hockey? Really, Cass?"

"Shh," I snap a little too harshly.

Emma has no idea about the turmoil I'm currently experiencing. And how could she? I've shared absolutely nothing about the years I lived with my dad in the trailer with anyone, even her. But I can't worry about her feelings right now.

I need to know if it's him. The images on the screen aren't helping at all. It's nearly impossible to figure out who's who. They're moving too fast, making it difficult to see faces clearly.

I lean forward, squinting my eyes as I try to get a clearer view. Emma probably thinks I've gone nuts. I'm rarely this excitable, and never when it comes to sports.

The camera zooms in on a man's back, and my whole body locks up. My heart skips a beat as I wait for him to turn toward the lens. The screen freezes, and then the commentator is back.

What the hell?

"Shit." The word falls out of me on a harsh breath.

I didn't get a good look.

The oxygen rushes back through my chest; the anxiety giving way to disappointment.

"Can I change it now?" Emma asks, completely missing my meltdown.

Which is good. That would only lead to questions, and I'm not sure I'm ready to talk about it.

"No. Not yet." I don't offer any explanation, and it's clear she's annoyed.

Emma sighs, but she doesn't change it. The man on the screen is talking about the play, and I hold my breath again for what comes next.

A name.

One simple name, but it has the ability to render me speechless. And numb. And sick to my stomach.

It's a name that has been haunting me for over ten years.

The camera cuts to a close-up image of the player they're speaking about, and my stomach bottoms out.

"Damn. Now that I'm here for." The sound of Emma's voice reminds me of talking underwater, muffled and hard to understand.

It's him.

Sure, I had a hunch it could be him. It's not like I didn't know he went pro. I even figured this day would come. But that hasn't stopped me from spending the years since he left avoiding any reminder of him. It was pointless.

His memory is etched into my soul, burrowed so deep that no matter what I do, he'll always be there. And that pisses me off.

He broke his promise.

He left and never thought of me again.

He didn't protect me.

I watch for a second, and I'm not sure I even blink. Now that my carefully constructed plan to erase him from existence is foiled, I can't help but hang on to every word as they discuss their guesses for what will happen during the playoffs.

The image on the screen changes to a video of him skating across the ice with effortless grace—the hockey player I had come to know so well.

Glad to see *he's* fared better than me.

"You okay over there?" Emma's tone is careful and concerned.

Am I that obvious?

Shaking my head, I turn to Emma. Her eyes meet mine, narrowing slightly to study me.

"Yeah. Why?" I answer as I hug my knees to my chest.

Real smooth, Cass. Now it's totally obvious you aren't.

She inclines her head. "Well, for starters, your shaking head, body language, and words. Everything seems to conflict." She widens her eyes in an *Are you going to argue?* expression. When I don't, she continues. "You look like you've seen a ghost. What's the deal?"

A part of me wants to make up some lame lie in an effort to

keep this one thing to myself. If for no other reason than to attempt a second try at erasing him from my thoughts.

Never gonna happen.

I take a deep breath and go with the truth. "I know him."

She blinks and splutters before finally getting herself together.

"Hold up." Her hand lifts. "You know who?" Her nose is scrunched, and her eyes are narrowed.

"Him." I drop my legs back down to the floor and point at his picture frozen on the screen as they continue to talk about just how incredible he is.

I once thought he was, too.

Two minutes later, Em still looks like a deer caught in headlights. Her green eyes are wide, and she shakes her head back and forth in disbelief. It looks like she has a halo around her thanks to her swaying honey-blonde hair. "You know that man? The absolute hottest guy in hockey."

I roll my eyes despite my turning stomach. "What do you know about hockey, Emma?"

"Answer the damn question, woman."

"Yes," I mutter before reaching toward the coffee table, grabbing my glass, and taking a long swig of the now warm tequila.

I don't even react as it burns, sliding down my throat. I'm officially numb.

"You know a professional hockey player?" she questions.

I nod, wondering how I can possibly get out of talking about it anymore.

In true Emma fashion, she jumps right in. "You need to start from the beginning. How am I just hearing about this?"

"Umm…"

It's not an intelligent way to bypass a topic you'd rather skip, but right now, my words escape me.

My brain's gone foggy.

Emma's lips purse, and she places the popcorn bowl on her lap. "No 'umm.' Talk." She grabs a handful of popcorn and shoves it in her mouth, looking like this is panning out to be quite the entertainment for her.

Placing the glass down, I close my eyes and try to think of a plausible explanation. My past is just that—my past. He was the boy I once considered my protector. In the grand scheme of things, it was only for a moment, and the sad fact is, he forgot about me.

It's heartbreaking.

Humiliating.

Typical.

I thought he was different. That—unlike my mom who had no choice because she died, leaving me alone with my drunk, negligent father—I meant something to Aiden. And that he'd choose not to leave me.

But he turned out to be no different.

Despite all that, I'm still not willing to share pieces of his past. Especially knowing how hard that past was. Like me, his life wasn't sunshine and roses. The only difference is, he made something of himself.

I exhale, feeling defeated and tired. "I just do. How I know him isn't the point."

"Then what is the point?" she asks around a mouthful of popcorn. Butter runs down her chin. She swipes it away, undeterred. Emma is a dog with a chew toy.

Lifting my hands, I bury my head in them. "I don't know," I groan.

I'm so off-kilter at the moment. I can't even think on my feet, which isn't normal for me. I've gotten good at spinning narratives, but tonight, I can't.

My stomach feels tight, and my heart seems to think I just ran a marathon. It's beating so fast. Before I can contain myself, the words slip from my lips. "I wish I could see him…talk to him."

See why he never came back.

A part of me knows…His hatred for his mom kept him away, but a part of me, a *big* part, wanted him to come back in spite of that.

Emma's eyes narrow in on me. "Then why don't you?"

Fear.

It's the first word to pop into my head. But as I think about her question and forget all about the past and how scared I am to confront him, the answer is actually simple for a change. I wouldn't even know where to start.

Finding him is easy enough, considering his schedule is plastered all over the internet, but gaining access to him would be much more difficult. They don't let just anyone past security.

"Call him?" she suggests.

I frown. Emma is not typically an airhead.

"How exactly do you think I'll find his number?" I roll my eyes.

"Google? Facebook...Insta? That's how I stalk people."

My palm hits my forehead. "He's not just anyone, Em. I doubt his information is public. You saw him and heard what they said about his skills. Millions of hockey fans are trying to get a piece of Aiden Slate."

"You're right. There's no way." Her lips are set in a thin line. She looks off to the side. "Except..."

I turn toward her fully, eyebrows raised in an *out with it* expression.

"I could." She sticks one shoulder out like she's a big deal.

I laugh without humor. Emma's always trying to lighten the mood, but I'm not into it tonight. Not when it concerns Slate.

"Yeah, okay." I make it clear by my tone that I'm not here for her shenanigans tonight.

She places the popcorn down and scoots closer to me, wiping her buttery hands on her pants.

"I'm serious. I happen to have some intel that he's staying at the hotel a few blocks away."

My eyes narrow in on my friend. Moments ago, she acted as though she didn't have a clue who he was. Just another hot hockey player. What's this about?

"How do you know that? Better yet, *why* do you know?"

"You forget I work there. The whole team is staying at the hotel.

I bet I can find out the room." She waggles her eyebrows as though we're embarking on a mission together.

This is the most exciting thing she's been part of. She forgets what something like this would do to her if it backfires.

"You'll get fired, Em."

She pulls her bottom lip into her mouth. "But only if someone finds out." She places her hand on my shoulder. "I can tell this guy means something to you. That isn't normal, Cass. You have to go see him."

I lean back and contemplate what she's said. Her idea is all sorts of risky for a million reasons.

"No. I can't put you in that position. This whole idea is crazy."

Crazy, because I don't know how he'd react. What would he even say if he saw me?

He never came back for me. Never bothered to visit the trailer park once he left. Never cared to check in.

He got his dream and never looked back.

As soon as I turned eighteen and graduated from high school, I got the hell out of there. That's when I finally came to terms with the fact that the ship had sailed. I'd never see him again. Our lives had gone in different directions, and he chose that.

Then there was also the day I legally changed my last name. Started a fresh life.

And effectively making it impossible for him to find you.

I push that thought away. I did what I did to shield myself. If I made it difficult for him, then I could convince myself he'd tried, and my actions prohibited it. I could lie to myself. Trick my brain into thinking he actually attempted.

It's pretty pathetic.

Why would I want to start the grieving process all over again? Why would I even consider setting myself up for rejection?

After all this time, it just seems like a bad idea.

Except all my efforts to forget have resulted in nothing. Maybe it's closure that I need.

Closure *I deserve.*

The thought of being around him again, albeit in a different setting, sends a thrill through my veins.

My mind buzzes with the possibilities. Would he be surprised to see me? Would I get an apology? Would he even remember me?

He better.

I don't know what I'd do if he didn't. For almost a year of my life, he was my reprieve from the hell I was living in, and I thought I was his. Sure, I was just a kid at the time, but I knew I was the only person he had. He has to remember me, right?

To be turned away by him would be another form of torture for that little girl he left behind.

But I'm not that little girl anymore.

He only knew me as Pippa, my middle name. I'm Cassidy, a grown-ass woman who can more than handle rejection.

You're also homeless and jobless...

Pathetic.

Yet as the tequila continues to flow and my inhibitions fade, the idea grows more appealing.

Liquid courage has a way of clouding judgment. A fact I know all too well and have always tried my best to stay away from.

Being rational is something I've had to be my whole life.

The desire to be nothing like my father gave me the strength to keep my head on straight.

But what would it be like for just a brief minute to pull down my walls and do something nuts?

Like showing up at the hotel of my childhood friend.

"I see you contemplating."

I sigh, giving in. "I think I'm going to go see him," I say, uncertainty evident in my voice.

Emma's eyebrows shoot up, and a mixture of surprise and concern etches across her face. "Wow. Okay. I mean...I said you should...but I guess I didn't think you'd actually do it." She worries at her bottom lip. "Are you sure, Cassidy? I know it was my idea, but maybe you're right. It's pretty late."

"It's now or never. The liquid courage will wear off by morning."

"Exactly. This isn't really like you. You're more—"

"Levelheaded?"

She nods vigorously. "You said it, not me."

I let out a sigh. "Maybe I want to be daring. Why can't I be more like you tonight?"

She's quiet for several minutes, still biting at that lip. "Do you?"

"Do I what?"

"Really want to be daring? Reckless? Crazy?" she asks, eyes opened animatedly.

"I do."

Em clicks mute on the remote and tosses it aside before she grabs her phone off the coffee table. The only sound in the room is the clicking of her fingers typing. My nerves intensify tenfold with every second that ticks by.

What the hell am I doing?

After a few seconds, she looks up, a smile spreading across her face.

"I don't know the exact room number, but I know the floor." She doesn't look up as she continues to type. "Not sure how helpful that will be, but he's on three." She finishes typing and places her phone down. "The rest of the team is on the fourth, so at least you won't be seen by any of them."

A distant memory filters through my brain.

Aiden always had little quirks.

Superstitions.

The third floor makes complete sense.

I don't say anything, just nod.

As a kid, I protected the little quirks that made him who he was as if they were my own. I was the only one who knew him and didn't taunt him. Even his mom ridiculed him, but not me. I knew what it was like to feel less than. So I never did.

If he's staying on the third floor, I have it narrowed down to which room he'll be in.

"You're really going to do this?" she asks, searching my face. I bob my head.

"Well, my contact says he's there right now. He arrived after dinner and hasn't left." *He has a game tomorrow. He wouldn't be anywhere else.* "Will you be okay?" she asks, and I wave off her worries with a dismissive gesture.

"I'll be fine, Em. It's just a short walk to the hotel. Besides, I can't let this chance slip away. Who knows when I'll get another opportunity like this?"

Emma sighs, her expression revealing a mixture of resignation and support. "Just promise me you'll be careful. If you need anything, call me. And please, don't do anything that could get you hurt."

"I promise," I reassure her, a mischievous grin creeping onto my face now that the earlier tequila is working its magic. "Help me find my shoes."

"No."

I stop looking for them and glance at her. "What?"

"Have you seen what you're wearing?" She drops her gaze to roam up and down my body.

I peer down at my outfit. Black-and-red-checkered pajama pants and a stained white tee. I squint. Is that butter? I pull the material up. Yep. Butter.

"Oh shit."

Emma runs into her room with a laugh, and a second later, she's tossing a top and skirt at me. I don't bother to look at it; I just strip down to my bra and underwear and change.

She has the decency to cover her eyes as I do, but in all fairness, I'm drunk enough not to care.

"Done," I say once I'm dressed.

Emma drops her hand and leads me to the door, where she hands me my coat.

It might be April, but Michigan's weather is a fickle beast. It's not unheard of to have all four seasons in one day. It's better to be prepared.

I wrap it around myself, the chilly night air hitting me as I step out onto the street.

Nervous energy courses through me as I turn and wave to her and start walking through the dimly lit streets on the way to the hotel.

My senses feel clouded by a mixture of anticipation and intoxication.

The rhythmic click of my heels against the pavement is drowned out by the buzzing in my ears, a constant reminder of the drink's effect on my body. But as the cool night air brushes against my flushed cheeks, the effect of the tequila drifts away.

The farther I get from Emma, the more sober I become.

This is a horrible idea.

This is by far the dumbest idea I've ever had.

My feet stumble, most likely my subconscious telling me to stop, but I don't. Because now that I have conjured up the idea that I might see Aiden, I can't let anything stop me.

My mind replays memories of the time I spent in my childhood with him.

We spent countless hours together. Endless hours under the tree.

There, he'd tell me about the fancy school he went to, and how he started skating on the very lake that rested beside the run-down trailer park. How, by a series of unlikely events, he ended up with a scholarship and then on the hockey team.

I'd watch him skate on the frozen lake daily, transfixed by his effortless grace on the ice. He was determined to make something of himself.

I made it my unofficial job to keep him company while he practiced, and in turn, he made sure I was fed and taken care of. *Protected.* The bond we shared was unbreakable.

Or so I believed.

He didn't come back for me.

He didn't protect me.

Those words have been my constant self-torture for years. Hopefully, after tonight, at the very least, I'll have that closure and can finally put Aiden Slate to rest.

The hotel looms ahead of me, its grand entrance beckoning me closer. As I approach, my eyes catch sight of a formidable figure stationed outside the door.

A bodyguard, maybe?

My heart skips a beat. A wave of nervousness washes over me. What if I can't get in? What if I miss my one chance to see him?

When I reach the main door, my steps falter for a moment. Doubt seeps into my mind, but I quickly brush it aside. If I want to have any chance of getting through this beefy man, I need to exude confidence.

Tequila, take the wheel.

Sucking in a deep breath, I move closer. That's when I notice that the figure isn't a bodyguard but a large older man dressed as though he's the doorman for the building. With a warm smile on his face, he pushes open the thick glass and lets me pass.

No questions asked.

They really need to up their hotel security game if they're going to have high-profile guests staying. Jeez.

Once I enter the luxurious lobby, I try to act like I don't have a care in the world. I need to blend in and pretend I'm supposed to be here.

I try my best to appear calm and collected, masking the nervous energy that's pulsing beneath the surface.

With a casual nod to the employee standing in the lobby, I stroll toward the elevators, praying that I won't run into any unexpected obstacles.

Stepping into an elevator, I sigh in relief to find it isn't one of those bougie places that require a room key to even move the elevator. I press the button for the third floor. The ascent feels excruciatingly slow, the anticipation building with each passing second.

The doors finally slide open, revealing a long corridor lined with doors leading to various rooms.

I might not know the exact room number, but I know it will be an odd number.

So that's the direction I'll head in.

I can't believe I'm doing this.

Since making my decision, I've sobered up. My small buzz is now completely gone and begging me to abandon this crazy-ass plan and return to Emma's place.

No.

I need to see this through.

Need to see him.

My heart pounds in my chest as I walk along the hallway, reading the numbers on each door. As I turn the corner, I see a man standing outside two large doors. The number beside him says 333. This is it.

This is Aiden Slate's room.

"Can I help you?" the man who must be part of the team's security, says.

I hesitate for a moment, not knowing what to say. If I tell him who I am, he might not want to see me. My mind races, desperately searching for a reason I'm here that will grant me entry. Summoning what little courage I have left, I take a step forward, giving the man a confident smile. "I'm here to see Mr. Slate."

His eyes narrow as he scrutinizes me.

He studies me for a moment longer. I'm sure he'll turn me away, but to my surprise, he nods. "Are you his appointment?" His voice is unreadable.

"Yes. Sorry, I'm a little early. I was close by." I can't tell if he's buying the shit I'm selling, but I've committed, so I'm not giving up.

Why am I so dumb? Why did I think this was a good idea?

Summoning every ounce of courage, I add, "Are you going to let me in?"

I hope I'm selling this.

"Sorry. Yes. He's expecting you." The man swipes a key and pushes the door open.

My heart beats so frantically that I think I might pass out. As soon as I'm ushered inside, I take a look around.

"I need you to sign a few papers. Standard protocol for these sorts of things."

"Okay," I say, even though I have no idea what's going on, and before I can ask, I'm being led to a round glass dining table where there are documents laid out.

What the hell did I just get myself involved in?

"Non-disclosure agreement."

Looking through the papers, it becomes very clear what this is. I'm meant to be his one-night stand for the evening.

My tongue feels heavy with the truth that I'm not his appointment and shouldn't be here, but all objections get lodged in my throat as the team's security leaves and Aiden Slate enters the room.

He looks exactly as he did on the TV, but different from before, back when I knew him.

Just as handsome, but like a fine wine, he's aged to perfection.

When we were neighbors, I was just a small girl, barely a teen. I knew he was gorgeous, but he was more like a big protective brother to me. One I certainly had a schoolgirl crush on.

Still, he was too old for me, and I was way too young for him to see me as anything but a friend. Now though…there is nothing sisterly about the way I feel when looking at him.

My heart races in my chest, and my cheeks become warm. It's the way my panties become damp that I know there has always been something special about Aiden Slate. He was the only person I ever felt safe with and now he awakens something inside me I rarely feel.

Want.

Desire.

Need.

I thought I was broken.

Apparently not.

I'm not a virgin, but my experience is limited. My pain-stained soul never allowed me to trust, but maybe this could be different.

He could be what I need.

Pushing my lust down for a minute because I need to see why he never came back, I wait for recognition to hit him. For him to look at me and smile, but there is nothing in his gaze. His expression is neutral. Almost bored.

Oh God…He doesn't recognize me.

Pain radiates through my body, piercing my heart.

You do look different.

My hair is darker now. It's a deep chestnut shade. Back when I lived at the trailer park, it was blonde. The same shade as my father's. I changed that the moment I turned eighteen. Plus, the last time he saw me, I hadn't hit puberty yet. I looked like a baby, a sickly skinny one at that. Now, I don't. *Yeah, maybe that's it.*

Despite my pep talk, my lungs feel tight.

It doesn't matter that I look nothing like I did before. The only thing that matters is that I'm not worth a memory.

All this time, I've thought of him. I thought maybe it was my fault I didn't get to see him again. That maybe since I changed my last name—no. That's bullshit. He could have found me if he wanted to. I was in the same place he left me for five more years. He never searched.

I can feel moisture collecting in my eyes, but I push it back. If I cry, I won't be able to talk to him. Maybe he doesn't remember me, but I still want to see if he's okay. Make sure he's happy. Because despite the fact that he never thought of me, I never stopped thinking of him, and I need to know before we part ways that he's happy. That way, I can finally leave my past behind me.

I debate what to do.

Do I tell him the truth?

Why should you?

If you're not worthy of a memory, why should you put your heart on the table and tell him it's you?

But I'm not ready to leave. I'm not ready to let him go. These feelings I have when he looks at me … I want it for a little longer.

A crazy idea pops into my brain. If he doesn't recognize me and never plans to see me again, maybe I can take this for what it is—one crazy little adventure just for me. A scratch I needed to itch.

Just once.

An escape from my memories.

And despite my anger toward him forgetting me, I do feel safe. When else will I have an opportunity like this again? To feel free, untethered to my past.

For one night, I can be someone else. Someone who throws caution to the wind and has a one-night stand with a stranger… except in this case, he's not a stranger.

But he doesn't know this.

He doesn't know it's me, so I can be everything he wants. And then I can go home and live my life, keeping this memory with me forever.

Liar.

No. I have to tell him, right? I'm about to speak when his gruff voice cuts through the thick air.

"What's your name?"

"Cassidy Baker." It slips from me unbidden. My name is out there. No turning back now. Squaring my shoulders, I prepare for whatever will be thrown my way.

"Well, Cassidy Baker, are you just going to stand there, or are you going to sign?"

chapter five

Aiden

WHAT AM I DOING?

The woman looks at me, her eyes wide. For a second, I wonder if Mike had it all wrong. She doesn't look like the sort of girl who knows what she's getting herself into. She's a deer in headlights, and that won't work. How the hell am I supposed to relax when this girl's anxiety is peaking my own?

But then I remember that I told Mike that I needed to be in control.

This is an act. *And a good one at that.* There's no mistaking the body language she's throwing my way.

She might appear timid at first glance, but the signs are all there. The way she bites her full bottom lip.

The rise and fall of her breasts.

The glossy sheen in her eyes.

Despite the glaringly obvious signs of desire, I'll confirm this is what she wants before we get started.

She can make the choice.

And I hope she agrees because there's no question, she's gorgeous.

Actually, that word is wholly underselling it. She's stunning. But none of that matters if this blows up in my face.

She blinks and opens her mouth to speak, but then closes it.

I narrow my stare at her, waiting for her to say something. When she doesn't, I do. "Would you like something to drink?"

She shakes her head. "No. I don't want anything to drink. But thank you."

I'm about to confirm that she wants to go through with this, but before I can say a single word, she leans forward, signs, and turns to face me.

Her shoulders are back, and she appears confident. Except I don't miss the way her hand shakes at her side. Or how her finger taps against the pen she still holds.

"Listen…we don't have to do this," I say, giving her an out. I will never take a woman to my bed who isn't sure. "You can leave, and we'll pretend this never happened."

"No." Her voice is silk and smooth, but more importantly, sure.

A confidence she hasn't had since walking into this room permeates the space, changing everything. I can smell how much she wants this. Wants me.

I'd be a fucking liar if I said I wasn't turned on by that fact.

I take a step, and the pen drops to the table with a clink.

"Last chance to back out, Cassidy." I grin, and her lips part into the sexiest smile I have ever seen.

The closer I get, the more I feel like the wolf stalking the lamb.

She shakes her head. "I'm not going anywhere."

Fuck.

My cock grows uncomfortably hard, and my need for this stranger intensifies.

"Clothes off." My voice is low and husky. "I want to see you." I grab my drink and walk over to the window that looks out into the small city, giving her a minute to undress and join me.

Birmingham isn't a large city, but the lights of the buildings still glow, spreading out to the edge where the darkness takes over. A siren in the distance rings out, but that's nothing new. It might not be as large as the city I live in, but it still doesn't sleep. There's constant activity. Unending noise.

It's the one thing I miss about a small town in the middle of nowhere.

Quiet.

Peace.

If only every other memory wasn't tainted.

I push those thoughts away, not wanting to go there. I focus on the lights. Where I live, Redville, isn't a large city by any means, but compared to where I grew up, it presents opportunities I never had in my youth.

Footsteps bring me back to this room. To the woman who should be naked behind me. My mind focuses on that singular thought. A beautiful stranger here has agreed to help me get out of my head.

Something I so desperately need.

I twist around to face her, my head tilting to the side. She's not made any move to get undressed. I lift one eyebrow, but she doesn't say a thing.

She holds my gaze, eyes sparkling in the soft twinkle of the battery-operated candles that Mike insisted on. I make a mental note to thank him for that touch because something about how the light shines in her eyes has my throat drying up and my heart racing.

What the actual fuck.

The coat she's wearing drops to the floor with a thump, and she places her hands on the hem of her shirt. Slowly, she pulls it over her head, and I suck in a breath. Despite her petite frame, she stands tall and confident in only a black bra and a skirt. She doesn't move. Doesn't turn her gaze from mine. She holds my stare, waiting for my command.

I'm practically salivating, which isn't like me. Typically, sex is transactional. It has to be, considering my status.

I know that makes me sound arrogant, but I'm not. It's the truth. A harsh one I've had to learn the hard way through the years.

Being a hockey star comes with perks and hindrances. Most women want me for the fame. The money.

This girl isn't much different. I might not be paying her, but she gets something out of it too. She gets to know she fucked me, and I get sex. Something about that just doesn't sit right with me for a moment. Even if I'm benefiting too.

It's not her fault. My people contacted her, but I can't help but feel the sting of knowing this isn't about her caring about me.

That pathetic, broken boy in me, desperate for the attention. Starving for affection.

I hate everything about this feeling, but I can't stop myself for what I say next.

"All of it," I demand, motioning toward her body and the last of the clothing covering her.

Cassidy's cheeks turn a dark shade of pink. She blinks several times before glancing down at her skirt. She doesn't make a move to take it off. Something about this has my misplaced anger melting away. This is just an innocent girl getting caught up in my internal battles. She's here to help, and I need to remember that.

She takes a deep breath, moving her hands to the waist of the skirt.

I don't know what she's playing at, but I can't say it bothers me. I like the act.

Timid.

Innocent.

It makes me want to do *really* bad things to her.

I want to corrupt her. Use her.

Good girl. Keep playing the part, little lamb.

There's no question in my mind that Mike must have conveyed

that I like control. I can only hope she keeps this up all night. It's exactly what I need right now. This will take the edge off.

Gone is the skirt, but she's still standing in front of me in her thong and bra. My lips tip into a smirk.

"All. Of. It." I repeat each word slowly and with a hint of menace.

Her eyes widen a fraction before her hands reach behind her back and unsnap her bra. It falls to the floor followed by her panties. I grin in complete satisfaction.

Fucking gorgeous.

Her tits are the perfect size. Full but not too full. Her nipples are pebbled, and I can't help but lick my bottom lip.

I motion to the floor. "On your knees."

She blinks, and for a moment, I think she'll object, but she doesn't. She drops to the floor, her perky breasts bouncing as she does.

Like the good girl she is, she doesn't move. She just waits for my orders.

Just how Mike described her.

She is perfect.

The right amount of shyness but a body of sin that tells of a hidden side I'm about to uncover. My dick strains at the promise of all the things I can do to her. *Will do to her.*

"Crawl to me," I command. She glances up at me, her chest rising and falling with her inhale of breath, but then she bites her bottom lip, and I know she's going to do everything I say.

My dick twitches at the prospect.

Fuck. It's been too damn long.

I'm reacting like a teenager. I need to pull it together. Control in all aspects is what I crave.

Slowly, she moves toward me, allowing that timid act to slip just a bit.

She's sexy. Sensual.

A fucking goddess.

When she makes it to me, she lifts to her knees, awaiting my direction. Without thinking, my hands dart out to her shoulders. I softly stroke her dark hair. "You're perfect."

The apples of her cheeks stain a pretty pink, but her eyes give her away.

Blue and glassy.

She likes this. Wants it.

I bet if I put my hand between her thighs, I'd feel the heat. She's probably soaking for me, and that thought has me needing more.

"Take my cock out."

Her hands reach out, and she fumbles with the button of my pants. The sound of her lowering my zipper echoes through the air around us, and I'm on edge with anticipation. She finds me hard and ready. One long and dainty finger runs up my shaft, and I can't help the way my dick jerks in response.

"I want your mouth on me."

Leaning forward, she licks the tip of my cock before wrapping her gorgeous lips around my skin.

The moment I'm fully engulfed in the warmth of her mouth, I take over, placing my hands on the back of her head to guide her pace.

I thrust in and out, and her small hands grab my thighs, nails digging into my jeans.

She's struggling to take me.

"Good. Now open your throat."

She does what I ask, and I gently stroke her head before picking up the pace again. "That's it." I push in deeper. Looking down, I watch her while I keep my rhythm and fuck her mouth.

Between sucks, she runs her tongue up my vein. I groan, loving the way she sucks my cock.

She gives me what I need. *Exactly what I need.*

I like the control I have over her when she's on her knees for me.

Finally, when my balls tighten, I pull out from her mouth with a pop. She sucks in air, acting like it's her final breath. I like it.

"Turn around and get on your hands and knees. Ass up."

I reach into my back pocket to grab the condom. I waste no time ripping the wrapper and sliding it on. I don't even bother taking my pants off.

This isn't about that.

This is just a means to an end to relax me.

Condom in place, I kneel behind her, rubbing my cock over her ass and through her folds.

She's drenched for me.

I slide a finger into her, and she moans at the intrusion, rolling her head back on a pant.

Curling downward, I hit the spot inside her that I know will make her come undone. Her hips push back, begging for more. I don't give it to her. Not yet.

I continue to stroke and tease her G-spot, wondering how far I can push her. Will she come all over my hand if I allow it?

Without a doubt.

But I'm not a generous man right now. She'll get her turn, but not before I'm inside her.

With that, I retract my hand, line myself up, and thrust, burying myself to the hilt.

Fucking heaven.

Just what I needed.

Pulling out, I let my tip rest just outside of her pussy. She wiggles back, wanting me to push back in.

"What do you need?"

She wiggles her ass, but I don't enter her yet, needing to edge her a bit more.

I swirl my hips, my cock tracing her damp skin.

"Please," she begs.

She speaks.

A smirk spreads across my face.

"You want me to fuck you?" We both know damn well she wants to be fucked. She craves it.

"Yes." My dick jumps at the breathy sound.

"You want me to use you?"

She pushes back, and the tip of my dick slips inside her.

"Game on, baby."

Driving my cock into her, I feel her muscles pulse around me. *Too fucking good.*

I wrap my arm around her, finding her clit, and rub it until she's a quivering mess.

"Be a good girl and come for me."

I start to drive my cock in and out of her, eliciting sounds that make me know she's close.

"Oh God," she moans, and it only incites me.

My thrusts are punishing. It's been too long. Well overdue. And this woman is getting the full force of my drought. Her pussy tightens, and my balls do the same.

I don't stop my pace as she unravels beneath me, making me fall over the edge too.

chapter six

Cassidy

H OT WATER CASCADES OVER MY BODY, THE STEAM ENVELOPING
me as I stand beneath the showerhead.

It does nothing to calm me.

Nor does it push down the bile climbing up my throat over
what I just did.

I lied to him.

Well…

Nope. There is no other way to spin this.

I lied.

Maybe not outright, but I withheld the truth. My name. Who
I am.

Why I let him fuck me.

I'm an awful person, and I don't know what to do about it.

Nothing.

You do nothing.

*It's a one-time thing. You slept with a man you will never see
again; it doesn't matter that your past is connected.*

Lies. Lies. Lies.

I scrub harder.

It's a feeble attempt. Nothing I do, no amount of soap, will wash away the remnants of tonight. Nor the memory.

I allow my mind to replay every detail. Every kiss. Every touch. Each one being wrong but oh-so right.

As the memories replay, my cheeks warm, and my skin tingles. Why did it have to feel so good?

It's never felt this way before for me. I thought I was broken.

After everything I've been through, I thought I was destined to never enjoy sex, my past and the memories never allowing me to be free enough to trust someone with my body, *but he changed everything.*

He's so much more than I imagined. And he proved that over and over. It wasn't a one-and-done. He took me over and over again. By the time he was done with me, my body was spent. I could hardly walk.

Now that I've had a taste, how can I move on?

There's no choice.

"Oh God," I moan into the steam.

This is bad. Very bad. I just wanted closure, and all I got was a slap in the face. He didn't remember me, and that's the bucket of ice-cold water that washes away the need for him.

We are two strangers who had a one-night stand. No biggie.

Now, I can go about my life.

Bullshit.

I meant nothing to him. Despite that hurtful truth, I let him inside me. I allowed him to consume me in ways I've never allowed anyone else. It was a night I'll never be able to forget.

And the worst part, I didn't even get what I came for…

No closure happened.

I'm cursed to have Aiden Slate haunt me for the rest of my life.

My heart hammers in my chest as regret rages a war inside me.

Can I just walk away with this memory? Will I even be able to enjoy it knowing it stemmed from a huge lie?

No. It's fine. It was an omission of truth, but it's not my fault he forgot me and didn't realize who I was. That's on him, right?

As the water courses over my skin, I still can't shake the feeling, though. The truth weighs heavy on my conscience, threatening to drown me in a sea of guilt.

It is my fault.

All of it.

With trembling hands, I lather my hair, the fragrant shampoo mingling with the steam. While it should relax me, each stroke feels mechanical. I'm going through the motions, attempting to wipe him away.

Nothing works. He's ingrained in me. Always has been.

That's the worst part.

Eventually, the water turns cold, snapping me back to the present.

Stepping out of the shower, I wrap a towel around my shivering body. I tiptoe across the cold tile because all I want to do is sneak out of here unseen and try to get my life back in order.

As I dry off, my reflection in the fogged-up mirror seems to echo the internal conflict raging within me.

Do I sneak out? Do I tell him?

I twist the soft cotton material surrounding me as I try to think of what he will say.

Shaking my head to myself, I decide against it.

That ship has already sailed.

We had sex, and there's no going back…it's fine.

It has to be.

Hastily, I get dressed, throwing back on my skirt and top that only hours ago were discarded on the floor when Aiden commanded that I strip. My cheeks start to flush at the memory of his dominance, a rush of heat warming my skin, but I push it away. This is not the time and place for that. One day, I'll cherish those memories of how Aiden Slate made me feel things I've never felt before, desire that I've never felt before, but that moment won't be now. No, it will be when I'm back at Emma's and am able to breathe again.

At this moment, I need to concentrate on the fact that I need to leave this bathroom and this hotel room, if I'm being honest.

There's no turning back, so I just need to face the music and get out of here unscathed. I check myself in the mirror one final time, determined to end this crazy one-night stand on the highest note possible.

As I step from the bathroom, my heart pounds. My gaze sweeps across the room, searching for any sign of Aiden. And there he is, sitting on the couch.

The first thing I notice is that he's more casual than before. Donning gray sweats and a black tee, he should look more relaxed, but he doesn't.

Instead, he's leaning forward, body stiff, and I can see the lines that have formed between his brows.

I follow his line of sight, and that's when I see what he's scowling at.

A bowl of assorted candies sits on the coffee table before him. He's glaring at it as if the bowl has offended him.

I don't make my presence known. Instead, I linger in the shadows, watching him.

My eyes fixate on his hands where they hover over the bowl. What's he doing?

Narrowing my eyes, I try to determine what could have him appearing so anxious. Then it dawns on me. It's the assortment of colors.

A memory pushes its way out of my subconscious. Aiden Slate sitting below the tree. His tree.

A box of Sweet Tarts in his hand. The box I got him because he told me they were his favorite, but as I watched him, he stared down at the box. His face tight. I remember asking what was wrong…

The same thing is happening now.

He's fighting the desire to pick them out, to sort them.

But eventually, the desire wins. Just like it did when we were younger.

Aiden Slate can't—won't eat any color but blue.

He begins his work, meticulously picking the blue out and separating them from the rest.

A mix of emotions surges within me—surprise, then comfort, for as much as things have changed, he's still the same boy I knew, which leads to an odd sense of relief.

With a deep breath, I move from the shadows so he can see me.

Aiden looks up, and our gazes lock. He furrows his brow and then looks down at the bowl. I don't need him to tell me how he feels. I know it deep in my bones. If there was one thing he hated back when we lived in the trailer park, it was people seeing his quirks.

No matter how smart or talented Aiden was, his fear of judgment clouded his brain.

He always felt that his quirks put a mark on him. His mother was the worst offender, but unfortunately, she was not the only one.

Other kids would mock him as well. It was always a way for them to ridicule and attempt to bring him down to their level.

I did my best to shelter him from those kids. From the nasty bullies who would do anything to cut another kid off at the knees, just to make themselves feel better about their pathetic lives.

It's sad that any kid grew up in an environment where that behavior became their method of protecting themselves.

The room is heavy with silence, and his features are hard when he lifts his eyes back up to me. The boy I knew is preparing for ridicule.

Something I would never give him.

Instead of the judgment that he expects, I simply smile.

The hard line of his jaw softens, and I see something familiar in his face…relief.

I move closer, my heart thumping like the wings of a humming-bird, as I sit down beside him. "You know," I begin, my voice light and teasing, "everyone knows that blue is the only acceptable color."

The sound of his exhale makes my shoulders uncoil.

I turn to face him. Only a few moments ago, his lips were in a straight line, but now they curl upward into a smirk. The tension between us dissipates, replaced by an unspoken understanding.

Leaning forward, I start to sort the bowl for him.

Removing the colors he doesn't like.

His hand reaches in, and we work in silence.

Just as we did so many times before.

chapter seven

Aiden

WHAT THE FUCK IS HAPPENING?

I'm sitting here, sorting Sweet Tarts with the woman I just used to fuck the tension out of me. We work in silence; her allowing me my impulses without judgment.

I waited for the words to come. The words that always came when I gave in to my needs…

What is wrong with you?

Why can't you be normal?

The screams of the past echo in my ears, but instead of taunting, I'm met with silence.

I watched her face closely when she found me sorting out the blues, and there was zero hint of laughter at my expense. She actually jumped right in to help. Something I've never allowed anyone.

Well…except…

I shake that thought from my head. Nothing good comes from looking back.

I've built a new life. One I can be proud of, despite all the things working against me. And I've done it by keeping my private life just that…private.

Now I've allowed this unknown woman into my space, and she's seen the things I do.

Control.

Sort.

Fixate.

What is going through her head?

We've been working in tandem seamlessly, the quiet not seeming to bother either of us. But now that we're nearing the end, the silence is suffocating. Is that when this peaceful moment between us will shatter with the questions she will undoubtedly ask?

That's not something I'm going to allow to happen. My secrets are mine, and I control the narrative. Besides, I don't think I could handle this woman poking around and uncovering just how fucked up I am.

I clear my throat and speak. "Thank you."

She turns to me, eyes narrowed, but I don't say anything.

Eventually, she shrugs. "It's no problem."

That's it. That's all she says. No questions. So I continue weaving my tale, just like I did at the beginning with Mike and the guys.

"It's part of my pre-game ritual. I'm sure it doesn't make sense to you, but all the guys have them. This is one of mine."

She blinks a few times, and I wonder what she's thinking. What's she going to say?

I'm full of shit.

Obviously, I have pre-game rituals. That part isn't a lie. This, though…it's not one of them. This is a compulsion I've had for as long as I can remember.

"I've heard about athletes doing that." She gathers up all the other colors, tossing them in her bag. My eyebrow lifts in question. "You aren't going to eat them, and I have a roommate who will. Why let them go to waste?"

I smirk but don't comment.

She isn't wrong. They would've hit the trash as soon as she left. And then, I'll clean the table, but that's a whole other thing, and now that I've thought about it, I can see the specks of sugar tormenting me from beside the bowl.

All of a sudden, she gets up and crosses the space. I have no idea where she's going, but a second later, I understand. She's grabbed the cleaning antibacterial wipes from the bathroom and is removing all traces of the dust left behind.

The mess is gone. I can breathe again.

"You know…" she says, and I prepare to hear something I don't like. "You could hire someone to do these things for you."

My shoulders straighten. "I said they're pre-game rituals. I have to do it."

She purses her lips, and I know she wants to argue with me, but she doesn't, and for some unknown reason, it puts me more at ease than I already was with her.

"I don't want people knowing my business." That's the truth. I don't need people to know about all the stuff I do because I have to, to function. I can pretend some of my stuff is superstitions but not all of it.

"You make them sign your NDA." She turns toward me. "Make sure you're—" She pauses, trying to find her words. "Comfortable. With the person. With the process."

Someone like *her*. Can I find a person who doesn't judge like she didn't? Hiring someone would pose too many questions. The applicants would all have to sign nondisclosure agreements, and someone would talk. It would get out.

They would look at me like I was a—nope. *Not going there.*

Plus, although her idea holds merit, it wouldn't really help my problem. I'm the one who has to do my rituals. That's the only way to calm my anxiety. It's not as easy as just having someone do it for me.

If only it was her.

Just her presence alone has worked magic over me. It's like she cast a spell, and the tension inside me dissipated.

Even now, when she caught me sorting, I didn't feel the usual shame that falls over me.

The only thing I felt was tension as I waited for the ridicule, but when no damaging words followed and she sat beside me, I felt at peace for the first time in years.

If only I could bottle her up, then I'd always have her calming energies.

A crazy thought pops into my brain. One that I should immediately forget because it's so asinine. But no matter how long I sit here, it just remains a constant thought.

She could do it.

She could be the person I hire. I'd let her think I'm hiring her to help me with my quirks, but in reality, I'd be hiring her to be near me. The thing is, I want her around. She soothes me and helps me. I just can't tell her the real reason.

Not that she'd judge me, but I can't run the risk of her saying no. Even in my own head, hiring someone for their presence alone sounds like a crazy idea. I'll just ask her to be my assistant.

Our eyes lock, and I see it. Her blue irises glaze over, the lust permeating from her.

"You could do it." The words are out before I've really contemplated all the consequences.

Her mouth opens and then closes. Her eyes blink rapidly all the while. She's speechless, and I have to admit, she's damn cute when caught off guard.

"What?"

I recline back, going for nonchalance. "You could work for me. I'd hire you to—" I take a deep breath, hating that I feel vulnerable, but I see no judgment in her eyes, so I press on, knowing she's perfect. "Help me."

"Work for you as what? Your assistant?" she asks, sounding skeptical.

I dissect the cynical tone she took on and realize my error. I'm about to say yes, but then something hits me—an assistant won't work.

Shit.

I would need her with me at all times. To truly help me, she'll need to be where I am when I need her the most. It's moments like now, at night and in the early morning hours, when I feel myself spiraling.

An assistant wouldn't be tied to my hip. They wouldn't share my space. That would bring about too many questions. It could stir up unwanted stories. The next thing I know, I'm mixing business and pleasure and taking advantage of my employees. It would reduce her to no less than an escort, and I won't do that to her. Or me.

"Yes. But no."

"I don't understand."

"I *would* hire you to be my assistant. You'd be responsible for all the typical things an assistant would do, but I'd also need you around all the time for moments like this."

"You want your assistant to stay in a hotel with you?" She raises her brow.

She's right. That won't work either. People *will* talk.

They will ask questions.

They'll find out my secrets.

Things I've avoided for years will come to the surface.

I can't have that.

I love the game, but I hate the spotlight in any capacity. I'm private for a reason. Nobody would believe that Aiden Slate, the man who avoids getting too close to anyone, would allow an assistant, much less a woman, to live with him unless she means something to him.

"You make a valid point. I can't exactly have people thinking I'm fucking you, which is exactly what they'd think. You can see how bad that would look. For both of us."

Her eyes grow wide, and her mouth drops open. "That would be worse for me," she says, swallowing. "I'd be labeled as a gold digger. Or worse."

"You're right, and it sucks. People have nothing better to do than pull others down." I run my hand through my hair. "As my assistant, your name would be run through the mud. You'll be with me at times that will make it appear as though I'm sleeping with you. There's no way to avoid those misconceptions."

"So what are you suggesting?" she asks, eyes mere slits.

What am I suggesting? I'm not even sure what other angle could be played. How can I have her with me at all times without the finger pointing and speculation? If she were my girlfriend, everything would be so easy.

I inhale sharply, having hit the nail on the head.

That's it. That's the answer.

"I'll say that you're my girlfriend."

She barks out a humorless laugh. "How will that work? If we were dating, wouldn't people, you know, like your friends, know?"

I rush ahead. "I'll say that we've been flying under the radar for some time, but we're ready to go public. It could work."

"You don't seem like the type of guy who *goes public*." She uses air quotes on the last two words.

I smirk.

"And you know this how? Checking up on me?" I'm teasing her, and it's baffling. I don't flirt. I don't tease.

But here I am, doing both.

"No," she squawks. "I haven't."

"I'll pay you to act as my girlfriend for the public, but in reality, you play the role of assistant behind the scenes."

"Let me get this straight," she says, leaning forward. "I'll pretend to be your girlfriend in public, and you'll pay me to help with your errands, rituals, and…" Her brows furrow as she drops her voice in confusion. "Have sex to calm you?"

"Fuck. No." I shake my head. "Sex is off the table after tonight. This was a one-time thing that my agent thought I needed. I would never pay for sex."

Why am I telling her all of this? It's not relevant. But I don't like the way she appears to be panicking.

"You'll pay me…just to assist you? In nonsexual ways." She confirms the last part, and when I nod, she lets out a breath of relief.

The truth is tonight was quite easily the best sex I've ever had. I'd love nothing more than to fuck her again, but I can't. She sees too much. I can't let anyone get that close to me, and sleeping with her again would most certainly blur the lines.

"I'll pay you well, Cassidy. All on the up-and-up."

She bites her bottom lip, eyes narrowing into slits. "I don't know."

"You don't know if you wanna work for me?"

She lifts one eyebrow, chewing on her tongue. "No. I don't know."

I have to refrain from laughing. She's a shit liar. The second I suggested paying her, her mouth dropped, and she was practically dancing in her seat. Sure, she was shocked, but there was something like relief that washed over her face. Which means she needs the money.

"Won't it raise suspicions with anyone? If I'm on the books." She uncrosses her legs and fidgets with her fingers. "If someone sees you're paying me, then the whole *you're paying me to pretend to be your girlfriend* will be hard to keep under wraps."

"Then I won't put you on the books. I'll pay in cash."

I can practically see her brain sorting through all of the details. Two sides of her warring over what to do. For a short time, I wonder if she'll reject the offer. Maybe she doesn't need the money. Maybe she's fine having a roommate.

"I have to think about it," she says.

That's better than no. I stand, heading toward the NDA she filled out earlier. "I'll need your answer after the game tomorrow. After that, the deal's off the table."

I pick up the paper and look at the name signed.

Cassidy Baker.

This will be either the best or worst idea I've ever had.

chapter eight

Cassidy

"**Y**OU'RE *WHAT*?"

Considering what I've just told her, Emma's reaction is not surprising.

It's not every day that a person accepts an under-the-table position to act as the girlfriend and life sorter to one of the NHL's hottest hockey stars.

"Cassidy, have you lost your goddamn mind?" she squeals. "I sent you to that hotel to catch up with the guy. Not to agree to be whisked away for God knows how long."

"It's just a few months. Until the Cup. The pay will be worth it, Em. I need it."

"You don't. You have shelter and food right here." Her arms cross over her chest, and she stares down at where I shove my few toiletries into a bag.

"I won't take up your space anymore. I need to do something with my life."

She pulls her top lip into her mouth. "Girl, you know there's always room on my couch for you. You don't have to go selling your soul for money." Her hands lift into the air. "You think this is the way? What about your goals?"

I didn't tell her about his quirks, just that for private reasons he needed me to play the part of his girlfriend, so her shock, of course, isn't misplaced. I made her swear to keep my secret because if it gets out that I'm playing a role, that will look really bad for Aiden.

If I didn't trust Emma with my life, I'd never have shared any of it with her. Being as I've been living under her roof, I had to give her a valid reason for leaving.

"You're being dramatic. I'm not selling anything. And he made it clear that he wasn't trying to have sex with me." I look up at my friend.

"This isn't like you. You don't have to pretend to be someone's girlfriend for money. You're beautiful."

I groan. "I shouldn't have told you."

"The hell you shouldn't have. When you come up missing, I'll be the only one who knows exactly who to point my finger at."

I snort. "Aiden Slate is not going to kill me. It's a short-term position and a chance for me to make some quick money." I shove the bag aside, jumping to my feet. "I could potentially save enough money to finally be able to go to graduate school. My only dream is to be a social worker, and you know I need this to make it happen." I give her a pointed look. "I'll be working toward my goals simultaneously."

She pulls a face. "I don't like it."

I purse my lips because Emma isn't usually this anti-anything. "Why not?"

Her head lolls to the side, and she scrunches her nose in contemplation. "It's a horrible idea. You're going to fall in love with him."

My mouth drops open. "You're insane."

"But you're not saying no." She sighs. "What exactly does this deal entail?"

She takes a seat on the couch beside me, and I pivot my body to face her.

"I'm not entirely sure." At my words, Emma makes a face that screams, *what the fuck*? I need to give her something, but not the whole truth—just a bit. "All he said is that to keep me busy, I'll be doing assistant things. He didn't exactly run down a list yet. It was a proposal. One I haven't officially accepted." I level her with a stern stare. "Obviously, that's not for public knowledge either."

Her left brow pops up. "What exactly are you assisting him with? His dick?"

I choke on my own saliva. "God, Em. No." My hands rub together on my lap, trying to calm my nerves. "I already told you there is no sex. I'm sure he's a busy guy. I'll run errands and stuff like that. Things devoted girlfriends do."

What I'll really be doing is anything to help him manage his quirks. Assist him in all the things his mind requires him to do to live. And from what I know of Aiden, it's a lot.

NDA or not, I wouldn't betray his confidence with that.

"He's very private, so he doesn't want people to know anything about his private life."

She narrows her eyes. "What aren't you telling me?" She purses her lips. "Does he have a red room? Something worse?"

If only she knew how close she was. He might not have all the equipment, but he enjoys the control that comes from dominance in the bedroom. Who knows how much farther it goes? We were in a hotel room, not his home.

That should terrify me.

It doesn't.

If anything, a thrill I've never had runs through me, lifting the tiny hairs on my arms. The thought of all he could do to my body heats me up, and that's surprising.

I'm not a prude by any stretch, but I didn't think the idea of being submissive would appeal to me.

God did it ever.

I crave it now.

When he told me to crawl to him, I about lost it right there. It was so hot. So sensual.

"Earth to Cassidy. Do I even wanna know what's going on in there?" she asks, tapping my forehead.

"Probably not." I sigh. "Anyway, in order to keep people from prying into why he needs an assistant, I'm going to play the part of his girlfriend."

"And you're okay with that? With pretending?"

I pop a brow. "Sure. Why not? He's paying me well enough."

Emma slouches back on the couch, staring off into space for several long moments.

"I'm worried about you, Cass. You're not the type of girl to run headfirst into something like this."

"I'll be fine."

She turns toward me, grabs my hand, and stares into my eyes. "Do you promise? Truly?"

I swallow because she doesn't know the depths of my hurt caused by Aiden. He's already abandoned me once, and I've carried that with me all these years. Will I truly be fine at the end of this?

I really don't know.

"I promise." My voice lacks conviction, but if she can hear it, she lets it go, instead opting to lift a brow like a concerned mother.

"Don't fall for him, Cass. You'll only get your heart broken."

Those words terrify me more than anything. I don't want to think about the damage that Aiden Slate could do to my heart.

I stomp those thoughts down deep. The money is something I need, and the job will be easy enough. I won't allow the past to ruin my future.

Jumping to my feet, I turn to face her. "Help me pack."

She lifts one eyebrow. "You have like three things."

"I have things," I say, sticking out my tongue.

She's not wrong. I'm wholly unprepared to play the part of Aiden's girlfriend. For one, he doesn't date, so when I show up on his arm, all eyes will be on me. They'll tear me apart and dig into my past.

Shit. I didn't think this through.

"Stop panicking. He's well aware of what the paps are going to do, Cass. He'll protect you if he wants to maintain his privacy."

Her words are meant to help ease my rising anxiety, but I'm not sure they do the trick.

I'm not sure I've thought this through.

With a sigh, I grab the small bag next to the couch and start rummaging through it, my hand bumping into the manila envelope I carry.

I'm not sure why I've kept it this long. I should have burned it years ago. Looking up, I notice Emma has walked out of the room.

Before I can stop myself, I pull it out and open it.

It doesn't take me long to find the first letter I wrote him. The picture I drew of an ice skate still mocks me all these years later, and it makes my heart lurch.

When I wrote this, I didn't have his address yet, so there was no place to send it, but I needed the connection. I needed my friend.

Unfolding it slowly, I allow my gaze to scan the words, tears filling my eyes as I read.

Aiden,

You just left. Like literally as I write this, I'm actually watching you through my window. I'm so excited for you. You are totally going to kill it. It's going to be epic. You're going to be epic. Okay, well, Dad's yelling at me. So yeah, I've got to go. Love you. See you soon!

My heart beats so hard. At the time, I truly believed he'd come back.

Now I know better.

How am I going to do this?

Let's hope Emma's right. I hope he protects our privacy because things might go horribly south if he finds out who I am.

chapter nine

Aiden

"**N**ICE GAME, SLATE." MASON SLAPS MY BACK ON HIS WAY TO his locker. "Might've been your best yet."

He isn't wrong.

I played a helluva game tonight.

"Thanks, man. We dominated for sure."

"Hell yeah," he whoops, swinging his white shirt over his head.

We wouldn't have had such a blowout if not for him. He's the best goalie in the league, holding the Renegades to a scoreless game.

He's also the reason our enforcers work overtime. He likes to run his mouth the whole game. I find it comical, but only because it's not my responsibility to defend our guys taking the heat for his chirping.

"You comin' tonight?" Dane asks, running his hands back through his dark hair. That's something I've noticed he does often.

Maybe I'm not the only one with *things*.

"Nah. I'm wiped," I say.

A large dramatic groan echoes across the space, and I turn to find Hudson shaking his head at me. "You need to let loose every now and then, Slate. That was your best game. Celebrate."

Typical Hudson. That man hasn't met a drink he didn't like. Or girl, if I'm being honest.

By his standards, I should already be popping a bottle, I was on fire.

Definitely my best game yet, and I have Cassidy to thank for that.

For the first time in a long time, I'm relaxed. Focused. My head was in the game and not even the chirping could throw me off. Maybe I should reconsider the no-sex thing because this is definitely the best I've played in a long time.

I shake my head, but as I do, I realize that it probably seems I'm answering Hudson. What was the question again? Oh yeah, celebrating with them. "Next time."

Hudson frowns, but he doesn't argue. He knows better. It won't change my mind.

"Whatever. Later, man."

I nod, allowing him to make his way out. This is one of my things. I'm the last to leave the locker room. Every time. I'm also the last on the ice and the last off the ice.

Why?

No clue. It's just my thing.

There's a pretty fucking long list of *things.*

From the piece of tape around my right wrist to the way I put my socks on before I play. The helmet kiss before skating onto the ice. Dunking my head in cold water to ground myself.

Sometimes it feels like my quirks are never-ending.

The need to check my gear three times. Not once. Not twice. Three.

Which is what I'm about to do right now.

As soon as the last guy leaves, I pack my gear. Counting all of my things and putting them in place. Three times. When I'm finally done, I finish getting dressed and make sure everything is perfect.

Then and only then do I grab my bag and head to the door. Just like every time, all the sports reporters and fans have given up on trying to get an audience with me.

They won't get anything anyway. I never speak a word to the press unless the coach mandates it. And I've never fucked a bunny. Well...not until recently.

I don't take chances of choosing the wrong woman. I've seen too many teammates get involved with drama I have no interest in. Fuck. That.

If not for Mike's personal recommendation of Cassidy, last night wouldn't have happened. She was vetted and given the proper legal documents ahead of time. She knew exactly what she was getting into. And she enjoyed it. Her pussy was so wet for me, and when she came, it was hard and long. It made me crazy with need. The need to control her. To fuck her again.

Shit.

This isn't good.

I'll ensure she takes the offer, and when she does, it's hands-off. Because I need her.

I pull out my phone and shoot off a message to Mike.

Me: Need a favor

Mike: Of course you do...

Me: Fuck off. You make bank off me.

Mike: *rolling my eyes so hard*

He's so damn dramatic. He's well taken care of, and that's the reason he's up for the challenge of dealing with me and my compulsions. He's one of the only people who knows, and he's gone above and beyond to ensure it stays private. For that, I owe him.

Aiden: Can you arrange for a buyer to put together a full wardrobe, accessories, and beauty shit for Cassidy?

Mike: First of all, who? What did I miss? Also, beauty shit! You do know I'm your agent, not your bitch, right?

Aiden: Shut up. And just get me what I want.

If it were anyone else, I wouldn't be such a dick, but Mike has been with me since I got drafted out of college. He knows I'm messing with him.

Mike: For fuck's sake, please tell me you didn't fall in love?

Aiden: Now I'm rolling my eyes...

Aiden: Did you see that game?

Mike: Sure did. But what does that have to do with the girl?

Aiden: She did that.

Mike: So many questions.

Aiden: Just do it. I'll fill you in later.

With that, I shut down my phone and throw it in my bag, not wanting to text back and forth all night. Because Mike would.

No. I'm going back to the hotel and unloading, and without a doubt, Cassidy will play the star in my mind while I do.

chapter ten

Cassidy

I'M BACK AT THE HOTEL TWENTY-FOUR HOURS LATER TO TELL him my decision. My hands shake at my side. The nerves claw at my gut.

The same man is outside Aiden's door.

He must realize I have no intention of knocking because he takes it upon himself to do so for me.

Shit.

What if he's changed his mind?

Can I do this? Continue to lie to him?

Bile rises up my throat, and my stomach clenches tight.

No. I can't.

I have to leave. *Now.*

I'm about to run away when the door swings open, and there he is with a towel wrapped around his waist, water droplets dripping down his firm pecs.

Holy. Crap.

"Your jaw's on the floor, sweetheart."

I snap my mouth shut, internally berating myself for ogling him so openly.

And what's with his swagger? He was always confident but never this arrogant.

Do I like it?

Yeah. I do.

But does he really have to be so damn hot? It's not natural.

I promised myself on the walk over here that there would be no more impure thoughts about Aiden Slate. One minute in, and I'm already failing.

How the hell will I be able to work with this man when I want to jump his bones every time I see him?

Easy, girl.

Get your head in the game.

But instead of listening to my inner ramblings and pulling my gaze away, I find my gaze drop to his lips.

Wrong move, *again.*

His grin is sinful, and I can't help but smile back.

"Glad you made the right decision." His confident voice makes my spine tingle. Okay, it's something else that tingles, but I refuse to admit that fact.

I clear my throat and swallow. "Who said I made a decision?"

His eyebrow lifts. "Haven't you?"

I sigh heavily, not wanting to have this conversation at the door. "Can I come in?" If anyone were to walk by and see me, they'd tell me to get a room with the way I'm staring at him. I need out of this hall.

He steps aside, motioning me in. Last night, I was too nervous to really take in the suite, but now, with my nerves taking a back seat to my libido, I can. Well, that is once I turn my attention away from the chiseled chest causing my heart to race.

Not only is it beautiful in here, but Lord, it's clean.

The place is immaculate, not that I expected anything different. When you crave control, it's in all things.

"I wanted to discuss the terms," I say, and he leans against the wall. My eyes sweep over the towel, just barely hanging off his hips. "Did you want to get dressed?"

"Not really."

"Oh…okay," I stammer, recognizing I need to get this conversation started and get out of here before I make an utter fool of myself.

"The terms, Cassidy." He smirks. "What is it you want to discuss?"

I shake my head to clear the ridiculous fog caused by his lack of clothing and sexy-as-hell tousled hair.

"Right? Okay…well, if I'm going to have to pack up my entire life, I'd like to know what to expect. You see, I realize if the story is to be that I'm your girlfriend to the public, I don't exactly…" The words catch in my throat, and he leans forward.

"You don't exactly what?"

"It's just that, I'm all right with pretending, but when this is done, I'll have a life that I need to get back to. I want to be a social worker, and if my reputation is soiled, no reputable employee will hire me."

He works his jaw.

"Why would your reputation be in jeopardy?" he asks, sounding confused.

"You're Mr. Hockey. Everyone loves you even though they don't actually know you."

"I guess you could say that, but how does this affect you?"

I have veered so far from where I started, and I need to get us back on track. "When we break up, since that's inevitable, what will we tell them?"

It's like a light turns on in his eyes, and I see the moment he's up to speed with me.

"That my schedule was hectic, and we were away from each other for too long. That we both mutually agreed that right now might not be the right time. We can cross that bridge when it comes, but I promise you, you won't be painted as the bad guy. I don't personally like to play the victim, either." He chuckles, but there is something off about it. "We'll work all that out, but you have my word that when it's all done, you will be able to walk right into any office and get a job."

I take a deep breath, feeling better now. "Thank you."

"Right, well…hopefully, this will actually help land you the job of your dreams."

It's so easy for someone like Aiden, someone who's well on his way to the status of legend, to walk through life. He's likely not even being boastful. It's a fact that if I become recognizable as his girlfriend, and things end on good terms, I could score a position for simply having dated a hockey star.

It's so messed up.

He chews on his cheek. "Social worker, eh?"

"Yep," I say, popping the p, not sure what else to say.

It's something I've wanted to do forever. Look after those kids who have been practically abandoned. The kids like Aiden and me.

"Didn't see that coming."

I tilt my head to the side. "Why? You don't know me."

He blows out a breath. "You're right. Just didn't expect that."

A steady thump lands on the front door of the trailer. The sound echoes through the space, shaking the walls around me. The knocking seems to grow louder as I stand from the couch to see who's there.

I throw the door open, and I instantly recognize the woman.

Mrs. Saber. The social worker from my school.

This isn't the first time she's been to the trailer.

I cross my arms as I stare at the woman who often comes over to check. "Hi, Pippa. How are you today?"

I roll my eyes. "Oh, I'm just peachy. Who called you this time?"

She chuckles softly, undeterred by my attitude. "Maybe I'm just here to check in."

Inclining my head down, I give her my best who you trying to fool face. "You're never here to just check in."

She throws her hands up in the air dramatically. If I didn't know her, I'd think she's annoyed, but she's one of the good ones. "Fine. There was a call. But I'm also here for you."

I nibble my lip, trying to think of who could have called her. Most likely my math teacher. I have class with her right after lunch. This morning, Dad was passed out, and I was so late getting to school that I forgot to pack a lunch…maybe that's it? Maybe she heard my stomach growl?

"You can talk to me. Nothing you say—"

"Can I?"

"From what I can tell, the house is clean, and you're eating, right?" I nod, knowing full well the only reason I'm not skin and bones is because I make sure I eat, but I can't let her know that.

"Your English teacher said you were upset. I just wanted to make sure you're okay."

Oh, there it is. She's not wrong. I was upset.

English is my first class, and on the way to school, I had a run-in with the asshat who lives a few trailers down. I got marked tardy, and to make it worse, I left my homework at home.

"Do school social workers usually do house calls?"

"No," she admits, and I'm almost shocked that she fesses up to it.

"Why am I so lucky…" There's a bite to my voice that I know doesn't belong there. She's trying. She cares.

At least one adult does. Not true. There's that nice old couple. The wife makes me cookies sometimes. If only they were my family. I'd much rather live with them.

"I know it may seem like a hassle, but I'm here to help. Please don't hesitate to let me know if there's anything you need or any concerns you have."

I look down, feeling a flicker of vulnerability. "Thanks. I guess it's good to know someone cares."

And I know she does. The thing is, I'm better here than living in the car again. Sure, things suck, but I can handle it. But maybe somewhere there's a child who can't.

Not everyone is lucky to have someone checking in, like Aiden…

"It's something I've wanted to do for a long time." I clear my throat. "Not like I can play the role of fake girlfriend for the rest of my life…" I raise a brow. "What else should we discuss?" I say, trying to get my mind off the day this will all end and we'll go our separate ways. Again.

"As a formality, I should probably remind you that you signed an NDA. For all intents and purposes, you *are* my girlfriend, and nothing about the way I live is to ever be spoken about by you to anyone."

My head jerks back, and I screw up my nose. "I won't… I wouldn't." I have to reel myself in and remember that he's just doing his due diligence. It's smart because he doesn't know me. Doesn't know that I'm the girl who's always held his secrets.

I take a deep breath, calmer than moments ago. "I won't air any of your secrets. Ever. You have my word on that."

"You want to remain in a positive light with people."

"Yes. It's imperative that I don't get a bad name through this."

He takes a deep breath. "You know I'll shelter you as much as I can."

His words hit me in the gut. He didn't shelter me before. *Will he now?*

Can I trust him?

No.

That's the thing about trust. Once it's gone, it leaves a hole that can't ever be filled.

But that doesn't stop me from not being willing to abandon him, despite the fact that he did that to me.

"But the media does like to tear women apart, so you never can tell. Since I've never dated before, you'll be under a microscope."

Wonderful. I have a feeling I know where this is leading, and I can't say it's not a bit humiliating.

"I have something for you," he says, moving toward the bedroom.

I'm not sure if I'm to follow him or stay in place.

"Cassidy, are you coming?"

My head lolls back on my shoulder. The last place I need to be with Aiden Slate is in a bedroom with him in a towel.

Lord have mercy, I only have so much willpower.

I won't even think about hooking up with him again until the terms of this arrangement are agreed upon. Or ever.

When I make it inside the room, I see that the bed is entirely covered in bags from various stores. Just as I thought.

He motions toward my outfit.

"You…you don't like how I look?"

Hurt flares, and my eyes mist even though I had just been thinking that same thing.

"No, Cassidy. It's not like that. I like your style. Please know that." His head falls back on his shoulders with a groan. "I'm only trying to protect you because people will judge."

I huff out an injured laugh. "I get that. I knew this was coming. It just doesn't make it any less embarrassing."

He closes his eyes and takes a deep breath. "You do realize I've never dated a single one of them, and I don't welcome the attention, right?"

"I do," I say, but that doesn't change the fact that people will expect a certain type of person, and the fact I don't fit that image is a real ego killer.

"We'll have several events to attend. I hoped this would be helpful, not hurtful. I was trying to do something nice…"

I can see the turmoil roiling behind his blue irises and swallow down the lump in my throat. "It was very nice. You didn't have to do it, but I appreciate it."

He takes a step toward me. Then two steps. He's standing right in front of me, and my whole body lights up.

His hand darts out, and he lifts it. For a second, I think he's about to move the stray piece of hair that has fallen on my face behind my ear, but then he drops his hand just as fast. Almost like he's been burned.

Ouch.

Figures.

I need to get my head in the game and remember why I'm here.

I'm not here for a relationship, only to fake one. I'm here to make my dreams come true, like he did all those years ago when I gave him the money he needed. This time, it's his turn to pay up, whether he knows it or not.

chapter eleven

Aiden

"**H**OW LONG DO YOU NEED TO GET READY?" I ASK, TAKING A step back. I'm too close to her. The desire to grab her, throw her down, and have my way with her is all-consuming, and I'm sure if I wanted to, I could, but I can't.

I might trust her with my needs, but I can't trust her with my heart. If she knew the full extent of my thoughts, she'd say the same things I have always heard when I've let my guard down.

No. It's easier to keep this professional, no matter how much I want her.

Her eyes narrow. "For what?"

"Since we won tonight and don't have a game tomorrow, a bunch of the guys are going out. Actually, I'm pretty sure the entire team will be there. Initially, I wasn't supposed to go, but I think it will be a good idea." I give her a second to digest what I'm suggesting.

"You think we should make our debut? As a... a couple? Tonight?"

I see the rising panic, and I don't blame her. All of this is a lot to ask, whether I'm paying her or not. To throw her into a situation with my teammates on night one is grounds for a bonus.

"I do. The guys need to meet you first. It will make it so much easier for you."

She takes several deep breaths, likely trying to avoid a panic attack. I'm throwing her right into the gauntlet. No better way to see if she can handle this. If she gets in good with my teammates, she'll handle the paparazzi fine.

I watch as stark determination replaces her fear. This woman is strong. Courageous.

Dangerous.

She's the kind of girl worth falling for.

God, you're not trying to fall.

"All right. I'll get dressed," she says, staring at the bags.

"Wear whatever you'd like. They're yours."

She starts going through the bags, and I have to admit that it makes me strangely happy that she's accepting the clothes so easily. I thought I'd pissed her off with the gesture, and she'd refuse out of independence.

It's a good sign that she's willing to go with the flow. It's exactly what I'll need from her in order for this to work.

"I'll give you some privacy." She doesn't look up from her perch on the floor, sorting through the products. "Take your time."

She doesn't acknowledge my comment, so lost in the task at hand.

I shoot off a quick text to the group chat. One of them will have the details. Hudson is most likely the party planner of the group.

Me: What are the details for tonight?

Hudson: WHAAAA You're actually showing your face?

Mason: Is the Stanley on the line? Are you being bribed?

Dane: You guys are assholes. Leave the man alone.

Me: What he said. Just send me the location.

Mason: Glad you're comin', man.

Hudson: Lux. It's a few blocks from the hotel.

These guys are the closest thing to family I have. They might be the only people in my life now, aside from Mike, who know anything about my quirks. They don't know all of them, but they know enough to know it's more than the typical hockey player superstitions. They never bring them up, which makes them solid in my book.

Of all the guys, Dane is the most like me. Closed off and reserved. He's the kind of guy you can trust. They all are. Just in different ways. He's one of the good ones, and those are hard to come by in this profession.

Everybody is out for themselves. And I get it. A lot of money is on the line in a sport where our playing time is limited.

I pull up my online banking and sort out my recent pay. Five hundred immediately goes into a separate bank account like it has for as long as I can remember.

I don't like the thoughts swirling around in my mind, so I shut down the app and throw my phone to the side. If we're going to this party, I need to get my ass in gear.

On my way to my bedroom, I pass the room I've arranged for Cassidy. The hotel suite has two, and I already made the primary one mine, so I'll have all her new stuff put in the other while we're gone. Our rooms are next door to each, which at this very moment seems like an awful idea, seeing as I just had a hard time keeping my dick in check as I caught her staring at me. I've vowed not to touch her, and I need to stick to that no matter how badly I want her.

And I do.

Thoughts of Cassidy's naked body responding perfectly to my commands filter through my mind, and I groan, rushing back to the shower since she arrived before I could fully wash off. *I'm going to have to take a cold one to calm down.*

This might be the one time my rituals will come in handy. I'll be too busy getting ready to think about her anymore.

Stepping under the frigid water does the trick. My dick is no longer running the show, and by the time I've washed myself in the order I like, I'm no longer acting like a teenage boy with a raging hard-on.

Thirty minutes later, I'm wearing a pair of jeans and a black T-shirt. My staple outfit, complete with Converses. I'm a simple man who doesn't give a fuck what anyone thinks. I make enough money to shroud myself in Gucci, but it's not my taste.

Growing up in a trailer and not having a dime to my name, I learned early on that would never be me. You can take the guy out of the gutter, but that doesn't mean he's going to lose every aspect of himself in order to fit in.

Not me.

When I'm ready, I head back out to the couch, and minutes later, Cassidy emerges.

My mouth dries at the sight of her. So much for having my dick under control.

"What are you wearing?" I practically snarl. *Real smooth.*

She looks down at the coral-colored mini dress with itty bitty straps. The front plunges into a V, showcasing a healthy amount of skin. It molds to her body like a second skin.

"A dress."

Standing from the couch, I move until I'm directly in front of her. "Obviously, it's a dress. But where is the rest of it?"

"You're being ridiculous, Aiden. I'm supposed to be your girlfriend. I have to dress the part."

I grind my teeth, annoyed that she's throwing my words back at me.

She has a point. But fuck.

That dress is all sorts of dangerous, and my teammates will make me want to fight. I know it.

Might as well get this over with.

Hudson rented out the VIP lounge at Lux Bar. It's an upscale club in town that's bursting at the seams. I was surprised to see a line outside that almost wrapped around the building, but we don't have to wait, VIP service and all.

It's one of the perks of the job.

I don't take advantage of it often, but I know my teammates do.

In every city we go to, no matter how big or small, all the bars fight to be *the* place where everyone who's anyone wants to hang.

This must be that place for Birmingham.

I follow Cassidy, my hand at her back, coaxing her through the crowded dance floor, heading toward the back where a set of stairs leads to the VIP lounge on the second floor. I don't miss the way every man's eyes follow her.

One by one, I shoot every man looking at her with a glare. One that has one clear meaning: *She's mine.*

It might not necessarily be true, but in a way it is. For at least the rest of the season, she's mine. Maybe not sexually, but mine, nonetheless.

That truth gives me a sense of control beyond anything I could imagine. Who knew that contracting a fake relationship would make me feel like this?

I grind my teeth together while that little voice in my head reminds me this isn't real, and it won't last.

"Yo, look who it is," Mason says, raising a fist that I bump with my own. "And who is *this*?"

Here we go.

I pull her to my side like I've seen some of the other guys do with their girls.

"This is my girlfriend, Cassidy."

Mason is mid sip when I say this, and the contents of his beer fly out, spraying all over my face.

I close my eyes and count to three, trying to remain calm.

This is the shit I hate about going out.

The noise.

The chaos.

The drunk idiots I call friends.

"Sorry, man," he yells louder than necessary.

Yep. He's already had too much. Not the first time.

"I'll get you something," Cassidy says, pulling out of my grip and heading toward the bar.

"Jesus, man. You could've given us a heads-up."

I don't respond, instead opting to take the offered beer from Hudson.

"She's hot as fuck. Got any friends?" Hudson says. Typical.

This time, I level him with a look, making it real clear with my eyes that I'm not opposed to murder.

"Hudson, I wouldn't hook you up with one of her friends unless I wanted Cassidy to cut my dick off," I reply, and Mason snorts.

Hudson has the audacity to act hurt. His bottom lip pouts out like a boy who lost his puppy. "What? I'm a nice guy."

Mason and I exchange a look. Silently deciding who's going to explain everything wrong with his comment. I lift my beer and nod for him to take the lead.

"For the first fuck and then you duck," Mason explains.

Hudson is a great friend and an incredible hockey player. But he's shit at relationships. He grins before taking a gulp of his own beer. He knows we're right.

Cassidy returns with a towel. "Here, let me do that," she says, laying on the whole "girlfriend" role rather thick.

The guys waggle their eyebrows and make obscene gestures while her back is turned.

Morons.

They may be mid-twenties, but they don't act a day over thirteen. All they think about is hockey, food, and sex.

"Tell us about yourself, Cassie."

"Cassidy," I correct, pulling her back to my side.

She grins up at me. "Not much to tell. We met at Starbucks,

exchanged numbers, and that's the story. I'm currently taking some time off before grad school, so I figured I'd follow Slate around for a bit." She winks at me.

I pull my bottom lip into my mouth. We hadn't discussed the specifics of how we met. Her on-the-fly thinking is a turn-on. She didn't miss a beat. Let's just hope we both remember this story later.

"Not sure how I feel about having a girl around all the time. Girls talk. You could ruin my reputation." Hudson groans.

"Poor boy, you worried if the ladies find out you fuck multiple a night, your dick will fall off?" Mason sticks his hand up for a high five, but I turn to Cassidy, trying to play it off like I didn't see it.

"Shut it, man." Hudson takes a long pull of his drink and sighs.

"Don't worry, boys. My mouth is shut. All your secrets are safe with me." Cassidy grins up at me before looking at each of my idiot friends.

Mason raises his hands in the air. "That applies to me too, right?"

She laughs. "I'm only here for the drinks. Speaking of which…" I hand her my beer, and she takes it. Got to hand it to her, she's good at this. Didn't even bat an eyelash about sharing a drink. I guess in the grand scheme of things, I did have my cock inside her. "Besides, no one needs to hear me gossip to find out shit. I'd say that exposé has your exploits pretty well covered."

It's my turn to choke out a laugh, and the others join me.

Not only is she hot as hell, but she's witty too.

If I were ever to settle down, I'd imagine it would be with some-one like Cassidy. Smart. Funny. Gorgeous.

What the fuck?

I immediately chase that thought from my head.

I'm not on the market now or ever. I like my privacy, and mar-riage and a family are not in my future.

We make our way toward the back and find the rest of the crew, plus a few additions. A couple of guys I can't stand are here, and I already regret this outing. Billy Lewis is the one guy I'd go to jail to put on his ass. He's an obnoxious asshole who has an inflated sense of his own skills.

He fucking sucks, which is why he's a reserve.

You can't tell him that, though. He's convinced himself he's a god.

As if the prick could sense my thoughts about him, he looks up. "Fuck, I didn't know you had it in you," he slurs.

"Had what?" I don't even try to contain the bite from my tone.

"A girl. Didn't think I'd see the day."

I take a step forward, and Cass's arm shoots out to stop me. "What the fuck does that mean?"

He shrugs like an arrogant ass and takes a drink. "You're a perpetual bachelor. I thought…"

"That's the problem, Lewis. You *thought*. Never been too good at that."

"Fuck off, Slate."

I'm about to knock this douche out, but Cassidy grabs my hand. "Let's go," she says, motioning toward the other side of the bar where Mason and Hudson are currently seated.

I nod before shooting one last glare at Billy.

When we're out of earshot, Cassidy turns toward me. "What was that about?"

I take a deep breath. "He's just a dick. Nothing I can't handle."

Her eyes widen. "It didn't look like you were handling it very well. Don't let him get under your skin. He seems like an ass. One who gets great pleasure out of taunting you."

I look down at her large blue eyes, rimmed in black. She's fucking gorgeous, but tonight, she's something else entirely.

"That he is, and that he does."

I smile, grateful she pulled me away. I rarely make appearances at these things, and none of the other guys deserve the night being spoiled because I showed up. I like control, and there's something about Billy that causes me to lose it. Every. Time.

He's slimy, and I don't trust him for a second.

This girl is good for me. Too good. I can get used to this.

But it's for a short time, and that's something I need to get through my head.

This is only to help me through the season. To help me relax so I can play the season of my life. Keep my spot on the team and win the Stanley Cup.

When that ends, so does this arrangement.

It has to.

chapter twelve

Cassidy

I SLEPT THE ENTIRE FLIGHT TO REDVILLE.

It's not that we were out late last night, but I've been exhausted with all the changes in my life.

It wasn't a long flight, only an hour, but I welcomed the time alone. Since Aiden flew on the team plane, he booked me a regular commercial flight and said he'd meet me at the airport when I land.

From the first night I met him to now, everything has been go, go, go.

After a late night last night, we were up early this morning, and Aiden was off to the arena for a one o'clock game.

I wasn't able to go, too much to do before uprooting my life to go with him to Ohio, but they won.

I caught a few glimpses on the TV as I packed up everything. Well, I packed up my new stuff. I assumed that since I was taking on a role as his personal assistant, I'd have to pack for him too, but he beat me to it. Every one of his shirts and pants were already in the suitcase and color-coordinated.

I make a mental note of the way he organizes his stuff. If I'm to be helpful to him in the future, I need to know how he likes things.

The little glimpses I caught of him playing were exhilarating. Game two was a blowout. The Saints move into game three with a two-zero lead.

I have no idea how the team even drank last night; today's game was insane.

Hockey is brutal.

From what I've learned via Google since agreeing to this crazy plan is that the hours of training are long, then every few days, they have a game, followed by after-hour commitments.

How they have the energy for that is beyond me.

But the team is known for being generous with their time in the community. Giving back to the city that has given them a home.

Watching Aiden in his element is nothing like the past. Sure, he was motivated. Determined. But he grew up. And he surely proved that he was more than good enough. No matter what his horrible mom tried to feed him.

Being near him again is crazy, but the thought of going to his home, the place he's made roots, is surreal. We always talked about what it would be like to get away one day, and now I'm headed to see how close to reality he was back in those days of dreaming under the oak tree.

It's a bit terrifying, if I'm being honest with myself.

Will there be anything that reminds me of our time together? If there is, can I pretend it's not there? On the flip side, if there's nothing, can I handle that? It's obvious he doesn't recognize me, but does he even think of the girl he once knew?

My breathing becomes heavy as my anxiety builds.

What the hell am I doing? I've allowed this whole thing to go too far.

I'm going to walk into his home because I lied. Not because he missed me or because he wants me there. Nope, it's all because I'm not ready to let him go. That's the truth. The ugly truth I try to pretend isn't there. But it is there. It hovers on the surface of every word I say, every look I give him.

I missed Aiden Slate, and I'm not ready to say goodbye.

If that makes me a selfish liar, so be it.

In my life, Aiden is the only person who makes me feel safe.

I need more time.

"You okay?" Aiden asks, side-eyeing me. "You look like you're about to pass out."

He sees too much.

Or you're just a shit liar.

"I'm fine. Just a little hungry."

Not a complete lie. I could eat. *I can always eat.*

"We'll grab something on the way. My car's just over there." He points off into the distance to where he must have parked. I'm still shocked that he offered to pick me up rather than just send a car service.

I crane my neck, trying to determine which is his. The BMW? Or something fancier. What has all this talent and money afforded him?

I'm actually kind of giddy. Why? Because despite the time that's gone by, I'm happy for my friend. The boy who saved me on numerous occasions. The one who sat for hours with me, talking about life and our individual futures, outside the dingy trailer park.

He pulls out his keys and hits a button. There's a beep signaling he's unlocked the car. I look up to find a white Jeep.

I swallow, emotion coming over me like a freight train. My heart thumps rapidly in my chest, and I'm practically in a daze as I jump into the passenger seat.

"What's wrong, Pip?" I hear Aiden's voice from behind me, but I don't bother to look up. Today's been a bad day. Worse than normal, and that's saying a lot.

When I got home from school, I found that the lights were off.

93

A side effect of Dad losing his latest job. Not showing up will do that.

They're still off, but at least now I have the money to turn them back on.

A trip to the pawn shop will do that.

But it was the last piece of jewelry I had of my mom's.

I don't know how I'm going to survive much longer like this. What happens next month if I can't find the money?

A tear leaks from my eye. I can't do this. "She lied."

"Who lied?" *he asks as he moves closer to where I am.*

I don't bother to look up. Instead, I focus my attention on my hands, twisting my fingers in my shirt. "My mom."

A few more steps echo in my brain before he sits beside me, and then my hand is in his hand. "What did she lie about?"

I shut my eyes, fresh liquid collecting behind my lids. "Mom said I was strong. That I'd be okay …when she was—"

When I stop speaking, Aiden squeezes my hand. "Was what?"

"Gone," *I whisper, hating to say the word.*

"Look at me, Pip." *At his words, I do. His arctic blue eyes peer into mine, begging me to listen.* "You are strong."

"No, I'm not. If I were strong…" *I stop, a sob lodging in my throat.*

His gaze continues to cling to mine. "One day, we'll both get out of here."

I nod at his words, hoping, praying for them to be true. "Pinky promise?"

"Pinky promise on my puck."

We both fall quiet, and then he breaks the silence. "You know, you never talk about her."

I look up at him, perplexed. "Who?"

A small line creeps up between his brows, and my heart rattles because I know who he's asking about. I'm just not sure I can talk about her. It's bad enough he already found me crying. If I open that door, I might never be able to close it.

"Your mom." Aiden's voice is soft like he's treading carefully over this topic. "Tell me about her."

I bite my lower lip, considering his request. "What do you want me to tell?"

"Anything that makes you happy, Pip."

I pause and swallow. "Did you know that all Jeeps have a secret?"

Aiden's eyelid twitches. He's getting annoyed. "Seriously, Pip. Deflecting again. Talk to me."

"I am."

He lets out an exhale. "Tell me about the secret."

"Nope. Your loss." I cross my arms at my chest and lift my chin in defiance. If he's going to act like this, I'm not going to tell him.

"Come on, don't be like that. Spit it out."

"Fine," I huff, and he raises an eyebrow for me to go on. "They all have a secret design."

"Design? What kind of design?"

"It could be anything. But every Jeep has one, and it's like a hidden treasure waiting to be discovered."

"How do you know this?"

I pause for a moment, my mind drifting back to when I was younger. "We used to have a Jeep when I was little. It was my mom's favorite car. She always told me stories about the secret character and how it made each Jeep special."

He looks at me with curiosity. "What kind of stories did she tell you?"

I take a deep breath; my voice feels like it might crack. "One of my last memories, actually. Together, we found the little symbol. It was a tiny lizard hidden on the side mirror. She said that the lizard was a symbol of strength and resilience, and that it would protect the people inside the car. She said I was that lizard. A symbol of strength." A tugging feeling spreads through my chest. "She said it's like each Jeep holds a unique secret, just waiting to be discovered. It's a reminder that there's something special in every ordinary thing."

I've only shared that with one person.

Aiden.

Did he drive this because of me?

No.

It's obviously a coincidence.

Jeeps are one of the most popular cars. No way he did it for you. He doesn't even remember you.

"Not a fan?" he asks, pulling me out of my thoughts by the bite to his tone. "Or was it not what you expected?"

My eyes narrow at his attitude. He's defensive, and I haven't even said a word.

"Not at all. I actually love Jeeps."

His hands have a white-knuckle grip on the steering wheel as he looks forward.

"What then? Did you expect a Bentley?"

I turn toward him. "You can drive what you want. I didn't expect anything. Maybe some would, but I'm not like other people, and you seem to keep forgetting that."

He turns and stares at me. I don't dare move. I want him to see that I mean it and that I'm a little irked that he'd think so little of me.

"You like it, then?"

I bob my head. "I love it. It's perfect. I'm a bit jealous. I kinda want my own."

His eyes narrow slightly, but after a few long, tense moments, his features relax, and he shakes his head, chuckling. "Let's get out of here."

While the atmosphere isn't quite as tense as it was moments ago, he still seems off. Lost in his own head.

What could he be thinking about? I wish I knew.

"You okay?" I ask, and he grunts. I chuckle awkwardly. "Is that a yes, Cassidy? I'm just fine?"

He turns to me and smirks, looking more like himself.

"Have I told you that you're a smart-ass?"

I smirk, but don't say anything, turning to the front and enjoying the ride.

We're on the road for twenty minutes before his phone pings.

"Will you check that to see who it is?" he asks.

I'm surprised by his request, but I pick it up to find he doesn't even bother with a password.

"Really?" I ask, lifting it into the air. "Do you know how dangerous this is? If you lost this, someone would practically have access to your entire life."

He lifts one brow, looking at me out of the corner of his eyes, one side of his lips tipped up.

"I don't leave that lying around anywhere."

I half roll my eyes. "Doesn't matter. You need to lock this down. As your executive assistant, I demand it."

He sighs. "Now you're my executive assistant?"

"I prefer it to assistant. That's below me," I joke, but he doesn't laugh.

Back is the mercurial Aiden, complete with a scowl and a tight grip on the wheel.

What's his deal?

"If I'd have known how bossy you were gonna be, I would've chosen someone else."

"No, you wouldn't," I respond. His comment stings, but I won't let him know I'm hurt. He might be in a mood, but it doesn't mean he has to act cranky with me.

"What?" He turns his head toward me quickly before turning back to the road.

I shake my head and plaster on the fakest smile I can muster. "Nothing. I didn't say anything. I'm just hungry."

Aiden nods, and one mile up the road, he pulls off the highway, heading toward a row of food options.

I don't call him out on his attitude because, with my luck, he'd turn it around to teach me some sort of lesson. He's very back-and-forth today, and I have to wonder if he's on edge about taking me to his home. I can't be the only one feeling a bit nervous about this step.

Fake relationship or not, his private space has never been shared. Ever.

"Can't have you starving. It's not good for anyone to go without food."

My chest is heavy with the weight of his words, and my stomach dives. Knowing our pasts, what he's just said is from experience. I know how much he means every word he's just spoken.

This short trip has already pulled on my heartstrings, which just has me questioning this whole thing more and more.

Too late now, Cass.

The Jeep takes a left into a little café. "This is one of my favorites. They have great sandwiches." He pulls into a spot and shuts off the car. "We can discuss the specifics of what your new position will include. Some of the stuff…" He pauses, and I know this is hard for him. He's not used to telling anyone.

Even in the past, he never told me. I just paid attention. The one thing I wished someone would do for me. My dad didn't care about anything that wasn't leading to him being three sheets to the wind. I didn't want to be like that, so I made a concerted effort to notice the little things. Especially with Aiden.

My stomach growls, and he shakes his head. "We can discuss it later. It's not important right now. You need food."

"That works for me."

We both get out of the car and head toward the restaurant. The café looks like a little cottage you'd find in the woods. Gray stone with ivy scaling up the sides. A cobblestone walkway leads to the red front door. When we step through, a chime rings, alerting everyone to our presence.

We don't bother waiting for a hostess to tell us where we should sit. Instead, Aiden walks right in like he owns the place, heading toward a table in the back. One that is hidden and obscured from the door. The few people in the place don't pay us any attention.

It's clear he's been here many times, and something tells me this is his spot, seeing as no one working here seems to find it weird that he's done this. Instead, an older woman lifts a hand and waves, all while smiling.

Once we're seated at the small, intimate table in the back, away from the other patrons, a man who has to be in his seventies shuffles toward the booth, two waters in hand.

"Mr. Slate. It's so nice to see you."

"Paul, I've told you to call me Aiden," he says, smiling up at the man, who waves him off.

"Different generation, son." He turns toward me. "And who do we have here? A guest. This is new."

I have so many questions about that. It's no secret that Aiden doesn't date, but surely, if he's been here often, he's come with someone.

"This is Cassidy. Cassidy, Paul owns Magnolia Café with his wife, Dorothy."

"Nice to meet you, Paul. You have a lovely place."

He beams. "It's been ours for forty-two years in November."

"Congratulations. That's incredible." I'm smiling because this man is so friendly and warm.

Something I'm not used to from most people.

Because your past won't allow you to trust.

"Thank you. What will it be for you two?" He looks back and forth between Aiden and me.

"I'll take my usual," Aiden says, not bothering to look at the menu.

I quickly glance at it and find *my* usual. "I'll have the Reuben and fries, with a side of pickles, please."

Paul looks at Aiden with a smile and wide eyes. Aiden quirks his brow before leaning back, and the man shuffles off again.

I don't even need to ask what that shared look was. I messed up. It hadn't even occurred to me that Aiden or anyone would find that weird.

Based on Paul's reaction, I'm almost positive he ordered the same thing. It's something we both always chose when available.

"That's...an interesting order," Aiden says.

"Is it?" I try to play it off like it's no big deal. "If you ask me, Reubens are entirely underrated."

"I got the same thing."

His eyes narrow, and I realize my blunder. It's something I've said a few times before. The part about Reubens being entirely underrated. Not only did I order something that was a mutual thing between us, but I'm using the same phrases.

Are you trying to get caught, Cass?

I don't react, keeping my face neutral and lifting my glass of water to my lips. After a few seconds, Aiden moves on to the topic he planned for us to discuss.

"About your responsibilities..."

I sit up straight and pull out my phone to take notes. He lifts a brow, and I bite my lip.

"I don't want to forget anything."

"Mainly, I'll need your help confirming certain things are always in place. I'll provide a list by tomorrow, and I'll ensure you know where everything is. The rest of it will be pretty basic. Run errands, like dropping my laundry off to the dry cleaner. Shopping for me if I have an event I need to attend. That sort of thing."

I nod, not hearing anything I didn't expect. The thing is, I know Aiden. I know him well, and he's leaving stuff out. It's fine. I'll figure out what still bothers him and if anything is new. I've always been good at seeing right through him.

"Outside of that, you'll be free to do whatever you want."

"Where will I be staying?" I ask, realizing we never discussed that.

"With me," he says.

My eyes widen, and I wonder what that means. We aren't going to have sex again, so where am I staying? "Do you have a second room?"

"I do."

I let out the breath I've been holding. But then another thought pops into my mind. He might not date, but it's clear he has sex. So if he's not having sex with me before games, will he have sex with someone else?

"Cassidy, look at me." I look up to find his brows furrowed. "Now speak."

Clearly, I'm not good at hiding my emotions. "Will you be having—" When I stop speaking, he lifts his hands and gestures for me to continue. "Umm. Will you be having any guests visiting to, umm, help you before a game?"

"No, I don't allow people into my home. It's my private space. Somewhere I can…"

His words trail off, but I know what he's getting at.

"Be yourself."

He takes a deep breath. "Exactly."

I'm being an idiot. I knew this about him already. I suppose I just needed it confirmed.

"And when we're on the road?"

"We'll cross that sleeping arrangement when we get there," he responds, shutting down the conversation. I welcome it because he might not have guests over, but he never said he wouldn't go somewhere else, and that's not something I want to consider.

The fact that the thought of him with someone else bothers me should be a huge red flag. One that should be screaming for me not to continue with this crazy plan.

The only problem is I can't walk away.

I'll take every second I have with Aiden because this will all end one day far too soon.

chapter thirteen

Aiden

Home.

It's the only place I feel safe and connected to my past. A past that most don't know about.

It's something I keep close to me.

It's personal.

We're finally here, and as the front door of my apartment swings open, I watch Cassidy's face closely. So many emotions are running through me. Each more concerning than the next.

Will she be impressed?

Will she be comfortable here?

Will she find it lacking?

Most importantly—why the fuck do I care all of a sudden?

It all goes back to my past and how much damage was caused. It was ingrained in me at a young age that I'm not good enough. I pushed against that with everything I had, but that little voice in the back of my head, that sounds a little too much like my mother, still whispers *you're not enough. You're not normal.*

My head is buried in my hands as I try unsuccessfully to push down the stress consuming me.

It feels like I'm drifting in the ocean, but I can't swim because the weight of the world weighs me down like an anchor. The need to get out of here presses against my chest, making it hard to breathe.

I'm almost eighteen, how is this my life?

Every day, I'm surrounded by kids my age with a world of opportunity, but not me.

I'm so close to my dreams but still stuck here because she won't let me leave.

Sitting here at the kitchen table, my hands tremble as I try to focus on my homework.

It's pointless.

I don't know why I bother.

The sound of my mother's steps has my back going ramrod straight.

I brace for her ridicule, knowing full well that whatever barb flies from her mouth will cut me like a sharp knife. Turning over my shoulder, I meet her gaze, and there's a disapproving frown already etched on her face despite me not even speaking.

But that's not what has her on edge. She's watching me…work.

Cringing over the kitchen being spotless. Because it is, not counting the makeshift desk I've set up on the kitchen table.

She's fuming over my assorted pens. The things I can't stop. The things she wants me to.

"You're such a mess, always obsessing over the smallest things," she sneers, her voice dripping with disdain. "Why can't you just be normal?"

I clench my fists under the table, my heart sinking with each word she utters. I know she couldn't possibly understand the constant battle that wages inside my mind.

I don't want to be this way. I don't want to need to have everything the way I do…

I want to defend myself, to explain it isn't a choice, that it isn't something I can just turn off.

But I can't.

The last time I tried to argue, she threatened to send me away.

Until I'm eighteen, I'm not safe. I need to apply to college. I need to get in, get a scholarship...

I'm stuck until I'm an adult. I can't risk her wrath.

Nobody realizes how hard I worked to get here. The obstacles I had to overcome.

"Wow," Cassidy says, taking a few steps into my place and turning in circles.

It's a top-floor penthouse with an open floor plan. A wall of windows lines the back and gives a perfect view of the town below.

Off to the left is the hallway leading back to my suite and the two guest rooms. One has been set up already with Cassidy's things. I allow very few people into my home, and none of them are there for long. One woman who was vetted by Mike. She cleans once a week, not good enough, in my opinion, and delivers food that she's prepped for the week when I'm in town. She also picked up and dropped off my laundry and, on this one occasion, prepared a room for Cassidy.

Now that I have an executive assistant, I can let her go, which will allow me more privacy in my own home. Not that she's ever here when I am. That's always been the rule. She's in and out before I get home. I've never met the woman, and that's the way I like it.

Mike says she's trustworthy with my things, and that's had to do, given my schedule. The fact is, I need help. I don't ask for it much because of the lengths I have to go to in order to reel my quirks in, but that's why I have Mike. He takes care of that shit for me.

He certainly nailed it with Cassidy.

Thoughts of the first night. Her crawling to me and the way she moaned as I touched her circulate on a loop, and I can feel my cock hardening beneath my jeans. I have to adjust myself without being seen, and it's not lost on me that I'm a grown-ass man who should be able to control his dick.

The idea of fucking her again is always there. This woman does something to me, and it's throwing me off-kilter. I've never had the urge to sleep next to another person, and right now, I'm having that urge with her.

Watching her twirl in circles, taking it all in, does crazy things to me. I've never wanted someone to see this place. To love it like I do. But it was important to me that Cassidy would. And she appears to, which makes me happy.

Yep. I made the right decision to keep this professional.

"This place is fantastic," Cassidy marvels, drawing me out of my thoughts. "I don't know what I expected, but this… suits you."

My place is incredible, in my opinion, but considering I'm one of the highest-paid NHL players, most would consider this underwhelming. Her genuine reaction makes me wonder what her background is. People who came from money wouldn't think much of my space, but Cassidy isn't proving to be like other people.

This girl could be anyone from anywhere. What do I really know about her? *Nothing.*

I wanna ask. I wanna know more about her. But if I pry into her life, she'll ask about mine, and that topic is off the table.

"Do you wanna see your room?" I ask, heading toward the dark hallway.

She follows me without a word as we make our way toward the back of the place. We come to the first door, which is farthest from my room.

"That room is used as an office," I explain, continuing on.

I don't bother opening the door to show her because there isn't much to see. A desk. Some files. A futon. That's it. I would consider myself a minimalist compared to my showboat teammates. When things have to be in a certain order to feel comfortable, you tend to have less, as not to have more to clean, straighten, organize, sort… the list goes on.

When we make it to her room, I pause for a moment. I didn't get to see what was done beforehand, and now I'm anxious, hoping

Angela took her time and made it feel cozy. The need for Cassidy to like this place is so intense, my stomach bottoms out.

"Aiden," Cassidy prompts. "Everything okay?"

I clear my throat. "Yeah. Fine." I throw open the door and step out of the way so she can make her way in. Just inside the door, I watch as her head turns around the room, taking in the space. Her space. She inhales deeply and exhales, sounding content. The relief is instant.

She turns to me and smiles. "Thank you. This is perfect."

I bow my head. "Go ahead and get settled. I need to leave for practice in two hours and have some stuff to do beforehand."

"Anything I can do to help?" she asks, placing her purse on the bed, made up of ivory bedding that blends in well with the pale gray walls.

I have to give it to Angela. She transformed this space expertly in a very short amount of time.

"Not right now. You'll need to come with me when I leave, but you should take some time to rest for now."

She nods, not needing me to elaborate. She knows I'll have some things I'll need done.

"I…I'll see you in a bit."

She doesn't say anything, jumping into action, getting her stuff in place.

I take one last look at Cassidy as she rifles through the bags sitting against the dresser, full of clothes waiting to be sorted. She looks at home already.

It feels right to have her here, and that thought almost pisses me off.

"Get your ass moving, Slate. What is this? Amateur hour? You're slacking, and it's pissing me off."

I practically growl, picking up my pace and slicing the ice with my skates. I'm headed toward the goal, ready to tell Coach to fuck off without words. Words will get you nowhere. Goals will.

Tomorrow is game three, which means today Coach gets to torture us during practice.

Mason comes from the left, trying to cut me off, but I pick, stopping in place and spinning to pivot before he even makes it to me. I easily maneuver around him, skating as quickly as I can toward the goal. When I'm close enough, I stop, take aim, and shoot.

There's your amateur hour, asshole.

"That's fucking better, Slate. Hit the showers."

One by one, my teammates head to the locker room as I continue to glide in circles as I wait for everyone to leave. Once I'm the last one still on the ice, I move to leave as well.

"What's up his ass today?" Mason says. Apparently, he was waiting for me to be done doing my thing. "We haven't lost yet. He should be in a better fucking mood."

I glance toward him. "Doesn't matter that we won. You know how he is."

He sighs. "I need a goddamn beer."

Before I step off the ice, I glance up into the stands where Cassidy sat during practice. People aren't typically allowed in the rink during practice, but Mike negotiated things with Coach, and she's allowed. There was pissing and moaning from some of the other guys, but they don't draw in the crowds like I do.

We start to walk, and as we do, we bump into Hudson, who's leaning against the wall in the hallway.

"You two coming tonight? We're grabbing drinks at Matteo's," he asks.

I lift my brow. "Really think you should be going out before our game tomorrow?"

"Worked well for us last time. You, of all people, shouldn't want to mess with a thing that seems to be working."

His comment gives me pause. I'm surprised he's referencing my "superstitions," although we both know it's more than that. It's a low blow because now that he's mentioned it, I have no choice but to stop by.

"If we get finished with dinner early enough." My jaw feels tight. Despite my words, I know I'll show up.

"Don't do that, man. You get a girlfriend and ditch your bro? What's that saying…bros before—"

"I know you're not about to call my girl anything but Cassidy…" I let the threat hang in the air.

He frowns. "You know I'm not that guy."

And he's right. I do. That's why he's one of my closest friends. The one who knows the most about me and my past.

I pat him on the back. "I'll try to make it."

He nods, heading toward the shared locker room. I follow him in but veer toward my private spot. I quickly make my way through, counting my pads and placing them in my bag. Once all the guys have filed out, Cassidy appears.

"Mike gave me the tour while you were warming up."

I need to give Mike a damn raise. He didn't need to do that. I could've gotten someone else to do it.

"What do you need help with?" she asks, ready to jump to work.

"Actually, I'm done here. Let me do my stuff, and then we can head to dinner. Are you good with that?"

She looks down at her outfit. "I'm good with it if you think this works."

I skim down her blush-colored sweater that hangs slightly off one shoulder, down to the tight skinny jeans that end right above a pair of beige ankle boots.

She looks fucking amazing.

"You look great. We'll keep it casual tonight."

Her cheeks flush, and a small smile graces her lips.

"Sounds good."

Forty minutes later, we head to one of my favorite burger joints.

We're seated at the back, my preferred spot, and already have our food.

"You said you have a roommate. What did you tell her you were up to?" I ask, popping a French fry into my mouth.

She fidgets in her seat, and that immediately puts me on edge. What did she tell this roommate?

"I told her I met a guy, and I was heading off with him for a bit." She acts like it's no big deal.

"You met a guy and ran off with him? And she didn't find that odd?" As soon as the question is out, I'm internally kicking myself.

I know better than to ask questions about her life. That only leaves me open to critique of my own.

"She found it more than odd. This is not something I do." She pats her lips with a napkin. "In all the years I've known Emma, I've never been serious with anyone. For me to come home and claim I met a guy worth uprooting my life for…yeah…she had questions."

"So what did you tell her?"

She smirks. "I turned on the TV and found a sports station playing highlights of your game. It was pretty simple after that."

One corner of my lips tilts. "Is she a fan?"

She lifts one eyebrow and frowns. "No. Emma does not speak sports…per se. However, she'd have to have her head in the sand not to know who you are. Considering you're easy to look at, her words," she quickly amends. "There weren't a lot of questions after that."

I chew the bite of cheeseburger in my mouth, take a sip of water, and consider this. "She didn't want to know anything about me?"

She chuckles. "She was too busy gushing about how good you look to ask any questions. There was a whole lot of cursing me and my luck and begging me to find her a hockey hottie." She shakes her head. "She practically packed my bags for me."

I take another bite around the smile that threatens to spread across my face. That conversation went much better than I originally thought. There is a bit of concern on my end about how easily Cassidy's family and friends stepped aside for her to run off with a stranger. Hockey star or not. Doesn't anyone worry about my motives?

Not your problem.

We quickly eat, keeping the rest of our conversation light. When we're done and headed out of the place, a light flashes, and I cringe. Normally, the press is not an issue. Hockey players don't get the same harassment as football or basketball, but apparently, this douchebag didn't get the memo.

Since I didn't expect this, I didn't prepare her or myself for any press hounding us.

Cassidy moves toward me, and I wrap my arm around her back, leading her through the fray.

"What's your name?" the man says, and I narrow my eyes. He looks familiar. "How did you meet? Are you two official?" He fires off questions at a speed that even if I weren't reluctant to answer, I couldn't. "Where did you come from? Why have we never seen you together?"

The more questions he asks, the more familiar his voice becomes. I know I've heard it before. Then it hits me. He's a local newscaster. New if I remember correctly. I think he was on weather before. He now covers sports, and by the looks of it, he's hungry as fuck for a story, and Cass and I are on the menu.

He hurls questions at us a million miles a minute, but to Cassidy's credit, she takes it in stride. She offers a smile and a cute little wave but doesn't say a word, allowing me to lead us to safety.

We get to my car, and I help her into her seat, shutting the door behind her and the never-ending questions. She's safe. I just need to get us out of here.

"No comment," I say, pushing my way to my own door.

I start the Jeep up and pull away on a groan. "I'm sorry about that. That doesn't usually happen."

She shakes her head. "I kinda figured I'd be subjected to

paparazzi." She blows out a breath. "If that's how it always is, no wonder you don't date."

The truth is that's one of the smallest reasons. She wouldn't understand the more important reasons. Nobody would. "Actually, hockey players don't usually have to deal with that."

"Well, that guy seemed to think there was a story," she deadpans.

"Regardless of whatever that guy thought, you did good," I say, glad to see she's not in hysterics like some women would be. "Handled it well."

Even better, she's not riding high on the spotlight. If she was, I'd be reconsidering this whole thing. Getting caught up in the limelight could change her mind about keeping this professional, and we can't have that.

"Wanna grab a beer with the guys?"

"I could use one about now. It's been a long few days."

I make a left and head toward Matteo's.

Long few days is right.

But regardless of that, I still feel calmer than I have in years, and I know I have one person to thank for that. Two if you include Mike for bringing Cassidy into my life.

I don't know what it is about her, but just her presence alone works better than a Xanax.

chapter fourteen

Cassidy

BUTTERFLIES SWARM MY BELLY, MAKING IT HARD TO WALK, BUT despite my apprehension, I square my shoulders and allow Aiden to guide me into the bar.

The air inside the large space appears hazy as my vision adjusts to the dim lights. The sound of laughter and the clinking of glasses echoes around me.

Despite the fact that I've met the guys already, I feel like the walls are closing in. Maybe this wasn't such a good idea. I'm still shook from that run-in with that reporter. I imagine that guy was low-key in the grand scheme of professional sports, but it still rattled me. I can't imagine how people dating football stars deal with it because if one local overzealous guy has me rattled, I'd never be able to handle a full swarm of paparazzi.

There is no preparing for that.

He places his hand on my lower back, leaning into my ear, and a shiver races up my spine.

"You okay?"

I nod, not sure my voice would work if I tried to speak.

This feels real. Too real.

Everything from the last few days is hitting me like a ton of bricks. It was nerve-wracking to go out with him in Birmingham, but at least I felt comfortable since I lived there. Now, in this new city, I feel like I've been thrown into the ocean without a life vest.

When I said yes to this crazy idea, I never considered what it would do to my psyche.

Being in his space.

Breathing the same air as him again.

I'm not prepared.

Not at all.

Being this close to him…

It brings everything back.

Today alone, the memories have been overwhelming. They've pounded at my brain, threatening to destroy the life I've made for myself.

I've moved on from my past. Made a life—even if it's not much, it's mine.

Can I really risk going back *there*?

I take a deep breath and look at the room around me.

Something I can see: The bar.

Something I can smell: The unmistakable fragrance of body odor.

Something I can taste: Nope. Nothing. But it doesn't matter, the trick worked.

I've calmed down enough to start walking.

It's funny that even now, his touch comforts me. After everything I've been through, I didn't think it was possible. I've tried to find contentment in my boyfriends, but it never worked. It's a bit annoying that my fake boyfriend gives me more comfort than any of the rest.

It's because it's him.

I shake my head, not wanting to think about what that means

for my heart. Instead, I pay attention to where I'm at. Making my way through this crowded place.

I'm shoved by some meathead who isn't paying attention, and my body stiffens. My legs turn to jelly, and that familiar fear creepy crawls its way in.

Aiden spins me around, crouching down to look into my eyes.

"Cassidy, look at me. I've got you." He pulls me into his arms, and his mint and leather scent washes over me. It instantly soothes me.

I stay in his arms for only a moment, allowing myself to fully relax, and then push away from him.

"I'm okay. I'm just on edge from tonight. It's been…a lot."

"We're going home."

My head shakes violently. I don't want that. I can't start this business relationship like this. Not on a freak-out that he's misunderstanding.

"I'd rather have the drink," I say, offering a smile that I'm sure misses the mark.

His eyes narrow, but he nods, stepping in front of me and grabbing my hand to lead.

It's hard to maneuver around the throngs of people, but lucky for me, Aiden guides us expertly through the crowd, attempting to get as close to the bar as possible. To get me the drink I so desperately need for about a million reasons.

They're all hoping and praying the bartender will take pity on them and ask for their order, but with a bar full of NHL players, they might be there for a while.

Good luck to them.

This place is insane.

Complete chaos.

So much so, that it's actually perplexing that Aiden, or at least the Aiden I remember, would ever be caught dead here.

But I guess, like me on his arm, it's part of the act. A well-constructed wall erected to keep him momentarily safe while secretly fighting a battle royale internally. One likely similar to what I'm experiencing.

My footsteps slow, but his hand tightens around mine and gives me a squeeze, urging me on.

"Come on. We're almost there," he says from beside me.

I lift onto my tippy-toes while trying to keep up the pace, looking to see where he's leading me. My anxiety ebbs when I realize we're headed away from the bar and the massive crowd standing around it.

The guys are in their own area, away from the mayhem.

Pulling my gaze away from the guys, I look at Aiden, studying his profile.

Yep, his calm nonchalance is all an act. Maybe someone less observant wouldn't see it, but I can tell by the tension in his jaw, the straight line of his lips, and his rigid posture.

He's walking a thin line, just barely keeping himself in check. This must be killing him.

Aiden has always hated crowds. He told me back at the trailer that he tried to work on controlling his anxiety, but he hated it. It looks like he's doing better than the last time I saw him, but at what cost to him? How will he suffer later?

The thing about the quirks that make Aiden unique is that every ounce of strength he possesses goes into controlling himself from exposing what he deems weakness to the outside world. This leaves him physically and mentally exhausted. The toll is hefty.

He ushers me through a roped-off area in the back, and I'm immediately on high alert.

Time to play the part.

His teammates are drinking already, likely well on their way to intoxication. They seem like good guys, but every single one of them knows that every girl in here wants them. The air reeks of arrogance and entitlement.

Sure, they're good-looking and another level of wealthy, but most women want so much more than that. They want stability.

Passion. To feel safe in all aspects. By flaunting their wealth—wearing their expensive, name-brand clothes and fancy watches and consuming top-shelf drinks—they're attracting the wrong girls who don't even know it.

Or maybe they do, and they just don't care?

It's kind of crazy. Over the last few years, ever since I saw that Aiden had gone pro, I've tried to keep far away from all things hockey. I didn't want any more reminders of him. Now that I'm here, I wish I knew a tad more about the guys. Wouldn't Aiden's girlfriend know a little more about hockey and the guys he spends most of his time with?

My heart rattles in my chest as we make our approach. I know that with every interaction, the questions will get more complex. More personal.

It all feels like a test. One I'm going to fail.

I'm trying to fool the world that I'm his girlfriend and not just a woman he's hired to keep him in check.

It feels like all eyes are on me, and I'm suddenly unsure that I can play this part convincingly.

Aiden must notice my hesitation because he stops walking, and I look at him. His brow is raised as he takes a step toward me so that we're toe-to-toe.

"You good? Because if you don't wanna do this, just say so." The bite in his tone shocks and confuses me. I get that my steps have been reluctant, but I said I was fine, so why the attitude?

Because you're not fooling anyone, that's why.

I'm sure everyone within a mile radius can tell you don't want to be here, present company included.

If I were Aiden, I'd be pissed too.

I blink several times, shift my weight from my left foot to my right, and cross my arms over my chest, mouth flapping open, likely making me look like a guppy caught in a net. I need to respond, but my brain is failing me.

Finally, I take a deep breath. "I've had a rough night," I say, glancing around, hating that people are now staring at us.

Can this get any worse?

Date number two and I'm already causing a scene. *Some help you are.* At this rate, I'll be fired within the hour.

"So…you wanna leave?" There's that bite again. He's definitely annoyed with me.

My face contorts, and my cheeks heat. If I keep up this behavior, we're going to get into a fight, as is people are starting to notice that we've stopped moving. I can only imagine what this looks like to the outside world since my body language screams defensive. Shit. I'm going to blow this sham of a relationship up. I'm about to answer, probably making this moment even worse for us, when he swoops down and pulls me into his chest, getting so close to me, I feel his breath skim across my nose. I glare up at him, and he smirks.

Asshole.

He leans into my ear for only me to hear his next words.

"Congratulations, Cassidy. We've had our first public fight. We're officially official to everyone in this room."

I pull away, eyes narrowed in on him. "What?"

"We've had a relationship in secret for some time. Arguments occur. We just happened to have one tonight, brought on by the stress of that asshole reporter." He glances around. "Every guy here hates the press more than the next. They'll sympathize and won't want to upset you by prying or poking at you." He bends down and places a chaste kiss on my cheek. "You're welcome."

I'm speechless.

That was…all an act? To save me from interrogation? The fact that he could read me so well…that he knew why I was struggling, just goes to show that he sees way too damn much.

I can't do this. Before the night's out, that little faux argument is likely going to be on social media. People were gawking at us. Thrilled to find that Aiden Slate is open to dating.

I could see it in their eyes. Hunger.

They were probably giddy at the prospect that we're already fighting.

Dear God, what is wrong with me?

It feels like my life is spiraling, and things that haven't bothered me in years are suddenly rearing their ugly heads again. I'm concocting stories about the women around me, making them villains when they're just here having a good time with their friends.

I'm losing my shit.

It was one thing to think I could pretend once or twice, but the reality is, I'm no good at it, which spells trouble. If I throw myself all in as the girlfriend. If I allow him to let me in piece by piece under falsities, and he ever finds out the truth…

"Hey, Cassidy. How's it going?" I hardly register that Aiden's friend, Hudson, has spoken. He bends down, waving a hand in front of me. "You alive down there?"

"Give her a break, man. This is new to her. Hell, some jerk of a reporter bombarded us on our way out of dinner."

His eyes widen. "Shit. That sucks," he says, running a hand back through his hair. "This is why I don't do relationships."

"That's why?" Aiden asks, snickering.

"Well…one of the many." Hudson smirks. "It's frustrating as hell. I bet you were ready to throw down."

"Now you know why I choose not to go out."

"I hate being here as much as you do. Not my scene." This time, it's Dane who speaks as he steps up to where we're gathered. He looks out at the throngs of people and frowns. There's something sad in his stare, and I wonder what his story is.

"Why don't you get your girl a drink?" Hudson says.

"I'll go with you," Dane offers before glancing at Aiden. "She'll be fine here. It's roped off."

Aiden holds my stare, waiting for me to give the okay. "Lord knows I want one."

He smiles. "Sure. I'll grab them with you. What do you want?" Aiden asks me.

I go right for the strong stuff. "Tito's on the rocks with some lime juice."

"Got it. I'll be back." He and Dane step away, and I'm left standing with Hudson and feeling awkward.

Hopefully, he doesn't try to make small talk before I've gotten my drink.

"I still can't believe you're dating my boy."

Great. So much for that. I escape one inquisition, only to be left to fend off another.

I straighten my back and prepare to be barraged with questions. "What's there to believe? He's a great guy."

He steps around so that we're face-to-face. He's handsome, in a boy-next-door sort of way. But he looks like he should have been an all-American football star as opposed to a hockey player, with his dirty blond hair and translucent blue eyes.

"That he is." He pulls one side of his mouth up. "He tells me everything, and this was a surprise."

"Turns out, I'm his best-kept secret." The irony of those words isn't lost on me.

It was his talent that got him here, but I wonder if anyone knows it was a girl from the trailer parks who rounded up the money to get him seen?

No chance he's shared that with anyone.

"I guess he doesn't tell you *everything*," I jest, lifting my brow, and he chuckles.

"So it would seem."

"Ah, there she is. The lady of the hour." Another player walks up, and this one, I can't remember for sure, but I think his name is Mason.

"Apparently, I'm the novelty act. Can't say I love the attention," I say, glancing at a group of girls who are currently staring daggers at me for no reason other than where I'm standing.

I offer up a wave, and they all huff, turning away.

"I like her." Hudson laughs.

"Who are we talking about?" Aiden walks up, handing me a glass.

"Me, of course. Not that you're surprised. I'm quite likable." I let my lips part and close my eyes as I sip my drink. The smooth taste tingles my tongue as it drifts down my throat. It's exactly what I need right now. An instant elixir.

From the corner of my eye, I watch Aiden. He lifts his drink to his mouth but doesn't take a sip.

I wonder if he limits the amount he drinks since he has a game tomorrow, or maybe he just doesn't drink a lot, seeing his past. I should try that.

Both our parents are alcoholics. His mom said and did terrible things while drunk. His decision might be about control, but there's no doubt some of the choice stems from her too.

She was always the hardest on him when she'd had liquor. Telling him how worthless he was. How he'd never amount to anything. I hate her.

As I take another sip, my brain drifts away from all that. The conversations around me revolve around hockey, which I'll avoid. I'm not really interested tonight.

"I'll be right back," I tell the group. Aiden looks up at me with narrowed eyes. "I'll be fine. I'm just checking my phone over there," I say, motioning toward a window with fewer people.

He nods, and I head off, pulling my phone out.

I check my email first as it's been a couple of days, and then I see a text from Emma.

Emma: You alive?

Emma: Hello! Are you alive?

Cassidy: Unfortunately.

Emma: Wow. That is extremely reassuring. You good?

Cassidy: Great.

Emma: Pulling teeth, I see. How's...being the girlfriend?

I probably should have come up with a better lie because her knowing it's fake feels like I'm breaking the NDA, but what choice did I have? Emma was not going to allow me out of her place without something.

I'm about to answer her when someone slides up next to me. I expect it to be Aiden, but when I look up, I find it's another player. Billy, I think his name is. I've met so many guys that keeping their names straight is hard, but I don't want to know him based on his vibe. Something about him is slimy, and he hasn't even said a word.

"What are you doing all alone?" His voice slithers up my spine, giving me the heebies.

My gut has never let me down. It's typically right on with my first impressions, and right now, alarm bells are going off.

"Not sure how that's any of your business." I don't bother to play the nice act. Something tells me this guy would run right over me if I did.

"Ahhh. I see," he grunts. "You're already sick of Slate."

My head jerks back, caught off guard by his words. "Who the hell do you think you are?"

He leans back, all smug arrogance. It probably works on some women, but to me, it's just sleazy.

"I can make you feel better."

"Doubtful, thanks." I turn to leave, and he grabs my elbow.

I yank it out of his grip, turning around to glare up at the creep.

"Are you always this much of a bitch?"

"Interesting choice of words when you're propositioning me uninvited."

He purses his lips. "I saw you alone and wanted to make sure you were taken care of," he coos, and it makes my stomach roil with disgust.

Memories crash over me. Ones I don't want to remember. Ever.

I exhale sharply, pulling myself from the nightmare, to find the guy's eyes trained on me. I do my best to compose myself so that I can get away.

"I'm a big girl. I am perfectly capable of being by myself." I take two steps, and he calls out.

"There's something about you."

I twist around, fear gripping me. Does he know? Will he tell? *No. He knows nothing.*

"What's that supposed to mean?"

He takes two steps toward me, but I hold my ground, refusing to cower. I did that once, and it did not end well for me.

"It means you have to have some secret. Something that makes you special. To capture his eye and tie him down…we all know there's something…"

"Leave me alone."

He doesn't stop, though. Instead, he continues on with his bullshit. "Then again, you might just be two of a kind. We all know there's something off about him."

Red.

It's all I see through the haze of rage caused by this asshat. Instinct to defend Aiden. The insinuations that there's a problem with him are enough to make me murderous.

"Leave me *and* Aiden the fuck alone." My voice trembles slightly as I try to maintain my composure. The dimly lit room seems to close in on me, the shadows dancing menacingly on the walls.

"And why would I do that?" he says, a cruel smirk playing on his lips. The way he looks at me makes a chill run up my spine. His gaze feels cold and hard as steel. It causes my heart to pound in my chest.

"I…" I start, my voice barely a whisper. I can feel the tension in the room, thick and suffocating, like a heavy fog making it hard to breathe.

This isn't just about him. It's about the past. Another time when I felt out of control.

His hand reaches out to grab me, his fingers closing around my arm like a vise. "Let me go." I try to pull away, but his grip is too strong.

I'm no longer in the bar.

No, I'm back at the trailer park, back to the place that broke my soul.

Back when Aiden didn't protect me.

chapter fifteen

Aiden

"T HE WAY I SEE IT, THERE'S SOMETHING YOU HAVE...SOMETHING special enough to entice the great Aiden Slate, and I want to know what that is—"

I walk up in time to hear Billy's words as he grabs Cassidy and traps her.

"Get the fuck away from her," I say, voice menacing. "Or I'll kill you."

Cassidy shakes her head frantically, blinking away tears that threaten to fall.

"Get your girl out of here." He's leaned back so casually, so fucking cocky, and I snap.

Before I can even process what I'm doing, I have him pushed up against the wall. My hand held tightly around his neck.

"Don't you ever fucking touch her."

"Aiden."

Someone tugs at my arm, but I'm too far gone. Too out of control.

I'm thrust back to another time, a different place.

One filled with pain.

"*Aiden*, please stop. He's not worth it."

Cassidy.

It feels like cold water is poured over my head. My memories fade away, and I'm brought back to the present.

I drop my hand locked around his neck and step back, breathing ragged.

"There will always be villains like him. Don't let him win."

My head snaps to Cassidy. "What did you say?"

Those words. I've heard them before. They aren't something I'll ever forget because, at the moment, they were profound. It's ingrained in my memory, never to be forgotten.

She blinks, tilting her head. "There are plenty of vain guys like him."

I stare at her for several moments, and she holds my gaze. My eyes roam across her face, and she shrugs. "He's not worth it."

I'd just been in my head, remembering things from the past. Clearly, I'm losing my mind tonight.

I shake my head, trying to brush off the anger still boiling under the surface. I need to get the fuck out of here.

I look toward the front of the bar, then the window. Hockey fans, mostly women, line the street outside.

They're everywhere. Like a swarm of vultures circling above, hungry for the kill. But instead of meat, they're desperate for a night with a hockey player. Most likely Hudson.

Shit.

On the few occasions I have joined the guys, this was not a problem for me. For one, I typically participate when they're going places the paps don't frequent for news. The times they were around, they were too busy trying to get the scoop on one of the other guy's escapades. Unlike me, they don't mind airing their laundry.

But mostly, I simply stay home, and for good reason.

If you don't go out, there's nothing for them to report.

But because of my "relationship" with Cassidy, the luxury of being a recluse is just beyond my grasp. To sell the story that I have a girlfriend, I have to periodically agree to outings.

I glance from the spectacle outside to the crowded room, searching for a way out of here.

"Can we go? I have a headache," Cassidy says, following my train of thought. "Or are we stuck here?"

I grab her hand, trying to offer a modicum of comfort. Tonight has been too much. She's just started, and already, I think I owe her a massive raise.

"I'm going to ask if there's a back way out of here," I say.

When I release her hand, a bracelet falls to the ground, and I bend to grab it. Cassidy and I do some strange dance, both going for the object. I win out in the end; picking it up and grabbing for her wrist to put it back on.

She tenses under my touch, going absolutely still. I slide up the sleeve of her sweater, and my breath hitches. My finger slides over her wrist and the scar that looks like it's been there for some time. The puckered flesh is still pinched despite the coloration that would suggest it's been years since whatever caused this.

"What happened?" My voice is low, like a winter storm building in intensity. My heart beats in my ears, and my chest tightens.

Most people wouldn't have this sort of reaction. But most people didn't grow up where I did.

"That's none of your business," she snaps, jerking out of my grip.

"Cass…"

"No, Slate. That's not what this is. What we are. Some things are mine."

She moves quickly, turning her back on me. Everyone has secrets, and clearly, Cassidy is not exempt.

The thought of what might've done that to her does nothing to settle the inferno within. Billy better stay well enough away because I'm a hairpin trigger away from giving the paps more than they bargained for.

I allow her to stalk off. She needs time, and I need the space. The closer she is, the harder it is to recognize that her secrets aren't my business. There's a reason we aren't sleeping together.

This has to remain professional. There is no future. Which means her secrets are none of my business. No matter how much I hate it.

I'll give her the time she needs to calm down. Not like we're going anywhere anytime soon.

There's no way out of here that doesn't involve overzealous fans and the flashing light bulbs of the cameras.

After what just happened and how Cassidy reacted, the last thing we should attempt is to leave.

Cassidy is new to this, so she doesn't realize we've stoked the fire to inferno levels. Showing up here, new girlfriend in tow, is big enough, considering it's me. An NHL player who has never had a girl on his arm. But it's guaranteed that someone in here captured our faux argument and the showdown with Billy.

Every gossip columnist or influencer in the area has arrived to catch a peek at her, and a pissed-off Cass isn't what I need them to see.

The truth is, I missed most of what was said between her and Billy. What I saw was enough, but her reaction seemed…intense. More.

Feeling concerned about her is not part of our arrangement. Worrying about what she's feeling and if she's all right are definitely not part of it. This has me feeling out of control. The exact opposite of why I wanted her to be my fake girlfriend.

But despite everything, I care. I don't like it, but I do.

Yeah, she's here to make my life easier. And bringing her around is a necessary evil, but I still want to keep her safe. To know her.

It goes against everything I normally do, but I'm not sure I can hold myself back any longer.

This is a problem. This girl does something to me.

She…she makes me feel. And feelings are things I want less of, not more.

Not one bit.

If I were smart, I'd keep her at arm's length. If I were smart, I'd have just told the world she was my damn assistant.

But no. I wasn't thinking. I was too busy protecting my secret.

I'm a fucking asshole because the longer I spend with this woman, the more curious I become. And as my curiosity is piqued, my resolve breaks down. Soon, I'll forget all the rules.

I'll be taking her to my bed.

Making her mine.

If only for one more time.

See, asshole.

When I go in search of her, I find her facing the glass window, looking out at the crowd of fans outside. Her head is pressed against the glass, and her breath fogs up the window.

"Shit," she mumbles. "It's a jungle out there."

I chuckle, relieved to hear her voice, soft and normal. Tired, but normal.

"There tends to be a crowd of women when Hudson is out. They don't want me, but we could be collateral damage."

"I'll probably regret this, but I think we should just rip off the Band-Aid," she says.

"It's been a night of Band-Aid ripping," I say. "Are you sure?"

"Can one ever be sure about these things?" A lopsided smile spreads across her face.

I grab her hand and pull her up, heading the way we came from, past the VIP section, until we are in the back hallway.

"Where—" she says, but I push open the back door, and she's instantly quiet.

The cool October air hits me in the face as I lead her outside. The chill in the air is a bit more than I was prepared for.

"Hopefully, none of your fans realize you've gone out this door."

"As I said, I don't have those types of overzealous fans."

"Only Hudson gets panties thrown at him." She laughs.

"Pretty much," I whisper, not wanting to tip off anyone lurking in the back alley. Since I don't go out, no one bothers with me, but now that I'm out, all bets are off.

I doubt they could see in through the front window, which I'm 90% sure was reflective glass, but you never can tell. They were more likely getting intel from someone inside that all the guys were here today.

This is the biggest problem with making the playoffs. Typically, life is low-key.

But once the playoffs start, and there's a shot at the Cup, all bets are off for any level of normalcy.

"The car is right around that corner. We'll have to be quick, but we can do it." I hold her gaze, trying to ensure she's on board.

"Let's do it," she says.

We aren't even a step around the damn corner before the painstakingly familiar sound of a camera firing and snapping away greets us.

It takes a mere second before a flash of light blinds us.

Someone from inside definitely tipped this guy off that we were here and that we were leaving.

Why does he have such a hard-on for me?

There are plenty of better stories out there. There's enough dirt on Hudson to fill a whole book, so why isn't he bothering him? That shit would put him on the national news.

I tighten my grip on her hand, and I don't miss the way she shakes. It could be from the cold, but I doubt it.

This shit sucks.

Hopefully, my touch will help ground Cassidy in her first real experience with these dirtbags.

Questions are shouted from all directions. There are so many here, I can't even figure out who's asking what.

"Come on, Aiden? Give me something," the asshole reporter's

voice yells out. "The girlfriend? What's your name, sweetheart? Why have you been keeping her a secret?"

I try to remain calm, but as my vision adjusts, and I search for a route to the car, my anger fuels.

Next to me, Cassidy stands tall, chin up despite the fact she's being assaulted with questions.

It's bad enough they do this to me, but to her…

I feel like a fucking selfish prick for thrusting this on her tonight. We came here so I could sell a story. One that keeps my secrets hidden. For my peace of mind.

Fuck it.

We're here now, and the story is out. Might as well cement the title of asshole thoroughly.

If I don't throw this dog a bone, he'll never stop.

The only choice I have is to give him what he wants. Something to splash across his website. Then I need to hope that's enough to appease him, so we can get the hell out of here.

Without a second thought, I stop in my tracks and lift her small, trembling hand to my mouth.

Placing a soft kiss on her skin, I look up and meet this douchebag's eyes.

"Rumors are true," I say, keeping my voice steady. "Now, can you let us go?"

Despite my words, he lifts his camera up and starts snapping away.

Great.

That didn't work at all.

Instead, I just riled him up more.

"Give him what he wants and get me the hell out of here," Cassidy mutters, low enough that nobody but me hears.

So I do just that.

I drape my arm around her waist and pull her closer.

I act on an impulse, moving closer. I turn her toward me and lean in until our lips are almost touching. Cassidy's eyes widen, and a surprised breath leaves her mouth. I won't take what she's not willing to give. Our eyes meet, and there's a silent conversation that only the two of us are privy to. Her pupils dilate and glaze over. That's my sign.

Her lids flutter shut just as I descend, a sigh escaping her as our lips touch. I'm tentative at first, but Cassidy opens up to me, and all sense is wiped away.

Camera's flash.

People yell.

Hell, the world might be on fire.

I don't fucking care.

At this moment, it's just Cassidy and me.

She claws at my jacket as my tongue circles hers.

There's no one here but us. We're completely oblivious to what's happening until I realize that it's gone completely silent.

There is no sound when moments ago, it was deafening.

I pull away, helping Cassidy steady herself, and when I look out at all the fans, who must have heard the commotion and wanted to see what was going on, welp, they're here now, and the crowd goes ballistic. The cheering echoes off the buildings.

"Now can we leave?" I say sarcastically, and the crowd laughs, thankfully starting to part so we can make it to the car.

We don't speak as I lead us to the Jeep, and as soon as we're there, I open the door for Cassidy, and then head to my side of the car, get in, and close the doors on the madness.

I take a second to breathe. To get my bearings before I look at her. I'm not prepared for what I see. Her body is rigid, and if I'm not mistaken, her jaw is tight.

"Cassidy, I—"

"Let's not do this here," she says, and I raise a brow.

She tries to mask her unease with a smile, but I can see the turmoil brewing. I know it all too well.

"I'm good. Can we leave?" She turns to the window, officially closing the door to any further talk about what just happened.

It doesn't matter, though, because I don't need her to say I shouldn't have kissed her like that. She might've been giving me the go-ahead signs, but she didn't speak the words. Yet again, I forced her into a situation she didn't choose. I know I messed everything up.

Because now that I've tasted her lips again, I'm not sure how I'm going to keep this just business. Assuming after tonight, she doesn't tell me to go to hell.

I'm fucked.

chapter sixteen

Cassidy

'M NOT GOING TO LIE…I'M A HOT MESS.

Yep.

That's me.

The idiot who pretended she could separate her emotions and work for this man. Someone who thought she could be subjected to the limelight, groped, and chased down, and not panic.

Hot. Mess. Idiot.

I know without a measure of a doubt, in order to help him, I will have to break my own heart.

I'd gladly fall on my sword to heal him. *To save him.*

The most tragic part of my misguided plan is that I've barely even scratched the surface of things to do for him. Ways to help him. It's become painfully clear that this Aiden is not the boy I once knew. He's changed.

Then there's the whole fact that I'm falling all over myself because of one damn kiss. One incredibly amazing kiss.

Aiden kissed *me*.

Again.

Sure, we already had sex, but this is different. Feels different.

That night lives in a self-contained vacuum.

Now I'm in his life, living in his home, and I no longer have the luxury to pretend he's someone else. After the first night, I took all my lustful thoughts, pushed them back in the corner of my brain, and remembered who he was to me and why I can't get attached. I pretended we were both someone else.

Tonight, Aiden Slate kissed me.

The boy I loved as a brother, a protector…he kissed me, and shit, now I want him to do it all over again.

Re-reading the letters I sent him had helped keep things in check since the night I slept with him. It's reminded me of why I sought him out to begin with.

But right now—my brain isn't listening, and neither is my libido. Something unlocked within me when his arms wrapped around my body, and he claimed me for the world to see.

It might've been fake, but it felt real.

Because damn, the man can kiss, and now I'm back to re-membering everything else he can do, and it has me on edge. Perspiration builds at my hairline. Palms sweaty. Legs pressed tightly together.

Thinking about the way he used my mouth—yeah, not going there.

Or the way he thrust—

God. Damn. It.

Nope.

Not going there.

I'm better than this. I'm *stronger* than this.

I pull out a letter, desperate to get my head back in the game.

It's all your fault. Everything. You lied. You never came back. And now my life is over. I'll never be the same.

I throw the letter as if it's on fire, all thoughts of anything carnal gone, replaced by pure fear.

The truth is, I've been careful what letters I've read.

I've sorted these so many times. I know which envelope goes with which memory, and I've purposely left that one in the box.

Right now, after the incident at the bar, him touching me, I can't go back to the past. Not *there.*

I can't accidentally let my brain think about all that again. I need to do something. Anything that can help take my mind off it. The only problem is, it's one in the morning. I can't sleep.

With a long, drawn-out sigh, I pull back the fluffy cream duvet and step out of the bed.

The floor is cold, so I grab a pair of socks from the dresser before I head down the hall.

Maybe I can find a snack in the kitchen. Something comforting. Soothing.

It's funny, I have barely had time to check out this place despite my curiosity. With the game schedule, we probably won't be here all too often, but that doesn't change the interest.

From the moment I stepped into Aiden's private space, I've wanted to explore every nook and cranny. Inspect every item on every shelf. I want to know him. This Aiden. The man he's become since leaving me behind.

I swallow, shaking off that thought.

It's eerily quiet as I head toward the kitchen. The fluffy cotton on my feet keeps my steps silent, which is good because I'd hate to wake him. His schedule is nuts, and he needs his sleep.

But when I turn the corner, I startle.

There he is in the kitchen, and what I find knocks the breath from my lungs.

Aiden Slate is standing with his back to me, in low-slung gray sweatpants, shirtless.

He must hear me because he pivots, lifting a brow when he sees me. But my eyes wander from his face, down his firm chest, over his well-defined abs, like some kind of oversexed voyeur. I swear drool is leaving my mouth, and I'm instantly embarrassed by myself.

"Couldn't sleep?" he says, leaning back against the counter.

"No," I say. "I didn't think you'd be up."

I narrow my eyes, finally taking in what he's doing. A sponge is in his hand and cleaning spray is on the counter right beside him.

"Are you cleaning?"

He purses his lips. "The kitchen was dirty."

Something tells me it wasn't. But knowing what I know about Aiden, it wouldn't matter if it's sparkling. His need to clean will overpower any other thoughts in his head.

A memory flutters in my brain.

Where is he?

I thought we were supposed to meet by the lake after his practice, but he wasn't there when I arrived.

His mom's car isn't here, which could mean he borrowed it, but who knows? Probably not. She never lets him have it. Instead, she makes him walk or take the bus...

He said he had something to tell me, but maybe it isn't that important.

I take a deep breath and think about what I should do.

Before I can think better of it, I take the steps up to his door.

They creak beneath my feet and make my heart pound harder with anticipation.

I hope she's not home.

When I reach the door, I take a deep breath and knock. When I do, it opens. It wasn't even shut properly.

This can't be good.

Tentatively, I step inside.

The smell of cleaning products fills my nose instantly. It's heavy in the air, invading my senses.

I glance around, and when I see him, my mouth drops open.

There he is, and it breaks my heart to see him like this.

He looks frantic. His chest rising and falling as if he had just run a marathon, but instead, he's cleaning the counter.

I move closer, taking him in.

With brows furrowed in concentration, he looks possessed.

From where I'm standing, I can see he's been at this for a while, probably the whole time I was waiting for him under the tree.

Every surface gleams.

It's like he's trying to erase every imperfection on the fake wood. But I know too well it's more than that.

This is his way of controlling whatever happened to him today.

Cleaning calmed him. It helped relieve his tension. Except once the compulsion started, it was tough to get him out of that state of mind. He'd clean for hours, going mad because it wasn't clean enough.

I won't allow his mind to do that to him anymore tonight.

I walk over to where he is and reach for the hand that holds the sponge. My fingers wrap gently yet firmly around his wrist. "It's clean. You can stop."

He shakes his head. "I can't."

I take a deep breath, knowing it's a losing battle for now.

"Then let me help you," I say, diving in and getting to work. "And maybe next time, I can do it for you? We can add this to my list of responsibilities."

He laughs darkly. "Even if you do, it won't stop me from making sure it's clean."

"That's fine. But I bet you find that it's to your satisfaction. I'm pretty good." I wink. "Now, what still needs to be done?"

"It's fine," he says, never ceasing to scrub.

"It's not. That's what I'm here for." I stare into the side of his head, and he finally turns to me and nods.

"The floors. You can help with that. All the dishes are done, and I'm almost finished with the counters." He glances around the room and sighs. "That's all that's left."

"Point me in the direction of the supplies."

His hand gestures to a door on the other end of the kitchen. It's a pantry, which surprises me that he'd keep supplies with his food.

"Right out back," he says. "Upper shelves, though, so let me know if you need any help reaching things."

I open the pantry door to find it leads to his laundry room. In the corner, well organized in bins and on shelves, are all his supplies. Labeled as they would be, alphabetically.

I marvel at the stark white room, with pops of color here and there. It's pristine. Gorgeous. Aiden. *This place is amazing.*

I grab the vacuum, plug it in, and get to work.

I'm lost in my own little world, bopping around to a song stuck in my head, finally getting to do my job. The reason he pays me. But it's not long before I feel his presence behind me. I glance over my shoulder to see he's leaning closer and shutting the vacuum off.

I twist around and when I do, his face, and his body are so close. I can practically touch his bare chest.

My heart hammers under my ribs, and I swear butterflies swarm in my stomach.

His nostrils flare slightly, a clear indication he's not happy. "You're doing it wrong."

I blink. *What?*

How can I be vacuuming wrong?

Despite the fact that the words are on my tongue, I don't ask what he means because it's not something I'd ever say to him. It's something most would say, not recognizing the effect that question could have on someone like Aiden. More ridicule for a man who ridicules himself enough.

He shakes his head. "It's fine. I'll take over."

"Could you show me? I'd like to know how you want it done. That way I can do it right."

It's as though his entire body exhales at those words. The rigid posture, gone. The blank stare that looks right through you, gone.

"Actually," he says, glancing around. "I think you're right. It's good."

When he turns fully toward me, the movement makes his pecs flex. I don't mean to lick my lips, but shit, I do.

His hungry gaze trails over my mouth, and he takes a step closer.

"Aiden." I don't mean for my voice to drop seductively, but it does.

For a second, I wonder if he'll kiss me again, but he steps back and takes the vacuum from me, essentially breaking the spell I was just under.

"Well… almost," he says. The compulsion kicks in, and my stomach drops. At least he tried. But in the end, he couldn't help himself.

A moment later, he's taking over. Showing me exactly how he likes it done.

Just like he did all those years ago.

And I don't know if I'm happy or sad that he's still the boy I loved.

chapter seventeen

Aiden

TODAY ISN'T GETTING OFF TO A GOOD START.

Everything has gone wrong. To the average person, they might not see it, but I do.

After the bar last night, I was all types of fucked up.

When I couldn't sleep, I thought about walking over to Cassidy's room and saying fuck it. It was so damn tempting.

Instead, I found myself cleaning.

Not that there was anything to clean.

I knew there wasn't. She knew there wasn't.

But it calmed me. And she got that.

There was no mockery in the way she asked me to show her how I wanted things done. Nothing on her face that told me she was judging. She just jumped in like it was normal.

After we were done, we went our separate ways, and I managed to get some sleep. *It was her presence.*

Today, however, is a whole other story.

It started this morning when my alarm malfunctioned. Instead of waking at 5:01 like I normally do, I woke up at 5:22.

It's been a shit show ever since.

Today is too important. I can't afford not to be on my A game tonight.

It's game three, but most importantly, it's the first home game since I brought Cassidy on. She'll be there watching. And something about that has me equal parts excited and anxious.

Despite the crap start due to the alarm, somehow Cassidy was able to calm me. After my morning workout, I saw the glass on the kitchen counter with three ice cubes in it.

How did she fucking know? It's probably a coincidence, but that move alone has me on edge. Did someone tip her off? Mike? If not him, who and how did they know? Thinking about my secrets getting out practically has me in hives.

It's just a coincidence. Three is normal. It's not overwhelming in the glass, but it's enough to do an adequate job of keeping the liquid cold.

I've been telling myself that on repeat ever since, but it's not good. I'm losing control, and I can't have that.

The worst part is I know what will calm me, or more like who.

I need her, and not in a way I care to admit. It makes me feel weak. Dirty somehow.

There's nothing dirty or wrong with mutually agreed-to sex.

Sure, she's my assistant, and she's meant to keep my life easy with her little fixes and ensuring everything goes according to my preferences.

Right now, everything is prepared to my liking on the kitchen counter. Everything I need is waiting for me so that I can start all my pre-game rituals before I have to leave for the arena.

This is where her duties end. So why do I feel like changing the terms?

Because you want her.

I close my eyes and try to push that thought away. It would be so easy to just say fuck it, tell her I was wrong, and that we should, in fact, have sex again. I refuse to be that weak.

Instead, I find myself leaving the kitchen and heading straight to my room. The blood rushes to my cock with every step I take.

By the time I'm behind closed doors, my dick is harder than steel.

Fuck.

How does she do this to me?

I head straight into the bathroom and turn on the shower.

Stripping out of my clothes, I step under the scorching water.

I fist my cock in my hand. No reason to postpone the inevitable, I won't be able to think straight until I get off.

Even with the water pouring down on me, I can see my cock leaking. I swipe my finger over it, collecting the liquid and spreading it over the crown.

I imagine the vision of her naked on her knees and crawling to me.

Her mouth dropping open as I feed her my dick.

Her puffy lips would be so full of me.

My body shudders as I imagine the feel of her tongue as she runs it over my skin.

Then I'd fuck her tight throat.

The sounds she would make when she wouldn't be able to breathe.

My eyes close as I grip tighter, thinking about the way she would take me. The way her perfect tits would swing as I thrust my hips faster.

I'd pull out, though, not wanting to finish in her mouth.

Then I'd bend her over and step up behind her. Her pussy would glisten with her desire as I line myself up.

I finally thrust inside. The feeling is sublime. Like nothing I've ever felt before.

Squeezing my cock harder, I move faster, chasing the high.

It isn't long before my balls start to tighten.

The shower becomes foggy with my breath as I pick up the speed of my hand.

My heart rate beats faster. I'm about to come.

In my head, I flip her over and imagine her lying before me. The look in her eyes as she begs me to fuck her again.

I grip tighter, my movements becoming jerky with my efforts.

The memory of her pussy taking me is enough to bring chills down my spine, and before I know it, I come in long hot ropes all over my shower floor.

Fuck.

She brings out a side of me I don't like, and despite the fact I'm putting on a show that she's my girlfriend (a bad call, might I add on my part), I can't touch her again because if I do, I might not want to stop, and that's not possible.

Hours have passed, and I have no idea where Cassidy is.

I need to head down to the ice soon. We've got to warm up before the game, and she's not here.

It's funny how fast you can become accustomed to something. I've only been with Cassidy for a few days, and it already feels like she's embedded herself in my life.

Like right now, I'm sitting alone in my apartment going over past footage. After my workout, I found the TV already on, volume set to 13. The perfect number. Not too loud. Just enough that my head is in the game while I watch. She arranged that.

Cassidy has a way of seeing my needs before I can even voice them.

She anticipates them with an insight I've never seen before.

Like when she knew I wanted only three ice cubes.

Now the TV.

How did she know I like odd numbers?

She only just started working, and she's already killing it.

The number of times she's anticipated my preferences without me telling her is strange. I do think she's incredibly observant, but some of this stuff that she's picked up on is downright eerie.

Am I that obvious? And if so, how the hell hasn't my secret gotten out?

Not that I'm complaining that she's cracked the code. For this to work, for it to be worth the risks, it's imperative that she knows me almost as well as I know myself.

I take a deep breath and lock my eyes on the screen, determined not to lose focus. I'm usually hyperfocused when it comes to playing or watching myself, but today, my mind is wandering. Normally, micromanaging all my mistakes is easy for me. Today, not so much. My mind wanders often.

Which fucking blows because this is important. It's how I'm able to skate at my best.

The relentless tapping of my foot on the floor pulls me away from what I'm supposed to be doing.

Fucking hell. Where is she?

Another minute passes, and I count the seconds as I wait.

I feel like I'm going out of my mind.

My leg drums harder on the floor.

I'm on the verge of falling off the edge.

Not a good place to be.

The last time I felt like this was right before I met her…

I throw the remote on a grunt. There's no use watching the damn replay.

I can't concentrate at all.

Jumping off the couch, I head toward my phone. I'm done with waiting and ready to call her when the door swings open.

"Where the hell have you been?" I blurt out before my brain's filter kicks in.

Smooth, Slate. Real smooth.

"I went to get you Sweet Tarts." She holds up the box, which from here is already open. "Sorted."

Fucking hell.

I'm a real dick.

I don't even know how to respond.

Since it's obvious I've lost all social graces, and I'm not planning on saying sorry or thank you, Cassidy strides up to me, her brows furrowed as she assesses me.

She reaches out and hands me the box.

Yep. All blue. Just as I'd assumed.

"We leave in twenty minutes." I don't say anything else, just storm out of the room like the asshole I am.

That went well.

chapter eighteen

Cassidy

O KAY, THIS WAS A HORRIBLE IDEA. HOCKEY IS BRUTAL AND watching Aiden get slammed against the glass over and over again makes it hard for me to sit in my seat.

Aiden has me sitting right by the ice, the glass directly in front of me. Close enough to taste the spray if not for the wall between us. Close enough to see every push, elbow jab, and flying fist, and duck as if it's coming toward me.

Dramatic much?

I feel like I'm about to hulk out and start shouting obscenities. How do people watch their loved ones play this sport and stay calm?

Loved one? Is that what he is to me?

I'd watched Aiden practice, sure, but I'd never had a chance to see him in action. This is something else entirely. He's gone over the terminology with me, but seeing it in play is just…wow.

The intensity. The strength. It's next level.

The crowd roars with excitement while I'm freaking out.

Some asshole from the other team cross-checks Aiden with his stick, slamming into him from the back.

And not a damn thing is done about it.

The refs skate on as if nothing happened, completely content to allow dirty players to continue on with their antics.

The crowd's energy is intense, and it should have me on my feet cheering.

Aiden spins around and shoves into a player, getting called out by the blind-as-a-bat ref.

The whistle is blown, and Aiden's skating off to the penalty box.

"Two minutes," the ref calls out, and Aiden throws his hands up.

The crowd cheers as though this is great news. Or maybe they're just celebrating the team's current score.

"Asshole," I mumble, and the girl next to me bobs her head.

"Total asshole. He hasn't called a damn thing all night." She turns fully toward me. "I'm Molly, Dane's sister."

A smile spreads across my face. I can see it. They resemble one another. Medium brown hair and bright green eyes. Both beyond attractive.

"You're Aiden's girlfriend, right?"

I stare at her for a moment until her words catch up to me, and I begin nodding like a bobblehead. "Yes. Yep. That's me. The new girl."

She chuckles. "You mean *only* girl. Aiden doesn't date." Her cheeks turn pink, and her eyes lower to the ground. "Well…until you, I mean."

I smile, hoping to ease her sudden worry. "Yeah, it's been a roller coaster because of that."

"Oh, I bet. The hockey tok is going nuts. You're trending all over." I wince. "Not a fan?"

I shake my head. "Not at all."

"I can see why Aiden waited for you."

Her words wash over me, and at first, I melt into them. The

thought of Aiden choosing me gives me tingles, but it's quickly washed away by the truth. A truth I can't share with Molly.

Instead, I smile.

"You don't seem to be a fan of hockey," she says, changing the subject.

"Is it that obvious?"

She laughs. "You look ready to either punch someone or throw up."

"It's violent. I'm just not used to it."

"It is, but the guys love it. Dane lives for it." She places a hand on my arm. "I promise, they can't feel much with all those pads. Your man's safe." She points toward the ice, and I turn in time to see a puck thud against the glass.

My body jerks back, and Molly snickers. "You'll get used to it."

I'm not sure I will.

"Keep watching. They're due to score, and Aiden is the king at making things happen."

She's right. No sooner does she say the words, and Aiden has a breakaway, skating like a demon down the ice, directly toward the opposing net. He doesn't even stop, simply slides to the side and pops it around the goalie's leg.

The crowd goes wild, chanting his name.

I smile, loving that he's doing what he always wanted to do. And doing it well.

A group of women are shouting, and it draws our attention. Molly groans.

"I'm a new-age woman who owns my sexuality, but something about them irks me."

"Who are 'they'?" I wonder aloud.

"Bunnies," she explains as if I know what that means. "Women who chase hockey players. Most of them only want the notoriety. Or worse, money."

A tall, leggy blonde stands, holding a sign above her head. I can't read it from here.

"They live to get the guys' attention. You'll see them after the game in the parking lot. They won't leave until the players do."

"They leave with the guys?"

"Some do," she says, eyes trained on the ice. "I told Dane if I catch him with one, I'll boycott the rest of his games."

I laugh. "How did that go over?"

She tips her head in my direction. "Do you see anyone else here for him?"

I glance around, but it's not like I would actually know who's here for whom.

"It's just me." She sighs. "We only have each other, and as much as my brother likes to act tough, he'd be lost without me."

People's backstories always interest me. As much as I hate to admit it, finding kindred spirits out in the world makes me feel not so alone. With everything Molly has shared, it has me wondering about her and Dane's.

Why are they alone? Where's their family?

I won't ask. For so many reasons, but mostly to preserve my own story. Asking questions opens the door for people to expect reciprocation. And while I don't truly know Molly, I like her.

The thought of lying to her any more than I already have, by simply allowing her to believe I'm Aiden's girlfriend, doesn't sit well.

Dane slams against the glass and locks eyes with his sister. He salutes her before rushing off to chase the guy with the puck.

I laugh, and she rolls her eyes.

We spend most of the game chatting about mundane things. Where she went to college. Her goals. I allow the conversation to remain fixed on her. It keeps me safe.

She's so easy to talk to. Funny. Smart. If her brother is even half as similar, it's not hard to see why he's one of Aiden's closest friends.

"Gah," Molly screeches. "Look, Aiden has a breakaway."

We jump up, and Molly cheers while I bite my gloved hands. The nerves intensify for no reason. Aiden's team is winning, and the game is nearly over. There's really nothing to be nervous about.

You want to see him succeed.

It's important to him, which means it's important to me.

With my eyes trained on the ice, I watch as he slices his way down the ice just like he did all those times on the pond. More proficient. Faster. But the same.

A defender from the other team comes up on him, but he doesn't seem to notice. He's too focused on one thing. The stick lifts into the air, he swings, and the puck flies right into the net.

And that's a wrap on my first home game.

chapter nineteen

Aiden

I STARE OUT THE WINDOW, TAKING IN THE CITY LIGHTS AND THE people walking below on the sidewalk even in the early morning hours.

Much like myself, this city doesn't sleep.

These people below are likely ending their night, while I fear I'm beginning my day. It's too damn early, but no matter what I do, I can't get my brain to shut off.

My best guess is that I'm still riding the high from the game three win.

But really, if I'm being honest, it's *her*.

Thoughts keep whirling in my head. I saw Cassidy at the game, talking effortlessly to Molly. They seemed to get along well, and that makes me happy.

It shouldn't.

I mean, yes, I need Cassidy to play the part, but she's doing it so well. Too well.

The lines are blurring, and I'm doing nothing to stop it.

Not to mention, my dick is constantly hard when she's around, which is really fucking with my head.

I need to keep the line drawn.

This must remain professional—*professionally fucked up.*

No more thinking about her on her knees, taking my cock in her mouth. No more daydreaming about bending her over—and here I go again. I'm like a fucking horny-ass teen.

These thoughts need to stop. The only thing I need to be thinking about is hockey.

We won, and I had a helluva game. I should be sleeping soundly. Instead, I'm focused on Cassidy.

Which leads me to one big question.

Did I make a mistake bringing her on? She's already helping me tremendously. Since I first laid eyes on her, I've led my team to three wins.

That should be enough for me. Who cares if she occupies my head far too much?

Which she does.

I want to know everything there is about her.

Where did this girl come from? And how does she know just what I need?

I sigh, closing the drapes and pacing the floor, mind racing from one thing to the next, landing on my constant.

"Fuck," I growl, pulling at my hair.

I've tried to turn on the TV, anything to keep my mind preoccupied, but I can't focus on it. They play highlights of our last game, and I don't care to see it.

I lived the fucking day. I don't need to hear some commentator who hasn't played a fucking day of hockey in his or her life, give feedback on every little play made.

It's fucking ridiculous.

The amount of fucks I've just given is an indicator that I'm spiraling. I need an outlet. A release.

I've even considered going for a run. But it's the middle of the night, and I need to work on getting back to bed. I need my strength.

You could always summon Cassidy...

See, there I go again. No. Nope. Not going there.

That's something I can't do. Waking her up in the middle of the night to fuck the insomnia out of me is more than crossing a line.

I lean forward, elbows on my knees and head in my hands, trying to refrain from slipping into my tics. Something to give me a semblance of control.

Control is what I'm grasping for at the moment. So many things are working against me, and it's making everything worse.

You need to practice restraint.

Apparently, in all ways.

"What are you doing?"

My head snaps up to find Cassidy, sleepy-eyed and hair swept over one shoulder, staring down at me with concern.

I hate that look.

I don't need anyone's concern.

My compulsions won't throw me over the edge and cause me to do something irrational.

They're fucking frustrating and annoying as hell but harmless.

I tear my eyes away from hers and do a slow perusal of her body. She's wearing a pair of short floral shorts that hang mid-thigh and a white T-shirt. She isn't wearing a bra, which is evident by her hard nipples poking through the thin fabric.

Fuck.

I snap my head away, trying to avoid needing her that way.

"I'm fine. Go back to bed."

"Clearly, you're not," she says in a tone that has me looking back at her.

She crosses her arms over her chest, blinking rapidly. Her cheek is sucked in as she appears to contemplate something.

"Seriously, Cassidy. It's all good. I couldn't sleep. Nothing more."

"Do you need—"

"Whatever I need, I'm not going to get. I just want to sleep."

"Come with me," she says, walking toward the kitchen and pointing at a chair, directing me to take a seat. I lift a brow. "Just do it." She offers a smile.

That gets me to do as instructed. Mostly out of curiosity. What is this woman up to?

She goes about opening the refrigerator and pulling out a gallon of milk. She lifts onto her toes, grabbing a mug from the cupboard.

The white tee lifts, and a patch of creamy skin peeks out. My dick hardens automatically, and the urge to ask her what she was about to offer before I so rudely cut her off slams over me. I had no choice. If she mentioned anything sexual, I wouldn't be strong enough to say no.

I close my eyes and count backward from ten, willing my over-active libido to sit down.

When I finally have things under control, I take one last deep breath and open my eyes. Cassidy places the mug of milk into the microwave, and my body tenses.

I watch, transfixed.

Warm milk.

When was the last time I had warm milk?

Years ago.

"Sometimes, when I'd feel stressed, my mom would make me hot milk. It always made me feel better. Do you want me to make you some?"

I look at her, surprised by her offer. "You don't have to do that. I'll be fine."

"No, really. It's no trouble at all. I want to help."

What are the fucking chances?

She places the piping hot mug down in front of me, and I just stare at it.

"Aiden…drink up. It'll help." She smiles warmly, but it melts from her face when she sees my reaction. "What?" she asks, nose scrunching.

I lift my head, eyes narrowed. "Why did you make this?"

"The milk?" she asks, cocking her head. "Doesn't everyone drink warm milk when they can't sleep?"

I've only ever known one person who did this. Not that I'll admit that to her.

Then again, how many people have I allowed myself to get close enough to, that I'd know something like this about them?

Not many.

Okay…none.

My shoulders relax, and I take a deep breath, lifting the cup to my mouth and taking a sip. My eyes close with a sigh.

That one sip assaults my senses, causing memories to come flooding back. The pain that I felt the moment I realized my dreams were beyond my grasp.

"Hey, what's wrong?" I don't bother to look up. I don't want her to see me like this.

I sigh. "Nothing you can help with."

"Try me."

"I missed the deadline to apply to college. She made me miss it." I bury my head in my hands. My body shakes with uncontrolled emotion. I need to control it. I need to—

I shake my head, pushing my past away to where it belongs.

"Thank you, Cassidy."

She smiles wide, and my breath hitches at the sight. "You're welcome."

Our gazes lock, and it's like we're in some sort of strange bubble. It's disarming.

It's not appropriate.

I pull my gaze away, breaking the connection.

I'm vaguely aware of Cassidy placing the milk back into the refrigerator and leaning over the counter, getting a little too close.

"Care to talk about what's on your mind?"

"No."

I don't bother elaborating. I don't need her to be my shrink. I need her to care for my needs in other ways. The milk was a surprising move, something I didn't know I needed, but I don't need any more from her tonight.

Not like this.

Not while thinking about my past. Or her splayed out naked on my bed.

Standing from the chair, I face her. "Thanks for the milk." And with that, I head back to my room, needing the space.

Needing to think with a clear head.

Lines can't be blurred, and sometimes Cassidy makes it difficult to remember that.

The crowd roars with excitement and anticipation, their cheers and chants echoing throughout the arena.

It's halfway through the third period, and despite our efforts, the scoreboard shows a tied score of zero to zero.

If we don't lock this up, we have to face them again, which is something I don't want to do.

We need to rally and prove we have what it takes to win this game.

Round two is on the horizon, so close I can practically taste it.

We need a victory today.

Shit.

Knowing what rides on this has my lungs tightening, making it hard to breathe.

Cass.

My gaze seeks her out, and the moment I see her, the pressure subsides.

It shouldn't help, but it does.

What that means, fuck, I don't even want to know right now, but as I see her waving and screaming what looks like my name, I can feel my adrenaline start pumping, but this time, it's filled with fierce determination.

The truth is, we've proven in the last three games that we have this in the bag. Now, we just need to bring it home.

Tightening my grip on my stick, I'm ready to face off in our defense zone. I look over to where Mason guards our net and then back to the puck.

With the speed I'm known for, I strike, winning the face-off and sending the puck to my second line defenseman Wolfe, who skates the puck behind our net to set up the play.

He passes it up our blue line, and I receive the puck with a burst of speed.

With adrenaline pumping, I glide across the ice, making my way to the red line, where I flip the puck into the Renegades zone for a dump and chase.

Dodging their defensemen, I send a perfect pass to Dane at the point.

Dane quickly passes the puck to Hudson, who's at the center of the blue line, for a quick one-timer.

The crowd roars fiercely as our plan works perfectly... but unfortunately, the Renegade goalie manages to block Wolfe's shot, deflecting it and forcing it away.

Fuck.

I skate toward the goal, needing desperately to save the play, and that's when I see an opening.

I go for it.

Without hesitation, I pull my arm back, hit the puck, and stuff into the goal.

The stadium erupts.

But I only have eyes for one person.

Which is a big problem.

chapter twenty

Cassidy

I T'S BEEN A GRUELING TEN DAYS.

I thought that since the Saints swept round one and had a break before their next game, it wouldn't be, but with the amount that they practice and how tough their coach is, the pressure is high.

The one thing that's been nice despite the rigorous practice schedule is not having to be on the road.

Being in Aiden's house for a long trek of time, we've gotten into a groove working together seamlessly, but now we're on the road again.

Tampa Bay to be exact. The Saints are playing the two-seeded Bulldogs.

As I walk into the hotel lobby, I find Aiden waiting for me, as per normal.

My mouth parts into a smile as I head in his direction.

A few of his teammates are nearby, so when I make it to where he's standing, I play my part, throwing my arms around his neck and giving him a hug.

It never gets easier to do this.

With my chest pressed against his, my heart beats rapidly. There's no way he doesn't feel it. The good thing about Aiden is that he wouldn't mention it even if he did.

Or at least I don't think he would. I only touch him like this in front of people, and he can't run the risk of letting people in on our secret.

As he pulls me closer, he places his lips right beside my ear. My body shivers at the proximity.

"We have a slight problem," he whispers for only me to hear. I pull back with a smile, pretending nothing is wrong. "Let's go to our room and put your stuff away."

"Okay," I respond, perplexed about what the issue is.

Together, we head to the elevator and then get off on the 9th floor. *Not surprising.*

Aiden is a creature of habit, after all.

As long as the floor is a multiple of three, Aiden is happy.

Neither of us speaks as he leads us to our room, but the moment he opens the door and I take a step into the living room, I realize the problem.

The room might be a suite, but it's a *one*-bedroom suite.

Which means most likely there is only one bed.

I move farther into the space and poke my head through the open door.

Yep.

One bed.

I turn back to look at the living room where Aiden stands with his arms crossed at his chest.

Sure, the room is large, featuring a couch, two chairs, and a small round dining table, but it still only has one bedroom.

My heart thumps in my chest at the thought of sharing a room with him.

Aiden unfolds his arms. "The hotel is fully sold out, and this was the suite they had booked for us."

I frown. "Shit."

He cracks his neck. "Shit is right."

I pace the small living room, trying to think of a solution, and then it hits me that this isn't really a problem. I've slept on much worse. "It's fine. We'll make it work. I'll sleep on the couch." It's not like I wasn't just living on the couch before this job, but I don't tell him that.

"Cass—" he says, but I shake my head.

"Aiden. It's fine. Now let me unpack, and we can talk about it after."

Walking to the closet, I'm about to ask him where his suitcase is so I can unpack it, but I see he beat me to the punch.

All his clothes are already in the closet. They are separated by color, which I already expected, but what throws me for a loop is that every hanger is perfectly spaced out.

I've helped with his laundry at his house. How did I not notice this?

Because you didn't, and most likely after you put his clothes away, he spaced the hangers.

I take a deep breath and then set off to unpack my stuff without disrupting his stuff. I can't have him off because of a dumb thing like hanger spacing.

It's bad enough that he's probably already stressed about the room situation.

Game one is tonight, and I need him to play his best.

When I'm finally done unpacking, I find Aiden cleaning the coffee table with a wipe.

I stand back and watch him. His brow furrows as he swipes, and when he's done, he grabs another wipe and starts up again.

He won't stop until it's been wiped down a third time. Things are such a process with him, and I have to wonder if anyone ever suggested he seek help to manage this better.

I can guess he'd likely be opposed to it because of the chance the media would get ahold of it.

Growing up with the kind of mom that Aiden had, it's no wonder he doesn't trust easily. He might think himself weak, but I think he's incredible. The fact he's managed without assistance for this long is hard to bear. The toll it must take on him.

"I'm going to clean the bathroom," he says, heading toward a door close to where the closet is.

Knew that was coming.

I'm getting good at recognizing all of his compulsions. Some are new, and I've had to learn how to maneuver around them. Every day, we get a little more in sync, and he eases up just a little bit, trusting me to complete each task.

"I'll do it. I'm already here." I pull out a pack of wipes from my bag that's in the closet and then take the few steps to the bathroom.

Everything still needs to be done, but it doesn't always have to be done by him. I'll wipe it down for him, and hopefully that will be enough. Sometimes it's not. Other times... well, I hope today is one of those times.

When I'm done, I step back into the living room. "What else can I help you do today?" I ask.

We're in his suite, closed off from everyone else so that he can have this time to be himself. To decompress. It's the time of day I love most because it's just him and me in the same room together. No distractions from outside people and things. No discussion of anything team-related. No lies about who I am or how much he hurt me.

"That should be it. Thank you, Cassidy," he says, swiping his hand back through his hair. I turn to walk away and go sit down at the table, but he speaks. "Can I ask you a question?"

I turn back around and tilt my head, wondering what's on his mind.

"Sure."

"What's your opinion of hockey?"

I blink. That was not what I was expecting.

"Umm. I don't know. It's fast-paced and very brutal." I watch as his lips thin. "But entertaining," I add quickly.

"Hmm." He narrows his eyes and takes a step toward me. "What do you really think?"

I blow a piece of hair out of my face, annoyed. "I'm still a shit liar."

"That's typically not a bad thing, Cass."

My back straightens as the reality that I said that out loud washes over me.

I take a deep breath and think back to the days when I used to sit and listen to Aiden talk for hours about hockey. I didn't know a damn thing about it back then, but he made me love it all the same. His passion was everything.

Those days are long gone.

"What does it matter what I think? You love it, and that's what truly matters. My opinion is moot."

His eyes narrow further in on me, likely trying to place my hostility.

I throw my hands up in the air. "Fine. If you must know, once I get past the way people plow into you, I enjoy it."

He smirks. "You worry about me?"

I roll my eyes. "If your season ends, what will I do?" He shifts, looking irritated for a moment, so I continue with the honesty. "I find it to be a fun sport. *You* make it fun to watch."

He exhales, and if I didn't know better, I'd think my words are somehow a relief to him.

"Now, is there a reason you asked?"

He turns around, wiping the counter…again. "Nope."

I sigh, not in the mood to pry things from him. "I'm gonna head down the hall to see if there's something I can grab to eat. Maybe there's something from the vending machine. Can I get you anything?" I say, motioning over my shoulder.

"No. I'm good. Thank you."

I offer a smile before exiting the room and closing the door behind me. I let out a harsh breath when I'm alone and out of view from Aiden.

It's getting harder to lie to him about who I am. When he's vulnerable, I want to soothe the lines around his eyes. When he's insecure, I want to praise him.

It's not my place, but I want to do it all the same.

He left.

As I'm walking around the corner, a man wearing a lanyard is coming toward me. I know he's a reporter, and he has no business being up here.

"Excuse me, sir. How did you get up here?"

His smarmy face pinches, and he looks down on me like I'm beneath him.

"I was given access." He tries to walk past me, and my hand shoots out as I step in his path.

"By whom?" I steel my voice, hoping to convey that he's not getting past me.

His hand lifts, waving around in the air. "I don't know." He scrunches his nose. "One of the players downstairs. He swiped his key for me and everything. Said I could find Aiden up here."

One guess says I know which asshole it was.

"No one should've given you permission to be up here. Hotels value their players' privacy. I highly doubt they would be happy to know a reporter snuck up here."

"I'm sorry…and who are you?" he sneers. "I was given clearance for an interview, so why don't you tell me where I can find him and run along?"

I huff a resentful laugh. "Apparently, you don't understand English. You can't be up here. If you want past me, you'll have to put your hands on me, and let me just give you forewarning that there will be severe consequences for that. Do you want to go down that road?"

"Who are you? You don't have any authority."

He tries to walk past me again, but I stand in front of him

holding my ground. He stares down at me, glare turning to recognition. "Oh, I know who you are. I've seen your face on social. You're that girl…Cassidy."

That girl? What a chauvinistic asshat.

"His girlfriend."

"Can I get a statement from you?"

"No. You won't be getting a statement from anyone. I'm calling security."

"What's going on?" Aiden says, joining us in the hall.

"Mr. Slate, I have some questions about the upcoming game. You swept round one, how are you feeling heading into round two with a two-seed?"

"Aiden, don't speak. You can go back to the room. I've got this."

I pull out my phone and dial the hotel number. When a woman answers, I don't bother with hellos and just cut to the point. "Can I be put through to hotel security, please."

"Can I ask what this is regarding?" she asks.

"This is Cassidy Baker in room 913. Mr. Slate is being harassed. A reporter with some balls of steel claims he was given clearance to come up to the floor. He wasn't by Aiden or me. I need someone to remove him."

The man's hands go up in the air. "Fine. I'll leave."

"You do that," I say, pointing toward the elevator.

The man stalks off like a ten-year-old boy being robbed of a popsicle. I make a mental note to get to the bottom of who he spoke to. I have my guess, but I need to ensure I'm correct.

If it's who I think it is, something more is going on here. He's got it out for Aiden, and I'll need to be sure that whatever game he's playing ends.

I huff, moving back through the door, and find Aiden pacing the room.

"How did he get up here? Who was he?"

I shake my head. "Some reporter. He said one of the players gave him access."

"Bullshit. No one would do that. They all know better than that."

I shift my weight from foot to foot. "I don't know how else he would've gotten up here. You need a room key to make it up the elevator. But it's fine now. Security is aware, and they're going to ensure that he's removed."

Aiden's shoulders droop, and a long sigh escapes him.

"Thank you, Cassidy. I jus—"

"Shh," I coo. "Don't say anything. Here, why don't you take a seat?"

I know this has him rattled. This is his sanctuary. His private space. And something like this can really send him overboard.

He takes a seat, and I come to stand behind him, placing my hands on his shoulders.

"What are you doing?"

"Giving you a massage." I start to work out the tight knots.

"Cass."

"Don't Cass me. I'm paid to make your life easier. Let me do that." I leave him no room to resist, instead kneading harder.

"I really don't know what I would do without you," he says, and my heart swells.

I've heard those words before, and they had the same effect back then as they do now. The air is thick, and a lump gets caught in my throat. All the good memories are chased away by everything that came *after*.

The lake.

That voice that feels like a million spiders crawling over me when I hear it.

The fall.

Aiden grabs my hand, pulling it forward, and I go still.

For one, his action completely catches me off guard. Two, he's staring at my scars.

"What happened here?" Aiden practically whispers. He gently slides his fingers over the scars, focused on the deep round one on my wrist.

"Nothing."

"You can tell me."

I jerk my arm away, feeling naked and vulnerable. "No," I say, refusing to go down that road. "They're just scars."

"Cassidy, I..."

I can't allow him to dig. "Please stop, Aiden. It was something that happened a long time ago. It's not something I want to think about, much less talk about."

That might be the most truthful thing I've said in weeks.

He stares up at me for longer than I like, and I squirm under his gaze. He can't possibly know what happened. There's no way. But he knows what it's like to be in an abusive situation. He's probably reliving his own right now.

The past has a way of holding us hostage, unwilling to allow us to simply float off, leaving the bad behind.

"What?" I say, but the word comes out breathy and all wrong.

He stares at me for a few moments longer, then shakes his head and turns away. "Nothing. It just...it just made me think of something. That's all."

I have an idea of what it could remind him of. Another time. Another place. Two broken kids banding together to survive.

Why did you leave me, Aiden?

There's a knock on the door, breaking into the moment, and I'm thankful for that. He sees too much, and it's getting dangerous. It's been dangerous.

Thankful for the interruption, I swing the door open without checking who it is.

When I do, I see Billy Lewis standing there.

He looks me up and down, his lips twisting up into a smirk. "Nice outfit." I look down, and that's when I notice through all the commotion, my shirt has risen up and is high enough that you can see my ribs. I must look like a mess. "Did I interrupt your pre-game fuck?" he asks like the asshole he is. "Does that come with a blow job, Charity?"

"Cassidy," I seethe, seeing red. *What a dick.*

This guy has some nerve, considering Aiden almost killed him the last time they were in tight quarters together.

"Billy…" Aiden says his name like a warning. "What do you want?"

"I just came up to see how you're doing and apologize about the other night. I had way too much to drink and was out of line."

Aiden cracks his neck but doesn't say a word.

"Anyway, sorry." Billy goes to shut the door but then stops. "I heard some douchebag reporter tried to get up here. I told him he wasn't allowed. He didn't listen."

He's such a freaking liar. I can tell by his smarmy expression. He knew damn well what he was doing, and he for sure told him to come up here. I don't know what this guy's angle is, but he's up to no good, and I'm gonna get to the bottom of it.

"What's wrong with you, Cinderella?" Billy coos.

My hands ball into fists, and I take a threatening step around Aiden toward Billy. I'm not sure what my plan is, but I want to inflict harm. That's for sure.

Aiden grabs me around the waist and pulls me back into his chest, whispering into my ear. "He's trying to goad you, Cass. Just fucking ignore him." He tilts his head up but doesn't remove his hands from my waist. "Do you need anything else?"

"Nah. Just came to ensure the dick wasn't still up here snooping around."

"I thought you came to apologize," I grit through my teeth.

He grins down at me, but despite the smile, nothing about the way he looks at me is warm or friendly.

"He's gone, and now you need to get the fuck out of here too." Aiden's voice is low and menacing, but the asshole chuckles.

"See you later on the ice."

"No, you won't because you don't even play," I snap, but the door is already closed.

He didn't hear me.

Aiden chuckles, finally dropping his hands. "Don't let him get to you. He's just trying to get a rise out of you. He's notorious for it."

"He's an asshole."

"That he is, but he's smart and has Coach fooled."

"He's not," I say, shaking my head. "One day, he's going to slip up, and I'm going to be there to see him fall."

Aiden pulls his lips into his mouth, trying not to laugh.

"What? He's awful, Aiden. He's exactly the kind of guy who takes advantage of women and probably kicks puppies. I can't stand him."

Aiden throws his head back and laughs, which is so unlike him before a game.

I narrow my eyes, and a part of my lips tips up. "Do you find something funny about assaulting women and puppies?" I ask, knowing he's nothing like that.

His hands lift. "I happen to be rather fond of both and find any type of assault on either one to be grounds for an ass kicking—or worse."

I half roll my eyes. "You need to get ready to head off to the arena." I go about tidying up the few remaining things on the table in front of Aiden. "Is there anything else I can do?"

He takes a deep breath, looking around. "No. I'm all good."

"All right. I'll see you after the game."

I'm halfway to the door when he calls out my name. I glance over my shoulder, not saying a word, allowing him to say whatever he's thinking. "I know I've already said it, but I want you to know how much I appreciate you intercepting that reporter. It would've thrown off my entire game if he had made it through that door."

"I know." I shake my head, sighing heavily. It was close. Too close. "I know," I repeat. "I'm going to speak to security and ensure nothing like that happens again."

"You're my girlfriend, not my agent." He grins. "I'll make the call."

I nod, and with that, I exit the room, my mind reeling with everything that's happened in the past few minutes.

He thinks about the past.

And a part of me wishes he didn't because it makes his leaving me behind even worse.

Nothing goes as planned.

It doesn't matter how hard the team rallies.

Aiden is off.

Has been all day, and nothing seems to be working to get him back in the right mindset.

I can see it from here, up in the stands. His face is tight, and his shoulders are rigid. He reminds me of a rubber band pulled taut and ready to snap.

This isn't how the game is supposed to be. But I guess I'm not at all surprised. He might not have said anything, but he hasn't been okay since the damn reporter made it up to the floor.

He's been about ready to lose it, and right now, it looks like he will.

I watch with wide eyes as Aiden checks the Bulldog defender hard. A fight is about to go down, and despite Dane skating over to stop it, Aiden is looking for blood.

The next thing I know, some guy on the opposing team is throwing a punch.

Then, it's complete pandemonium as a full-fledged fight breaks out. My heart rattles in my chest as I watch in horror as Hudson and Dane jump into battle.

The ref blows his whistle and breaks it up.

It takes a few minutes before the players are separated, and then Aiden and the defender who punched him are being sent off to their penalty boxes.

This is going to be a long game.

Hours later, I'm waiting in the room for Aiden to return.

They lost.

And I'm not sure what to do to help him.

Back at the trailer, after a loss, I'd find Aiden sitting beneath the tree. It didn't matter the weather. He was always there.

"Penny for your thoughts." I take a few steps until I'm right beside where he's sitting.

He tilts his head up, catching my gaze.

The look he gives me makes my stomach feel hollow. He looks lost and completely out of control.

Pulling my gaze away, I see his hands in his lap. His fingers tap his thigh as he mumbles something to himself. I can't hear the words, but whatever he's saying can't be good because his jaw is tight as he mutters them through clenched lips.

"What's going on?"

He doesn't speak, doesn't acknowledge me.

"Aiden, I don't know what's happening. But you'll get through this if you need me. Just take a breath, remember that—"

"Cut the shit, Pip, you aren't Mrs. Saber."

The fact that he knows the social worker I talk to takes me off guard, but I guess it shouldn't. He's been around multiple times when she's stopped by.

I take a deep breath, knowing he doesn't mean to snap at me. That's not Aiden. Aiden would never hurt me. "I'm just trying to help you." My words come out slightly above a whisper.

"I don't need your help."

"What do you need?"

"Just sit with me." At his words, I plop down beside him, leaning my back against the bark of the trunk. "Your being with me is enough."

The door opening of the suite has my memories drifting away and thrusting me back into the present.

I watch as Aiden walks in. His presence alone sucks up all the oxygen from the room.

He pushes his sleeves up and addresses me on the couch.

"I'll sleep on the couch." He grunts, barely giving me the time of day.

Aiden is stuck in his head. He needs time to calm down. I want to object to the notion that I'd ever let him sleep on the couch, and I will, but right now, he needs a minute, and that's exactly what I'm going to give him.

Standing, I turn to him and nod. Keeping silent, I cross the space toward the bedroom. Once there, I sit on the bed and try to keep busy.

I can't imagine how hard this is for him right now.

Me being in his space when he tries to silence the war going on inside himself.

From where I'm located, I can hear the slight mumbling as he talks to himself.

Most likely berating himself.

It crushes my soul.

After a few minutes, the mumbled words die down, and I hear a door open and close. The bathroom. The faucet turns on, and then a few moments later, there's more noise, rummaging, a curse.

The words he said all those years ago play on a loop in my brain.

"Your being with me is enough."

I kick off the bed and stand.

Enough time has passed. I'm going to him.

Crossing the space, I head out to where he's sitting on the couch, but this time, there's a pillow and blanket beside him.

I sit beside him. Giving him a second to adjust to my presence.

From the corner of my eye, I can see his shoulders drop, and then he moves to recline back into the sofa.

The breath I didn't realize I was holding trickles out of my mouth as I lean back too and get comfortable.

The silence envelops us until he finally breaks it. "What are you doing out here, Cass? You should go to bed."

I turn to face him. "Not without you."

Aiden doesn't respond at first, and the only reason I know he's alive and not stone is the rise and fall of his chest. "I'm not sleeping in a bed with you."

"You already did."

His jaw locks, and I can see the tension radiating throughout his body. "That was before. And there wasn't any sleeping," he grits out through clenched teeth.

"We're both adults. We can sleep in a bed together without touching each other." I arch a brow in challenge. "Seriously, though. You had a long game; you need your rest."

He lets out a long-drawn-out sigh. "Fine. But I doubt I'll sleep."

Knowing I won this battle, I don't stay around to gloat. If I do, I run the risk he will change his mind, and Aiden needs his rest. Instead, I head off to the bedroom and get on my side of the bed.

It's not a few seconds later that the room lights go off, and then the sheets are pulled back.

The bed dips as Aiden slips beneath the covers.

Despite it being a king-sized bed, it feels small. Every move he makes, I feel in my bones. Every dip and turn makes me hyper-aware that if I reach my arm out, I can touch him.

My heart rattles in my chest, and my body tingles with his proximity.

I try to calm the butterflies in my stomach.

But it's no use; their wings flap.

How am I ever going to fall asleep?

The room is relatively quiet with the exception of our breaths. If I strain my ears, I can hear the cars on the street, but it's only a faint hum in the distance.

I listen to see if he's awake like me.

The only sound I hear is that of Aiden's soft inhaling and exhaling.

Guess he was wrong.

He did fall asleep.

chapter twenty-one

Aiden

I HAVEN'T SLEPT THIS WELL IN YEARS, AND IT DOESN'T TAKE A rocket scientist to know why.

It's her.

The moment I laid down beside her, I passed out.

It's almost as if she's drugged me.

Obviously, she didn't, but fuck, she's like no one I've ever met before.

My lids crack open, and I blink a few times until my vision clears.

There she is, fast asleep. She's placed a small pillow between us, and I can't help but laugh.

If she thinks that would stop me, she has another thing coming.

The only reason I didn't make a move is because I'm her employer, but shit, if I weren't, no pillow would stop me from having her.

I stifle a groan. *Too bad I am.*

Unfortunately, as much as I'd love to lie here for another second and watch her, I need to get up.

Coach wants an early practice this morning, and seeing how poorly we played, he's not wrong.

The truth is, yesterday I let the outside world affect my playing, but I'm done with that shit.

I have one day to get my act together before game two.

Which is exactly what I'm going to do.

The day off yesterday was exactly what I needed to get my head back in place. I just need to keep it up.

Now back on the ice, we're leading the Bulldogs by one in the second period.

As I'm skating up the ice from my own blue line, my grip tightens on my stick. I pull back and pass the puck up the ice.

It glides toward Hudson, but it's intercepted by the Bulldog's center.

The asshole has a breakaway, and he scores with ease.

Fuck.

This doesn't bode well for us. Now we're tied with the Bulldogs, and we can't risk another loss.

Skating back to center ice, I stop before the face-off to talk to my line.

"That one is on me. We'll get it back."

"We're with you," Dane responds.

I head back to the center of the ring for the face-off.

The ref drops the puck, and I win it back to my defenseman.

Dane skates up to center and dumps it in, but the Bulldog defenseman gets the puck and carries it off.

As he's rushing up the ice, I notice he's not paying attention to my side. I take full advantage of his lapse and quickly steal the puck back from him.

Hudson quickly catches up to me for a two on one. I'm on the left, and he's on the right.

I pass to Hudson, who immediately passes back to me to confuse the goalie.

Time stands still as I release the puck.

My heart thumps rapidly in my chest as I watch it glide across the ice.

The roar of the crowd echoes in my ears as I score on a wide-open net.

After the goal, my teammates rush toward me. We huddle together, screaming in celebration before skating off so the next line can take over playing.

"Nice rally, man," Dane says, hitting my back. "I see whatever was fucking with your last game is gone."

At his words, I can't help but seek her out. A moment later, I find Cassidy in the stands. Her smile radiates even from here.

"I want to get me some of that magic you're getting." Hudson laughs.

"Shut the fuck up," I grunt.

It's true, it's all Cassidy.

Although nothing has happened with her, being in bed, near her has certainly worked its magic.

I don't know what it is about this girl, but one thing is for certain, bringing her on was the best decision I've ever made.

chapter twenty-two

Cassidy

IT'S SO GOOD TO BE HOME.

The past few days in Tampa were trying to say the least.

The Saints won game two, but if I'm being honest, how well they played or didn't is the least of my problems.

The proximity was killing me.

Sharing a bed was torture.

When you want a man as much as I want Aiden, not jumping his bones when he's only a breath away is no small feat.

Don't get me wrong, I love being with him, and as much as I want to spend every minute around Aiden, to soak up our time because it will inevitably end, right now I don't.

I need a break from that man.

Like tonight, I'm exhausted and would love nothing more than to get in my pajamas, crawl into bed, and watch all the romantic comedies I can find. I don't know what's wrong with me today. I'm just off. I need to distract myself with anything that will make me laugh so I don't burst into tears.

But that's not in the cards for me.

Tonight, I get to lay on the charm and pretend I'm Aiden's girl. The only problem is the lines seem to blur far too easily for me. I need to do better at protecting my heart.

Aiden Slate has already crushed it once, and I refuse to allow it to happen again.

Which is likely why I'm in this foul mood. Our last few times together, he listened. He wanted to know things about *me*, and that does horrible things to my head. It makes me think things that I have no business thinking.

Grow up, Cassidy.

My phone rings, and I see Emma's name lighting up the screen.

"Save me," I say, sounding whiny and tired.

"Dare I ask why you need saving?"

I groan. "I'm meeting Aiden at a trendy lounge bar downtown, where they're having a small VIP meet and greet." I turn up my best peppy cheerleader voice, infusing each word with faux excitement.

"That sounds fun. What's it for?"

I sigh. She would find this sort of thing fun. "It's an annual fundraiser that raises money for a different charity each year. A bunch of bigwig moguls with way too much money will be there, flexing their wallets for a chance to rub elbows with some NHL greats."

"Aw, poor Cassidy. You get to walk among the elite. I'm so sad for you."

I rub at my temple. "My head already hurts from all the egotistical talk I'll be subjected to."

"Try to have fun, Cass. I know this is out of your element, but you're capable of fun. I've seen you bust out a dance or turn on the charm when needed. You've got this."

"You're the worst pep talker."

She chuckles. "I really only called to bust your balls for not updating me on all things Slate. I need to live vicariously through you, and you're not being a team player."

"You're ridiculous. I'll call you tomorrow and update you on all the nonglamorous shit I've been up to."

And I will. I'll tell her everything aside from the specifics on Aiden. Despite everything, I won't sell him down the river. Ever.

"Fine. Go have your fun. I'll just be over here binge-watching some cheesy vampire show with an annoying heroine who I'm just waiting for them to finally kill off."

I snort. "You have fun with that. Talk soon."

"Byeeee."

Clicking the button, I end the call and throw my phone into my clutch. I need to figure out where the hell I'm going.

Since I had to come on my own, I've been instructed to enter from the side door that's not open for the public, and one would think that would be easy to find.

It's not.

I've almost walked the entire building when I finally find said door. On the back of the building, not the side.

I blow out a harsh breath and inhale a cleansing one before I knock.

"Name?" a burly man with a deep voice barks from behind a slot in the door.

I give the bouncer my information, and now I'm being escorted in by another hulk of a man, wearing a black-collared shirt with the lounge's emblem over the left chest and a pair of gray slacks. His beefy arms flex as he walks, and I wonder how many years he's been doing steroids because there's no way this isn't manufactured.

"Right through there, Miss." He sweeps his hand out, gesturing for me to walk around a set of heavy velvet drapes.

The lights are dim, and blues music circulates through the room, a saxophone carrying the weight. It's a moody, sensual ambience, which seems strange, considering it's a bunch of dudes standing around talking about guy stuff.

I nod to the guy. "Thank you."

He leaves me alone, and I take a second to collect myself and acclimate to the vibe of the place. I need to be prepared to play a part like a seasoned actress, and tonight, I'm not feeling it. With one final round of inhale and exhale, I go to step around the curtain, but familiar voices stop me in my tracks.

I shouldn't eavesdrop.

I know it's wrong.

But it's Aiden and a part of me just wants to listen to him for a bit. To hear him in his element talking about things that excite him.

That motivate the enigma of a man.

The things that make him who he is today.

That's all I want. To know him as he is now. Because no matter how much I wish it were different, we're not the same people we were back home.

"How do I end this, Mike? I'm out of my element here."

"You're really hung up on this. You know it's not healthy, Aiden. You have to focus on hockey. Your team needs you."

"I know my job, Mike. I'm more than capable of handling my shit."

"I don't think you are. This was supposed to be easy. Something to help you loosen up. She's got a hold on you that's not healthy. You need to let her go."

Aiden sighs. "You're probably right."

Mike chuckles. "Not for nothing, you're kind of a big deal. You should've seen this coming a mile away. Just do what you're doing. The cards will fall as they're supposed to."

My stomach bottoms out, and bile rises up my throat. I want to leave. I want to run.

I didn't want to come to begin with, but now the entire night is spoiled. I couldn't even fake it if I wanted to.

He's trying to get rid of me.

Again.

I'm not sure why I'm surprised. He's Aiden Slate. The man who takes and gives nothing back. The man who makes promises and doesn't keep them.

He left you behind without a second thought.

I stomp down the sadness and allow anger to take its place. I'm taking care of him like I always did. I'm helping him to relax and to be on his game.

Why am I not good enough?

He left once before, and I'd be a fool to think he'd stick around this time if I told him the truth.

I'm going to march in there and quit. Tell him what I think of him.

Except why should I? This is a paid position, so why should I walk away from that? I shouldn't. He's going to have to grow a pair and end this himself.

My hands ball into fists. I'm about to ditch this party and claim a stomach bug when someone comes barreling through the curtain right into me.

I cry out as my body pitches back, falling toward the ground, but I never hit. Strong arms wrap around me, saving me from being hurt and making a complete and total ass of myself.

"You're late," he says, grinning down at me.

"And you're a bull," I quip, allowing him to help me stand.

I run my hands down my dress to straighten out any wrinkles. "A bull?"

I look between him and the curtain and make a face. "Yeah, a raging bull. You came through that like I was a matador holding the handkerchief."

He laughs. "Where have you been?"

"Well, this is the city, and traffic at this time of night is not exactly light. Then it took me a moment to find the entrance." I sigh heavily.

"I'm sorry. I should've called to check on you." He shakes his head. "I could've met you at the door."

"You're right. You should've. A gentleman would have." I meant the words to be teasing, but they came out anything but.

His eyes narrow in on me, and I know it's because of how I'm acting. It can't be helped. My hackles are raised, and contrary to the role I'm being paid to do, I'm not a great actress.

"I really am sorry, Cassidy. I got stuck talking to the senator, and then Mike found me. I lost track of time."

"You don't need to apologize to me. I'm the hired help. It's just business."

His head jerks back. "What's going on with you? Are you all right?"

"Yes," I say, motioning back toward the lounge. "Let's go. You have places to be and people to swoon."

Without giving him a chance to speak, I shoulder past him, making it clear I'm done talking. I'm pushing my luck. I need this money, and my attitude over something I have no right being pissed about, will cost me this position early if I'm not careful.

We spend the rest of the night walking around the room, and I play my part as the doting girlfriend. I hold on to his arm. I take special care in helping him conceal his compulsions, and at some point, I even forget about earlier and begin to enjoy myself.

"Cassidy, are you enjoying the playoffs?" asks some wealthy businessman, whom Aiden has been talking to for the past twenty minutes, bringing me into the conversation.

I bob my head. "Yes. I find hockey to be fascinating. It's so much more than just a sport."

The man's eyebrows fold inward. "Is that so? I'm curious to know what you mean."

I take a sip of my champagne. "Well… it's not every day that players engage in arguments in the middle of play. Hell, it's even encouraged." I think back on the last game and how physical it got. How the crowd cheered louder when helmets hit the ice and fists started flying. "Hockey is like some sort of mix between MMA and golf."

Aiden snorts next to me.

"Seriously, those are your comparisons?"

He's not making fun. He's genuinely entertained.

"I must admit, I knew little about the sport until I met Aiden. I couldn't claim to be well-versed in any sport to be fair." I shrug. "Those are the two it reminds me of. It's brutal and vicious but intoxicating to watch."

Aiden's eyes hold mine, and a mixture of amusement and something else lingers just under the surface.

"It's been a pleasure, Cassidy." He holds out his hand, and I extend mine. His handshake is pleasant, not overly done like most men tonight.

He's not trying to show dominance. This is a sign of respect.

"Thank you for humoring an old man."

I offer a smile. "The pleasure is all mine, sir."

He smiles back warmly. "Aiden, take care of this one. You've got yourself a keeper."

"Thank you. I'll do my best."

The man nods before making his way over to Aiden's coach.

Aiden whistles low. "You won him over. It's not an easy feat."

"What do you mean? He seemed lovely," I say, glancing up at Aiden. Under the glow of the soft light, Aiden's dark scruff looks almost like salt and pepper. Distinguished. Handsome as hell.

Aiden chuckles. "He doesn't love women."

I pull a face. "I didn't get that impression at all."

"It's the truth. He finds them to be below himself. Very misogynistic."

My eyes find the man across the room, and I notice his back is turned to the coach's wife, effectively shutting her out of the conversation.

"Guess you never can tell a person's true colors."

His eyes narrow as though he finds double meaning in the words. In this particular moment, there are none. I'm truly floored to hear my radar was so far off.

"Would you like another drink? One more before we hit the road?"

"Sure," I say, offering a small smile before he walks off, heading toward the bar, leaving me standing at a high-top table alone.

I glance around the room, taking in all the smartly dressed men and over-the-top dresses the few women wear. It's practically a runway show full of models and actresses. They glide across the floor, backs straight, and heads held high.

I stuff down the insecurities rising to the surface. Aiden could've asked anyone to do this job. Why me?

Because you keep his secrets and don't judge.

Women like this wouldn't be all right with his quirks. They'd sell his story to the first person offering a sizable amount of money.

"Has Aiden told you your ass looks fabulous in that dress?" A smooth male voice caresses the back of my neck, but it's not good chills that spread across my body. My hackles rise at the sound of Billy's voice. I look over my shoulder.

"Aiden wouldn't be so crass."

He purses his lips and makes a face. "Aiden is a moron. Although…maybe he's not," he says, tapping his chin. "He has you to take care of his every need. Are you a girlfriend or a glorified ho?"

"Don't you dare say another word," I bite through my teeth. "You had the audacity to comment on my ass, which was mistake number one. But you and I both know if I were to tell Aiden everything that's been said here tonight, your ass would be laid out across the floor before you even had a chance to offer an explanation."

He chuckles, low and threatening. "You overestimate Aiden's level of care for you. You're dispensable." He glances around the room. "These women would take him away in a heartbeat if he gave them one chance." Hate blazes in his eyes. "Aiden isn't the god he thinks he is."

"Let me tell you something right now, dickhead. I don't need Aiden to fight my battles. You touch me…you come near me… you say one fucking word I don't like, and I'll end your career so fast." I hold his stare. "You understand."

"You're just easy pussy. One that he'll tire of."

I feel like I've been punched in the gut. Everything Billy has said plays on my insecurities masterfully, and he doesn't even realize it. Except I'm not that fragile little girl who Aiden left in that run-down trailer.

I'm strong.

I'm fierce.

I take a step toward him, getting as close as I can without causing a scene.

"You will apologize in a manner that I deem worthy, or tomorrow, you won't have a fucking job. I'll have your name plastered all over the papers. Sexual harassment. Misogyny. You name it, and I'll ensure every newspaper and media outlet in this fucking city smears your name so gloriously, you'll never work again."

Billy's face turns a shade of red I can't name.

"Everything all right, Cassidy?" Aiden says, swooping in and handing me another glass, but this time, it's a martini.

I'm typically not a martini girl, but tonight, I need it.

I look back at Billy and offer a menacing smile. "Yes. Everything is good. Billy was just telling me how sorry he was for bumping into me. Weren't you, Billy?"

He clears his throat, looking at Aiden. "Yeah."

"Let's get out of here." I place my glass down and then walk away with Aiden right behind me. All the while, I think of what was said and how close to home he actually was.

I head out to the curb to look for his car. Since I didn't come with him, I'm not sure where he parked.

If I were smart, I'd slow down and wait for him to catch up to me, but the truth is I need air and space after my run-in with Billy.

My adrenaline courses through my body. It feels like my heart might explode from my chest.

Despite my labored breathing, I walk faster, not watching or thinking where I'm going, just needing to get far away from the party. I take a step, and before I know what's happening, I'm falling forward.

My hands reach out to brace myself as I start to crash face-first into the sidewalk.

"Cass," Aiden's voice breaks through my haze as I see him running toward me.

Getting my bearings, I find that I'm lying on the concrete. But I'm okay. Luckily, my hands stopped my fall from being worse.

"Are you okay?" he asks as he moves to crouch so our gazes can meet.

"I think so." I feel like a huge idiot, but as I take stock of myself, I'm pretty sure I didn't do any real damage.

His brow furrows. "What happened?"

"Misstep."

"You need to pay better attention," he grumbles. He looks mad at me, which makes zero sense. Men are so confusing sometimes. "Let me help you up."

His arms reach out, and then he's lifting me until I'm on my feet. The moment I am, my ankle gives under the weight.

In a split second, I'm cocooned in warmth. I blink. What the heck?

That's when I realize that Aiden's strong arms have wrapped around me. Before I can object, he's lifting me effortlessly off the ground.

My heart beats frantically in my chest at the proximity of our bodies. The fresh, minty smell of his soap infiltrates my nose as I bury my face into his shirt.

"What are you doing?" I squeak out.

"Making sure you get back home in one piece."

"I don't need your help." Jeez, I sound like a toddler having a tantrum, but my crushed ego can only take so much. Having Aiden come to my rescue runs the risk of shattering me into pieces.

He leans closer, his lips tickling my ears. "Remember you're my girlfriend. You shouldn't be objecting so much," he whispers.

"I might be your girlfriend, but that doesn't mean I want you carrying me around like a sack of potatoes."

"And I'll stop once I get you home and see if I need to call the team doctor."

My mouth opens and shuts. He's being ridiculous. Surely, he's not really going to call the team doctor. "Are you serious?"

"As a heart attack."

I roll my eyes at him. How can this get any more embarrassing? As if the universe could hear me, it answers in the only way it can. At that moment, the sky opens up, and big droplets of rain begin to fall on us. Soon, the water is cascading down. My dress is getting drenched and clinging to my skin.

Aiden stops moving, and I tilt my head to see what made him stop. He's looking down at me, heat in his stare.

It feels like he's undressing me with his eyes.

A shiver runs up my spine, and I start to tremble in his arms.

The chill causes my nipples to pebble, and that's when I realize what he's looking at. My skintight dress is now clinging to my body like a second skin.

Aiden looks at me like a hungry predator, and I'm his prey.

My pulse pounds, and as he stares at me, he leans closer.

I think he might kiss me.

I hope he will.

Closing my eyes, I move closer.

Waiting.

Waiting.

Then I hear a car door open, and I'm placed into the car.

And just like that, I'm thrust back into reality.

And I feel like an idiot.

Again.

chapter twenty-three

Aiden

I T WAS A GRUELING FUCKING PRACTICE. COACH WAS NONE TOO pleased with our last few games. First, we lost game one, and sure, we eventually won game two, but it was close, too close. It should've been a blowout.

Personally, the first game against the Bulldogs is probably the worst game I've played in my career.

I was still out of sorts from the reporter trying to gain access and then from Billy picking at Cassidy. Something is going on with him. He's always been an asshole, but he's been abnormally bad lately.

He wants her.

Too fucking bad. Never happening.

When this contract ends, the last thing I need is for her sticking around and dating a teammate. Not that I think she would. It was pretty clear that she despises Billy. Probably more than I do, which is saying something.

If I'm being honest, it's more than that. Something about

Cassidy feels safe. She takes care of me in ways I never knew I needed. I can trust her.

There's only one problem, I can't stop thinking about touching her. Kissing her. Fucking her.

Last night, when I held her in my arms, I almost lost it. The way her dress clung to her, the way her perfect nipples pebbled under my touch.

Fuck.

Thankfully, she wasn't hurt. Just a twist, but being that close wasn't a good idea.

Now I need to get my head out of my ass before Coach catches me zoning out.

Fifteen minutes later, I'm skating drills when I see Billy talking to Stefan. As I go by, I shoulder check him.

"The fuck, man? What the hell is your problem?" he yells to my back.

I smile. Good. Come at me, dick.

I loop around to see him skating at me. His helmet hits the ice, followed by his gloves. I follow suit, throwing off my gloves and stand tall. Hoping to convey that I'm not playing around.

"You know exactly what my problem is." I skate closer, getting into his face.

We've drawn a crowd, but nobody attempts to get between us. They wouldn't. Nobody loves Billy, and nobody would get in my way when I'm this angry.

"You think I didn't hear the fucking shit you said to Cassidy?"

"The hell? I didn't say shit."

"You did," I grit through my teeth. "And if she doesn't report you, I will."

"For what? Talking? Fuck you, Slate."

"Harassment, asshole. You and I both know you've been beyond inappropriate with her. She has every reason to contact Coach or even higher up."

"Are you seriously threatening me? I'm your fucking teammate. You're taking some broad's side?"

I shove him, and a couple of the guys move closer, likely to back me up if fists start flying.

"I'm warning you right now, if you don't apologize to her and make things right, I'll help her go to the proper channels. You're second string. A nobody. This team doesn't need you."

"Fuck you," he seethes.

"You're expendable."

He bares his teeth, and I laugh. "Aw, does that piss you off? Do you want me to lie to you and tell you that you're special?" I huff a condescending laugh. "I can't help that you're a subpar hockey player. Get your shit together and apologize to her, or I'll make sure you're off this team by tomorrow."

"You wouldn't dare." His words come out pathetic. Feeble.

"I have Coach on speed dial. Want to test me? I have plenty of time to watch you fall."

His face is the color of a tomato as he looks from guy to guy, trying and failing to find an alliance.

"You know what... drop to your knees and put your stick over your head."

"No way. I won't do that."

"You will," Hudson says, coming to my side. "Or I'll go with Cassidy to report you."

"Like you're one to talk, Wilde. You're the biggest player on the team." He shakes his head, crossing his arms over his chest. "Plus, I didn't do anything."

"That's not what I'm hearing. Now do as you've been told by your superior and drop and raise your stick."

The asshole finally complies, and the rest of us get back to drills. An hour later, Billy is still on his knees, arms shaking. I skate over to him.

"Done being an idiot? Ready to apologize?"

He nods.

"Words, Billy."

"Yes."

"Everyone's dismissed," Coach barks out, stalking off the ice.

Hudson slides up next to me. "Do I even want to know what all that was about?"

"You're just now asking me? Hours later?"

"I would've gone with whatever you said, and I wasn't gonna question you in front of him." He pulls off his helmet. "Color me curious."

"I don't like his attitude. And I don't like how he talks to Cassidy."

Hudson lifts a brow. "What did he do?"

"He's made some very sexual comments. Things that made her extremely uncomfortable. He's lucky I didn't kick his ass."

Hudson whistles. "I would've just kicked his ass and got it over with."

"Humiliation sounded more fun."

He chuckles. "You really like this girl?"

There are only a few guys on the team that I hate to lie to, and Hudson is one of them, but there are just some things he can't know. My relationship with Cassidy being one of them.

"Yeah. I do." It's all I offer, and he doesn't press.

"Do you think he's going to apologize?"

"I don't care what the fuck he does, as long as he stays the hell away from her and doesn't make another comment to her. I don't want him to even look at her."

"I think something's up with him," he says offhandedly, and I turn to him, curious.

"What do you mean? Color me curious," I say, smirking as I repeat his words.

He grins. "I don't know. He's just been abnormally shifty as of late. He's up to something, and I wanna know what it is."

"Yeah, I got the same impression."

He's definitely up to no good, and I have a feeling it's centered around jealousy. The douche wants nothing more than to be the center of the media. The team's top dog.

He's far from it.

His entire career has been mediocre at best.

"I'm gonna keep an eye on him," Hudson says.

"Same. Good practice," I say, changing the subject.

We bump each other's fists, going our separate ways. He'll be long gone before I'm even through my second ritual.

At some point, I really need to seek professional help to work through this. Having Cassidy is a godsend, but I can't live like this. It's too much.

I slip down onto the bench, shoulders hunched, exhaustion falling over me. All I want to do is go home and ask Cassidy to give me a massage, but I can't. It's becoming too easy to rely on her. I might be paying for the service, but the more time I spend with her, the harder it gets.

You like her.

I do. And that's the fucking scary part.

chapter twenty-four

Cassidy

I GATHER MY THINGS, PREPARING TO LEAVE THE ARENA. NOT wanting to stay home all day while he's at practice, I hopped a ride with him, and plan to do some shopping and then get an Uber home when I'm done.

He'll be busy all day. His coach has been on the whole team to make sure they win.

"What do you plan to do today?"

I look over my shoulder and see him striding over to me. Coach must have given them a break.

When he's only a few feet away, he raises his arms in the air to stretch.

As he moves, the black Henley he's wearing lifts, giving me a perfect view of his well-defined abs and the delicious V that disappears into his shorts.

The man is simply perfection. It's just not fair.

I look away, clearing my throat in an attempt to get myself under control.

"I'm going to walk around and do some shopping, and when I'm done, I'll just head back to your place and get everything situated. That way, when you get home tonight, you can just relax."

I turn to find Aiden in my space, holding my purse out to me.

My entire body shivers at his nearness, and I feel myself flush.

Is he aware of my reaction? Is this another thing I'm obvious about?

"You don't have to do that," he says.

"Yes, I do. I know you're likely still going to have to do some things yourself but let me try to help you." I hold his stare. "That's why I'm here… right?"

There's so much meaning in that question.

Do you want more?

Are you falling for me like I'm falling for you?

Do you know who I am?

"Okay," he says, pulling me out of those dangerous thoughts. "I'll see you tonight."

I smile and give a quick wave before heading out the door, making a mental list the entire way down to the first level of all the things I need to do. I'm so caught up in planning that I nearly run headfirst into Billy.

Dread pools in my stomach at the sight of his smarmy face. He's the last person I want to deal with today. I have too much to do, and he's sure to ruin my entire day.

"Watch out," I say, pushing past him.

"Wait, Cassie, can I talk to you for a minute?"

"It's Cassidy," I snap, not bothering to stop.

"Please." Something in his tone has me stopping and turning back toward him. I have one eyebrow raised and a fist on my right hip.

I swipe my hand out, motioning that he has the floor.

"Thank you," he says, which sounds all wrong coming from him. "Listen, I just wanna apologize. I went way too far. I should've never said any of those things."

My eyes narrow, running over his face for any indication that this is some kind of joke. When I don't find anything off, I grow even more suspicious.

"Are you sick?"

His head juts back a bit. "What?"

"Are you sick? Ill? Dying?" I snip. "Something's off with you."

He chuckles, raising both hands. "I'm fine. I just owed you an apology. I'd had too much to drink that night and went too far."

"You can't blame alcohol, Billy. You've done plenty of shitty things completely sober."

He swallows, nodding several times. "That's true. I'm just sorry."

My eyes narrow further on Billy, as I try to find a hidden agenda, but today, he just appears repentant. Which puts me on edge. I can't let my guard down. It wouldn't be the first time I did...

That time didn't end well for me.

"Okay," I say, not having the words.

I can't forgive him. I hate the asshole, but I can at least acknowledge his attempt at making things right.

"I appreciate that. Have a good practice."

He offers me a tight-lipped smile. "See you around."

God, I hope not.

I'm halfway through my shopping trip when I remember to call Emma. I've been a horrible friend as of late. Too preoccupied with a guy who doesn't even know who I really am, to even remember the person who knows all my secrets.

Well... most.

I pull up her number and click to call. It rings twice before I hear her huff down the line.

"'Bout time you keep your promises, Cass the ass."

I snort. "That's a new one."

"Yeah, well… I haven't had a reason to bust it out until now. I need gossip," she whines. "I'm dying over here."

"Not much to tell. I've been busy playing keeper to the NHL's sexiest player of the year while being tormented by his team. Well… only one major asshole. But I set him straight."

"That's my girl," she praises. "Wait… what? Who's the asshole?"

I sigh. "He's inconsequential. You'd likely not even know him. Billy something or other."

"I'll be looking him up and sending him a shit sandwich."

I choke out a laugh, and the elderly lady next to me throws the stink eye my way.

"Please don't. He actually apologized today. Which was odd."

"Sounds like he came to his senses."

I purse my lips. He doesn't strike me as the kind of guy who recognizes his faults. Something in my gut tells me there's more to it.

"Anyway, tell me more. Have you scored with the hockey hottie?"

"That would be a no, Em. This is entirely a business relation-ship. Outside of gawking at his biceps and well-defined back mus-cles, it's strictly platonic."

She grunts. "I'd jump all over that. Make it not platonic," she suggests. "Put the moves on the man."

"That's called assault."

"Yikes. Okay… well, strike that from the plan." She's quiet for a minute. "Maybe try at the truth?"

"Which is?" I practically whisper, dreading the thought of air-ing my truths.

"You like him. You want more."

"Ugh," I groan. "That's not happening. I'm not in the business of putting my heart on the line, Emma, and you know that."

"Maybe that's your problem. You're too guarded."

I purse my lips; despite the fact she can't see my reaction to her less-than-appreciated comment. "And you're too opinionated today."

She chuckles. "I only want what's best for you."

Sighing deeply, I grab a gallon of milk from the cooler and place it in my cart.

"What's best for me is making money and getting off your couch permanently."

"I don't like it. The couch isn't the same without you."

I laugh. "I miss you too."

"Call me when you get the lady balls to tell the man that you love him."

"I don't."

Good God. The thought of Aiden hearing those words gives me the chills. He'd run for his life. Love isn't something that Aiden is comfortable with. Never has been. Which shouldn't be surprising, considering his upbringing. The man didn't have love from the person who should've loved him above all others.

It pissed me off then, and it still pisses me off today.

"Whatever," she singsongs. "I'll catch you later."

I end the call, shaking my head. Emma is a character. One I cherish immensely. But she's far braver than I am. Unafraid to be herself. To put her love on her sleeve and offer it to the first man she falls for. She'd own her feelings without thought.

That's not me.

I'm petrified to own up to who I truly am. The thought of spilling my feelings gives me hives.

I spend the rest of the day grocery shopping, folding laundry, sorting it in his closet the way Aiden prefers, and trying to forget all about Emma's suggestion. I almost miss the sound of the door creaking open and Aiden's heavy footsteps padding down the hall to begin his rituals before dinner.

He won't have much to do today because I've done all that I could for him.

"Someone's been busy," Aiden says, sauntering into the kitchen in a fresh pair of black joggers and a gray short-sleeve Henley shirt, not even ten minutes later. "It smells delicious. What is it?"

"Pasta Bolognese. Your fav—"

I slam my mouth closed, recognizing my near-fatal error. Of course, I know what Aiden's favorite food is. It was something he told me long ago. But he hasn't told Cassidy. That slip could've cost me greatly.

"It's one of my favorites," I amend. "I hope you like it. I should've asked before."

He blinks, narrows his eyes, purses his lips, and for a moment, I hold my breath. Did he catch my blunder? Is he working it out?

"I haven't had pasta Bolognese in a long time," he says, eyes zeroing in on me.

I squirm under his gaze, wondering what he's thinking. What's to come? Will he throw me out or welcome me with open arms?

I shrug, trying to play it nonchalantly. "It's quick and easy. I've been so busy today, I had to choose something fast."

He nods and looks away. I breathe for the first time in minutes, shoulders slouching when his back is turned.

"How long until it's ready?"

"Now. If you want to take a seat, I'll put some on a plate for you," I say, moving toward the stove where I have the piping hot pasta waiting.

I measure out three cups and cut a piece of garlic bread into the perfect square, just the way he'll want it. When I set the plate down, I watch him closely. He takes his first bite, and I relish at the way his eyes close around a moan. I can't stop the wide smile spreading across my face.

"This is incredible. I knew you could cook, but this is something else."

"I learned early on," I admit. "I spent most of my life cooking."

"You've clearly mastered cooking. It's so good," he says, and I blush under his compliment.

"That comes with a lot of hard work," I say, chuckling.

He takes a bite, eyes never straying from me. "Tell me about yourself. Something you're comfortable sharing with me."

Internally, I panic. What in the hell can I possibly say that wouldn't tip him off? He knows so much about my early years, so I decide to artfully pass over those, and go straight to the years in which he's been absent.

"I've had a host of odd jobs. Mostly to save up money for grad school. I want to be a social worker." I take a bite of pasta, trying to determine how much to say.

"Yeah, you said that before, but I have to ask, what drew you to it?"

Is there more to that question? Is he on to me?

Dear God, Cassidy. Pull your shit together.

I'm going to give it away myself by worrying. He doesn't know who I am. If he did, there's no way he'd have kept quiet.

Right?

"Cassidy?" Aiden says, pulling me back to him.

"Hmm?"

I just sound dumb. I try to stop my cheeks from reddening, but it's no use. They're on fire.

Aiden smirks. "Social work. What drew you to that?" he says, reminding me of his question.

"I want to work in child welfare or provide therapy to kids who come from abused and neglected homes."

"Why?"

Shit. Shit. Shit.

There's something in his tone. An unspoken question.

Or you're making it all up in your head, bound and determined to be caught.

No.

I take a deep breath and try to formulate how in the heck to circumvent this. I can hardly say *well, growing up in a trailer park with an abusive alcoholic parent who chose any vice presented over caring for their child…*

That wouldn't give it away or anything.

I need to rein in my emotions. Especially my fear. I've got this.

"Where I grew up, it made me have a special appreciation for the homeless. One of my first days here, walking through Redville, I saw a mother with a small child. The little girl most likely had only one outfit to her name. A pair of holey pants, dirty shoes, and a tattered coat. Her only other possession, a raggedy teddy bear." I take a sip of my water, trying not to cry, picturing the mother and daughter.

The story is true. Every bit of it. The little girl reminded me of myself, and that was like a knife through the heart.

Except I did have a home, a really shitty one, but it's more than that little girl had.

"I hoped that the money I handed her would go toward food for the little girl." I lower my head, shaking it back and forth.

The story might only be an alibi for Aiden's sake, but it did have a hand in fortifying my decision. The fact it's not entirely the truth bothers me.

The reality that I have to continue to lie to Aiden hurts.

"What about it made your decision?"

He's a dog with a bone, picking apart my life and uncovering the layers of Cassidy.

"That moment made me question, if the system hadn't let that little girl down, could things have been different? Could she be somewhere warm, with a fresh, clean set of clothes and food in her belly?"

He nods but doesn't say anything. Something in his far-off expression makes me wonder… could he be thinking about me? About Pip at this moment?

"Anyway, I started volunteering at a local foster care agency and just saw more devastating situations. I heard horrific stories from the children there, and I wanted to make a difference." I inhale. "So yeah… that's why I'm here pretending to be your girlfriend," I say, shrugging one shoulder. "I figure all the lies are worth it in the end."

He swallows around a mouthful, nodding more.

"I think that's an admirable goal. I have no doubt you'll do well." I hold his stare. "Children don't deserve to be punished for the actions of adults. They deserve love." His eyes drop to the table. "Unconditional love."

I know he's thinking about his mother and how horrible she was. He might've gotten out and made something of himself, but that didn't make his life easy.

"Children deserve their parents' time and effort. I hope to ensure that for many children, including my own one day."

Aiden's eyes darken in a way that sends liquid heat pooling low in my belly.

"I'm sure your parents are proud, Cassidy."

I can't contain the humorless laugh that bubbles up. "I doubt that. Good or bad. I'm on my own. I have been for a long time."

His eyes narrow. "I'm sorry if I hit a nerve."

"You didn't and don't apologize. You did nothing wrong." I place my fork on my half-eaten plate and stand from the table. "I'm gonna clean up. You should get ready. It's about time for you to watch your game films."

And with that, I pick up the plate and walk away from the room, needing space from Aiden.

That conversation got a little too real.

chapter twenty-five

Aiden

I watch as Cassidy leaves the room, head held high despite the heaviness of the conversation we just had. I am entirely fascinated by Cassidy's many layers. There's so much to this woman, and I feel like I've only scratched the surface. She buries her emotions so deep. It's a wonder she has any relationships. They're likely few and far between, as the wall she's erected appears to be fortified by stone.

What did her parents do to her? It was clear there's bad blood there.

It makes me think about my own past, and my stomach sours.

Whatever I can do to help Cassidy realize her dreams, I'll do it. Why?

Because she's been a lifesaver in the short time I've known her. Because she deserves it.

Because she makes me think of—I shake my head. Nope. That's ridiculous.

I go about my nightly rituals, cleaning the kitchen, but this time, I don't linger as long in the room. I do a quick clean before heading into the living room to prepare to watch the film.

Within moments, Cassidy stands in front of me, brow furrowed. "You're done in the kitchen already?"

"Yep."

"Are you okay?"

"I am." I smile.

Her eyes narrow, clearly confused by how fast I cleaned the room. *So am I.*

She walks to the back of the couch, hovering back there, for what, I'm not sure.

Then her hands rest on my shoulders. "Are you sure you're okay? Do you want a massage?"

"I'm fine. And that's not your job."

"It'll help."

She has a point, but as my assistant, isn't massaging crossing the line?

She waits for my signal of what to do, and on a resigned sigh, I lift my right hand, and with that, the massage commences.

I groan at the way her knuckles knead my aching muscles. For not being a licensed massage therapist, this woman does it expertly. Her touch removes all of my worries and the need to organize or sort. I'm able to relax and melt into the couch.

I start the footage, and admittedly can't even focus. My concentration is solely on the way her nimble fingers move across my shoulders and down my back. My cock hardens, and I shift slightly to hide my reaction to her touch.

I don't want to make her uncomfortable, and I don't want her to think that this is not appreciated.

I shake off the thought. Allowing myself to unwind.

When she's done kneading my tight muscles, Cassidy taps my shoulders.

If I need something, she attends to it so I can focus. Tonight, it doesn't feel right to order her around.

"You're off duty starting now," I say as she looks at me.

Her eyes narrow, but she doesn't speak. I pat the spot next to me on the couch.

"Let's watch a movie instead."

At this, her eyes widen, and her mouth gapes. Her reaction is warranted. I'm stunned. This might be the first time in my entire life that I've forgone some of my rituals.

It's probably even more confusing to her since I've gotten past games already on the screen. But as I take in her adorable features, I know I want to spend time with her, doing something that's not work-related.

"Are you sure? I mean…"

For a second, I expect my need to win out, but as I stare at her, I find that I don't at all regret my decision.

I lick my bottom lip, thinking about how cute she is at this moment. Unsure. Confused.

Beautiful.

"Positive."

She takes a seat next to me, and the smell of her floral perfume washes over me. It's a scent that I've come to know as all Cassidy. It's more than pleasant. It's intoxicating. With her this close, it's all I can do to keep my hands to myself.

"What do you want to watch?" I'm waiting for her to say some dreaded romantic comedy. I don't want to, but I will watch one. For her.

"Something with action."

I stand corrected.

Once again, Cassidy has me off-kilter. She says and does the absolute opposite of whatever I think she's going to do. I'm constantly on my toes with her, and I like it more than I should.

"Something with action… well, all right," I say, smiling like an idiot.

I put in one of my all-time favorite movies. There's been a

constant debate about whether this movie is a Christmas movie, and for some reason, I can't wait to get Cassidy's take at the end.

"*Die Hard*? I love this movie," she squeals.

Fuck. Me.

"You've seen this?"

"Who hasn't? This is a classic." I turn toward her, eyeing her as though she's a strange animal.

"What?" she asks, incredulity clear. "I like movies, Aiden, and this one is special."

She looks away, but before she does, I catch a glimmer of something resembling trepidation.

"Anyway, let's watch the movie," she says, suddenly acting strange.

"What's that?" I ask into the side of her head.

She peers over at me, and that niggling feeling comes over me again.

"Why did you get weird?"

Her eyes close for a moment. "I didn't get weird."

My eyebrow lifts. "You got weird. Why?"

She blows out a harsh breath. "I was just settling in for the movie."

Lie.

When you've grown up around the best liars the world has to offer, you quickly learn how to spot one a mile away. I should press. I should find out what the hell's going on with her, but I just wanna watch the movie.

By the way she's alluded to her past, I'd harbor a guess that she's had a terrible upbringing. Maybe there's a story there with the movie? Something triggering. I don't want to bring up bad memories, so I decide to drop it, opting to just enjoy myself.

We're both riveted to the screen, and I can't stop smiling at how many times Cassidy has quoted some of my favorite lines. This girl is an enigma. One I wholeheartedly want to figure out.

With every moment I spend with her, something shifts.

"So I have to know… which is it? Christmas or no?"

She grins before rolling her eyes. "Does it really matter? It's a kick-ass movie. Who the hell cares if people think it is or isn't a Christmas movie? I'll watch it any time of the year."

"If someone feels that strongly that it's not a Christmas movie, I let it pass. To each their own."

"Exactly," she says. "I like it no matter what."

I grin manically because that is a non-answer if I've ever heard one. I stand by what I said. If someone says it's not a Christmas movie, I won't argue with them. But I say yes.

"Okay, but really. Which one?"

Her head lolls back on a groan.

"Why do you men always have to make big deals out of things that aren't?"

I guffaw, playing at hurt. "*You men*? I'm shocked you'd make such generalizations."

"I've yet to meet a man who doesn't demand you choose a side where *Die Hard* is concerned."

"Everyone has an opinion, and yours can't be that generic."

She laughs. "I don't personally think of it as a Christmas movie, but then again, it wasn't something *I* watched around Christmas. You and me—"

She stops mid-sentence, staring off into space.

"You and me," I press, but she swallows and waves her hand.

"We're just different."

It's all she says, and it makes zero sense in the context of our conversation. She snaps her mouth shut and turns away, acting strange yet again.

"What's next?"

Just like that, she shuts down any possibility of me prying by moving on to the next topic.

I turn on some lame drama, and I'm not at all surprised when Cassidy dozes off.

The TV plays a political show, but I don't pay any attention. I'm lost in thought. My mind races from Cassidy's reactions tonight, all the way to tomorrow's game.

Typical.

My head is always yo-yoing from one thing to the next.

At some point Cassidy nestles into my side, laying her head on my shoulder, and all feels right in the world. My mind eases and eventually clears; all I can focus on is her steady breathing. This feels familiar.

Like home.

I grind my teeth, so fucking tired of thinking of the past.

Right now, I'm just going to bask in the moment with Cassidy's warm body next to me. Because at the end of the day, this is what my life is now, and nothing can change that.

chapter twenty-six

Cassidy

T HE MOUTHWATERING SCENT OF EGGS AND BACON HAS ME
stirring awake. For a moment, I think I'm dreaming. I pop
one eye open and immediately sit up, scanning the area.

I'm on Aiden's couch, with a blanket wrapped around me. He
hadn't woken me last night when I fell asleep watching the movie.
He took care to ensure I was comfortable, though, and I was.

That gesture warms me from the inside.

"Wakey wakey, Sleeping Beauty. Breakfast is almost ready."

I blink several times, completely confused by what's occurring. I've never seen Aiden cook here, and definitely not for me.

I wipe the sleep from my eyes. "I'm supposed to be doing these
things for you," I say, and he smiles.

"You were sleeping pretty peacefully. I didn't wanna disturb you."

"That's my job."

He half rolls his eyes. "You've taken such great care of me,
Cassidy. It's the least I can do." He flips bacon on the stove, looking like he's done this a thousand times.

"If you want to get ready, it'll be done in a couple of minutes."

I jump from the couch, rushing toward the back to get my toothbrush and a few other accessories to pull myself together. I chance a glance in the mirror and grimace.

I'm sure there are people who look worse in the morning, but this is not how I would want Aiden to see me.

He never cared about those things.

I shove that thought away. He isn't the Aiden I once knew... or is he?

When I'm finally presentable, I make my way to the small dining nook, taking a seat when it's clear Aiden has finished cooking and doesn't need help. I watch as he dishes out eggs, bacon, and toast onto a plate and slides it to me.

Having him do this makes me uncomfortable. I'm not used to anyone taking care of me. It's what I do for others, but it's rarely reciprocated.

Aiden has never been like the other people in my life. He always made sure I was taken care of before himself. It appears some things haven't changed, and that makes me smile.

I smother it, not wanting him to pry into my internal musings.

"Are you ready for your game tomorrow?" I ask, lifting the fork to my lips and popping a piece of bacon into my mouth.

"I am, but I'm most looking forward to the break after."

"You're on a break now," I deadpan. The Saints haven't played since Tampa. Tomorrow they play game three.

I wonder if practice will be as grueling as it's been if they win tomorrow's game. Maybe if he's stuck in practice all day, I can try to spend some time with Emma. It's not that long a drive to Michigan. Maybe I can have her come here, or I can go there.

Perhaps if I can visit her, I could start looking around for an apartment close to the university too. Or better yet, maybe I could start researching some online programs to get started. Something that would allow me to work while taking classes.

It's a dream I've had for so long, but I've never felt like it was a possibility. I have watched friends navigate the process, leaving me behind. Most of them are now gainfully employed, earning substantial salaries, while I am playing the role of a lifetime, pretending to be someone who I'm not.

It's been a blessing I didn't see coming.

I'm being paid well by Aiden. Not well enough to pay for school and a place of my own, but soon. Assuming he keeps me for a few extra months after the playoffs and doesn't go through with what I overheard him say to Mike.

Something felt different last night. He didn't do all of his rituals. Sure, he cleaned up, but it was different. It wasn't as intense.

Then when he would normally watch old footage of himself, he watched a movie with me instead.

He cuddled with me. Took care of me. Could he still throw me aside that easily?

Nope. Don't go there.

The truth is, I still don't trust him. Not fully. It's funny how something that can take seconds to break takes forever to repair.

"Listen, I don't need you to be at the game tomorrow," he says, and my face falls before I have a chance to control it.

Disappointment settles in, as I had just been hoping for more time. Could this be the start of the end of our professional relationship?

"It's not like that, Cassidy. There's a huge charity event... one that I truthfully forgot about. Well, I guess it's not that I forgot about it, I just didn't plan on going." He groans. "But Coach made it very clear that it wasn't optional." He shakes his head, tapping his knuckles on the table three times. "Anyway, it's a very fancy gala. One that will require a new, expensive tux and the whole nine yards for you."

"What?" I say, eyes narrowing.

"I'll need you to attend...obviously. You'll need to work fast in order to make this all happen."

"Wait. Umm. When is it again?"

"Sunday night." He grimaces when my eyes widen.

"You mean tomorrow?"

"Yeah, but don't worry, the game is early."

"Umm…wow. Okay." I start to internally panic because no way in hell can I afford a new dress for such an event. "I don't know if I have anything—"

"I'll handle that. This is part of our arrangement, Cassidy," he says, as though reading my mind. "I'm going to leave you the number to a personal shopper who Mike recommended, along with the address. I'll get ahold of her today and ensure she contacts you to make an appointment."

I nod like an idiot, trying to make a mental list of all the things.

"She'll likely want to work fast too, as this will be a social event that any stylist would kill to be part of in any capacity. With you being the girlfriend who everyone is watching, it shouldn't be a problem at all," he says.

Damn. People will move mountains for him.

I continue to chew my eggs while I sort through everything.

I'll need to set up hair.

And makeup.

"Whatever you need, Cassidy, just use my name and my credit card. If anyone gives you a hard time, I'll reach out."

I purse my lips. "This isn't *Pretty Woman*, Aiden. I'll be fine."

He smirks. "I have no idea what that means, but I'm sure you'll tell me."

I shake my head once, being defiant, and he chuckles.

There will be paparazzi everywhere, which means people will be judging me, and that thought has me panicking all the more.

"You're stunning. You have nothing to worry about."

The way he reads my mind always manages to throw me off-kilter. Aiden has always had a way of knowing exactly what I'm thinking and how I'm feeling.

"I know you could do your own hair and makeup and look gorgeous, Cassidy. I just don't want you to have to worry about it. It's so last minute, I'm willing to pay for someone else to take that stress off you." He holds my gaze, staring into my eyes. "You deserve to be pampered just as well as every other woman who will be there. More so. Go all out. Get a manicure and a pedicure. A wax." He grimaces. "Whatever you need."

My heart warms with his words and how good he is to me. He doesn't have to do this for me at all.

He can't have you wearing a subpar dress and looking a mess. You're pretending to be his girlfriend, fool.

My good mood sours instantly at the reminder that this is all a sham.

He reaches across the table, placing his hand on top of mine. "I know this is asking a lot. Are you okay with it? If not, I can make up an excuse for you not to go."

I shake my head adamantly. "No, I can definitely make this happen. I was just thinking about everything that needs to be done before Sunday. I could kill you for waiting until now."

He grins. "Lydia is the name of the shopper. She's wonderful, and Mike trusts her. I'm sure she'd be willing to help set up all the other appointments too. Ask her. I will pay her well."

I smile, but it's forced.

His life is so out of my realm. Having people jump through hoops for you isn't something I've ever known. And aside from this time in my life, pretending with Aiden, it likely will never happen for me again.

"I'll give her my sizes. Please have her arrange for a new tux for me as well. Like I said, I'm sure she's great considering the recommendation, but I'd like you to oversee what she chooses for me. I trust your judgment more."

My cheeks heat. "I'm not really sure that I know anything about expensive tuxedos, Aiden."

He grins. "I know you won't disappoint."

My stomach turns, and I plaster on the fakest smile yet.

"I can manage. I've got this."

I jump up from the table, fumbling with my plate, needing to clean up quickly and run through the rituals so I can get started on my large task ahead.

Aiden stands and moves beside me, turning me toward him and getting up in my space.

"Leave it, Cass. I can do this."

Our eyes meet and hold for several seconds. Aiden's hand lifts, and he slowly moves a piece of hair over my shoulder, dragging his fingertip across the curve of my neck. I shiver under his touch, eyes closing with a sigh.

Without conscious thought, my body moves closer until our chests are practically touching. I inhale deeply, soaking in a scent all Aiden.

When my eyes open, he's staring at my lips, eyes dark and turning with something that looks a lot like desire. My lips part, and my chest rises and falls quickly.

"Cassidy." He says my name like a prayer, and I know without a doubt he's thinking what I'm thinking.

This is meant to happen.

I lean up on my tiptoes, and everything happens quickly from there. He grabs me around my waist, pulling me taut against him. Our mouths crash together, a tango of teeth and tongues. This is something between the first night and the kiss for the paparazzi. Passionate. Heated. There's nothing soft about this kiss.

It's pure need and desire wrapped up in a tiny bomb that's just detonated, burning us both. The flames lick up my legs and over my belly, up my spine and across my shoulders. I feel his touch everywhere, but it's not enough.

I claw at his shirt, wanting the thin fabric between us gone. I'm lost in the moment, wholly prepared to throw our agreement to the wind and give myself to him. Fully.

Aiden groans, pulling away slightly. Our breaths mingle, my heart beating out of my chest.

"I…I don't want to stop, Cass."

"But we have to."

He doesn't need to say it. I know he's right.

"It's not like that. It's not about our agreement. It's…" He rocks back on his heels, eyes shifting around the room.

At the mess.

His compulsion to clean won't allow it.

I don't want to make him feel bad, so I swallow down the disappointment, put on the best fake smile I can manage, and dive into cleaning.

His hand darts out, stopping me again. "No. You should go."

"Oh…okay, well…you're probably right. Lots to do," I say lamely, sounding awkward as hell.

"I'll see you later."

It's all he says before pulling out his phone and firing off some texts. Once he's done, he gets to cleaning up.

I should pull myself together before heading out, but the need to run outweighs what I look like.

Before I know it, I'm in the elevator, and then once I get to the lobby, I'm rushing outside, gulping in the fresh air, likely looking on the verge of a crisis. And the onlookers thinking that would not be wrong.

A war is brewing inside me. I can't keep up the lies. It's not fair to either one of us.

A horn honks, and I realize I'm in the street.

"Hey, lady, you got a death wish or something?"

My hand lifts in apology as I rush back to the sidewalk, the angry taxi driver mumbling obscenities loud enough for everyone around to hear while rolling up his window.

An elderly woman walks by me, holding out a five-dollar bill, and I look at her like she has three heads.

"Get yourself a hot sandwich, dear."

My mouth flops open. Does she think I'm homeless?

She places the money in front of me, waving goodbye.

"I'm…I'm not homeless," I yell, glancing around to find that, thankfully, nobody else was around to witness one of my lowest points.

I glance down at my pants, recognizing that I'm in pajamas. My hair is likely a fright, and I'm sure I look like a hot mess.

Rock. Bottom.

What if someone from the press was lurking around out here to capture that? I'd have Aiden all over the news for all the wrong things. I'd embarrass myself and him. The last thing I want to do is go back in there, but I can't be out in public like this.

Clearly, Aiden was too wrapped up in his compulsion to notice the way I left. Maybe I can sneak in without being seen.

Unlikely.

Oh, the horror I feel at this moment. I've been at rock bottom, or so I thought, but this doesn't feel much better. This is embarrassment personified. I was mistaken for a homeless person. Albeit by a woman whose glasses were thicker than my hips, and her age is likely three times higher than mine, but still.

I'm losing control. The longer I keep this secret bottled up inside me, the worse it's going to be when my house of cards comes crumbling down.

I have to come clean. I have to tell Aiden the truth. The question is, when?

Do I do it before the charity event? Or after?

So many decisions need to be made, but I know without a doubt, I can't keep this up.

My days with Aiden are numbered, and that makes me want to cry more than anything. I've enjoyed being with him again, and I don't doubt that when the truth of who I am is revealed, I'll lose much more than this job.

I'll lose Aiden.

Again.

chapter twenty-seven

Aiden

SUNDAY CAME TOO QUICKLY.

Now I'm back on the ice, playing game three against the Bulldogs.

The problem is I'm a complete mess.

For one, my head isn't in it.

I've spent the entire afternoon glancing at where Cassidy typically sits, missing her presence. The worst part is it hasn't gone unnoticed by anyone. The jumbotron has caught me doing it often, according to Coach, who's about ready to kick my ass.

I'm slammed into from behind, and nothing is called. My anger flares as I spin on the dickhead from the opposing team, skating after him without any thought to where the puck is.

I lower my shoulder and throw him into the boards, earning myself an immediate penalty.

"What the fuck?" I say, throwing my gloved hands up. "Were you fucking blind a moment ago?"

The ref ignores me, calling out my penalty.

I refrain from telling him to go to hell, knowing that will surely send Coach over the edge.

"Do I even want to know what's happening out there?" Dane asks as I take a seat next to him in the penalty box. Apparently, both of us are feeling violent today.

"What are you talking about?"

He lifts a brow. "You've been skating around like a lost puppy. Constantly checking the stands. She's not here, dude. Get your head in the game."

I pull a face. "I'm not acting like a lost puppy."

"Dude…you're acting exactly like a puppy dog," he says, curling his upper lip.

I'm not gonna sit here and continue to argue with him, especially because I know he's not entirely wrong.

Over the course of time since Cassidy entered my life, I've become more and more dependent on her. But it's not just that. Of course, her help with my rituals has been a game changer, but even if she didn't do any of that, I would want her here.

I need her here.

The calm she brings.

And calm is one thing I've been low on in this lifetime. Constantly waiting for the other shoe to drop doesn't allow for that.

"Where is she, anyway? Everything good with you two?" Dane asks, pulling me from my thoughts of Cassidy.

"Everything's fine. She's running errands for the gala."

I'm not entirely lying. She is doing just that, but the whole part about her being my girlfriend makes me feel bad.

I allow very few people into my life, and Dane is one of them. Lying to him is one of the worst parts of my current position.

"Let me guess…you just sprang it on her this morning."

I shake my head, pursing my lips. "Yesterday."

He whistles. "You're lucky she didn't castrate you. Do you have any idea how much work goes into these things for a woman?"

"I didn't peg you for a guy who cared about those sorts of things."

"I'm not. But Molly likes to harp on me every time I spring these events on her at the last minute."

Dane and Molly have a relationship that I've never experienced from family. They only have each other and they rely heavily on one another. She's his constant, and he's hers. If not for Molly, Dane would probably be off the team and a raging alcoholic. His words. Apparently, it runs in the family.

"I just told Molls about it too. She's not currently happy with me. She said I should know better." He shrugs. "She should know better. It's not like this is her first rodeo with me."

"No shit." I chuckle. "I'm finding it is not easy to book someone for hair and makeup this last minute."

I have no idea if that's true. I haven't spoken to Cassidy about it since she left me standing in the kitchen.

"I have someone," he says, and it's my turn to lift an eyebrow.

"You have someone?"

"A college friend's sister works in the area. I know if I made a call, she'd hook you up. Molly already has an appointment, but I bet she'd squeeze Cassidy in too."

I nod a few times.

"I scheduled the works for Molly since she's coming with me as a favor. It's the least I could do."

"Probably a good idea. You owe that girl your life."

"Truer words have never been spoken," he says, head forward, waiting for his time to be up. "I'll make the call after the game."

"Thanks, man."

We fist-bump, and then I get to my feet. My time in the box is over. Dane has longer. Hell, the way he beat the shit out of the Bulldogs right wing, I'm surprised he's still in the game.

I can't help but chuckle at how ridiculous that conversation was. Makeup and hair in the penalty box? Yeah, that wasn't on my bingo card.

The rest of the game is intense, but I'm more focused. The talk with Dane helped me get my head back on the ice. We managed to pull it off, but it was too close, and Coach was not happy, which made for a rough night finishing stuff up.

I've just completed my post-game rituals, and I'm walking out of the locker room when I see a frustrated Mike heading toward me.

"We've got a major problem."

I stop in my tracks, trying to determine what said problem could be. These days, the list is mounting to unmanageable lengths.

"What is it?"

Based on his posture and the paleness of his skin, I begin to panic.

"I know you're finally getting settled and feel good about how things are, but this has to end. It wasn't supposed to be a long-term deal, Aiden."

I huff out a breath.

"I'm tired, and I don't wanna talk about this tonight, Mike. Call me tomorrow."

He takes a step into my path, stopping me from leaving. "That's not acceptable. Do you have any idea how much damage it could cause if this got out?"

"I'll take care of it," I say, trying to move past him. I just wanna be home.

"No, you won't. You'll allow me to handle it. You can't give her any reason to out your personal life." He runs his hand back through his dark wavy hair roughly. "Give me time to dig something up on her. Something we can use to get her to go away."

What if I don't want her to go away? What if some broken part of me refuses to see things how they actually are? A damaged man, desperate to paint a picture in my head that's vastly different from reality.

"Aiden," Mike drawls, likely seeing the look on my face.

Despite my every attempt to avoid getting close to people,

Mike wormed his way in and knows me better than I'm comfortable with most days.

"I will take care of it, Mike. I promise."

He takes a deep breath and blows it out harshly. "Fine. I'll allow you to handle this, but make it fast, Aiden." He huffs a humorless laugh. "She's a loose cannon. Desperate women will do heinous stuff to get what they want. You have to be careful."

"I will be."

Mike half rolls his eyes, making it clear he doesn't like this one bit.

Well, neither do I, Mike. Neither do I.

It's going to be a long night.

chapter twenty-eight

Cassidy

"C ASS, WHAT'S WRONG?" MOLLY ASKS FROM THE LOUNGE chair next to me. "You've been off all day. This is supposed to be fun."

Today's the day of the gala, but that's the last thing I'm thinking about.

Aiden and Dane set up an entire spa day for Molly and me to get ready for the event. We've had massages, facials, manicures, and pedicures. We're waiting in the quiet room, sipping on mimosas, and relaxing in the flickering faux candlelit room, waiting to be called for our hair and makeup to finish up the day.

I turn to look at her. "I'm just tired. It's been a long couple of days."

Not a lie. Trying to arrange for a dress and tux at the last minute was not easy. There were very limited choices, considering my build is not typical. Everything was either too big or not curvy enough.

When you're small with curves, everything needs tailoring, and with these dresses, it's not easy to find a tailor at the last minute.

Luckily, Lydia, Aiden's shopper, was incredible and pulled off the impossible.

My dress is divine, and his tux will fit him like a glove.

But that's not why I'm in this mood.

Aiden has been off.

After the night we watched *Die Hard*, I thought things were different, but then we kissed and well, everything has gone to shit since.

Last night, after I got back home, he practically ignored me, and it's been the same this morning.

To make matters worse, he's insisted on doing things himself and has been overly meticulous, taking twice as long to finish a task.

He's been cold and distant, and when you're sharing a space with someone like that, it makes everything awkward.

Something is eating away at him, but he won't say what. I fear it's because I kissed him, which is making me feel sick.

"I feel you. Thankfully, I knew Dane would pull this on me, so I ordered a dress months ago and put it on his tab." She chuckles. "The dipshit didn't even notice. That or he just never said anything." She sighs. "Not that he ever would. I don't take advantage of his money."

I smile at Molly. In the short time I've known her, it's become very clear that she and Dane are good people. No part of me ever thought Molly would mooch off Dane. She does so much for him.

"What are you going to do with your hair?" Molly asks, eyes wide and a goofy smile plastered across her face. "I think you should leave it down and curl it. With that plunging back, it'll look fantastic.

"I was thinking the same."

"Have her put some highlights in. Something to make it pop." She wiggles around excitedly. "Ooh…maybe add some extensions to make it even longer."

"You think she'll have time for all that?"

"Doesn't hurt to ask. Let me handle it. Janine and I have a pretty good relationship. I bet she'll be happy to do it."

"Do you think Aiden will like that?"

As soon as I ask the question, I want to snap it back in and keep my mouth shut. Since when do I care what a man thinks about me? I like me, and that's all that matters.

Except the truth is, I do care. I want him to look at me like he has before. Like I'm the only one in the room. Something he wants to own. Possess.

I want him to ask me to crawl to him. To take him in my mouth. To—

"Earth to Cassidy," Molly calls, clapping her hands and laughing.

I blink several times, shaking my head. "What?"

"You just spaced. Looked like whatever you were thinking about was spicy. You were practically drooling."

My cheeks heat, and my nose scrunches. Oh, how fast my mind slips down to the gutter.

Aiden has a way of pulling that out of me. My inner vixen begs to be unleashed.

But that can't happen. He's made that clear.

"Oh my God. I was not."

She smirks. "You were totally drooling."

Molly throws her head back and laughs. "Not that I can blame you. The relationship that you and Aiden have is drool-worthy. I hope I'll find a guy who makes me look like that one day."

If only she knew the truth.

Fairy tales aren't real, and believing they are will only set a girl up for disappointment.

"Molly, girl, you're up." A woman with long black hair enters the room, smiling widely at Molly.

"Hey, Janine. Any chance we could switch things up today?"

The woman tilts her head to the side. "What did you have in mind?"

Molly turns to me and grins. "This is my friend Cassidy, and she needs the works today."

Janine bites her lip, walking in a circle around me. "What were you thinking?"

She doesn't address me, continuing to have a conversation with Molly. It doesn't bother me. I'm enjoying the break from decision-making.

"Some dimension with her color?"

Janine picks up a brush from the counter. "I think you're right. Okay, Cassidy, you're up."

———◆———

I've been staring at my reflection in the hotel mirror of the massive suite he got me to get ready in for for the past ten minutes.

The transformation is a bit of a shock.

Every imperfection I've ever fussed over is absent. Not because it's been covered by makeup or hidden underneath well-placed hair. Janine and her crew have an uncanny ability to highlight every one of my best features, making the flaws disappear.

My eyes pop with the colors used to line my eyelids, making them look uniformed and bright. My lips are full and pouty. Something I didn't even know was possible. My cheeks are the perfect shade of pink, and my eyebrows are impeccably sculpted and filled in, just enough that they stand out more than usual.

But it doesn't stop there. My eyes travel down my body, marveling at the dress. The beautiful gown Lydia chose highlights my hourglass figure, unlike any other dress I've ever worn. It hugs every curve of my body, accentuating my breasts and waist. The sapphire hue complements my skin tone and brings out the color of my eyes even more.

I twist just enough to see the open back that scoops right above my butt. I gulp. I don't know why, but I'm so nervous.

What will Aiden think?

Did I overdo it?

Will he think I'm trying too hard?

Or will he feel the way I do? Caught up in the whirlwind that has always been Aiden and me. Whether he knows it's me or not.

I'm still the same girl, transfixed by the boy who continuously finds ways to save me.

My eyes water, and I quickly lift my hands, fanning my face, to stop the tears from falling. I refuse to let the hours of work that went into this go to waste. My inner turmoil surrounding Aiden will have to wait. Tonight, I need to continue to dupe the whole world in more ways than one.

I take a deep breath and glance at the clock. It's time. I need to get downstairs and face Aiden.

If I know one thing about Aiden, it's that he will not abide tardiness.

I take one more deep breath and blow it out, giving myself a last once-over in the floor-length mirror before making my way down to the lobby.

The elevator drops me on floor two and then I head to the marble staircase that will lead me to where he said he'd meet me.

With my hand on the railing, I practically tiptoe down the stairs, praying to God that my dress and feet don't get tangled up. The last thing I need to do is take a fall and end the night before it's even begun.

Most of the way down, my eyes are trained on my feet for obvious reasons. But when I lift my head, I find Aiden at the bottom, staring up at me with a look that has my belly flopping and my toes curling. There's no way to misinterpret that look.

Hunger.

"Cassidy, I…" His eyebrows furrow and his mouth pinches.

The shift in Aiden comes so quickly that I'm left a little off-kilter.

"We need to get going," he says, turning his back on me.

I start to internally panic. Something is most definitely wrong.

"Is everything all right?" I call out, and he stops.

He shakes his head before twisting around to face me once more. "No. I mean…yes. Everything's fine. You just…caught me off guard."

I blink a few times, trying to read the room. His emotions have been all over the place in a matter of seconds. I'm not sure where we've landed.

"I caught you off guard. How?"

I walk down a few more steps but stop when I'm almost at eye level with him. The advantage of looking down on him helps me feel more secure.

For years, when I'd go toe-to-toe with a man, I was always being looked down on. It made me feel small and helpless. Right now, that feeling is absent. Not that Aiden ever made me feel that way. He didn't. The awful boys I encountered left me feeling insecure, and it's difficult not to revert to those same insecurities, even after all this time.

"I just…you look…" He shakes his head again. "Ready?" He turns his back to me once more, and I'm growing angry with each dismissal. This reaction is not what I was expecting.

Cool indifference is the worst reaction he could have to me.

I stand on the bottom step for a moment, disappointment washing over me.

The high I was feeling moments ago dashed away in a heartbreaking beat. The way he's acting is so similar to my father all those years. If he wasn't screaming down at me, he was ignoring my existence. And here's Aiden, doing practically the same.

This is how tonight's going to go?

Wonderful.

chapter twenty-nine

Cassidy

W E'RE IN THE BACK OF A TOWN CAR, THE PARTITION BETWEEN the driver and us is raised. We're alone and the air feels thick with emotion. Stifling.

Aiden hasn't said a word since the stairs, and I'm not sure how I can fake happiness tonight. This is awful.

"Is there something wrong, Aiden? Did I…do something to upset you?"

His eyes narrow in on me, lips pursing. "No, why do you ask?"

I huff out a laugh. "Well, you just got weird back there." When it appears he doesn't know what I'm talking about, I explain. "Back at the hotel. You were rude, Aiden."

He blinks a few times, licking his bottom lip. "I'm sorry, Cassidy. I'm having some current issues, and they rattled me."

"Do you want to talk about it?"

He blows out a breath. "Not really. I don't want the night to be ruined."

"Did I do something?" I ask again, nervous he knows what I've been keeping from him.

Petrified that everything is about to blow up in my face.

He groans, throwing his head back. "No. This has nothing to do with you. It's a personal matter. Something to do with my family."

The mention of his family has my stomach twisting. The list of issues they could bring to his door is extensive. More than likely, it involves money. It always does with them. That or one of them has gotten into trouble and will bring a storm of press to ruin his life.

"I'm really sorry. I know you don't want to discuss it, but just know I'm here." I avert my gaze. "I have a complicated relationship with my dad. I understand how family drama can eat away at a person."

"I'm sorry to hear that, Cassidy. Truly. I wouldn't wish it on anyone."

"I got out. I ran so far away from that life and never looked back," I admit.

"I'm so glad you did." He smiles, and I can't help but smile back. He's so incredibly handsome. "Sometimes, we have to leave our old life behind to find ourselves. To thrive."

The mention of his leaving and knowing that I was part of the casualty in order for him to thrive assaults me with mixed emotions. On the one hand, I'm willing to sacrifice in order for Aiden to have the life he deserves. On the other hand, it hurts that I meant so little to him that he was able to throw me aside.

"By the way, you look incredible." I blush under his compliment. "I should've told you that earlier. Family drama or not, there's no excuse."

My eyes lower to my lap. "Thank you. They did a pretty impressive job. That's for sure."

He narrows his eyes and slams his lips together.

"What?" I ask.

"You don't see it. Do you?"

I lick my bottom lip. "See what?"

"How gorgeous you are. Every day. It's not about what they did, Cassidy. They simply highlighted what you look like every morning when you wake up."

I'm speechless.

This is the kindest thing that anyone has ever said to me. The best part? I know without a doubt he means what he says. As much as it overfills my cup, it also makes me awkward. What do I even say to that?

"What should I expect tonight?" I ask, the need to change the subject immediate.

I'm so incredibly uncomfortable with compliments, and more so when they come from him.

"It's a stuffy gala with a bunch of people who have far too much money. It'll be ostentatious and over-the-top." He relaxes into the seat, the heavy moment gone.

"Will there be paparazzi?"

"There will be a few media personnel, but it's very limited, and they are under strict rules. They will not be approaching you. They're only there to report on the event."

"They'll still be watching," I murmur.

"Someone's always watching, Cassidy. Nothing to worry yourself about. You'll be fine."

He grabs my hand and squeezes, and I'm shocked when he doesn't remove it. He allows his touch to linger.

"You'll do fine. I dare say they'll likely write about you, though."

My head snaps to his. The grin on his face catches me off guard. He's so damn attractive.

"You're without a doubt going to turn heads." He chuckles, shaking his head. "I really should have asked to see your dress before tonight."

"Would you have changed it?" I say, trying to contain my smile.

"Yes. Absolutely, I would have."

"You don't like it?"

"Why does your mind always go there? Of course, I like it, and so will every other man and woman there."

"It's a good thing we're just pretending then. Isn't it?" As soon as the words slip from my mouth, I regret them.

Why do I always find a way to ruin a good moment?

Aiden's smile drops from his face.

"I guess you're right."

———— ·◦· ————

Aiden couldn't have described this event any better. Ostentatious is almost underplaying things.

We're in a lavish hotel ballroom underneath ten massive chandeliers. Crystal teardrops falling toward the ground, shimmering like diamonds. In the middle of every table is a crystal centerpiece that extends five feet into the air, overflowing with a mix of roses, hydrangeas, orchids, white larkspur, and delphiniums.

A string quartet plays in the corner, filling the room with a classical melody that no one, aside from the few dancing on the dance floor, appears to pay any attention to.

Aiden has been tied up, discussing his take on the Stanley Cup with some congressman that I'm not familiar with. Not that I mind. I'm completely preoccupied with the opulence of the place. It gives me a moment to stare in wonder without any of them recognizing how out of my element I am.

It makes me wonder what things were like for Aiden when he was first introduced to this world. Were his eyes as large as mine? Did he marvel at the money that must've gone into putting on this event?

"I apologize for keeping you from your beautiful date, Aiden." The gray-haired man, dressed in a black tuxedo with a black bow tie, says, offering a smile to me.

"I don't mind at all," I say, smiling back. "I've been enjoying the music."

The man offers a slight bow. "Slate, you shouldn't keep her waiting. *Dance.*"

Aiden turns to me with a lifted eyebrow. "Would you like to dance, Cassidy?"

No.

"Yes. I'd love to."

He extends his hand to me, and I place mine in his.

I allow him to walk me to the center of the dance floor, all the while cursing myself for saying yes.

What was I supposed to say? I was caught off guard.

The truth is, I'm a shit dancer. I don't know how to waltz, or whatever it is these people are currently doing as they move around us effortlessly.

"What's wrong?"

I lean in so that others won't overhear. "I...can't dance. Not like that."

He lets out a breath. "You'll be fine. Just allow me to lead."

When did Aiden Slate learn to dance?

The current song stops, and Aiden gets into position. As soon as the first note sounds, we're off and moving.

I'm doing my best to keep up with Aiden's effortless moves, and surprisingly, I find I'm not so bad as long as I follow him. He spins and twirls me all around the floor as people whiz by. I hardly notice them, though. My eyes are transfixed on Aiden.

He pulls me tighter into his chest, and my breath hitches. We're so close. Our mouths are mere centimeters apart. If I leaned in just a touch, our lips would touch.

The want builds, and I see it in him too. His eyes have darkened to deep pools of black. His breathing has accelerated, his chest rising and falling quickly. The music comes to a halt and so do our feet. My eyes remain fixed on Aiden.

"Cassidy, I—"

Someone claps as they approach us. "I must say, you two look fantastic out there. The media is buzzing about it."

I turn to see Mike, the man I know as Aiden's agent.

Aiden's focus on me shatters as he turns to address Mike.

"Nice to see you. Where have you been hiding out?"

Mike shrugs. "I just arrived. Hadley accosted me at the door."

I have no idea who Hadley is, but Aiden seems to. His eyes widen, and he attempts to hide a smirk.

"Did she now?" Aiden says, mirth evident in his tone.

Mike purses his lips, bobbing his head. "Sure did. I'll be hiding for the remainder of the evening."

"Aiden, would you mind if I cut in for a dance with Cassidy?"

Aiden lifts an eyebrow but steps aside, waving a hand out to give his blessing.

"I must admit, I'm not very good. Aiden simply ensured I remained on my feet," I say, eyes lowering to the floor.

"No problem. We'll take it slow," he says, grabbing my elbow and ushering me to the farther side of the room.

The music begins, and Mike takes my arms and places them where they need to be and we're off. He's not as skilled as Aiden, and it becomes evident quickly that our steps will be slower and shaky.

I'm concentrating on the moves when Mike speaks.

"Who are you?"

I stumble at his words, eyes flying to his. "Excuse me?"

He gets closer to me, and I have to stop myself from jerking away and making a scene.

"I know you're not who you claim to be."

"What are you talking about?" I ask. A boulder settling in my gut.

"We were expecting someone the night you showed up, but it wasn't you. I spoke to my contact, and apparently, the girl who was supposed to meet Aiden had a minor car accident and never made it to the hotel."

I try to continue to dance but instead step on his toes as I try to develop a story on the fly. "I was sent instead."

He shakes his head. "Come on, Cassidy… that is your name, right?"

I stop, pulling out of his grasp while dancers call out in anger about our sudden move.

"Of course my name is Cassidy. I am who I say I am."

"You might not be lying about your name, little girl, but I know you weren't meant to be in the hotel that night."

The gig's up.

"What do you want from me?" I ask, my voice hard.

"The truth," he says, eyes fixed on me.

"I'll tell you everything."

He shakes his head back and forth. "Not me. Aiden. You'll come clean to him now, or I will."

He turns to leave, and my hand juts out, grabbing him. Mike twists around, looking down at my hand around his arm, lifting a brow.

"Please. Not here. I don't want Aiden's image to be impacted by this. Allow me to talk to him in private so we can devise a plan that won't come back on him."

Mike's eyes narrow in on me, and he sucks in his cheeks. After a few painstakingly quiet moments, his features soften.

"All right. I'll give you twenty-four hours. If you haven't told him by then, I will."

I wrap my arms around my waist as Mike walks away, leaving me in the middle of the floor.

My heart pounds, and my palms sweat.

I knew this day would come, but I'm not prepared for it to be here so soon.

Everything is about to change, and I'm petrified.

I'm going to lose Aiden again, and my heart can't handle that.

Not now. Not when I know who he's become.

A man so much better than I could've ever imagined.

I'm falling in love with him and that's the most heartbreaking of all.

chapter thirty

Cassidy

THE NIGHT CRAWLS BY AS AIDEN RUBS ELBOWS WITH THE CITY elite. I've been introduced to far too many people I'll never remember. We've eaten, drank, danced, and now we're back to schmoozing. And every moment was brutal.

To pretend everything is all right when I'm dying inside is the hardest of all the lies. I've been silently freaking out, trying to determine the best way to break the news about who I am to him. Mike made it very clear. I have twenty-four hours to come clean, or he'll tell Aiden himself.

I can't allow that to happen.

I've watched Aiden so closely tonight, soaking in every last memory that I can. It's likely that when he learns the truth, he'll want nothing to do with me. All this time we've spent together will be like the past, discarded and forgotten, while he moves forward with his dreams.

You'd think it would be hard to keep the resentment at bay, but it's not. I've seen Aiden's struggles. I've witnessed how hard he's had to work to get where he is. And if what he said earlier is half as bad as I suspect, he's still running away from his past.

"He's very good at hiding how uncomfortable he is…isn't he?"

I turn over my shoulder to see Billy, eyes trained in on Aiden like a snake in the grass, except he's not even trying to stay hidden.

Gone is the repentant act he'd been playing as of late. In its place is something devious. Calculated.

"What the fuck are you up to, Billy?"

He turns his head, looking down at me with a wicked half-smile. "You'll see. Everyone will."

My blood freezes at his words.

"I don't know what you're playing at, but you need to stay the hell away from me and Aiden."

"Aw…are you afraid of little ol' me?" He barks out a humorless laugh. "I'm harmless if you stay out of my way."

"Get away from me right now. I don't want anything to do with your sick and twisted mind games."

The most sinister smirk spreads across his face. "You have no idea who Aiden Slate is. But I do. I know far too well, and one of these days…very soon…he's gonna fall from that ivory tower he thinks protects him."

"And how would that be?" I take a step into his space, the anger fueling my actions. "Let me guess. You're single-handedly going to ensure it happens."

"I don't think I need to. There are plenty of players in the game. Aren't there…what's your name again?"

The blood drains from my face. The way he said that, and his facial expression have me teetering on the edge.

Does he know who *I* am?

"What's going on?" I hear Aiden's familiar voice, but my eyes remain fixed on Billy's, trying to determine what his words mean. Is he only messing with me? Or does he know my secrets too? When I don't answer he says my name, but it's Aiden's hard tone that has me peeking over my shoulder. But Aiden isn't looking at me. His glare is fixed on Billy.

"Nothing," Billy answers before I can say anything. His nonchalant tone takes me off guard. You'd think Aiden hadn't just used his *I'm going to kill you,* tone. "I was just complimenting her on this dress. She looks rather beautiful." He turns to Aiden. "Don't you think, Aiden?"

Aiden takes a threatening step forward. "I think you should refrain from making comments about my girl."

Billy chuckles darkly. "Have a good night."

He turns around and walks off like there wasn't about to be a throw-down in the middle of a black-tie event.

"What is it with that asshole?" I say under my breath.

"He's a spoilsport. Pissed off that he's not as good as he thinks he is."

I lift an eyebrow. "That he is."

Aiden blows out a harsh breath, rubbing at his chest. "I don't give a fuck about anything he says or does, but I don't want him anywhere near you."

"That makes two of us," I say, inhaling deeply. "I just don't understand him. You know, he did apologize to me for being an ass at one point, but he just continues to be an ass."

Aiden bobs his head. "I don't think he knows any different. From what I understand, he comes from a rich family who was able to buy his way to the top of whatever he wanted. But it isn't working that way in the NHL. Coach sees he's a subpar athlete that made the team because Billy's daddy plays golf with the team's owner."

I clench my teeth, baring them. "That explains a lot."

Aiden chuckles, but it dies off quickly. "He was right about one thing."

I raise an eyebrow, highly doubting that there's anything Aiden could say to convince me that the guy was right about something.

"And what would that be?"

"You look absolutely stunning."

I grin. "I don't remember him saying stunning."

He smirks while lifting one shoulder. "Regardless, you are."

"Thank you," I say, cheeks heating and eyes dropping to the floor.

Aiden's finger comes under my chin, lifting my head until our eyes meet.

"Dance with me." He holds his hand out, and I put mine in his, allowing him to lead me to the dance floor.

This night has been full of anxiety and fear, but for a few moments, I'm going to bask in this moment with Aiden. Hand in hand, we shut the world out as we twirl around the room, lost in each other's smiles.

Whatever's to come for me tomorrow, I'll deal with then.

Tonight is for us.

The end of the night came far too quickly. We've said our goodbyes to everyone that Aiden wanted, and now we're making our way to the door.

"Great night, Aiden," Mike says, clapping him on the back. "Thank you for the invitation."

Aiden smirks. "Of course. No way was I going to be subjected to this bullshit alone."

"Get some rest. You have some big days coming up." Mike looks at me when he says it, and I have to force myself not to react to his words. They're a veiled threat, and I hear them loud and clear.

The clock is ticking, and you better come clean, so I don't have to.

"Cassidy, it was a pleasure," he says, and I nod.

"It was nice to see you again." Despite his threats, I can't help but appreciate the fact that Mike has Aiden's back. He needs someone in his corner.

We're heading toward the door, but there's a commotion just on the other side.

"Holy hell. Who let the mob through the gates?" Mike says.

"Well, there were quite a few celebrities at the event. Maybe they got wind that the star of that new Netflix show is here?" I mutter back.

One of the attendants comes rushing in. "It's crazy out there. Fans are rushing the gates. They're looking for the cast of *The Note*. I'm not sure I can get your car through them, sir," the young man says to Aiden. "I'm going to go try to find someone to help clear them out. This is private property. They shouldn't be here."

He rushes off, cursing under his breath.

"I'm calling the police," Mike says, pulling out his phone and dialing. Someone answers on the other end, and Mike gives them the rundown on what's occurring, along with the address.

"They're sending a couple of cars that are in the nearby area over now." He huffs, running a hand back through his hair. "I think it's best if we hold tight until then. Unless you want to brave it?"

Aiden sighs, head falling back on his shoulders. "I just want to go home. This is fucking ridiculous."

"I don't think it's a good idea for you to go out there," Mike says, glancing out at the chaos. "The police will be here soon."

Another couple comes up from behind us, getting a good look at what's transpiring beyond the door. They're older, more refined. The man is dressed like Aiden and Mike in an expensive black suit. The woman has on a gold, sparkly, floor-length dress that was likely expensive. She turns to me and smiles kindly.

"Monsters, all of them," the man says, shaking his head. He turns to his date, who I assume, because of the massive ring she's wearing, is his wife. "What do you want to do, my love?"

She smirks. "No one knows who the hell we are, Alfred. Let's make a run for it."

I smile to myself at the excitement that was evident in her tone.

"I couldn't have said it better. Could be fun to have our spotlight moment."

"I've always wanted to be in lights." The woman turns to me and winks.

Hearing the playfulness and obvious love the two of them share makes my heart swell. It's in the way they speak to each other. The secret smiles they share. It's what I hope to have one day.

They clasp hands and rush out into the swarm of fans together. But before the doors close behind them, I don't miss the chilling words that ring through the air.

"Aiden Slate…" I look toward the voice talking, and a shiver runs up my spine. It's him. The local reporter who has it out for Aiden. This man has got it in his head that Aiden will be the story that will make him national news. It's disgusting. "I want to know about your rituals."

When no one answers, the vulture presses on. "Why did you keep them a secret?" My head snaps to Aiden. His shoulders tense, and the color in his face drains. "Are you embarrassed?"

"Fuck," Mike swears under his breath.

The crowd might be here for some Hollywood star, but this guy used the mob to his advantage to sneak in and go after Aiden.

He knows about him.

I turn quickly toward Mike. "What do we do?"

He blinks several times, biting his lip, lost in thought.

"It was Billy," I say. "He all but admitted that this would happen."

Mike lowers his head, shaking. "This isn't Billy." He looks back up. "It's your mother."

Aiden flinches at the mention of her.

"That bitch," Mike says. "I swear to God, if I get my hands on her." His words trail off because I'm too focused on Aiden.

"Was this your family problem? She threatened this. You?"

He nods. "I've been paying her a shit ton of money to keep her away." His head falls back on a deep sigh. "I recently cut her off and told her there would be no more." He huffs a humorless laugh. "She threatened to expose me."

"You should've allowed me to take care of it," Mike says, sounding beyond angry. "You never listen to me where she's concerned."

"Stop," Aiden snaps. "Right now, I don't want to hear another word. I want to get the fuck out of this place."

Aiden's practically shaking. I grab his hand and squeeze, letting him know I'm here. I won't leave his side.

Seeing the hold that woman still has over Aiden makes me murderous. I vow here and now that I'll find her myself. She won't get near him ever again.

chapter thirty-one

Aiden

I WANNA VOMIT.

My palms are sweaty, and my head is spinning.

How could she do this?

That broken child in me hoped that I'd be more important to her than money. That all the threats had just been a desperate attempt to see how far she needed to push, to get me to cooperate. I thought when I finally put my foot down and refused, she'd back off—all talk, no action.

I was wrong.

She has only ever cared about one thing. Herself.

Drugs, alcohol…whatever provided a quick fix of dopamine.

She's a piece of shit, and I swear I'm done.

Done chasing her love.

Done being surprised by her selfishness.

Just fucking done.

Mike got the bastard removed and staff from the hotel helped to usher us to the safety of the Town Car without incident. We're heading toward my house, Cassidy, Mike, and I all in the same vehicle, nobody speaking.

It's been like this since we left.

Nobody knows what to say.

Mike's been on his phone typing away, likely working on damage control with my publicist.

"What a fucking mess. He's going to run with this story as far as he can go," Mike grumbles, throwing his phone to the seat. "We need to get ahead of this."

I huff a humorless laugh. "Damage is done, don't ya think? What can we possibly say?"

"We can spin this. Make it solely about pre-game rituals. Really push your superstition."

Cassidy squirms next to me, and I look over to see that she's chewing on her bottom lip.

What's going on with her? I know it might be in part from the bastard reporter, but it's more than that. I know it. I also know that she likely doesn't want to discuss it in front of Mike, so I don't ask. We'll be home soon enough, and I'll ask her then.

"How do you want to handle this, Slate?" Mike asks again.

"I want to get some sleep. To think on it," I say, running a hand back through my hair, hating the products that have it stiff. The need to shower and wash it and this fucking shit show of a night down the drain is at the top of my must-do list. "Just have Jane make a statement that the information was given by an unreliable source. A mother who I've been estranged from for years. Throw her in the river for all I fucking care. Air her drug addiction. Then tell them I'll make a formal statement regarding all of this by midafternoon tomorrow."

"That won't be soon enough, Aiden. He'll push. His social media post is already going viral. By morning, it will make national news. They'll want your side of the story."

"Too fucking bad, Mike. I pay you and Jane a massive

amount of money to handle this shit. Handle it. Buy me the fucking time I need."

I'm spiraling, and Mike can see it.

His hard features soften, and he nods.

"I'll take care of it."

The car pulls up to my apartment, and I'm desperate to get inside. To shut out the world and all the gossip swirling around about me.

"Get some rest and call me when you're prepared to discuss this," Mike says and turns toward the driver. "I need you to drop me off at the office."

I feel horrible. Mike will be up all night dealing with this. He won't sleep.

Not that I will.

The second we get inside my place, I'll turn on the television and torture myself with every single bit of bullshit they're spewing, courtesy of the woman who carried me.

She's no mother.

She's a parasite.

I've just cleared the threshold of my place and shut us inside when Cassidy's hand extends, palm up.

I glance at her outstretched hand and then back to her face. Her head tilts, and I know she's waiting for something.

"What?" I say, nose wrinkled.

"Give it to me," she says.

I narrow my eyes, trying to determine what she could possibly be talking about.

"Give you what, exactly?"

She sighs heavily. "Your phone, Aiden. Give me your phone."

I continue to stare at her, completely dumbfounded, but she explains.

"There will be no TV or looking at your phone. None of that. You've had enough for one night. We can deal with all of this tomorrow."

"Don't you think I should know exactly what she said? To be prepared?"

She purses her lips and shakes her head. "Aiden, what difference is it going to make?"

"Typically, a good defensive strategy is key not to being slammed by the media and having your career ruined."

I'm practically reciting Mike verbatim from prior threats where my mother is concerned.

"Your defense is going to be simple," she says, taking a deep breath.

She looks like a seasoned publicist at this moment, with a slightly more empathetic demeanor.

I lean back against the door. One eyebrow lifted.

I have no idea what she could possibly be thinking, but I'm curious to hear what she has to say. If one thing is true about Cassidy, she never ceases to amaze me.

"Well, you obviously can't make it a bad thing. Too many people in this world are afflicted by the same struggles. You don't want to alienate them or make them feel as though they should be ashamed."

My mouth drops open. It's not like I have some warped idea that I'm the only person in this world that has compulsions, but I've been too consumed with trying to conceal my own to consider how someone would feel if they knew I'd been hiding them out of embarrassment.

"Go on," I say, giving her the floor.

She stands up tall and dives right in. "You're going to own it, and you're going to tell them you weren't purposely hiding anything. Your focus is on hockey and playing well, and you're just living your life."

"I'll tell them that, yes, I have rituals, but so do other hockey players," I say, cutting in to offer more ideas.

Things that are genuine among all the white lies I'll inevitably tell. Because the truth is, I was hiding my compulsions. I grew up being told they were weak. That I was weak. My mom drilled into me that the behaviors I had were not normal and that normal kids would think I'm strange. They had me convinced that the world was against me, even as a child. So I hid those habits as much as I could to protect myself from the harsh world.

The thought of those years and all the abuse washes over me, pressing down like a weight on my chest, threatening to suffocate me.

"But you admit that it's not all rituals. You're going to have to be honest. And tell them how you've just recently made the decision to seek help to manage your compulsions."

I clear my throat, but my words still come out hoarse. "I am?"

She bobs her head once. "You are. First thing tomorrow morning, you're going to research doctors and call the best."

I know she's right. I do need help. As incredible as Cassidy has been, she won't be here forever. I have to find ways to control the urge to sort everything. I need to simplify my rituals, because right now, they're overpowering my life and making it difficult to get basic tasks and work completed in a timely fashion.

"You're going to look into that camera, which will act as an extension into every person like you out there. You'll tell them that there's nothing to be ashamed of. Anxiety and compulsions can be life-altering and difficult to manage, but they do not define you. You can be a fantastic doctor, or a lawyer, or even a hockey player, and still deal with all of this." She takes a deep breath. "You're going to tell them that you're confident that there are ways to get help."

I look up into Cassidy's eyes. "I wanna help people like me, Cass. People who don't have supportive families. People who don't have the funds to chase down the best care. I wanna help. I need to."

She smiles at me. "Then you will."

I blink a couple of times, taken aback by how confident she is. How determined to help.

"How?" It comes out as barely a whisper.

"You could start a blog or a website where resources or information are compiled and distributed."

I chew on my lip, mulling her idea over. It sounds like a lot of work, something that I'd love to offer, but will likely not be able to facilitate between my compulsions and hockey schedule.

"When am I going to do that? As much as I'd love to do something like that, I just don't see how."

She inhales and exhales harshly, lips pursed. "You can create the material and build the site on the off-season. Maybe I can even help run it for you."

I'm stunned. I'm entirely speechless.

Who is this girl, and why does she care so much about helping me?

Sure, I'm paying her, but this is above and beyond.

Cassidy is committing herself to work with me after the season is over. I know she needs the money, but it's not about that with her. I know it isn't. She genuinely cares, and I'm not sure what to do with that.

When you've lived your life being treated like a nuisance by the people who are supposed to love you above everything else, you tend to believe nobody cares.

The number that woman did on me throughout the years settles over me, and that pain in my chest intensifies. Her abuse through the years made all my compulsions so much worse, and there are no repercussions for it.

She lifts her hand to my cheek, wiping away a tear I didn't even know fell.

"Please don't," I say, my voice full of emotion. "I don't need you to pity me."

She frowns, shaking her head. "These are things that someone else should've done for you years ago, Aiden. Your mother…" She grits her teeth and inhales sharply. "She's a horrible person, and what she did is unforgiving."

This woman, who I have only known for a short time, has been kinder to me than anyone else has my entire life, apart from one person.

Sure, Mike and my teammates have had my back, but it's different. My friends know nothing of my past, and while Mike does, I pay him a significant amount of money to be on my side.

Yes, I pay Cassidy too, but it's a short-term contract. Nothing that she's offered to me today is expected, yet she's willingly stepped in and formed a plan. One that has my long-term best interest in mind.

One that speaks directly to me and to people like me. She understands me down to my core, and I don't understand how that's possible. Not when the very person who gave me life has treated me like nothing more than a stranger they've been saddled with.

The years of neglect. The years of abuse. The years of being told I was damaged have done a number on me I didn't even fathom until this moment. The small, beating organ behind my ribs shatters. I slink to the floor, head between my knees, working on my breathing.

At the end of the day, I have no one.

Not a single person in my corner for the long haul. Cassidy will leave me eventually. They all do.

I'm drowning in a sea of grief, caused from years of abandonment. The heavy burden of knowing I'm nothing more than a meal ticket to the woman who gave birth to me is crushing.

Cassidy falls to her knees in front of me, placing her hands on the sides of my cheeks, but I don't dare lift my head.

"Aiden, look at me," she commands. "I'm not them. I won't hurt you."

I lift my tear-stained eyes to meet her. I should be ashamed that she's seeing me like this. But I'm not. Cassidy makes me feel safe. Something I can't say about too many other people.

"Do not let her break you any further," Cassidy says, holding my stare. "She doesn't get to have this much of an impact on you."

"You don't understand—"

"I do." She cuts in. "I understand more than you know." Her head falls back on her shoulders as she looks at the ceiling. "God, I wish I didn't, but I do. Fight through the pain, Aiden, because you are loved. No matter what you think. You. Are. Loved."

My head shakes back and forth. "No, I'm not."

She places her fingers under my chin, holding my head in place when I attempt to look away.

"Yes, you are. Aiden, your teammates love you. Your fans love you." Her hands lift into the air as her head swivels around the room. "This entire town loves you." Her face turns hard and somehow, I know whatever she's about to say is about my mother. "You don't need her approval, and you sure as hell don't need her false love. You never have."

I don't even think. My body moves without permission as I lunge forward, pressing my lips to hers. Cassidy goes still for a moment, apparently shocked by my actions.

Me too, Cass. Me too.

It doesn't take long before she melts into me, returning my kiss enthusiastically. Our tongues tangle in sync as if we've been doing this our whole lives. I explore every inch of her warm mouth in a dance that's equal parts sensual and feverish. The need for more is so acute that I need to pull back before I take it too far. But it's not me who pulls away. It's Cassidy.

"I'm sorry, Cassidy."

"Don't apologize," she says. "Please don't apologize. I wanted it every bit as much as you seemed to need it."

I blink, taken aback by how sincere she is.

She wants this.

I want this.

Why the fuck do I continue to hold back?

"I'm here for you, Aiden. Whatever you need, I'll be here, but I'm not who you think I am."

Not who I think she is? What does that even mean? Of course, I know little about her, but do I care? The answer is simple. No.

"I know who you are, Cass." I point at her heart. "Everything else is inconsequential. I know *you*."

Her head lowers and shakes. "You don't. I've hidden who I am because I'm ashamed."

It's my turn to lift her head to me. "Haven't I done that too? You've only been privy to my secrets because I needed help."

"You'd change your mind if you knew."

I consider what my hard lines are and voice them.

"Have you abused or abandoned a child?"

Her brows furrow. "No. Never."

I nod. "Did you have anything to do with my mother leaking my private life to the press?"

Her face hardens to stone. "Absolutely not."

"Are you a bad person?"

Her face pales. "What?" The pitch of her voice catches me off guard. She places her head against mine, and our breaths intermingle. "Sometimes, Aiden. But only when I have to be."

"Did someone hurt you?"

"*Nobody will ever hurt me again.*" She responds, and I breathe her in, hearing the determination and strength in those words. One day, I will uncover the story behind this moment, but not now. Not when I'm in this headspace. "But I'm here with you now, and everything is perfect."

Is that permission to take things further? Is that her way of saying she wants more?

I can tell by the look on her face she wants me to kiss her again, and God, I'm a bastard, but I want to. The only problem is, if I go there, I don't think I'll be able to stop and that is dangerous territory.

For her.

For me.

I weigh the pros and cons so quickly, and it's not even a question. If she says yes, I'll take whatever she offers.

"I need you, Cassidy, but I don't want you to do this because you feel sorry for me. Or because you have some warped idea that you owe me for something."

"None of that is true, Aiden. I don't feel like I owe you. What I'm offering is coming from a place of want. I want you."

My breath hitches at her proclamation. I move to a standing position, with Cassidy on her knees in front of me, "I'm the one who drew the line in the sand, and if you want to keep those boundaries up, I completely understand—"

"Aiden," she says, "what aren't you understanding? I. Want. This." She licks her lips and swallows. "Don't overthink this, Aiden. I'm yours if you want me. Let me take care of you."

I watch through hooded lids as her hand reaches out and pulls down the zipper of my pants…

Carefully, she removes me from the now tight confines of the material.

Heat rushes through my veins and straight to my cock, as her small hand finds me. My thick erection proves my desire for this woman.

I want this.

I want her.

I know it. And she knows it now too.

A shudder reverberates through my bones as she places her tongue on the head of my dick and trails it down. Licking the crown and down the shaft.

Tasting my full length before swallowing me whole.

"Fuck," I groan as I hit the back of her throat.

Flexing my hips, I push in deeper. And like the good girl she is, she takes me, all of me, every single inch.

"So good."

As if my words fill her, she moves up and down on my length.

Each pass down her throat has my balls lighting and tightening.

I throw back my head.

A primitive sound escapes my lungs as I sink my hands into her hair and thrust myself in deeper.

Her tongue slides over the tip, once, twice, and on the last swirl, I erupt. My dick jerks in her mouth.

I push her off me. "Not in your mouth."

She swallows. "I want you."

chapter thirty-two

Cassidy

THE WORDS SLIP OUT UNBIDDEN, AND I'M ABOUT TO TAKE THEM back, but his eyes darken, and it's not out of anger.

It's pure lust.

He bends down and places his lips over mine, not going any further than that. He's putting the ball in my court. Giving me the opportunity to choose.

I lift to a standing position.

In a flurry, I'm swept off my feet, and he's carrying me to his bedroom. Once inside, I'm practically tossed on top of the bed.

"Take off your dress," he commands, and I jump to work.

Within seconds, I'm lying bare in front of him. His eyes rake over my body slowly, and I wiggle under the weight of his gaze.

He leans down, hovering just inches from my mouth. "Tell me I can trust you." The words whisper across my lips, and I shiver.

"You can trust me, Aiden."

His lips slam to mine.

As his mouth devours me, I can feel his hands running all over my body. His touch is amazing, but no matter how good it feels, I can't help but replay his words.

Tell me I can trust you.

I don't have the heart to let him down right now.

He needs me.

And I'll do anything to give him what he needs.

Aiden stops the kiss. Pulling away from my mouth, he trails a path down on my skin.

Licking.

Sucking.

Teasing.

Across my jaw.

Down my neck.

Over the swell of my breasts.

He stops there, sucking my nipple into his mouth. His tongue caresses the hard peak.

Then he's separating my legs farther.

My breath comes out in ragged bursts as I wait for him to touch me.

It feels like my heart will explode. Like it will beat right out of my chest.

I'm wound tight.

Needing relief, needing for him to touch me.

And then it happens.

I feel the soft caress of his fingers. He trails through my slickness, until he reaches my clit. He plays me like an instrument. Strumming me until I'm panting and pleading with him. His mouth replaces his hands, his tongue swiping against my clit.

Pleasure zips through me.

My thighs tremble.

I'm so close.

About to fall over the edge when Aiden stops all movement.

A groan escapes my mouth as I lift onto my elbows to see what he's doing, and what I see knocks the air out of my lungs.

Aiden is between my thighs, his gaze steady, staring at me.

I follow his gaze, looking down to see what he sees.

His hard cock is at my entrance. The ruddy crown is close enough to enter me.

Aiden moves his hips slightly, running his cock through my wetness, coating his skin with my desire.

Teasing me.

Torturing me.

"Please," I beg, and he answers my plea by moving another inch, spreading me wider, but he doesn't breach me.

Not yet.

He's prolonging the moment. Drawing it out.

Aiden grabs my ass, and lifts me until I'm impaling myself with his cock.

"Fuck. You feel so good," he groans. The husky rasp of his voice makes me quiver.

Pulling all the way out, he rubs the head of his cock up and down my slit, then he slams back in. Pushing all the way to the hilt.

My mouth falls open on a gasp. The noises escaping me are primal and desperate.

He moves his arms, grasping my legs, giving him the perfect angle and an even better view. "I love how you feel around my cock. How you look as your pussy takes me so deep."

His fingers bite at my skin where he holds me.

"Aiden. Please. Harder." I beg for more, and he happily obliges. He pumps in and out of me like a crazed man. He slams into me so hard that I cry out, arching my back.

My walls squeeze around him.

He drops one of my legs and uses his free hand to bring me over the edge. "Oh God. I... I'm coming," I moan as my orgasm spreads through my body, tearing through me with a ferocity I've never felt before.

My eyes close as Aiden slows his pace, pumping inside me.

He thrusts a few more lazy strokes until he jerks, falling over into his own abyss.

⸻

The early morning light gleams in through the blinds, making me aware that I must have passed out last night.

In the fresh light of the day, I realize I'm in Aiden's room.

I'm lying in Aiden Slate's arms, feeling like the world is mine one minute and fearing it's all about to collapse in another.

The truth is, I should've been honest with him.

I should've come clean about who I am.

I tried. I truly was prepared to spill the truth, but when he laid out his list of hard lines, I was so caught off guard by the last one that the truth about my identity was not even on my mind.

I know Mike gave me a timeline to tell him, but surely, with everything that went down, that window is no longer relevant. I'm sure even he can agree that right now isn't ideal.

Soon, though. I'll tell Aiden soon.

Today, I'm going to hang on to him with a white-knuckled grip because last night changed things for me.

He might not know my name, but he knows *me*.

And I know who Aiden Slate is. Not the boy who left me all those years ago, but the man who he became.

"Mike's been blowing up my phone," Aiden grates. "Can we just tell him and the world to go the fuck away?"

I chuckle. "We can, but it will only make things worse for you. I think we need to face the day and weather the storm that woman has created."

"Do you have any thoughts on how to go about it?"

I mull over some ideas and land on what feels like the most obvious.

"Hear me out," I say, popping up to my knees and bringing the blanket with me. "I think it's high time you brought some other people into your inner circle."

He narrows his eyes in on me. "I already have. Dane, Hudson, Mason..."

I shake my head. "No, Aiden. They might be your friends, but you haven't allowed them to truly see you. Have a conversation with them. Tell them the truth before you tell the world. Allow them to stand by your side and support you." I grab his hands, lifting them to my lips. "Allow them to shoulder some of this burden with you."

He swallows and appears to be organizing his words. I'm prepared for him to push back and give every excuse in the book as to why he doesn't want to involve them. To my surprise, he doesn't do any of that.

"Okay. Let's do it."

An hour later, Dane, Hunter, Mason, and Molly sit in Aiden's place for the first time.

Dane whistles. "Dude...this place is awesome. No wonder you kept all of us Neanderthals out."

Molly and I share a look. She already knows what's coming. She rounded up the troops for me by contacting Dane and making it clear that Aiden needed them.

I had explained to Aiden the dynamics between Dane and Molly, which he seemed to know already. He thought going through Molly was a great way. Not that Dane wouldn't have come on his own if Aiden asked. Molly is Dane's keeper. She organizes him and his schedule, which is a feat.

"Thank you all for coming," Aiden starts. "I'm sure you've all seen the reports."

Hunter nods. "I'm not understanding the big deal, truthfully. We all have rituals. Why is this asshole focused in on you?"

Aiden takes a deep breath and dives in. He tells them about his past and how his mom treated him. He opens up about how much his compulsions run his life. That it's more than a few pre-game rituals. He also shares with them his plans to start a website to help others in his position who have limited resources or whose families aren't supportive.

"I'm…speechless, Slate. This is a lot to take in," Dane says, running his hands back through his hair. "I mean…how the fuck have you kept all of that from us?"

"I've had some help," he says, glancing over at me.

The only part he hasn't come clean about is me, and that's because it wasn't something we discussed before they all arrived. That's a big lie. One that implicates me and threatens to ruin the relationship I've built with Molly. She's been made to believe I'm Aiden's girlfriend. The whole world has.

That's not something we want to get out. When it's time for things to end, we'll figure out the story and how to do it, so neither of us suffers.

Not that it can be avoided. The truth is, when this is all done, it'll shatter me.

"Can you press charges?" Mason asks. "I mean…the bitch abused you. It might've been years ago, but the effects are still something you deal with." His face is like stone. "It doesn't seem right that she gets to just walk away after all the damage she's caused."

"Not that he thinks you're damaged," Hunter says, glaring at the side of Mason's head.

Aiden chuckles. "I know that's not what he's insinuating."

He licks his lips and settles back in his chair. "Blackmail maybe, but I'm not sure I want the media circus that would come from bringing about charges. Let's be honest, the statute of limitation has most likely long since passed. Plus, if I do, that's playing into this reporter's goal," he admits. "I want her to go away for good. I never want to see her again."

Everyone nods, understanding why he'd feel that way.

"What now? How can we help?" Dane asks.

"Support me. Tell everyone about my character on the ice and how my life is dedicated to getting better for my team. That the compulsions are something that I've controlled so that I can play the best hockey possible."

"Obviously, we'll say that," Mason says.

"Really, I just wanted to tell you all the truth before everyone else hears it. It didn't seem right for you to all learn these things with the rest of the world. You're my friends. My circle. You deserve to know the real me."

Hudson stands up and walks toward Aiden, patting him on the shoulder. "We've always known you, man. Rituals. Compulsions. Whatever it is that you battle on a daily basis, it doesn't define you."

"He's right," Dane says. "We all have our things we battle, but at the end of the day, we're the same guys you call friends."

Aiden smiles, and for the first time since the news broke, he looks peaceful.

Whatever his mother set out to do, she failed. She can't break him. He's too strong for that. All she's managed to do is make him that much more of a force. In the end, he'll come out on top, and she'll still be the freeloader, looking for her next free ride. The only loser is her.

There's a buzz signaling someone is here.

"Mike," Aiden tells the group. "He's here to spin the story my publicist wants me to recite."

Dane shakes his head. More to himself than to us. I wonder about him. What's his story, and why does he seem to be the serious one of the group?

"Just be real, man. I promise you that you won't regret being honest in the long run. Spinning stories works for a short time, but lies have a way of catching up with you." This time, it's Hudson who talks. Do all these guys have secrets?

Something about that thought unsettles me.

Likely guilt surrounding my own lies.

More likely, the threat of my secrets coming to light. Because they will.

I can only hope that when they do, Aiden understands my motives were pure and forgives me, because the thought of saying goodbye to Aiden Slate doesn't seem possible.

Aiden's press conference was incredible. He shut down his mother's attempt to make him look bad by turning everything around and showing the world what a villain she is. I couldn't be prouder of his bravery and honesty.

Aiden and I have been researching professionals to help support him. Someone who can teach him real coping mechanisms to cut back on the time it takes him to complete his rituals. Things to help curb some of the impulses.

Aiden's phone pings, and I know something is wrong. His face contorts, turning red. He throws his phone across the room.

"Fuck."

I jump as the phone collides with the wall, creating a cracking noise that doesn't bode well for the device.

"What's wrong?"

My entire body is locked up, fear for what he's about to say, making my stomach roil.

"It was him. Lewis was involved."

My eyebrows tilt inward as I try to decode his words.

"Billy Lewis?" I ask.

Aiden's head turns to me, and he nods once.

"Oh my God. I knew it," I say, mostly to myself.

I had a feeling that slimeball was gunning for Aiden. I just didn't know how he planned to make his life hell.

"Apparently, he went digging into my family. The fucking creep actually drove to my mom's and quizzed her about me."

I blink, stunned by the lengths Billy went to. "How do you know?"

"My attorney reached out to my mother and threatened to press charges for blackmail and extortion. She doesn't have money to go to court, so according to Mike after they interrogated her further, it came out that Lewis was behind things."

The need to find Billy and strangle him is strong. He's a snake. A fucking creep.

"How are you going to be able to play with that guy?" I ask, seriously curious how Aiden plans to keep himself from harming the asshole.

"I won't. I'm going to Coach now and giving him my resignation if it comes down to that. I'm a free agent. I'll go to another team before I'm forced to play on the ice with that fucker."

I bob my head, knowing that's the only answer.

"What do you need me to do?" I ask, feeling a bit out of my element.

Things are already so different now that Aiden's situation is out there. I can be more open about helping. He doesn't need to hide it.

If one good thing has come from this, it's that I can tell it's liberated him in ways that were necessary for him to live a normal-ish life.

"If you could just take care of dinner for tonight, that would be good. I'm going to be starving, and I don't want to have to go out today. Or tomorrow. It'll be best if I can lie low for a bit until the interest of the media dies down. Or at least until my next game."

"Makes sense. I'll handle dinner." I stand from my chair and make my way toward Aiden, placing my hand on his shoulder. "Whatever you need."

He smiles up at me. "Thank you for everything, Cassidy. I'm not sure how I can ever repay you."

"You don't owe me anything." I sigh. "I'm going to go shower. I'll see you later."

He places his hand over mine on his shoulder and squeezes.

"Good luck," I say, making my way toward the back, thinking through my grocery list.

The conversation that Aiden is about to have could be a tough one. Billy Lewis is third string and not a key member of the team, but he's also on contract. I'm not sure how hockey works, but I can't imagine getting rid of Billy will be that easy considering the money they likely paid him, even for third string.

I want to make Aiden something that I know he loves. Something that will comfort him during a time he needs it most. I've recently cooked his favorite, but I also know he equally loves lasagna, so I'll get everything I need for that.

It's not lost on me that I'm using the distraction of what to make for dinner to keep me from panicking about the conversation I know I need to have with Aiden.

The longer I wait to tell him the truth, the worse things are going to get.

After everything he's been through, he deserves nothing but the truth from me.

But is now the right time? With everything he has going on hanging over him?

I'm between a rock and a hard place, unsure what the right move is. Mike hasn't given me any indication that he's going to spill the details to Aiden, and that's likely because he has bigger things to handle at the current moment.

No matter, I can't leave fate in Mike's hands. I need to come clean.

If tonight ends up being the right time, then so be it.

chapter thirty-three

Aiden

I T'S BEEN A LONG FEW DAYS.

The night that I shared my truth with the world, I came home exhausted and ready to fall into bed. Cassidy had prepared one of my favorites, and I had to choke it down.

Not because it wasn't delicious, but because my stomach was in knots.

Coach understood where I was coming from, but his hands were tied. It's not up to him to decide about that. It's something he has to talk to the owner about, and we all know that as good of a guy as he pretends to be, money talks and any amount that's thrown away isn't something he's going to jump at.

He knows my worth and what I bring to the team. I'm sure he'll come to the right decision, but it won't be overnight.

For the time being, Billy has been put on leave for personal misconduct that impacts the team and organization. Luckily, the Saints have a clause that allows for disciplinary action for players who disrupt the team in any manner. The Coach appealed to the owner that Billy's conduct brought unwanted stress and media attention to the program.

I told Coach I wouldn't play on the ice if he was there. He assured me he's on my side, and he'll do whatever is necessary to keep me on the team.

Tonight, is a game day, and I'm stressed.

It'll be the first time playing since my private life was aired, and I know all eyes are going to be on me and not for the reasons they typically are.

It's uncomfortable and unwanted.

The door opens and Cassidy walks in, wearing my jersey, with her hair pulled into a high ponytail. She looks beautiful. There's something about her wearing my number that feels right.

"I came to give you a massage," she says, smiling wide.

I know the smile is forced. She's nervous about tonight too. We discussed it this morning. But she's doing her best to reassure me, and she'll never know how much I appreciate her for that.

"Thanks, Cass. I could use one."

She nods, heading to her position behind me.

Her hands land on my shoulders, kneading deep. For a small woman, she's a force. Her hands are firm and her ability to get deep in the muscle is something that men have struggled with in the past.

"That feels incredible," I moan.

I could really use something more, but I'd never suggest such a thing to Cassidy. She means more to me than a quick blow job to help work out my nerves.

The days of seeking out a woman to tend to my needs in that way are over.

She might've willingly come for that purpose, but it just doesn't sit well with me. It's so out of character for the Cassidy I've come to know, that I have to question why she'd sign up for that to begin with.

There are a lot of women who would, and I'm not saying there's anything wrong with that. Men love sex, so why can't a woman?

It's just not Cassidy.

"You okay?" she asks, bending down to my ear.

A shiver races over me at the feel of her breath on my neck.

"I'm good."

"You know," she says, moving away from my neck. "I could cut your tension with a chainsaw."

My back stiffens at the phrase. I've heard that before, but where?

"You okay?" she says, voice taut.

"Yeah…it's just…" My words trail off because it's just a phrase.

"Time to go," she says, patting my shoulders.

I look up at the wall clock to see she's right. I need to get dressed and head to the arena.

"I'll see you after the game," she says, smiling and making her way out of the room.

I watch her go, unable to shake the feeling that I'm missing something.

But what?

It's time.

I step out of the locker, the last one on my team, as always, and then start to head toward the rink.

The sounds of my skates on the rubber echo in my ear.

It's been a rough few days, but I'm ready to get back out there.

The feeling I get when I glide across the ice, is what I need right now.

My anticipation builds the closer I get, and when I'm finally at the entrance, I glide onto the ice, the cold air and familiar smells hitting my face.

I skate across the smooth surface, meeting my team where they're already skating because I'm always the last of us out here.

When I come to a stop, I hear the roar of the crowd.

Cheering.

"Slate!"

"We love you, Slate."

I glance around to see why the chanting is growing louder.

When I do, the arena erupts in cheers.

A sea of enthusiastic faces, some painted, others holding signs.

Squinting, I try to make out the words, and when I do, my heart pounds in my chest.

Thank You.

You're not alone, Slate.

We love you, Slate.

We're with you.

Each person here, reminds me that I'm not alone. That maybe I don't have the family I was born into, but I do have a *home*.

I raise my stick, and they cheer louder.

At that, my team huddles around me, and I've never been more ready to play.

"For fuck's sake, ref. You plan to make a fucking call today?" Dane yells out from the penalty box, taking his chances by calling out the ref for the second time in the past few minutes.

"You sure you wanna poke the bear, Sin?"

"I'll do more than poke if he doesn't start using his eyes and that fucking worthless whistle of his."

I chuckle, knowing that Dane is about to lose his shit if this continues, and it will likely result in more stints in the penalty box.

We're both waiting for our time to be over so we can get back on the ice and end this fucking game. It shouldn't be this fucking close.

The Bulldogs are assholes, and the refs seem to be blind to it. The cross-checking is out of control, but it appears the only calls today are going to be made on us. Go fucking figure.

"It's fucking bullshit. They're getting away with everything."

I grin over at my friend. "You sound like a whiny bitch."

Normally, Dane Sinclair is more the type to let his anger simmer beneath the surface, but something is up with him today, because he's letting it all out.

He glares at me before breaking eye contact, shrugging. "Molly's rubbing off on me."

I roll my eyes. "You and I both know you whine far more than Molls does."

"Whose side are you on?"

"Hers. Every time." I grin. "If not for her, you'd be a bigger asshole."

He bobs his head. "No question. Fair point."

My eyes search the bleachers until they land on Cassidy and Molly. They're chatting about something animatedly, Cassidy's hands flailing in the air like they do when she gets excited.

My stomach twists, telling me that I'm bothered. I just don't know why.

Maybe it's all the eyes on me. Knowing what they know. Feeling their possible judgment.

Or maybe it's something else entirely.

"Slate, you're up."

I fist bump my friend and skate onto the ice, ready to push down this unnerving feeling and get my head in the game. These Bulldogs need to be snapped, and I'm in just the mood to do it.

chapter thirty-four

Cassidy

My throat burns today.

After yesterday's game, I thought we'd be able to rest.

But Coach wanted everyone at the arena bright and early today.

The team is so close to winning this round, he doesn't want to take any chances. Which means practice on top of practice.

Which also means despite it only being noon, it's been a long day.

Hell, it's been a long week.

I've been walking on eggshells over when I'm finally going to talk to him about who I am.

I've tried.

Lord, have I tried. But with all the shit being spread around about him, the words have been locked inside me and no matter how hard I try, I can't say them.

Especially not now. They need to win this round. It's important. If I tell him now, he could lose the game.

That is something I can't let happen.

Plus, the truth is Aiden needs me right now.

You're not ready to lose him.

I'll talk to Mike, ask him to give me more time. Aiden isn't in a good place emotionally and winning the Stanley Cup is so important to him. Surely, Mike will agree that now's not the time.

Chickenshit.

Despite the voice screaming at me to tell him, I don't.

Instead, I follow him into his place, heart still racing from the game.

We're just inside the foyer when he stops abruptly, causing me to nearly run into his back. I'm too preoccupied with my own thoughts. I halt, letting go of the door. My hand moves to my heart as the door swings shut with a bang, causing me to jump back and shriek.

Aiden turns. Slowly. Eyeing me like prey. My eyes widen at the look I see on his face. I don't have time to act, and he's moving closer. His steps are slow, measured. And my heart is hammering in my chest.

There's nowhere for me to go. No time to act. Not that I want to run away. It's not fear that has my heartbeat racing or my body warm all over.

It's the heat in his intense stare.

I tilt my head up to meet his gaze, and despite the sexual tension, he looks tired.

There are bags under his eyes, and his brown hair is ruffled from the cold water he dunks his head in after a game.

Another habit I've grown to love.

The scruffy version of Aiden is my favorite version of him. Right after a game is when he's his most free.

It reminds me so much of when I was a kid, when I looked at him like he hung the moon from the sky, and he looked at me with eyes full of love, the type of love you would give a little sister or best friend.

Maybe that's it.

Maybe the reason I keep silent is fear that when he knows he won't just be mad, but he will also be disgusted. He only ever looked at me like a sister, and if he's thought of me at all through the years, that's likely how he's remembered me.

Not like this.

Not like he wants to devour me on the spot.

A shiver runs up my spine, and I look down at the floor, breaking our eye contact.

He moves one step closer, and we're chest to chest. No space separates us. I can feel the heat from his body. His breath tickles my face.

"What's wrong?" His hand lifts, and the rough pads of his fingers touch my skin, bringing my head up. Once again, we are staring at each other.

I blink my long lashes, eyes roaming over his chiseled face.

"Nothing. Just tired."

"It's been a long week." He drops his arm to his side and then grasps my hand. "Come with me."

I follow, allowing him to lead the way. When he pulls us into the living room, he stops before tilting his head down, signaling for me to sit.

"If you don't want me to fall asleep, I should probably not sit. After the day we've had, I'm not likely to make it long."

He chuckles. "Just sit, Cass. You look dead on your feet."

"That bad, huh?"

He smiles. "You never look bad."

Despite my insistence I'll fall asleep, I sit, and God, is it exactly what I need.

My feet ache, and I'm bone-tired, which leads me to wonder how he's managing.

Aiden takes the seat beside me, his arms reaching out to place my legs over his.

"Comfortable?"

I turn to face him and find him smiling a small, contented smile.

A long way from where we were only hours ago.

Aiden needs hockey.

The release. The happiness. The control. This is something he can't get anywhere else. It always has been and always will be.

I smile back, unable to stop my lips from spreading when I see him so relaxed.

"You played great today at practice, and yesterday…just wow," I say, needing him to hear that from someone other than his coach and teammates.

Every one of them has a carload of family and friends at the games to support them. For Aiden, it's only me. Well…and his legion of fans.

He bobs his head. "I really did, didn't I?"

"Cocky much," I tease, wrinkling my nose for effect.

"Not usually. But yesterday—yeah. I kicked ass."

Coming from most other people, the words would sound arrogant, but not with Aiden. He's not boastful when he says this. He's matter of fact. And he's right; in the time I've been with him, cocky isn't a word I'd use to describe him.

A laugh bubbles up through my mouth. "You did. Kick-ass."

I watch as his tongue moves across his bottom lip, and I want to lick his lip. Hell, I want to bite it.

"It's because of you."

I blink, having missed what he said. "What?" I was way too focused on him licking his lip and so many other impure thoughts that I won't even acknowledge right now.

He reaches out, placing a loose strand of hair behind my ears. "I said…it's because of you, Cassidy."

My heart somersaults in my chest at his words, beating so fast, a part of me wonders if it will explode. "No, it's not," I whisper back because this feeling is too much.

Hearing Aiden say this is too much.

"Yeah. It is, Cass." Lifting my hand, he brings it up to his lips and kisses my knuckles. "Ever since you agreed to this crazy plan, my life—my life has been better."

My hand begins to shake in his grasp. "Aiden." So many words rush through my mind, but all I can manage is his name.

"I don't know what I'm going to do when you're gone," he mumbles as he moves his free hand and kneads at his temples.

The harshness and unmanaged control that Aiden possessed when I first arrived is absent. Today, he looks like a different man. A man who knows his struggles and is trying every day to master them.

He looks comfortable. Happy.

How can I ever take this look away from him? How can I risk it?

I'll do it after they win the round.

You have to. You have no choice.

The truth always finds a way to come out.

As much as I'd love to bottle up this moment and keep things just like this, I refuse to live in a lie. It's not fair to either of us.

I hold his stare and smile sadly. "Whatever you do, tell me you won't forget me."

He narrows his eyes on me. "I'd never forget you. I—"

"Pinky promise on your puck?" The words rush out, desperation taking hold.

His brow furrows. A strangled look passing over his face. At first, I'm not sure why his mood has changed. But when his jaw locks and he drops my hand, I realize what's happened. What I've just said.

It's not the sort of thing you'd forget.

A simple promise exchanged by two friends. One born out of hope and fear of being forgotten.

"Aiden…" I start, trying to work out what I'm going to say.

I knew this day was coming, but I didn't want it to be like this.

"What…" He shakes his head. "What did you say?"

My mouth opens, but words don't come out. I'm suddenly speechless. Unable to form words. My heart hammers in my chest, and panic threatens to overtake me.

"Let me explain." My voice pitches.

I watch as Aiden funnels through a series of emotions. Confusion. Shock. And now… anger.

"What"—he draws the word out—"the fuck did you say?"

I shake my head, trying to think of something to say, anything to say.

Where did you go?

Have you missed me?

Please don't hate me.

"I-I—"

"You what?" His voice rises and his hands lift to his sides. "Speak, Cassidy, because my mind is going to some very dark places right now."

"Please calm down and let me start from the beginning."

"There's only one thing I need you to say, and something tells me you know exactly what that is."

"Aiden."

He jumps up from the couch. "Who the fuck are you? Is Cassidy your real name?"

"Yes. My real name is Cassidy. You just…"

My head lowers to the ground, shaking back and forth.

"Goddammit. Look at me," he bellows. "Just say it."

My head pops up, and my mouth opens and closes, tears collecting in my eyes.

"Say it," he repeats, taking a step toward me, face turning red. "Just fucking say it."

"Pip," I yell. "Is that what you want to hear, Aiden? My name? It's Cassidy. But you know me as Pip."

His face drains of all color. His mouth drops open, but he only allows me to see the emotion for a second before he's doing what he's always done to protect himself.

Building a fortress around himself.

He straightens his back and crosses his arms, erecting the walls he so often uses.

Never on me.

Until now.

"I'm sorry." My voice is low and tormented, the words sputtering out as my cheeks dampen.

What else can I possibly say? There's nothing to excuse what I've done. The secrets I've kept. I was wrong.

"You think you can run, but one day, I'll catch you."

His expression is terrifying, stone-cold eyes that look right through me.

There's no warmth. No signs that point to fond memories of the girl I used to be. He looks at me like I'm a stranger.

Worse.

He looks at me with pure hate. The way he used to look at her. The one person who deserved his loathing. His mother. The first woman to betray him, and now I'm no better than her.

"Please talk to me," I beg, taking two steps to close the gap between us.

He doesn't move, but he certainly doesn't reach out to me.

"Please," I ask once more.

"What was this? Some ploy? For what purpose?" He huffs a humorless laugh. "Cassidy. What the fuck? All this time, I thought this was…that *we* were a sweet collide. Something big and strong and unbreakable. But this wasn't a collide. You fucking *shattered* me."

Disdain drips all over my name, and it's not lost on me that he doesn't call me Pip. Because to him, that time in our life is long gone.

"Aiden, I didn't mean—"

"Are you like them? All the others that have tried to get close to me. To use me? Just want a piece of the player."

"No. Of course, not—"

"Then why didn't you tell me?" he snaps, each word that leaves his mouth sounding harsher than the last.

I'm trembling. My entire body shakes from the chilled atmosphere. The only noise in the room, as he waits for me to speak, is the chattering of my teeth.

"It wasn't supposed to be like this. I only meant to see you. To tell you who I was."

"Then how did I end up inside you, Cassidy?"

The way he says it is meant to be crass. To make me uncomfortable.

"Stop," I bite out. "Don't do this."

He laughs bitterly. "Answer the fucking question."

I swallow down the lump forming in my throat.

"When I got there, the guy at your door mistook me for whoever you were waiting for. I lied to get in. It was my only chance to see you."

I can't stop my voice from quivering, my breath coming out harsh and choppy until I'm spiraling into a panic attack.

A thing I can see: Aiden. His nostrils flared. Jaw hard as stone.

Something I can smell: His cologne. But instead of calming me, it makes my heart lurch in my chest, a fresh set of tears cascading down my eyes. I'll never bury my head in the crook of his arm or find comfort in his embrace again.

Something I can hear: My own sobs.

"You didn't even remember me," I whisper, fresh tears running down my face, forcing me to blink them away. They flow like a river, the salty taste landing on my lips. "You left me. I wasn't even worth remembering."

"You think I forgot about you?" he sneers.

"Yes."

"You think I'm that much of an asshole?" He doesn't even give me a chance to answer. "You don't know shit."

He stalks off toward the kitchen, leaving me standing alone, cradling my chest with my arms.

A few seconds later, he's marching back into the room with a piece of paper clutched in his hand. "You know *nothing*," he says, tossing a piece of paper at me.

He doesn't say another word. He doesn't even look back as he storms out the front door, slamming it shut behind him.

I'm left alone in his house, the paper he held moments ago, now clutched between both of my hands, as my trembling somehow intensifies.

My entire body goes limp as all my strength bleeds out of me. And then…I'm falling.

When I land on my knees, my head falls back on a strangled cry as I allow every last emotion to pour from me until I'm nothing but an empty vessel. A crumpled mess, lying alone on the hard floor.

chapter thirty-five

Aiden

THE ANGER BUBBLING UP INSIDE ME IS LIKE NOTHING I'VE EVER felt before.

I want to punch a wall.

Throw something.

The betrayal cloys at my chest, making me itch and my skin pull taut. I need to get the fuck away from her.

I head straight out the front door, to the elevator, and toward the exit. My feet not carrying me quickly enough.

The muggy air hits me in the face the moment I step outside, and I feel like I'm suffocating.

I suck in a lungful of air, not giving a shit about any people passing by. Let them look. Let them watch my breakdown.

I don't care anymore.

How can *she be her*?

Pip. *My Pip.*

Moments from the past rush at me like a freight train as I start to walk, needing to put distance between us.

There's no destination. I'm just allowing my feet to guide me. My head is lowered, and my hands are balled into fists at my side. But the farther I walk, the more my shoulders slump, and my hands relax.

I'm a shell of a person.

Betrayal oozes from every pour. But there's also this strange feeling of relief.

Pip is alive.

Shouldn't that matter for something?

Fuck.

A war rages inside me.

My emotions are all over the place, and I don't know what is up or what is down.

When my feet stop, I'm at the local hole-in-the-wall bar a few blocks from my apartment, and I know exactly who I need to text.

Dane.

He'll help me forget.

Me: Need you. Now.

Dane: Is this Cassidy?

The mention of that name causes a sharp pain in my chest. My hand flies up over my pounding organ, surprised to find it still beating.

Dane: Did you steal your man's phone?

Me: Seriously. Meet me at Dickies.

Me: And don't mention that name again...

It doesn't take long before the seat beside me at the bar is being pulled out. The sound of the metal scratching the floor grates at my ears.

"You look fucking awful."

I turn to look at the teammate who has quickly become more than just a friend, but family.

"I feel awful," I groan. "My head is pounding."

"Nothing a drink can't help." He peers down at the half-empty tumbler in front of me, lifting one brow. "Looks like you already started."

I lift my glass up in a mock cheer.

Dane's eyes narrow in on me. "What's going on? Drinking this early in the day isn't like you."

"Too much to deal with," I respond with a grimace. "I just wanna forget. Why don't you help me with that?"

He lifts his eyebrow. "All right." He lifts a hand, signaling for the bartender. "I'll have whatever he's having." He lifts up two fingers. "We'll take two."

The redheaded, middle-aged man nods before grabbing the whiskey bottle off the top shelf.

For the next thirty minutes, we drink together in silence. My eyes remain trained on my glass, and he appears to watch whatever's playing on the TV behind the bar. The silence is good. It's why I chose this place.

This is the type of place you come to forget. Everyone within these walls has something they're running from. Even Dane.

"You didn't call me here to sit in silence," Dane says, breaking the peaceful moment.

"I'm good with it. Just make sure I get home…" I shake my head. "No…not home… anywhere but there."

He purses his lips, watching me far too close for my liking.

"What's going on, Slate?"

"I no longer know what to think. Or how to even answer that question," I admit. "You wouldn't understand anyway."

"Try me," he says, never turning away from me. "We all have our secrets, Slate. You're not the only one."

I let out a deep sigh. "I wouldn't even know where to begin."

He sits back, crossing his arms over his chest. "I find the beginning to be the easiest."

I huff out a breath. "Shit, that would take forever."

"I have time. No place to be."

I pick up the glass, inspecting the rim, feeling wholly uncomfortable with Dane's focus being on me.

"Does this have anything to do with Cassidy?"

"No. I don't even know..."

I was about to say I don't even know her, but I'm not sure how much I want to confide in Dane yet. I'm still trying to make my way through the mess.

As I think about all the shit that went down back at my house, all I can do is groan out, "Fuck!"

He nods as if he finally gets it. But I know without a doubt he doesn't. How could he? It's too complicated.

I never told him about Pip. Never told him about my home life at all, really.

"Your mom, then?" he asks, continuing to guess.

"No." I lift my hand and run it through my hair. "But...yes."

His head tilts to the side. "Not following at all, buddy. You lost me back at fuck."

I huff out a humorless laugh. Not at Dane, but at the situation.

"It has to do with where I grew up. My past before hockey."

"All right. I'll bite...what secrets are you harboring, Slate? Is there a body we have to bury?"

For the first time since leaving my apartment, I laugh, but it only takes a second to dry up on my lips as I take a swig of my drink. I brought Dane here, and I should've known there were going to be questions. Hell, if I were him, I'd have already pried it from his mouth.

It's time for someone to know.

"Cassidy isn't who I thought she was."

His eyes widen, but he doesn't interrupt. Dane has known me long enough to know I don't share my life, my secrets, or my past with anyone. The fact that I'm talking to him now means that shit is really bad. That I'm at rock bottom and need help clawing my way back to the top.

"I didn't grow up the way you think. I obviously explained most of this already when I told you about my mom. But what I didn't tell you was that there was this girl…"

"Isn't there always?" He huffs, taking a long pull from his whiskey.

If I didn't have a mountain of problems, I'd dig into that a little more, but there will be time to uncover Dane's secrets later.

"Not the way you're thinking. She was younger. Much younger. I was younger," I clarify. "This girl was like a little sister to me. She saw me. Understood me. Never judged me."

I give him a small, sad smile as I lift my glass to my mouth and take another swig.

"Her name was Pippa. I called her Pip. She was this little thing, but she was strong. Fierce." I sigh. "She was…she was like me." *Or maybe even better. Before she got caught in her lies.*

"Like you how?" His eyes squint as they bore into the side of my head. I can see them out of the corner of my eye.

"Getting to that…"

"Sorry. I guess I'm just invested," he blabbers. "Continue."

"We were both alone. We had parents, but they weren't around. We bonded. Became our own family of sorts." I let out a breath. "We were there for each other." I turn to look at him, thankful I chose such a dark place.

It allows me a modicum of safety. I don't feel so vulnerable because a part of me is hidden in shadows. Just like he is.

"I know it sounds weird, but she was my best friend. A twelve-year-old, but she lived a life most couldn't comprehend, and so had I. She's the reason I'm a hockey player."

He pulls his mouth off to the side, confusion evident. I can practically hear the questions rattling around in his head.

How could a girl be the reason you play?

"She loaned me the money to try out for juniors. My mom—well, she fucked things up for me, and Pip gave me a second chance…"

"Wow. A twelve-year-old girl gave you the money?" He

whistles. "That's…pretty cool, honestly." He shakes his head. "Have I told you that I hate your fucking mom?"

I laugh because Dane looks like he would strangle her if she walked into the bar at this moment.

He's a great friend. Someone I know I can trust with my secrets.

"What happened to her?" he asks, voice lowered as if it was the one question he was nervous to ask. "This Pip?"

"That's something I've wondered for a long time," I admit. "I never saw her again once I left. Or at least that's what I thought until…"

"Oh boy…why do I get the feeling you're about to drop a bomb?"

I take a deep breath. "She's Cassidy. Cassidy is Pip."

He whistles, nodding.

"It all makes sense now," he says, and I narrow my eyes in on him. "This is why you jumped into a relationship in five minutes. I knew there was more to the story. You don't go from swearing off relationships to in a serious relationship that quickly."

Fuck.

More secrets. More lies.

How do I tell him this?

Rip off the Band-Aid. That's how.

"That's…not exactly the truth. I thought she was a puck bunny when I first met her."

His lips slam shut, and he makes a face.

"I didn't know it was Pip when I first met Cassidy. Mike…" I say, trailing off.

"Jesus…what does Mike have to do with this?"

"He thought she could help me unwind. That…Cassidy could. And she did."

"He hired you a puck bunny?"

I shake my head. "No. There was no money exchanged. The girl was supposed to just like sex."

He shakes his head. "Let me get this straight…she was the puck bunny that Mike sent to you? Was it an accident?"

I run my hand back through my hair on a groan. "I'm not explaining this right. She was never the bunny. She found out I was at the hotel and tried to sneak in to see me. Security thought she was the bunny and let her in."

He chuckles. "And she just went along with it?"

I nod slowly. "It worked. She got me out of my head but also had this calming effect on me."

"Because she knew you." It's not a question. He's just working things out loud.

"At the time, I didn't understand. I just knew I needed her with me." I swallow, preparing to tell the truth. "I hired her."

His eyes look like they're about to bug out of his head. "For sex?"

My head falls back on my shoulders. "Not like that. That wasn't part of the deal. I hired her under the guise of needing her to manage some of my quirks. But, to the outside, she had to play the part of my girlfriend. That way, it wouldn't get out why I actually hired her."

"I don't get that. Why did you need her to be your girlfriend?"

"A lot of my…quirks happen after hours. I didn't want people to think I was banging my assistant." I groan. "At least that's part of it. The truth is, I just wanted her around."

"You were trying to keep it a secret from everyone."

I bob my head. "I was embarrassed. It was taking over my life and getting me more into my head."

"It's nothing to be embarrassed about, Aiden." He holds my stare. "We all have our things."

"I know that now," I say, offering a smile to my friend. "She helped me realize that. Her being around gave me the peace that Pippa had given me all those years ago. I didn't put two and two together. She looks so different now than she looked back then. Plus, I didn't have any pictures; Pip was only in my memories. So while she felt safe and familiar, I didn't know it was her. All I knew was that whatever was happening between Cassidy and me, the way she made me feel…I didn't want to let her go."

"And then you just found out the truth…"

I sigh. "Yeah."

He lifts his glass to mine, and we clink them together, each taking a drink, allowing the weight of what I've just shared to fall over us.

"What did she say?"

I'm quiet, and Dane shakes his head. "You didn't let her explain, did you?"

Dane, always the great defender.

"No. I wasn't in the headspace to think straight."

He lifts his brow. "She said nothing. Or you just stormed out?"

"She said I didn't remember her. I freaked out and left."

"Because you did remember her?"

"I might have not recognized her, but of course, I remembered her. She was the only bit of hope in my life." I hold Dane's stare. "I could never forget Pip."

He sighs, taking another sip and draining his glass. "I don't think it's just about that, man. She was bothered that you didn't realize that she was Pip."

I blink several times, allowing what he's just said to sink in.

"She was around twelve when I last saw her. How could I have known?"

He shrugs. "You need to talk to her. She's back in your life, and for the first time since I've known you, you've looked happy when she's around. Are you really willing to throw that away?"

"Fuck. I don't know."

He waves down the bartender and asks for the bill. I try to put my card down, but he brushes me off. "I'll take care of this. You need to go talk to her."

I swallow down a lump. "Yeah, I do."

But first, I need to see how this happened. How did this slip past everyone?

I stand to leave, and Dane nods at me, not saying anything. What else is there to say? We both know where I'm going.

First, I need to make a call. There's only one person who could have known or should've known.

I'm out the door, heading home, but find myself heading in a different direction first. As I walk, I pull my phone out of my pocket and dial his number.

Mike will have the answers I need.

"What's up? Everything okay?" His voice sounds edgy, like he's anticipating something. "Your mom off your back?"

"This isn't about her. It's about Cass."

He sighs. "She finally came clean?"

"So you knew?" I snap.

There's no hiding the anger in my voice.

"Calm down, man, I only just realized. I gave her an ultimatum."

This just pisses me off more. How long has he known? What ultimatum?

"Explain."

"I found out right before the gala." He breathes heavily down the line, and for a moment, I think he isn't going to elaborate. "I spoke to my contact. The one who knows the girl we'd set up to meet with you. He mentioned how he saw his favorite girl and that she had apologized for bailing on me."

"She never showed," I say, mostly to myself.

That had been a question circulating for me. Had Cassidy somehow arranged the switch? Did she know when she got there that she was to have sex with me?

"She asked him not to use it against her in the future," Mike continues. "He relayed the message. It didn't take a rocket scientist to put two and two together that Cassidy wasn't the girl I sent to you."

"And you didn't think to tell me immediately? You're my agent, Mike."

"Listen, Aiden…you were doing so good. I just wanted to give her the benefit of the doubt." He grunts. "I wasn't about to take the chance of telling you in the middle of a room full of people to have you freak out and cause a damn scene."

I blow out a harsh breath, understanding that decision.

"I approached her on the dance floor. Told her she could tell you, or I would. She had twenty-four hours, but as you know, shit hit the fan, and I was a bit preoccupied."

"What if her motives had been like my mother's?"

And there it is.

The truth behind my anger.

What if she didn't come for me, but for my money?

"She's not your mother, Aiden. You know better than that. The woman has done nothing but try to help you."

I swallow down the lump that keeps lodging in my throat.

He sighs. "I'm just glad she came clean. I was not looking forward to that convo."

"Hardly," I snap, thinking back on how it all went down.

Pinky promise on your puck…

She could've pinky promised on anything else, and I likely would still be with her, none the wiser. But that phrase is all Pippa. The words she said before I left.

"What do you mean, she didn't tell you?"

"She didn't tell me. What else is there to say?"

"But you know. So—"

"I figured it out all by myself. There were signs I should've seen weeks ago."

"How? What are you talking about?"

"She's Pippa, Mike." I make a strangled noise. "She's Pippa."

"Fuck," he bites out. "I don't even know what to say."

Me either.

"I thought she would tell you that she wasn't the girl we thought she was, but I never realized she knew you. Weird. Come to think about it, she seemed almost relieved when I demanded it."

"I think she tried. A few times. I wouldn't let her," I admit.

After the gala, she told me she wasn't who I thought she was. I told her I didn't care. That I knew who she was.

Maybe I did.

Maybe a part of me knew all along.

I saw her, but I wasn't ready to admit it. All the little things she said over time pile on top of me.

It's only business.

A warm cup of milk.

The conversation about my Jeep.

The whole time, she was trying to tell me, and I was too blind to see.

Or maybe I didn't want Cassidy to be Pip. Didn't want her to be the girl I left behind. My best friend. The girl who I looked at like a sister.

Guilt pounds against me, and I succumb to it.

chapter thirty-six

Cassidy

I'M NOT SURE HOW MUCH TIME HAS PASSED, BUT I'M STILL IN THE same position I've been in since he left me. I'm curled into myself on the floor, shivering from the cold seeping through my bones.

This was always going to happen. It was inevitable.

I had hoped it wouldn't come down to this. That I could've been honest, not forced to spill my truth. That he would have let me explain…

You lied.

You gave him reason to question your motives.

Not once. But twice. Hell, I broke it over and over again. Every word I said, every look I gave reiterates this.

After everything he's been through at the hands of his shitty mom, trust doesn't come easy. And what I did shattered whatever trust I've built up.

The moment I slept with him, my original reasons for being there were moot. Pip, the girl he knew, disappeared soon after he left.

Aiden Slate doesn't trust anyone, and he trusted me. He trusted Pippa back in the day, and he trusted Cassidy. In one fell swoop, I destroyed that for both versions of me.

I saw the hate in his eyes.

The disgust.

I broke more than his trust.

I'm an awful person.

And for what?

Love.

Because that's the truth of things. I fell in love with Aiden.

I couldn't just leave him. Couldn't abandon him like everyone else does.

I hoped he was falling for me too. And even if he wasn't, I wanted anything he was willing to give me.

Any tiny scrap.

Bile crawls up my throat, and I run to the bathroom.

My knees hit the cold tile as I open the lid and dry heave.

Nothing comes up, though. My stomach is empty.

My life...empty.

I sit there for a minute as tears pour down my face. Waiting for my turning stomach to spill its contents. It doesn't. Even my body is intent on keeping me miserable.

In pain.

Suffering.

After a few minutes, I stand, making my way to the sink and turning on the faucet. I splash cold water on my face, and the chill is enough to snap me out of my stupor.

"Why did he leave me?" I ask my reflection in the mirror, but the poor, sad, heartbroken fool doesn't respond.

Not that I need her to. I know what I did. I deserve his hatred.

You don't know shit.

Those were the last words he hurled at me before storming out of my life.

What could he have meant?

Curiosity gets the better of me, and I wipe my hands on my face to rid myself of the extra water clinging to my lids. I'm in search of the little slip of white paper he threw at me, and I find it lying on the floor.

I pick it up, and despite the size, it feels heavy in my hand. I turn it over, staring at it, but mostly delaying. Whatever this is… it feels important. An outcome that will most likely change me forever. And that thought alone makes my breathing ragged. My heart races. My palms sweat.

I turn it over again. This time, I read the words.

A website is scrawled across the top, followed by a username and a code.

My name and his number creating the username. Pip13.

What is this?

Under it says, "…with interest. We're even now."

What the hell does that mean?

There's only one way to find out. I make a mad dash for my room, snatching up my laptop and typing in the information.

The website sends me to a bank account, and my heart stutters before resuming the pounding quality it's taken on since my secret was exposed.

I'm not sure what I'm going to find, but my fingers type in all the information quickly.

You know exactly what you'll find.

My hands shake as I wait for it to load. The screen refreshes, and a bank account dashboard pops up.

The balance of $60,000 flashes back at me, and my eyes narrow in on the screen.

Confusion settles over me as a million questions run through my mind.

Whose money is this?

Why did he give me the details?

I press the profile information and start to scour the site.

Under the profile setting, I search for the account details.

Aiden's name is at the top, but beneath it, under a heading for account nickname, is a name I haven't seen in years. Pippa Johnson. The name I gave him long ago. The only name he knew me as.

My eyes well with tears, and my heart slows.

Seeing that name brings about a host of emotions. It's what I went by before I escaped the hellhole I grew up in. I changed my last name to my mother's maiden name the second I got away. All the reasons I left Pippa behind crash over me.

The abuse.

The neglect.

The hurt.

The betrayal.

The accident.

This money is for me.

You forgot about me.

You don't know shit.

My eyes blur as I stare at the computer screen.

This entire time, he didn't forget Pippa. At least not entirely. He was keeping money aside for me.

With interest. We're even now.

I look through the transactions to see that the account was opened almost ten years ago.

Ten years ago was the last time I saw him. He opened it a month after he left. It shows a deposit of only twenty-four dollars.

I open the next one, and there's no activity other than a deposit of five dollars this time.

The next month shows the same thing. It's pretty much small deposits every few months. A few dollars here and there.

I keep going. Over the next year and a half, slowly the amount increases.

From five to ten dollars a month to twenty…by the time four more years pass, the amount is now over three hundred until a lump sum was deposited.

A grand total of thirty-six thousand was placed in the account.

I furrow my brow. Why did he deposit so much? I squint my eyes, and then something hits me. That was the year Aiden would have graduated from college.

I google my question: What year did Aiden Slate get drafted to the Redville Saints?

As I suspected, the dates match.

From there on out, every month like clockwork, he deposits five hundred a month. Five hundred dollars every single month to come to a grand total of sixty thousand dollars. The last deposit was only weeks ago.

I had told him to pay me back with interest, and he remembered.

He kept his word.

Even if he didn't know where to send the money or how it would get to me.

Liquid wells in my eyes, the words on the computer screen becoming blurry with unshed tears.

He never forgot me.

Aiden never forgot me.

Almost every month of every year since he left, he's been paying back my investment.

I should've told him the truth.

Should've trusted that our bond was too strong to be that easily forgotten.

I've ruined everything.

chapter thirty-seven

Aiden

M Y PHONE KEEPS RINGING, BUT I IGNORE IT.
I don't have to look to know who it is.

It's her. Cassidy.

She's been calling for over an hour.

Back in the days when I knew her as Pippa, if she wanted your attention, she stopped at nothing to get it. She'd search until she found me. She was a determined little shit then, and it appears not much has changed in that department.

Despite myself, a small smile spreads across my face before I force it away.

I'm not ready.

To smile.

To answer the phone.

To forgive.

It feels like I'm still spiraling out of control, and I need to rein myself in. I need to be in a better headspace. To think about what

I want to say. Nothing good could come from lashing out without thought.

I'm not my mom, and I refuse to act like her.

So instead of calling her back, I go to the one place I can find solace when my brain is a mess.

I take a seat on the small bench outside the local ice rink.

Ever since I was drafted all those years ago, I've come here. It's the closest thing I have to my tree and my lake. I left everything behind, but I kept some of the memories.

That time of my life was a nightmare, but the ice was my solace.

Since as far back as I've been able to remember, looking at the ice has calmed me, and even now, years later, it still does.

It all began at the lake.

I found a new home in my college rink, and now, here, this place is my peace. Normally, I'd go in, but I'm not in the mood to see anyone. Right now, this bench outside the building will have to be enough.

Closing my eyes, I can see the ice in my head. I like to watch the kids skate. To see the joy it brings them, just like it did me. Watching them laughing on the ice, surrounded by family and friends, and the enjoyment they find makes my world feel not so empty.

I can't explain it.

For me, the ice has been a symbol of many things.

Freedom. Skill. Determination.

But it was never about laughter.

When I was young, it was an escape, then it was a means to an end. Now, it's about the control I yield on the ice.

The longer I sit here, the looser my muscles get.

It's like I can think because I'm most relaxed.

And the more I think, the more I know I handled things really bad.

She lied, and I have every right to be angry, but I shouldn't have walked away.

That's the very thing everyone else has ever done.

It's what she probably thinks I did back then.

Because you did.

Her voice haunts me.

Promise me you'll never forget me.

And I did.

I didn't recognize her the day she walked into my hotel room. Didn't realize the significance of the moment.

Her wide-eyed gaze had nothing to do with the famous hockey player in front of her. No, when I think back on what she looked like that night, the truth hits me square in the chest. She was a deer in headlights. Her past had come back to haunt her even though she chased it.

She had to have been absolutely gutted. Heartbroken.

She gave me the last of what she had, possibly the money that would allow her to eat that week, and I couldn't even be bothered to remember those eyes. The same ones I looked into time after time.

And despite the heartbreak I likely caused, she gave up her life to help me. She kept her secret in order to be by my side. She never asked for a thing. Not even money. That was something I supposed.

That has to mean something.

She's nothing like my mother. A user. Someone who set out to take from me.

"Ugh," I grit through my teeth, pulling at my hair by the roots.

I slept with Pippa. *My Pip.*

The girl you spent years looking for.

The girl you missed with all your heart.

Yeah, she lied. But she also gave me hope. Always put me first. *Loved me unconditionally.*

For her to lie, she must have felt she had no choice.

Shit.

A part of me wants to forget everything. To go back to being naïve to her identity. It occurs to me that it's not even an option not to speak to her again. I can't do that. Having Pip back in my life is all I've wanted since we parted. I can't give up on her.

I need to see her. To let her explain.

Leaping to my feet, I turn to leave and stop short.

As if conjured by my mind, she's there. Cassidy found me.

She stands tall, trying to appear together, but I know she's nervous. Her upper teeth are worrying her bottom lip, and her fingers tap the side of her leg.

"Penny for your thoughts?" she says, repeating words she's spoken before. In another life. "Or in this case…60,000."

She knows.

That's why she's here.

Cassidy knows that despite how it might have appeared, not a day has gone by that I haven't thought of her and what she did for me.

"I shouldn't have lied to you. I'm so sorry, Aiden."

I shake my head. There's too much to say, to talk about, to ask. "Not here."

She nods, understanding clear on her face.

I begin to walk, and she trails close behind me. When we're out of earshot of others, I start my questioning.

"How did you know where to find me that night?"

Had she been searching for me? Was this all planned?

"Isn't it obvious?" she says, but I don't look back at her. I keep walking, and she finally continues. "I saw you on TV. Heard you were in town." She clears her throat. "My friend works at the hotel, and she let it slip you were staying there." A strangled noise flies out of her mouth. "But please don't get her in trouble. It's my fault. Not hers."

I don't like that a member of the hotel staff told outsiders where to find me, but in this instance, I wouldn't say anything to the hotel.

"If I'm being honest." She pauses, and I don't think she's going to finish, but she presses on. "I've intentionally avoided anything that would remind me of you. For years." She huffs a humorless laugh. "That night I'd been drinking and seeing your face on the screen…affected me. You actually haven't changed at all. Not much. I'd know your face anywhere."

There's sadness in her voice, and it makes my stomach drop. She recognized me, but I didn't recognize her. She doesn't say the words, but they're there, hanging over us.

I want to say she's wrong, but she's not. I haven't changed much. Still too focused on hockey. Too focused on my own shit to realize who stood right in front of me.

These last few months with her, I feel I have grown. I've begun to care about things I never did before.

We walk in silence the rest of the way back to my place. Both of us seemingly lost in our own thoughts.

I wonder what's going through her mind. Could she be stuck in the past? The days of Pippa and Slate? Or is she thinking about us, only hours ago, wrapped in each other's arms?

Cassidy and Aiden.

It's only a few blocks from the rink, but it feels like miles away as we trudge in silence. We're each able to keep our space, but when we enter the elevator, the tight quarters swallow us up when the doors shut us in, and it feels like the walls close in on me. Suffocating.

The soft music filtering through the small, confined space feels taunting. Like it knows there are a million questions on my tongue. Questions I can't ask until we're alone.

When the elevator jerks to a stop, I allow her to go first. To lead us toward answers. I follow to the door of my penthouse apartment, dragging my feet when I should be sprinting to the truth.

I'm nervous.

Scared.

What if I don't like what I hear?

What if I do?

Where will that leave us?

Is there an "us"?

"Fuck," I say, pulling at my hair. The pressure presses down on me.

"Are you okay?" she asks, and I grunt in response.

When we enter the foyer, it's dark. The small city gleams in the distance, providing a scrap of sight.

I don't bother turning on the lights as I pace the living room. I'm on what's likely my tenth lap of the room when she walks up to stand in front of me, stopping me in place.

"I know I was wrong." Her voice shakes, and the need to reach out and grab her is intense. But I don't. I can't.

"Why did you do it?"

Her lips tremble, and her shoulders shake with barely contained sobs.

"Why didn't you tell me who you were?" I ask, trying to control my voice.

She sniffles, brushing away stray tears. "Honest answer?"

"Always," I grit through my teeth, attempting to rein in my emotions.

"At first, I was upset." She drops her gaze to the floor. "Devastated."

I swallow that fucking lump that won't go away, hating the hurt in her tone.

"But then something shifted. Something was…different from before."

I tilt my head to the side, confused by her words. She just told me, not too long ago, that I haven't changed.

"I saw the way you looked at me. It was different. You weren't the boy who left me behind, Aiden." Her voice pitches, and she takes a moment to compose herself. Her chin tips up, and her eyes meet mine. "The way I felt when you looked at me like that…it's not normal for me to feel that way."

"What way?" My voice is thick and husky, and I know it affects her when she closes her eyes and inhales deeply.

"Like you saw me. Cassidy." She inhales and exhales before

finishing her thought. "Not the little girl you used to look at like a little sister."

I nod slowly, recalling that first night she crawled to me.

God, did I want her.

It had been a long time since I've felt that. Hell…I'm not sure I've ever wanted someone like that.

"The way you looked at me changed things. I didn't see you as that boy. I saw Aiden that night, and I wanted him. Wanted you." She shrugs. "I said fuck it. One night. I'd allow myself one perfect night with you."

She crosses her arms protectively over her chest. "That was all it was supposed to be. I debated telling you while I showered. I was going to, but then I saw you…"

"Sorting," I say, remembering that night all too well. "And…"

"And I was brought back to our childhood. I couldn't not help you. You were my only safe place. You were my home, and when you left, you took that with you. I know it was selfish, but I just couldn't let you go…"

"I get why you came to the hotel." I shake my head, clearing the jumbled emotions away. "I even get how we ended up…together." I give myself a moment to untangle my thoughts. "But you could've stopped there. You could've turned down my offer and then turned your back on me. Hell…you could've told me who you were…but you kept up the lie week after week."

Her face falls, and as soon as it does, I want to soothe her pain and take my cold words back. But I need to know why.

"I wanted to say something." Her head falls back. "So many fucking times. But every time I got close, something would happen. Something that would have you needing me, or worse. Something would happen to trigger you, and I couldn't rock the boat more. I wanted to be there to help you calm down. To show you that you had someone in your corner."

"How was this supposed to end?" The question is practically a whisper.

"I would have helped you, and eventually, when I felt like you were going to be okay, I would have let you go." A tear slips down her cheek, and without thought, I reach out and swipe it away. At the touch of my hand against her skin, her eyes close. "All I cared about was you, Aiden."

"And what about you?"

Her eyes flutter open, and her lips turn down. "I'm used to being second."

Each word she says feels like a dagger to my heart. For the first time since she's come back into my life, I see that broken little girl.

"You'd put my happiness before your own?" I mutter, understanding dawning on me.

She's falling back on old habits.

"Yeah. Every time, Aiden."

I take a step until our chests practically touch. As I look down at her, all the anger melts away. All the fears surrounding why she lied and why she was here disappear.

She chooses me.

I know she lied, but hearing her reason, hearing her truth, I can't be mad.

"I have to be honest with you, Cassidy, leaving Pippa—you—behind has eaten at me for years."

A sob catches in her throat, but I don't stop. She needs to hear this.

"I understand why you lied. I'd have probably done the same thing in your place. A moment more with you would be worth it."

I reach out and touch her soft hair, placing a piece behind her ear. I lift my other hand and place it on her jaw. My fingers caress her soft skin.

"I never meant to leave you. Not for good. I wanted to come back for you. But shit was hard, and I couldn't risk my mom interfering with what I was building."

"I understand." Her lips tremble. "I'm sorry for lying. I'm sor—"

Leaning down, I silence her with my mouth, not allowing

another apology to leave her lips. She has nothing to atone for. She's done the one thing no one else has ever done for me…

Care.

She put my needs before her own. Something that my own mother couldn't be bothered to do. How could I hold her lies against her?

I push every one of my own apologies into my kiss.

I'm sorry.

I'm sorry I left you.

I should've come back for you.

Our tongues tangle, and so do our bodies. This kiss is different. It's putting the past behind us and forging a future. One in which Cassidy and I can be honest with each other. Be there for the other.

She said she'd put herself before me, and I know she means it. I'd do the same for her, and I won't stop until she believes that. Until she knows I care.

More than she can ever understand.

This might not be love, but it's something monumental. The start of what could only be life-changing.

chapter thirty-eight

Cassidy

HIS LIPS CRASH AGAINST MINE, HUNGRY AND DESPERATE. It's as if he can't get enough of my taste, and the truth is, I can't get enough of his.

My arms lift until they wrap around his neck, fingers sinking into his disheveled hair. His in turn roam my body, stroking down my back until he cups my ass in his hands, pulling me closer to him.

Once flush against his hard chest, he deepens the kiss, if that's even possible.

We're all tongues and teeth as he shows me without words that he still wants me. That despite everything, what we have is more.

Soon, the kiss becomes more heated, and I barely grasp the fact that he's walking us through the hallway and into his room. It isn't until the back of my legs hit the bed that I realize where he's led us.

"I need you," he grits out against my lips, his hands moving from my body and letting me go. I want to protest at the lack of his warmth, but then the sound of his zipper echoes through the air with a promise, and my heart beats faster.

Need courses through me at an intensity I've never felt.

He pulls his mouth away from me, and a whimper escapes, my eagerness to resume evident. But my whining is short-lived as he shucks off his jeans, giving me a full view of what's to come. I'm staring at his long, hard cock, and my tongue darts out to swipe across my bottom lip.

That hunger only grows with every second that goes by.

My mouth waters at the sight. The desire to drop to my knees and take him in my mouth washes over me, but before I can, he's sealing his lips against mine again.

Aiden's hand reaches toward my sweatpants and pushes them down. I only break the connection for a moment as I kick them off and lift my T-shirt up and over my head.

I'm standing naked in front of him, offering myself to him. His lips moves into a smirk.

"You're mine," he growls, and then he pushes me back until I'm lying half on the bed, legs dangling off.

He steps up, and I part my legs for him, giving him room to stand. He grins down at me, and a shiver runs up my back.

"I'm going to devour you, Cassidy. Every fucking inch."

With that promise, he drops to the floor in front of me, grabbing my legs to hang over his shoulders.

I dig my heels into his back as his expert tongue licks right up my folds. My head falls back, and I practically come undone from that one move alone. The man knows what he's doing as he strokes every inch of me with that tongue.

A groan escapes his mouth as he feasts, drawing a line from my ass to my clit, inserting one finger to skyrocket the pleasure. He takes me to the edge but stops just as I'm about to fall over.

"You're going to come on my cock," he practically growls,

pushing to a stand. He positions himself at my entrance but doesn't put me out of my misery.

"Aiden," I groan. "Please."

He only smirks as he slides his cock along my skin.

"What do you want, Cass? This?" he asks, gripping his dick in his hands while rubbing it against me. No matter how close he gets, he doesn't breach me. He just teases. Tortures.

The building pressure makes me delirious with want.

Pushing my ass up, I try to coax him inside me, but he's not having it. Instead, he grips his dick harder and rubs the head on my clit. Circling me. Driving me insane.

"Aiden," I say again, making it clear I'm about to take care of myself.

He rocks back and forth a few more times before he aligns himself with my entrance.

On one thrust, with no warning, he fills me.

I cry out at the feel of him taking up every inch of me. My walls expand to accommodate him, and he's still for a moment, allowing my body time.

Like this, with nothing separating us, I can feel every inch of him, and I love it.

"Fuck," he groans through clenched teeth before he's rocking his hips back and forth. Slowly. Methodically. Until he's picking up speed and slamming into me.

"So fucking good." His head is turned down, and I follow his gaze.

He's watching us, completely enthralled by the vision in front of him.

He's pumping inside me, stretching me to the limit, and he gets a front-row seat to it.

I lift onto my elbows, and from this angle, I too can see, and I understand the glazed look he's wearing. This is intoxicating. Erotic as hell.

What I'm seeing makes me grow even wetter. I can't take

my eyes off where our bodies meet. How his cock disappears inside me. My hand palms my breasts, squeezing, and Aiden's eyes darken.

"You like that?" his husky voice, warm like honey, slides over me, making my body shiver. I don't respond; the only sound leaving my mouth is a moan. "You like watching me fuck you?" He motions with his head toward my hand. "You like touching yourself?"

My head falls back on a moan, eating up every single dirty word he says.

"Answer me," he demands, thrusting harder. Deeper.

I love when he's like this.

Commanding.

In control.

This is how he is on the ice too.

He stops moving and a mewling noise escapes me. He pulls out until the crown is the only piece of him still inside me.

My gaze trails up, and I see his rigid length glistening back at me with the evidence of my arousal.

"Please," I beg.

"Please what?" he challenges, and he smirks when my body quivers beneath him.

"Please fuck me."

He shakes his head, lifting one eyebrow. "You never answered my question."

"Yes." My voice cracks. "Yes, I love watching you fuck me." I lift my hips until more of him is inside me. "More."

"Dirty girl," he growls, finally giving in to my pleas.

He thrusts deep, bottoming all the way out. His movements are fast and hard, driving me toward orgasm.

He must sense I'm close because his hand reaches between us, finding the spot I need him most. He's circling me, rubbing and teasing me, all while picking up the speed of his hips, pounding inside me as if he can't get enough. The pleasure is almost unbearable.

"Aiden," I practically scream.

He works my clit harder, giving me the needed pressure, and finally, a climax works its way through my body, washing over me until I'm shaking in ecstasy.

I push myself against him, riding out my orgasm as he finally gets his own release. When we're both sated and thoroughly exhausted, he collapses on top of me. The full weight of his body weighs me down. I never liked it in the past, but with Aiden, I feel safe, desirable, and most of all, loved.

This moment changes everything for me.

I only hope he feels the same.

chapter thirty-nine

Aiden

I HOVER OVER HER FOR A MOMENT, LOOKING DOWN INTO HER beautiful face. Something's different. There's a change in her. She's breathless, her eyes wide and sparkling with an emotion I don't think I'm ready to name.

I lick my lips and push my weight into her a little more, trying to break the intensity. A burst of air escapes her, and she taps my shoulders, spluttering.

"Wow." She giggles as I roll off her. Now that she's beside me, I pull her closer so that I can wrap my arm around her. "That was incredible." Her words come out in a pant. "Until you smothered me."

My lips tip up into a smirk. "I aim to please. And smother apparently."

She laughs at that, her body shaking against me. "Jeez. What am I going to do with you?"

"As long as you're naked, I don't care." I lean down and place a kiss on the top of her head. The room is silent for a minute. Both of us letting our breaths regulate.

A few more seconds pass before she moves. "Where are you going?" I ask, not ready for her to get up.

"I gotta pee."

I bark out a laugh. "You do that. I'll be here waiting."

She raises her hands in mock annoyance. "Men."

"You love it." I grin at her.

Her translucent blue eyes sparkle at me. "I do."

The bed dips, and I feel her get off and head toward the bathroom. I swallow, taking in her naked form. It never gets old looking at Cassidy. She's breathtaking.

I watch until she's out of sight, shaking my head to myself. There's no way I would've ever thought she was Pip. She looks nothing like the girl I knew. Sure, there are little moments when I can see that version of her. That fire and the protective instincts that, even at thirteen, Pip possessed. When I left, she was barely a teen. It was right after her thirteenth birthday. She wasn't a mature-looking thirteen-year-old. She was a kid.

Now, she's all woman.

Poised. Passionate. Fucking gorgeous.

Despite the change in her looks, she's the same girl. The same selfless girl who always put me first. The same one who always had my back. And maybe that's why I had an immediate connection with her.

The part that hurts is that she never thought I had her back.

Pip thought I betrayed her. Thought I took the money she offered and ran, never thinking about her.

There's so much we need to talk about, but I don't know where to start. We've crossed a line that complicates things. It's not just Pip and Slate who have things to work out, but Aiden and Cassidy. The same people, yet different issues.

My jaw gets tight, and the need to do something to take my mind off the turmoil is all-encompassing.

I close my eyes to fight off the headache that often presents itself in moments like this. When my anxiety spikes.

It's like she left the room and took all rational thought and my control with her.

This is what she's always done for me. Something about her acts as a balm to my chaotic soul. It was like that when I knew her as Pip, and it hasn't changed since I've known her as Cassidy.

"Penny for your thoughts?" Her voice cuts through the air, and I pop my eyes back open.

"Too much," I admit with a sigh.

She pulls the covers back and slips in beside me, cuddling into my side.

"Better to rip the Band-Aid right off. Or at least that's what my mom always said."

I lift an eyebrow, huffing, as I turn my gaze to the ceiling.

"She probably makes a good point." I inhale deeply, giving myself a couple of moments to gather my thoughts before turning to face her again.

Our eyes lock. And I hold her stare.

Her face looks pale, and she worries her bottom lip. It's as if she's afraid to have this conversation. But there's no reason to be frightened. I've already forgiven her.

I lean forward and plant my lips on hers, hoping to ease her unease.

"No need to bite that lip," I say, offering a small smile.

"You okay?" she says as I pull back, putting a little space between us.

"Yes. Everything is fine."

She chews on her cheek, searching my face. "So you're not mad at me?"

I clear my throat, looking down at her naked body. "I'm pretty sure I already proved that."

She smiles, cheeks staining a pretty shade of pink as I stare at her body unabashedly.

"Well, some people like angry sex. I thought maybe…"

"No," I say, shaking my head. "True. But no, Cass. I'm not angry and if I was, I wouldn't have used you like that."

She nods.

"You…haven't called me Pip," she says, biting on her cheek again.

She noticed that.

"It's because I'm still coming to terms with it, but in truth, I'm not sure you'll ever be Pip again."

Her face falls at that, and I feel like a bastard for how the words came out. I didn't mean it like that. "You misunderstand," I say, pulling her toward me.

"So explain it to me. Please," she whispers that last part.

"You're so much more than that. Pip is the little girl I had to leave in order to survive. I don't want you to be her. I want you to be Cass. Because Cass isn't a little girl, she's an incredible woman. A woman who sees me. The man that I've become."

She pivots her body closer to me. "But I'm still that girl. Deep down, I'm still that broken girl you left," she whispers.

Those words break me a little more. The picture my mind conjures of that little girl, sitting by our tree, all alone crying…it damn near breaks my heart in two.

"I'm sorry I left you. You have no idea how sorry I am."

"You thought of me. That's got to mean something." Her voice still sounds broken, and I don't like it.

I shake my head. "It wasn't enough, though. I should've tried harder to keep in touch. To ensure you knew I hadn't forgotten."

"How were you supposed to do that? You were eighteen, and your mom was a monster. Coming home would've set you back. Could've destroyed all you worked for."

Which is the very reason I stayed away. It's why I had to. But there were other ways.

"I could have called. I could have contacted you."

"How?" she asks, placing her hand against my cheek. "You

knew I didn't have a phone. It was hard enough to keep the lights on, let alone pay a phone bill and have food."

"I should have figured out a way." I clear my throat. This conversation is harder than I thought. "Fuck, Cass. You thought I abandoned you…"

She leans her forehead on my shoulder, breathing in deeply.

"I did. But I also believed you had a good reason."

I sigh heavily, shouldering so much guilt.

"At the time, I thought I did, but now, they all feel like pathetic fucking excuses."

The truth is, I fell into a routine. One that I enjoyed. And I pushed my past behind me. Pip included.

"So tell me about what you were doing. Where did you go?" Her voice is full of curiosity. There's nothing bitter about it.

My eyes glance up to the ceiling before looking back down.

"The day I left, I hopped on a bus. As I told you, there was a tryout. I impressed the coach, and it basically changed my life. What you did allowed for everything that came after boarding that bus, Cassidy."

She smiles wide. "That's all I wanted for you."

I huff a laugh. "I won't lie and say it was easy. I needed money in a bad way, so when I wasn't playing, I was working. A lot."

She bobs her head. "What did you do? I wanna know everything."

I place a kiss on her cheek and tell her everything she wants to know.

"My options were really limited. With no formal education beyond high school, and with the fact that I couldn't work during the day, it was tough. I took a job working nights stocking shelves at the local grocery store. I worked from midnight until six o'clock. Some days, I had to go straight to practice from the store. It was brutal."

"Shit," she says. "I can't imagine."

"Yeah, it sucked there for a bit," I admit. "But I couldn't

complain. I was getting a chance that few kids in my position would ever have at their fingertips."

She tsks. "When did you sleep?"

"I didn't. When I tried, it was wherever I could lay my head."

"Aiden. Are you serious?" Her voice is full of distress. Her eyes wide with shock.

"I'd crash after practice, sleep a few hours, eat, and then work. If I was lucky, I'd get to shower after practice. That was my life for two years. It's not that I wanted to disappear…"

"You just couldn't do both. You had hockey. If you wanted to play, you had to prioritize."

I swallow because it's not lost on me that I'm about to admit that yeah, Pip was not my priority. But I can't lie to her. I won't.

"Yeah."

"You had to choose—" she says, but I cut her off.

"I shouldn't have."

She shrugs. "But you had to. I understand. It's not easy to hear, but I understand, Aiden." She blows a breath through her teeth. "What happened next?"

"I got into college. I got accepted to play on the hockey team, and after that, I was in deep. I saw my goals were closer than they had ever been, and I just couldn't mentally go back to that place. I had to look forward. To stay on track."

"I understand."

I know she means that, and I appreciate how supportive she's being, but it doesn't make me feel any less of a shit. I chose my happiness over ensuring she was okay, and that makes me the world's biggest dick.

"You had to be focused. You couldn't risk it," she says, making more excuses for me.

"It was selfish. I should have—"

"Stop. You did what you had to do. I probably would have done the same thing if I was presented with that opportunity. We had to do what was best for our survival back then, Aiden."

"No, you wouldn't. Because that's not you, Cass. Never have been, never will be. You gave your last dollar to me so that I could chase my dream. That could've been the difference between you eating or not for a week."

"You don't know that."

She looks away, looking uncomfortable, and that makes my stomach drop. How close to an accurate picture did I just describe? I can't think about it because it will make me rage.

"You're a good person," I say, placing my hand under her chin and turning it so that she's looking at me.

She furrows her brow, a look passing over her features that I can't decipher, but it's quickly gone. "What?" I ask, confused by the expression on her face.

"Nothing. I was just thinking about what I would have done if you'd called. What I would've said." She smiles, a closed-lip bullshit smile.

She's lying. But right now, I don't want to ask. I can't risk ruining this moment because I know one thing for sure.

I don't want to ruin this. Not now.

Not ever.

I'm falling for Cassidy. If I haven't already fallen.

chapter forty

Cassidy

IF HE ONLY KNEW.

He thinks I'm a good person. But I know the truth.

My hand reaches beneath the blanket, and despite the fact that I shouldn't, I can't help but touch the scar that lies there on my arm near the juncture of my wrist.

Blood. So much blood.

I have to stop the bleeding.

It pools on my skin, but it won't cease.

I rip my shirt above my head, tying it around the wound, praying it will help.

Something tells me it won't.

This pain will never go away.

The one that holds my secrets. One of many scars, but this one is the only one you can see with the naked eye.

How fitting that it would be the one to brand me for a lifetime.

I'm not sure what to say about what he just told me. I never knew why he stayed away. I had my suspicions, but it turns out that none of them were true. They were little lies the broken girl inside me whispered to keep me rooted. To keep me beholden to my circumstances.

That broken girl didn't want me to see that I deserved so much more. That I too was capable of escape.

Now I know Aiden's reasons, and it helps me to understand a little better why he did what he did.

It doesn't erase the pain I felt. The hurt of feeling like I wasn't enough.

The truth is, nothing will take away that pain, but it will help me heal. Will help dull it over time.

The process started when I first saw him again, and every day, it gets better. After this conversation, it will only happen quicker. I needed to have this talk.

We can't get back all the years lost. All the time lost to the lie hurts.

In life, there are crossroads, and you can never know where they will lead you, but I do know that I had to do what I did, and so did he. It's a truth I can live with.

It doesn't erase the past and everything that came after and between this moment. And that's the part that haunts me now.

My mind shifts back to how I lied to him about who I truly was. Because I was afraid. Because I didn't want him to send me away.

If only I could go back, maybe I could have changed something. Maybe things could have been different. Maybe I never would have had to—

"Why are you crying?" The rough pad of his finger touches my skin and brings me back to the present. That's when I realize a tear has slipped down my cheek. One he's collected on the tip of his finger. He tilts his head toward me. "What's going on in that beautiful head of yours?"

A sob bursts through my chest, unbidden. "I'm a horrible person."

His eyes go wide, and his mouth drops open. "You aren't." He says it with so much conviction that a girl who hasn't done the things that I have might believe him. I don't. I know better.

"You wouldn't know." My voice quivers as I think back on my past.

He sits up, bringing me with him. He's staring into my eyes, trying to convey that he means what he says.

"Not true, Cass. Despite everything, I know you."

Another tear falls. This time, he doesn't wipe it away. It collects on my lips, and he moves quickly, crossing the small space and placing his mouth on mine, tasting my sadness. A sob catches, and I shudder against him.

When he pulls back, he inclines his chin, asking what's going on without words.

"It feels like I'm being ripped in two sometimes. Like I don't know who I am. I should have told you the moment I walked into your suite." My head shakes, and a puff of air bursts from my lips. "I should have told you it was me."

Aiden is silent, his jaw tight and brow furrowed. What's he thinking? If only I had a way of being in his head and being able to read his thoughts. Too bad I can't.

"I was scared," I say quickly, filling the silence.

He still hasn't spoken, and the silence haunts me.

All the memories, our memories, the past month, every single minute I've spent with him, play out in my head as I wait for him to say something. Anything.

I know we just had sex, and he said he's not mad, but now I'm scared. I'm afraid that despite his kisses and touches, despite his words, it's all going to crash around me. I'm worried that right now he's second-guessing his feelings.

My heart hammers in my chest, and I close my eyes.

I can't lose him.

The rational part of my brain tells me I won't, that he already forgave me. It was in the way he kissed me today. The way he's held me. Still, we can't always be rational. Sometimes those intrusive thoughts can't help but form.

"I just wanted—" I start, but my words die in my throat. "If you knew. If I told you, would you have—"

"No."

My eyes open at that. Knowing that everything is based on a lie and the only reason I'm here is that lie. It hurts, because a part of me thought that if I was honest, maybe he would have seen me as more than Pip.

"You had to do it. I'm happy you did," he says, shocking the hell out of me.

My mouth drops open, and then I quickly close it. "Wait. What?"

"I know why you did it now. You didn't come to my suite to trick me. Things just got out of hand. I was expecting someone else and really didn't give you ample time to process anything." He huffs a humorless laugh. "I didn't remember you. I'm sure your mind was in a million places, all the while I was shoving NDAs in your face." His head falls back on a groan. "I understand how things could've moved really quickly, and after…the ship had sailed."

I nod because he's painting a pretty accurate picture of how the night went.

"I could have told you afterward. But…" My words trail off as I try to figure out how to say this. "That night, with the sorting, old habits just kicked in. I wanted to help." I shrug. "The more time that went by, the more I wanted to be with you. To continue to help you, and there was no way you would have let me if I was Pip."

He chews on his cheek, breathing in deeply and blowing it out through his nose.

"You're right, I would never have let you put your life on hold for me because you deserve to live, Cassidy. You deserve to chase your dreams."

I huff out a humorless laugh. "There weren't many to chase, Aiden. And like I said, I wanted to be here with you."

He shakes his head, mumbling something, but finally looks up and holds my stare. "If I knew the truth, I'd never have let you do any of this. I would've sent you away."

My face falls, but I don't turn away from him. I refuse.

"The thing is, I'm glad I didn't know, because things changed. I got to know Cassidy. I got to know *you*. And I don't regret any of it. I don't want to change any of it."

We both move, coming together, lips sealing together. It's a long kiss. A passionate one. But it doesn't last long before Aiden pulls away, leaving me practically panting.

"Talk and then…" Aiden leaves the possibilities dangling on a mischievous grin.

We both go quiet for several moments. The air feels heavy with all the truths we've both exposed. I'm raw from my confessions.

"Tell me about what I missed," Aiden says, breaking the silence.

"Oh jeez. No." I try to laugh, but the truth is, I never want to think about my time in the trailer after Aiden left again.

It's a miracle I've made it this far with all the shit I had to endure in my teens.

My father alone. Not to mention—

"Cass." Hearing my name has me pulling out of the dark thoughts that threaten to send me back to a horrible place.

"Yeah." The word slips out as a whisper.

"Come here." He pulls me close, back into his body, until I can rest my head on his chest.

I love being in this position. Love hearing and feeling his heartbeat. Knowing he's here and safe.

Peace washes over me. Like I've found home. Because that's what Aiden is to me. Home. He always has been since that first day I saw him.

"I want to know what I missed," he says into my hair.

"You mean how I paid the bills? Fed my dad?"

His shoulders stiffen, and his entire body goes rigid. I'm afraid I've ruined the moment when he relaxes and says, "If that's what you want to tell me."

I pull away, gaze locked on his chest. "I don't. My time back then…" I shake my head, trying to push away the errant thoughts running through my mind. "It's in the past. I lived. I made it out." I look up and into his eyes. "I don't want to go back there."

His eyes search mine, and I wonder what he thinks he'll find.

"I missed so much, and if you want to talk—"

"I don't. Not about that." I clear my throat, trying to calm my nerves. "I'll tell you anything you want, but just not about when you left."

If my words affect him, it's hard to tell. His features are frozen, no emotions play on his face, but the thing is, I know Aiden. He needs to process.

"If that's what you want."

It's all he says, and I nod.

Right now, he's processing what I just said. Or what I didn't say. But soon his silence won't be enough for him. My insistence that I don't want to talk about it won't be enough. He'll want to know the truth, my truth. And God help me when he does.

chapter forty-one

Aiden

FOR THE FIRST TIME IN MONTHS, SCRATCH THAT—*YEARS*—I wake, and I'm not instantly attacked with things I need to do.

It's a soft hum in my brain that I need to get up and start my list, but instead of jumping up and rushing into things, I look over at the clock. It's nine in the morning.

No. Not nine, it's nine twenty.

I almost want to laugh. How the fuck did I manage to sleep this late?

I give in to the urge and laugh because I don't know the last time this happened.

The last time I woke this late, let alone did so on a time that wasn't an odd number. It's coded into my brain, and despite everything, my body just knows.

Except for today.

Last night, I forgot to turn my phone back on. I turned it off when Cass and I were talking, but the compulsion to turn it back on was lost somewhere between our intense discussion and worshipping her body.

Apparently, even my mind can agree that being with Cassidy is better than lists and rituals.

"What's got you laughing over there?" she says from beside me, and I turn toward her.

She looks cute when she's half asleep. Her hand thrown over her head, hair fanning across the pillow.

"Nothing. Go back to sleep."

"Can't now," she says, lifting to a seated position. "Once I'm up, I'm up." Her head swivels around, eyes half closed. "What time is it?"

"Past nine."

"Holy shit. We slept until nine? *You* slept until nine?" she corrects, because Lord knows, Cass doesn't have my fixation with waking at a specific time.

She, of course, abides by my schedule, but when she's not micromanaging me, she definitely doesn't live a rigid life.

She never did.

And it feels comforting that she too hasn't changed all that much from the girl who once was my best friend.

Now she's more, and I like it that way.

"Hence why I laughed," I say, shrugging one shoulder.

She pulls her hand away from her face, and I'm met with wide eyes and a puzzled look.

"Are you okay?" She reaches out and touches my forehead. "Are you sick?"

I chuckle, playfully slapping her hand, before grabbing and bringing her dainty hand to my lips, placing a kiss there. "No, Cass. Just happy."

With that, she rewards me with an earth-shattering smile. One that I swear lights up the room.

"What do you have planned today?" I ask, wanting to know all her plans.

"Whatever you need me to do, but other than that, nothing. I'm free," she says, smiling.

Luckily, we have no game today. There's no practice either. Coach has a lot on his plate with all the drama that went down. But I do have an idea. There's only one place I want to go, and I want her to come with me.

"I want to take you somewhere."

She lifts a brow. "Cryptic much?"

"You know me." I wink, stifling a laugh.

This girl lights me up. Makes me want to smile nonstop.

"Well, I need some information. What do I need to wear? When are we going? That kind of stuff." She lifts both hands, moving them like a scale.

"Casual." I purse my lips, trying to think about what a girl would wear. "Warm, though. Bring a sweater. Even if the weather outside is nice."

She licks her lips. "Interesting."

I jump forward, tackling her softly back to the bed. Her screech turns to giggling, and I realize it's a sound I never want to go away. I place a kiss on her lips. "Let's grab a bite to eat and then head out. An hour works?"

She smiles up at me, her bright eyes shining in the sunlight. "Works for me. I'm low maintenance."

"One of the things I love about you." As soon as I say the words, her eyes go wide, but she quickly recovers and jumps out of bed.

"I'll make it fast," she says, voice a bit shaky.

Fuck.

What a dumbass thing to say. It's too damn soon to be offering proclamations of love. The truth is, I do love Pip. Always have.

But I'm not sure I'm *in love* with Cassidy, but I'm definitely heading in that direction.

I can tell this thing between us is special, and who knows what that will lead to? Maybe love. But I'm not ready to put a name on it yet, it's still too new.

I hear the water running as I head toward the kitchen to start the coffee.

I dive right into cooking, making us both eggs and toast. A quick breakfast before we head out. I take the chance to meticulously clean the kitchen while the food cooks. When I hear the sound of her footsteps, the food is plated and ready to go.

The best part? You would never know I cooked. Nothing is out of place. Everything is in its correct position.

I might have overslept, but I'm obviously still *me*.

Not that I thought I could change overnight, but Cassidy's presence in my life has definitely helped with some of my smaller quirks.

Rome wasn't built in a day after all.

But for her, I'd like to change. Be the man she needs, not the one who left, and if conquering my shit is the means to being that changed man, so be it. I'll do whatever is possible.

After the playoffs are done, and hopefully, I have a championship under my belt, I'll look into it. Find the right person to help me.

"This looks delicious," she says, biting her bottom lip.

"Sit," I say. "We only have a little time left."

Cassidy sits beside me, and we both dive in to eat.

We keep the conversation light, and before long, we finished.

Cass does her best to help me clean, and I try my hardest to humor her, letting her help me until she excuses herself to get dressed. When she does, I go over the counters again, until they are the way I like it, and then I head to shower.

Once I'm dressed, I find her in the kitchen waiting for me.

"Ready?" I ask.

"Sure am," she responds, a hoodie hanging over her arm.

Together we head out of the apartment, down the elevator, and then out into the street in comfortable silence, both just happy to be next to each other.

Downtown Redville is quiet on Sunday mornings; most of

the city is locked away in their homes, enjoying a peaceful end to the weekend.

"We're going to walk. Are you good with that?" I ask.

She nods. "I could use the fresh air."

I take her hand in mine and lead her in the direction of our destination. I'm nervous about this. I've never cared what anyone thought of the things that are important to me, but this is Cass—Pip—and I care so fucking much.

"So…any hints?" she asks, and I clear my throat, pulling myself out of the doubts that are creeping in.

"No."

I peek over at her, and she's chewing on that lip.

"Stop that. You're going to make it bleed," I say playfully.

She purses her lip and narrows her eyes up at me. "You are not funny."

"I'm plenty fun."

"Nope." She shakes her head.

"You weren't saying that last night," I tease, and she stops short, scrunching her nose. She's about to fire off a witty rebuttal, but I lean down and kiss her.

Something I'd never thought to do in public before reconnecting with her.

When she sighs into my arms, I laugh against her lips and then pull back. "Only a few more blocks."

The sunlight beams down on us. Cass wears a pair of sweats with a T-shirt, but in her arms, she carries a hoodie, something she will need shortly.

A block later, I stop, motioning toward where we are.

She looks up, recognizing the bench where she found me yesterday. The confusion is evident on her face. "Back to the bench?" she asks comically.

"Nope." I point toward the building a few feet past the bench. "In there."

Her head tilts. "And what's in there?"

"You'll see." I grab her hand and pull her toward the building.

"Okay. Fine." She rolls her eyes. "Let's get to it, then."

Together, holding hands, I lead her into the Redville youth center. Then I walk us down the long hallway until we enter the ice rink.

The moment we step inside, the cold air hits us in the face, and Cass shivers beside me.

"Happy I told you to bring a sweater?"

"Yep." She pops the p as she drops my hand and puts on her hoodie for an added layer.

Once she's done, I lead her down to the rink, where we head to the benches next to the ice.

I wave to Coach Joseph, who returns the gesture, turning toward the team and saying something we can't hear. A moment later, a bunch of kids skate toward us.

"What is this?" she asks, turning toward me with a huge smile.

"This, Cass, is the youth league I sponsor."

"Really? This is awesome, Aiden."

She hasn't seen one of the most special parts of it, but then one of my players turns, and she sees the team's name.

The Pipsqueaks.

chapter forty-two

Cassidy

MY HEART BEATS IN MY CHEST LIKE A DRUM AS I TAKE IN THE
words written on the back of the boys skating in front of me.

The Pipsqueaks.

It feels like I might faint. My mouth opens and shuts, and I
turn to look at Aiden.

He has a mischievous-looking smile on his face, like he knew
this would be my reaction, waited for it, and by the way he's smiling, he loves it.

I stare at him for another second, trying to find the words I
want to use, but I'm speechless. Nothing comes out at first. I just
stare.

"Not what you expected, right?" His voice is teasing, and it
makes me close my lips before a laugh comes bubbling out.

"No. Not at all." I turn to look back at the little kids. They appear to be around four or five years old, if I had to make a guess.
"Why are they called the Pipsqueaks?" I ask, my voice low.

My brain screams it's a coincidence, yet my heart says there are no coincidences. That the name has to do with me.

Aiden moves closer to me, and when he's standing right beside me, he places his hand on my face.

I lean in closer, loving the way he touches me. The way he can always calm my racing heart.

"I thought it would be obvious. For you," he answers, and a kaleidoscope of butterflies instantly takes flight in my belly.

I knew it. I just needed him to say it. To make this all real. To prove that I'm not lost in a dream.

"I sponsor the team. I actually sponsor the whole rink, teams, and all. All of the kids here wouldn't be able to afford the lessons, gear, etc.…."

"You do all of that?" I say, voice full of awe.

"I do."

I take a deep breath, processing everything that Aiden has done in the years since we've been separated. Just how much of me he's integrated into his life.

It's endearing. Heartwarming.

It makes all those doubts and feelings of betrayal feel so ridiculous. While he might not have come back, he never forgot, and that means everything to me.

"How old are the players?" I ask, trying to keep the emotion out of my voice.

"This group is my five-year-olds, but I help kids all the way through high school."

Tears well in my eyes, and I quickly turn away from Aiden so he doesn't see.

He's helping kids like him. Kids who don't have an outlet, and he's giving it to them.

"I'm giving them a chance. The same chance you gave me," he says.

My vision goes spotty again, the unshed tears threatening to fall.

"How did I not know that?" I whisper more to myself than to him. With all the time we've spent together, I should have seen something. Some papers.

But this whole thing comes as a huge shock to me. I feel like I've been sitting in the dark, and the light just turned on.

"For the same reason people don't know anything about me, I'm a private person."

I nod, turning back to face him. "Yeah, I know that, but wouldn't I have known since I work for you?"

"I don't announce my involvement. Sure, I volunteer in the off-season to help them learn to be better players, but I don't take credit for funding it."

"Why not? It's amazing what you're doing."

"I don't do this for the accolades. I do it for them. For these kids, who by no fault of their own would never be able to play hockey without help."

I blink, taking in a deep breath. He doesn't want to draw attention to their situations.

"I understand. It's the same reason I want to be a social worker."

He nods in confirmation and understanding. "To help the kids like us."

"It's amazing, Aiden." I look around. "Truly."

His lips part into an earth-shattering smile.

"Come on, let's go meet the team named after you."

It's my turn to smile wide.

His hand reaches out and takes mine, and then he leads us down to where the ice meets the concrete.

"Hey, Slate!" A small group of boys scream as they skate closer to where we are. "You playing with us today?"

"No, bud. Can't do today." One of the little boys pouts at his words. "But I have someone I want you all to meet. This is Cassidy. My girlfriend."

I think my heart explodes with the reference. In the past, when he's referred to me as such, it's always left a bad taste in my mouth. The lies made me feel like I was choking on it.

But now, in the fresh light of the day, and the fact that he now knows I'm Pip, I feel elated at the moniker. Today, it feels like anything is possible. Like this isn't some sham. He chooses me. Cassidy.

"And what's your name?"

"I'm Sam," the little boy responds, holding up his hand.

"It's nice to meet you, Sam."

One by one, each child comes over and introduces themselves to me, and then when there are no kids left, Aiden orders them to do drills.

I can't help but laugh when he does. He's such a natural coach. Yes, he's controlling, but his voice is so filled with love and serenity that the kids thrive under his guidance.

He's exactly the person he needed all those years ago.

He didn't have that. Sure, eventually he had the coach that pushed him, but by then he was a teen.

At this age, Aiden had to teach himself how to skate.

He had no one.

What he's giving these kids is priceless.

And if my heart wasn't filled with love already for this wonderfully complicated man, it's now bubbling over.

I watch as the kids skate, leaving Aiden to talk to an older man, maybe in his late fifties.

These little kids are naturals, skating with ease. More importantly, you can tell they love the game. Live for it.

Just like Aiden.

Finally, I pull my eyes away from the game and find Aiden and the man making their way toward me.

"Cass, I want you to meet Coach Joseph. Joe, this is my girl, Cassidy."

"Nice to meet you," I say, extending my hand so we can shake.

"Nice to meet you too. Happy to see Slate happy." His words

are filled with fatherly love. Like he genuinely cares for Aiden. I immediately like the man.

"How long has this facility been open?" I ask, trying to make conversation.

The coach's eyes widen, and Aiden inclines his head down. "I told Cass my involvement."

He looks over at me and then back at Aiden. "I can speak freely?"

Aiden nods and says, "Yep."

"That's a change." The older man grins, turning back toward me. "The ice rink and youth group have been around for the last six years. Give or take."

I mentally do the math. Like my deposits, Aiden started this shortly after being drafted to the Saints.

"It's amazing." I turn to face Aiden. "You're amazing." I mouth, only for him to see.

"It's the least I could do," Aiden says, shrugging. "These kids will do great things one day."

"Don't sell yourself short," Coach Joseph tells him, before turning to me. "We have multiple age groups here practicing, running drills, but it's more than that. We give these kids everything they need for the best chance to succeed. Skates. Equipment. Lessons."

"You give them the best shot at a happy life," I say, understanding wholeheartedly what happens here.

The coach nods. "It was great meeting you, Cassidy. I gotta get back to it."

"Nice to meet you, Coach." I smile and listen to his goodbye to Slate before he pats him on the back proudly and skates off to help the kids.

I chuckle, unable to keep the happiness from bubbling over. "You're really amazing."

"Just trying to pay back my investment." He winks, and I melt—that single action is so sexy.

My stomach flips in the best way possible, and the need to get him out of this place and back in bed is too intense.

"You did that and so much more," I say.

"It's the least I could do." He looks around, and I can see how proud he is.

"Coach Joseph is right. Don't sell yourself short, Aiden. This," I say, motioning around. "All of this. It must cost a fortune. Not many would do that."

"There's only so much money I need to live off; the rest, it goes to give these kids a chance."

I throw my arms around him at that, kissing his lips. I hear the giggles as I do, but I don't care.

I love this man.

chapter forty-three

Aiden

Tonight, I'm back in Tampa for game five against the Bulldogs. If we win this round, we advance to round three of the playoffs.

That puts only two teams standing between us and the Cup.

The atmosphere in the locker room is always intense, but today, even more so. Everyone focuses on getting ready for the game. Getting their head into the right headspace to dominate.

It's what I've been doing since I arrived at the rink.

I have a different method from the rest of them. Always have and they've always respected it.

My teammates are all in a huddle, laughing and joking around as they get ready.

I'm in my private space, just out of sight, slowly working through my pre-game rituals of taping my hand, righting my socks, and mentally preparing myself.

Knowing Cass sits in the stands ready to watch me makes today feel different.

Sure, I've played in front of her before, but this feels different. Probably because it's really official that we're actually a couple.

We're dating.

We might not have said as much, but that's what this is. I want to be with her, and she wants to be with me. And this will be the first time she's watched me since.

I take a deep breath and try to steady my nerves, finishing the last of my stuff before joining my team.

Coach steps forward, coughing once to get our attention. We all know better than to have him do it a second time.

"Don't lose this one, boys."

That's it. That's the talk, and I can't help but roll my eyes before laughing.

Coach typically has plenty to say. There have been times we've been pushing the clock, almost late, because of his long-winded speeches. Today, he keeps it short and sweet, and I can't say I'm not happy about it.

After his less-than-serious pep talk, everyone heads out of the locker room, and I trail them.

The last one.

I can hear the screams of the crowd.

My heart beats out of my chest, adrenaline pumping through my veins as I glide onto the ice.

I skate to the center and look toward the stands. Knowing the general vicinity of where she'll be, it doesn't take long to spot her. Cassidy's head is tilted back on a laugh, clearly finding something the person next to her has said funny. She's fucking gorgeous.

My eyes trail down her body and stop on her chest. She's wearing my jersey, and my cock goes rigid in my pants at the sight. How the hell does something so simple have this much of a reaction on me?

Fuck.

With her hair thrown up into a bun, she's a wet dream.

I shake my head. Not the time for this.

I'm standing on the ice, waiting for the game to begin. *Get your head on straight, Slate.*

Focusing my attention forward, I wait for the game to begin. My heart pounds with anticipation as the people in the stands stomp and make noise. Then it happens. The moment I'm waiting for. The puck drops, and I explode forward, my skates cutting into the ice with precision.

This is what I love.

The thrill of the game.

Controlling the puck.

The cold air rushes past my face as I push my body to its limits, racing toward the opposing team's goal.

Time passes, plays attempted, but finally sixteen minutes into the second period, I get my opening.

Surveying the ice, I analyze the best path to the goal.

My gaze drifts out toward the opposing defenseman moving to block me.

He's searching for my weakness, and I'm searching for his.

That's when I see it.

It's crystal clear what I need to do.

I spot a small gap, a sliver of opportunity, and with a burst of speed, I dart toward it, leaving the defenders in my wake.

The crowd goes crazy as I break away, careening toward the goal, weaving between the opposing team. My stick works the puck until I'm almost there.

The roar of the crowd builds with every move I make. Adrenaline surges through me.

I take my shot.

Goal.

The crowd erupts, but I only have eyes for Cass as I search for her up in the stands again.

No matter the mayhem around her, she stands out among

the throng of people. She's standing, waving her arms in the air, going crazy, celebrating me.

———•◦•———

As the horn echoes through the arena, it's official—we won.

Spent and exhausted, I head to the locker room.

Before long, I've completed my end game rituals, my hair wet from the ice water dunk, and I'm dressed and ready to go home.

Since this is an away game, I won't see Cass until we're both back home, but that won't do. I need to see her.

I grab my phone and shoot her a text.

Me: Head to the hall outside the locker room.

Cass: Already here. Waiting.

Her words make me smile. Of course, she is. She always anticipates my needs.

Good thing too, because I want to at least say goodbye before I get on the plane with my team to head back to Redville tonight.

I take one step outside the locker room, and I see her standing there waiting for me.

Gorgeous.

Fucking stunning.

And in my jersey.

Fuck.

My dick is rock hard as I take her in.

I turn to Coach, standing next to Hudson. "Coach, I need to take care of something. I'll be fifteen minutes."

"You've got five," he responds as he walks toward the bus.

Hudson looks over from me to Cass and laughs. "Bro, you better hurry. Not sure you've got time before Coach castrates you." He shakes his head, walking away.

"Fuck off," I say to his back as I grab Cass's hand and start pulling her in the opposite direction.

"Umm. Hi to you, too." She giggles, allowing me to drag her off.

"No time for hello," I say as I find the door to the storage closet and fling it open.

The moment we're inside, I slam the door shut, and we are bathed in darkness.

"Take your pants off," I command. I can barely see her, but I can hear her intake of breath.

"What?"

"You heard me. Pants. Off. Now. I need to fuck you in my jersey."

She scrambles beside me, and by the time she's stepping out of them, my eyes have adjusted to the dim lighting coming in from under the door.

The jersey is short enough that I can see the outline of her pussy. "Where's the light in this place? I want to see what's mine." I reach behind me and find the switch.

As soon as it's on, I get exactly what I want. A clear shot of her glistening skin. "Fuck. I want to taste you so badly, but I don't have time. This is going to be fast, Cass. But, fuck, I need to be inside you now," I rasp.

"Think this is a good idea?" She laughs, but it's strained. I can tell she wants this just as bad.

"This is the best idea I've ever had. Now, be a good girl, and be really quiet. I need you to turn around. Hands on the shelf."

She follows my orders and gets into the position I told her to. Once her hips are tilted back, I step up behind her and run the pad of my fingers over her hips to caress her skin.

At the move, she presses her rear back against me.

With my free hand, I lower the zipper of my jeans and pull my cock out.

In the background, I can hear the team laughing. But I don't have time to think about that before I'm stroking myself from root to tip and getting in position.

As I run myself against her, she lets out a moan. "Not another sound."

I position my hard length, pressing against her core, and she quivers against me, her body trembling with want.

It's then and only then that I finally push inside her.

My mouth latches onto the back of her neck as I pull out and thrust back in.

Her back arches up to meet each of my strokes as I take her from behind.

I know I need to be fast, but I slow my pace. The feeling is too sublime to rush it, despite Coach's threat.

Time stretches slowly as I leisurely retract from her greedy pussy. I pull myself out so only the crown is inside her. I hover for a second, her soft moans begging me to fuck her.

Someone calls my name, and I groan, knowing I'm pushing my luck.

Fuck it.

I slam back in, picking up my pace, fucking her brutally against the shelf.

She mewls. "Cass," I growl. "Quiet."

I pull her closer until there's no end and no beginning to where our bodies meet.

It isn't long before her walls shudder around me, and I follow her over the edge. I plunge deep inside her until I'm flooding her with my cum. We're both breathing raggedly.

"Wow," she breathes out, and I laugh against her neck as I pull my still hard cock out.

"Wow is right." We both right ourselves, her placing her pants back on, me putting my cock away.

"Listen, I'm going to open this door and leave. You stay in here until you can't hear our voices anymore."

She nods.

I'm sure the idiots on the other side know exactly what went down, but I don't want to embarrass her like that. I can play it cool on the bus and insist we were talking. If they see her, hair wild and face flushed from what we just did, there will be no denying it. And while I don't care, I suspect maybe Cass would.

I place a small kiss on her cheek, and I turn to leave. I open the door and step out of the closet before I turn to her. "See you in Ohio, babe." I wink and head out to meet the team.

chapter forty-four

Cassidy

NOW THAT THEY HAVE MOVED ON TO ROUND THREE, AIDEN has some time off before his next game.

Tonight, I've planned a lazy night for us. Something that isn't easy for Aiden.

I kept it simple with dinner and a movie, hoping that it would stay close enough to his typical routine, that the promise of relaxation isn't an impossibility.

I'm sitting next to Aiden on the couch, and he has Netflix fired up, tasked with finding us something to watch. He's shifting through old movies, and I about squeal when he lands on *The Goonies*. It's one of my favorites, and I can't help but smile. He doesn't know the significance this movie has for me, but still… what are the odds that he'd stop on that one?

It's a sign from my mom.

Her way of telling me that she's happy for me. For us. That I'm on the right track. At least, that's how I like to look at it.

"Let's watch that," I say, clapping my hands together.

"*The Goonies*? You like this one?"

I bob my head and smile. "It was my mom's favorite," I tell him. "I haven't seen it in so long."

He clicks the button but doesn't start the movie, sitting quietly next to me, looking lost in thought.

I turn to face him, and his expression turns serious. I tilt my head to the side. "What's wrong?"

"You know, you never really talk about her. Not now and barely back then. Other than her love for Jeeps, nothing."

I raise a brow. "As if you ever talk about yours," I challenge, knowing there is no comparison. We don't talk about our parents for different reasons. At least where my mom's concerned.

"It's different. I have no good memories with mine. But you... and your mom...that's different. From what I gathered back then, she was a good mom. You loved her."

I nod at his statement. "She was." Closing my eyes, I remember her, the way she used to smile down at me. How she'd sweep me into a hug that felt warm and perfect. A single hug from her could turn around a bad day. The love she had for me is what carried me through on the worst of days. I knew she was looking down on me with all the love in her heart, doing what she could to keep me safe.

She was warm and caring. So completely opposite of my dad.

"She taught me to love."

Opening my eyes, I reach up and swipe a lone tear that fell.

He offers me a sad smile. "She must have been amazing."

My lips remain pressed together, but I smile. "She was." I huff, motioning toward the TV. "We used to watch old movies together all the time. It was our thing." I shrug because I really didn't want tonight to turn into me crying. Yet here we are.

"I remember you always liked them. Movies," he clarifies.

"Still do. They remind me of her." I smile, taking a cleansing breath. "She was my best friend. And then she was gone."

He nods. "Cancer, right?"

"You remember." I hold his stare, another tear building.

"I remember everything about you, Cass. Every word you ever told me as Pip…I remember."

He looks at me intently, and I wonder what's going through that head of his. Is he thinking the same crazy thoughts going through mine?

What are we doing here?

Is this more?

Do we have a future?

Do I want a future?

I do. I want nothing more than forever with him, but I'm too scared to say that. To admit it out loud. Because if he doesn't feel the same way, it might break me in two.

It was one thing to work for him, then to sleep with him, but now I want forever, and I'm not sure he does.

"Same," I say, hoping he can feel the truth in those words while simultaneously trying to get myself back on solid ground.

I lift my hand to run it through my hair, combing my fingers through the strands, and then place my arm down. My eyes catch on my sleeve, seeing that it's rolled up.

Aiden's hand reaches out, and he takes my wrist in his hold.

The rough pads of his fingers draw a circle over my scar. "What's that from, Cass?"

I try to pull my wrist away, but he won't let me. "It's nothing."

Aiden shakes his head. "It's not nothing. That wasn't there when I was with you at the trailer park."

I rack my brain for something to say, something close to the truth. "I fell," I finally say. Not a lie. But also, not the whole truth.

"Bullshit. This isn't a simple cut. This is a deep one. Deep enough to leave a scar."

"I said it's nothing." I turn away, pulling my arm from his hold, not wanting him to see through me. To expose my secret. That's the one thing I don't want him to know. Ever.

"Come on. Pip. Talk to me."

My head snaps toward him, and for a reason I can't quite place, I crack.

"Oh, now I'm Pip? This whole time, I've been Cass. But now what…" I cross my arms over my chest. I stand, pacing the floor.

I know I'm lashing out, but I can't stop myself. "Everyone has secrets. Even you," I accuse, and his head jerks back.

"So something did happen," he says through his teeth.

"That's not what I said."

But it is.

This is my secret.

A secret I'll carry to my grave.

My heart rate picks up, and suddenly, I feel like I can't breathe. I'm careening headfirst into a panic attack, and I need to stop it. I can't let him see me like this.

If I do, he'll realize there's more to this scar than I'm letting on. He's already onto me.

My own guilt and shame threaten to suffocate me.

Something I can see: My hands, as they twist the cotton of my shirt.

Something I can hear: The soft hum of the dishwasher running in the other room.

Something I can smell: Aiden's woodsy cologne; it makes my mouth water.

When my pulse slows, I take a deep breath and take a seat, looking up at him. Concern lines his face. I move closer. So close that I'm practically on his lap.

"I just don't want to go back there," I admit with a sigh.

His eyes are narrowed in on me. "Let me share your burden."

My head shakes. "I'm not ready." I'll never be ready, but I don't tell him that.

He takes a deep breath and nods. "Promise you'll tell me one day."

I don't want to lie to him, but it's my only chance to turn this night around. To get us back to the easygoing night I had planned.

"Pinky promise on your puck." I wink, trying desperately to be playful.

"I still can't believe you said that while trying to hide your identity." He chuckles, his face relaxing, signaling it worked.

"I think deep down in my subconscious mind, I knew I would never have the balls to tell you the truth, so it took the ball out of my court."

"I think you might be right. But I'm happy it did." He smiles, pulling me toward him.

"Me too." I scoot even closer, but I rise and sit on his lap this time.

My pajama shorts bunch at my thighs.

And then I'm leaning in, placing my lips on his, needing to get to this part of the night.

His mouth meets mine, and we open to each other. Tongues swiping, tasting.

It's divine and exactly what I need to rid myself of the thoughts that threaten to run rampant in my brain.

The longer we kiss, the more heated I get, and it's not long before I'm squirming on his lap, rubbing myself against him.

"Need you," I say against his lips.

He chuckles. "Then have me."

I pull away, looking at him, and then I'm pulling my shorts aside while he's freeing his cock from his sweatpants.

"Put me inside you. Fuck my cock, Cass. Take what you need."

My entire body crackles with need. His dirty words do things to me that threaten to make me come undone.

I move my hips until I feel the head of him at my entrance, and then I'm sinking down.

He lets out a long, primal groan as I fully engulf his cock in my heat.

"So good," I moan as his cock fills me, stretching me to the hilt.

Slowly, I rise back up and then slide back down, impaling myself.

I continue at the same pace.

Up.

Down.

The feeling is amazing.

Looking into his eyes is sublime.

Every time I rise up and slide back down, his eyes darken. He wants to take control of the pace, but he's letting me lead, and my heart warms.

I know how hard this is for him. To give up control.

The closer I get to my orgasm, the faster I move.

His fingers bite into the exposed flesh of my ass as I ride him hard.

My walls quiver around him as I chase my climax.

With one thrust up by Aiden, I find it; careening over the edge, I come so hard, I see stars.

Aiden's eyes close as his fingers grasp onto me, and I feel him jerk inside me. Pulsing as he comes. He falls over the edge, and I ride his cock until every last drop of him has been spent.

Every moment with Aiden is perfect.

I just hope our past never interferes with it.

"You awake?" My eyes flutter open at the sound of Aiden's voice.

The early morning sunlight streaming in through the window, makes me squint at where he's standing beside the bed.

"What time is it?" I groan, not ready to wake up.

"It's ten."

I pop up off my pillow at his words. "Ten? Are you serious? Why did you let me sleep so long?"

His lips tip up into a smirk. "'Cause you looked so cute. Plus, you needed the rest."

He's right. I've been exhausted.

"I did." I stretch my hands over my head, a yawn escaping my mouth. I didn't realize how exhausted I was, basically running on fumes, because of his schedule, but now that I've been able to rest, it hits me like a ton of bricks. "Thank you."

"You're welcome. Now get up."

I roll my eyes. "Jeez, bossy much."

"Yes."

I laugh. He's being ridiculous but also cute and sexy. I love when he gets bossy.

My tongue licks my upper lip.

"Whatever you're thinking over there, stop. We have plans."

Plans? What's he going on about? I furrow my brow. "What plans?"

"It's a surprise."

"Another one?"

The last time he had a surprise, I found out there was a team named after me. Which I loved, so now I'm even more excited to see what he has in store for us.

Kicking the sheets off, I move to stand, but Aiden's hands push me back on the bed until my head rests back on my pillow.

"Hey!" I playfully scold.

Aiden looks down at me, like the cat who got the canary. He's practically salivating at the sight in front of him, namely me, naked on his bed.

"You're insatiable."

"Only for you." He lowers his head, taking my nipple into his mouth.

"Aiden."

"Mmm?" He continues to suck, feasting on me.

"Don't we have to go?"

With a pop, his mouth is no longer on me. I want to groan in protest, but I'm also curious about what we're doing today.

"To be continued…"

This time, when I stand from the bed, Aiden doesn't object, he steps out of the way, and lets me leave the room to get ready.

I'm showered and dressed within twenty minutes; hair blown out too.

I learned at a young age that quick showers are imperative. Especially when the hot water barely works, and there's only enough for a five-minute shower.

Now, years later, I still don't waste the heat.

When I walk into the kitchen, I find Aiden sitting at the countertop of the island. He must hear my footsteps because he pushes the stool back and strides over to me.

"Ready?"

"Yep."

"Good." He leans down and takes my lips with his. I sigh into his mouth. Every time he touches me, it feels like a heavenly dream, one I never want to wake up from.

My eyes close, and I wrap my arm around his neck to deepen the kiss. He laughs against my lips and pulls away, making me whimper. "Now that I've done that, let's go."

"You suck." I playfully stick my tongue out at him.

He laughs at that. "I do. And I promise if you're a good girl today, I'll do just that."

That makes me groan. "Tease."

Now I'm all hot and bothered and being forced to leave. Mean man.

"Okay, enough stalling, though. Let's go."

Aiden reaches his hand out and takes mine in his. Then he leads us out of the apartment and to the elevator.

Within minutes, we're back in his Jeep and driving to God knows where.

It isn't until we're pulling up to a small college that I know where we are. But the question is why.

"What are we doing here?"

Pulling over and into a spot, he throws the car in park. Then he's pivoting in his seat to look at me.

Our gaze locks. A world of emotions plays within his beautiful blue eyes.

Reaching out, he takes my hand in his, lifts it to his mouth, and places a kiss on my knuckles. "You said you wanted to get your master's in social work. Redville University has a great program."

"We're here for me?" My heart hammers in my chest.

"Yeah. I thought we could look around. Speak to admissions."

"You want me to go to school in Redville." My words come out low, almost a whisper. Almost like I'm afraid to voice my question for the fear it might not mean what I hope it means. Does this mean he wants more? That he sees a future here.

I'm scared to hope.

"I do."

If someone had told me when I first started this insane journey with him, that we would be here right now, looking at a school for me, I'd have said they were crazy.

But here we are.

Now the question is, what to do with this?

Is there a future here?

I hope so.

But the truth is, we still have secrets between us.

Secrets that might ruin us.

chapter forty-five

Aiden

T HINGS HAVE BEEN GOOD.

Of course, practice has been as grueling as ever, but what did I expect when we're about to start round three of the playoffs? While in the past we've had a good team, we've never gotten this far.

But we have a shot this year.

Only a few days are left until we head to New York to play the Empires, so as much as I want to spend time with Cass, it's been hard. Today, I asked Coach if we could have an early practice. That way, I can surprise Cassidy with a fun day together.

I never thought I'd be this guy.

The type of guy who changes my hockey schedule for a girl. I've always been so closed off about dating, but I realize now that I wasn't closed off to the idea. It was rather that I had never met anyone I wanted to change for.

With Cassidy, I want to be a better man.

The thought scares the fuck out of me, but it's true nonetheless. I want to put her needs before my own.

Be the man she deserves.

Which is why we're currently in my car, and I'm taking her on a date. "Where are we headed?" she asks from where she's sitting in the passenger seat.

"It's a—"

"Surprise. Yeah. Yeah. I know." A dramatic and playful sigh escapes her mouth.

"If you know it's a surprise, why bother asking?" I make a turn, bringing us closer to our destination.

It's funny how little she's changed all these years. She didn't like surprises then, and she doesn't like them now.

"To be difficult, of course." She laughs, and the sound warms me. Moments like this with her make all the bullshit better.

I continue to drive, and it's only another five minutes before we're pulling up to an amusement park.

It's not a large one, only featuring a few games, a small roller coaster, and a Ferris wheel, but it's still fun.

When I throw the car into park a moment later and look at her, I know I picked the right activity for our date.

Both of us step out of the car, and I make my way to her, grasping her hand in mine and leading us to the entrance.

Once we have the tickets in hand, we start to walk, and I point in the directions for the different activities.

"I love this." I turn to face her, and she looks around with the bright eyes of a woman remembering the first time she ever saw the neon lights. "The way the signs glow. The vibrant colors. The sounds and the laughter. And don't get me started on the smells. I swear I can smell the funnel cake from here." She inhales deeply, most like inhaling the sugar-sweet smell that permeates through the air. "I love this."

"I know."

She furrows her brows at my words. "How?"

"Back in Michigan" —I don't specify when, but by the way her features tighten, I know she knows I'm referring to when she was a kid— "you told me about this carnival you went to and how much you loved it. I remember you saying it was enchanting. Actually, you used the word dazzling, and it made me laugh. Well, this isn't a carnival, but I figured it's basically the same thing."

"I love it. I love the freedom, the fun, the possibilities. It's like anything can happen at a carnival or, in this case, an amusement park." There's almost a sparkle in her eyes, and I'm happy to be the one that put it there.

"Let's go see what trouble we can muster up."

"I never said trouble…"

"You forget I know you, Pip." I wink before leading her past a popcorn stand and toward the games.

We spend the next thirty minutes laughing and playing.

From basketball to shooting ducks, we try our hand at every single one. I win Cassidy a few prices, and in typical Cassidy fashion, she hands off the giant stuffed animals to the kids who lost.

She's something else.

Her need to put everyone first always wins out.

"Where to now?" I ask as we walk away from the ring toss. No matter how hard I try, that's the one game I can never win.

There's no question that it's rigged.

Laughter breaks out beside us, and I pull her in the opposite direction. Together, we look around, walking by each ride. All the lights flash around us. Each attendant tries to lure us to the ride they're monitoring.

When Cassidy sees me looking at the teacups, she shakes her head.

"No way. That will make me sick. How about the Ferris wheel?" she asks, and I nod.

"Anything you want. This is your night, after all."

She stops walking and turns to face me. "Anything?" Her lips tip up into a smirk.

I wrap my arm around her back and drop a kiss down on her head. "Mind out of the gutter."

"Fine. But then you must stop touching me. 'Cause I always have my mind in the gutter when you do."

With one final peck, I drop my arm and point in the direction we need to go.

"Come on," I say, interlocking our hands and letting her pull me toward the ride.

There's a short line. Nothing crazy, which is nice. Cassidy stands beside me as we wait our turn. She looks so happy and at peace.

We both needed a fun night before the crazy starts again.

Who knows how round three will go.

The Empires are a good team. I'll need to keep my head in the game with no distractions if we're going to win.

When it's our turn, we sit beside each other, her body flush with mine. It's almost as if she's sitting on my lap.

It's not like Cass to be clingy, so I wonder what's up but as we start to make our ascent, she doesn't say anything, so I chalk it up to the fact that maybe she doesn't like heights.

It isn't until we're nearing the top that she finally speaks.

"I saw this movie once." Cass bites her lips. "It's called *Fear*."

I pivot my body to see her better, and when our gazes lock, I lift my eyebrow. "I know the movie. Please don't tell me this is another movie that you watched as a kid with your mom."

Her eyes go wide, and it makes me laugh. They look like they might explode from the socket. "Oh my God, no. Jeez. What kind of weirdo do you take me for?"

Inclining my jaw down, I give her a look. "You really want to know the answer to that?"

"Not really." She rolls her eyes. "As I was saying…"

"Yes, please go on. I'd love to hear where this is going. Nowhere good, I assume." I know exactly where this is going, but I can't wait for her to say it.

"Well, since we're on a Ferris wheel, and we're not moving…I was thinking…"

Wouldn't take a rocket scientist to know what scene she's talking about from that movie.

Can't say the idea doesn't have merit, so I'm more than willing to oblige her, but I'm still going to give her shit.

"I know exactly what you're thinking, and *they* were on a roller coaster."

"Same difference," she huffs out, most likely annoyed by my taunting, but she's so damn cute when she's like this, I can't help myself.

"The thing is, I—it's always been a fantasy of mine." She doesn't finish the sentence, so I do it for her.

"To have your pussy played with in public at an amusement park."

"Aiden." The shock is evident in her voice. I'm not sure why there's shock since it's what she wants.

"What?" I shrug. "If you want me to play with your pussy up here, where anyone can see, I'm going to need you to say the words."

"Fine," Cassidy huffs out. She then rolls her eyes at me. "Aiden Slate, will you make all my fantasies come true and play with my..." Her hand reaches up and covers her face. "Play with my pussy."

"Your wish is my command."

With that, I lean forward, placing my mouth on hers and kissing her senseless.

Since we're stuck at the very top of the Ferris wheel, we should have a bit of time before anyone can see us, but I don't want to risk it, so as I deepen the kiss, I place my hand on the exposed flesh of her thigh, trailing my finger under the hem of her shorts until I'm able to push the cotton that covers her pussy aside.

A shudder runs through her at my touch. Her hips lift to urge me to move.

I do.

Swirling my finger over her clit.

A sexy moan escapes her mouth at the contact, but I don't worry about being caught. The music playing covers her cries.

"Is this what you wanted?"

"Yes."

My fingers dip down to her opening.

Her lids flop down as I push one finger inside her.

"Can anyone see?" she whispers.

"Oh, now you care." I laugh as I start to pull my finger out.

She shakes her head back and forth, lifting her hips to thrust my finger back in.

"No one can see us," I tell her, and it's true. Despite the flashing lights of the ride, it's still too dark to see anything.

I pull my finger out, lifting it to my mouth to taste her, then I lower my hand back down and push inside her.

One finger.

"So wet for me. I bet you'd like it if I let you ride my cock up here."

At my words, she spreads her legs wider, giving me better access, and I take advantage of that, thrusting into her roughly.

I slam another finger inside her as I move my thumb to her clit, fucking her tight pussy while working her bundle of nerves at the same time.

Her sounds make my dick hard. My cock throbs in my pants, begging for release, but this is about her. Her fantasy.

"Open your eyes, Cass. Let me see you come."

Beautiful blue orbs meet mine, pupils dilated and desperate for release.

I pick up my pace, and her eyes roll back as her walls clench around me.

A tortured cry flies from her mouth as she comes.

"Good girl."

<hr>

The past few days have been a mess. After my date with Cass, practicing became extra grueling, which, in turn, brought extra stress to both of us.

I know why I'm stressed, but I'm not sure what's bothering her. I'm missing something. This just can't be because of me.

I know I'm a lot to handle, but this is something else.

A huge something at that.

Something she said days ago keeps playing out in my head. I try to push the thought away, but I can't.

Her words torture me.

Everyone has secrets…

What the hell is that supposed to mean?

I need to get my head in the game, because yesterday, my playing was certainly affected.

Yes, we won game one, but we lost game two, and I was definitely the weak link. Something that has never been associated with Aiden Slate.

Today, I have a minute to myself, not something that happens often, but I'll take it.

Cass is God knows where, doing God knows what.

Knowing her, she's at the market picking up my Sweet Tarts.

I smile to myself.

Even now, after everything, she's still always going out of her way for me. Taking care of me.

My smile drops from my face as my mind wanders back to those fears creeping in. I wonder what happened to her. Who hurt her?

Trying to distract myself, I set off to do some of my pre-game rituals. I need the comfort they provide me.

I've already cleaned, so now I need to watch the footage from my last game and analyze what I could have done better.

Everything.

That's what.

There's not one thing that could help me because I just sucked, plain and simple, and that's a hard pill to swallow. I let my team down.

Reaching into my pocket, I pull out my phone.

"Slate. What's going on?" Mike answers. "You all set for today?"

"Yes, but that's not why I'm calling."

"Okay," he says, and I hear him typing on the other end. "What's going on?"

"Your guy…"

"You're going to have to be a little more specific. Which guy?"

"The PI," I say. "I want to know what info he found when we looked into Pip."

Mike grunts. "There was nothing. She completely disappeared after she turned eighteen."

I groan, running my hand through my hair. "There's got to be more."

"What do you mean?" His voice is hard. Questioning.

"Forget it. I'll talk to you later. Also send me your guy's number," I say, hanging up.

We already exhausted that, and I need to organize my thoughts before I bring Mike or anyone else into it.

Or I just need to let it go.

I head over to the living room, sit on the couch, and cue up the footage to watch.

My knee shakes like it always does as I watch, but today the sound of the bouncing grates on my nerves like nails on a chalkboard.

I can't get my head in the game. Changing positions, I lean forward, placing my elbows on my thighs. Maybe I won't be annoyed by the sound in this position.

Unfortunately, it does nothing to sort my head.

All I want is to know what Cass is hiding.

What secrets can she possibly have?

A lot.

Knowing where she came from and the type of people she was surrounded by, I can only imagine the endless possibilities.

What I don't understand is why she's hiding things from me.

For years, I wasn't a part of her life. A million things could have happened during those years. Too many things.

And even though I did a background check on Cassidy Baker, I don't know if I missed something.

Except that's not true.

I did one on Pip…and that didn't find anything. Because in the time I knew Pip, I never even realized her real name wasn't Pip. Hence the issue Mike had locating her.

I was such a selfish prick during my senior year of high school when I met her that it didn't even dawn on me that Pippa wasn't her real name.

By the time I had the resources to look into Pippa, she was already eighteen and gone.

That's when I ran into a dead end, and I certainly wasn't going back to Michigan to find out from her dad.

The truth is, that would have been a dead end.

I know in my heart that she never would have told him where she was. Hell, I'm sure she changed her last name the moment she had the chance.

I look back at the TV, but the image of me skating down the ice isn't computing in my mind.

It's like I can't even see the screen.

My brain is too jumbled with horrible thoughts.

Pressing pause, I move to stand and do what I absolutely should not.

I head to Cassidy's room.

A voice in my head is telling me not to be a jackass. Not to snoop. She'll open up to me when she wants to. When she's ready. But the other part of me is desperate to know.

The room is completely spotless. Not a thing out of place. The bed is made and not a single personal item is left out on the dresser.

She hasn't slept in this room for weeks but still keeps her stuff in here. The fact that she respects me enough to ensure even her own space is kept spotless isn't lost on me. She's always caring for me.

I don't know what I'm doing in this room, but I can't stop myself from running my hands over the dresser. Not a speck of dust.

The next thing I know, I'm crossing the space and heading into her closet.

Pulling open the door, I look toward the clothes hanging. I stare at them, wondering if I can ascertain anything from them.

Who am I kidding? What the hell am I going to find from looking at her clothes?

It's all sweatpants and leggings. Nothing fancy to be seen aside from the clothes I bought her.

What does that prove?

Nothing.

It doesn't give me any glimpse into the life she led before me other than to tell me she lived a laid-back life before coming to stay with me. One she had no choice over. With limited funds, she was just barely making ends meet.

Despite knowing I should leave, I find myself sifting through her stuff.

It's wrong.

I know it is, but still my mind is set, and I can't fight the compulsion.

There's nothing to see until my eyes land on the suitcase sitting in the back of the closet.

I move toward the back and pull it out to set it in the middle of the closet floor. When I open the lid, it's empty. All the contents have been removed. Except… there's a zippered compartment I haven't checked, and something tells me there's something to be found.

Even if I wanted to, I can't stop myself. The sound of the zipper opening echoes through the small walk-in closet like a freight train. The chance of being caught speeds up my heart. My hands are moving before my brain can catch up to tell me to stop. To give her the privacy she wants.

Bingo.

Inside the zippered compartment is a manila envelope.

I flip the top open, knowing there's no going back. I've seen it, and now I can't turn away. It's calling to me. Begging me to open it.

Inside is a stack of letters.

I grab one and turn it over, inspecting every aspect of it.

It's addressed to me, but there's no physical address. It just says Aiden Slate.

I'm about to put it back until I realize it's not sealed.

Don't open it. Don't you dare do this!

My mind screams for me to stop. That I know better. It reminds me how betrayed I'd feel if she did something like this.

She lied to you.

Opening it up, I pull the paper out.

Aiden,
It's been one month, and it's official. I'm worried.
I never heard from you. I'm scared.

Placing the card back in the envelope, I pull out another one. This time, it's months later.

Aiden,
I can't believe you haven't reached out. Where are you? I haven't heard anything. Not one word. I was going to ask your mom, but when I got there, I chickened out. I wish I knew where you were so I could send this.

It feels like the oxygen is being depleted as I go, one by one, through them all. So far, it's as expected. The truth of the hurt I caused right there in writing. I grab another, and this one is different.

This letter has smudged black writing on the cover. It's as if someone's hands were wet and touched it.

I pull it out and read. My stomach drops when I see the words.

It's all your fault.

Everything. You promised you'd protect me. And you lied. You never came back. You forgot about me, and now I'll never be the same.

Fuck.

What happened to you, Pip?

chapter forty-six

Aiden

IT'S OFFICIAL. MY LIFE IS UNRAVELING.

The last game I played, I wasn't on my A game, but today, I just plain sucked. If I keep playing like this, it'll seal the deal that my career is over.

It's practically a joke, and I can tell by how my teammates look at me that they want to call me out.

Coach has given me some leeway after everything that's happened the last few weeks with my dirty laundry being aired, but even he looks pissed.

Best of seven.

I just keep repeating this to myself.

The loss hurts, but I can redeem myself.

The question is… how?

No matter how hard I try, I can't get Pip's letters out of my head, and I'm falling apart at the seams.

I keep thinking if I go back and read more, maybe I can find out what she's holding back, but there's been no opportunity.

Hell, I'm lucky I even read as many as I did.

No longer than a second after I put the letters away, I heard the front door to my apartment open. I dashed out of the room and met her in the kitchen, and thankfully, she was none the wiser.

The problem is her words written on that card hang over me like a black cloud.

I try to shake it, but I can't, and my game is off because of it.

She blames me…

But for what?

As I'm skating off the ice, my stomach feels like it's filled with rocks. Fuck that, heavy boulders are weighing me down.

"Slate," my coach yells as I make my way to the locker room. "What the fuck is going on with you?"

"What's going on with m—" My words cut off, and I shake my head. I'll get nowhere lashing out at Coach. "Listen—"

"No, you listen," he snaps. "I gave you the benefit of the doubt after the shit hit the fan that you'd be able to handle your personal bullshit because I feel for you. I can't even imagine what it's like to have to deal with a mom like yours, but this shit has to stop. You have to get it together. It's affecting your game, and in turn, it's affecting your team."

My jaw tightens. Nothing he says is wrong, but it still sucks to hear it. Mainly because it's not as simple as *handling my bullshit*. This is my life. One that's been nothing but a fucking travesty. Something he and most on my team will never understand. They didn't live the life I did. They had loving families handing them everything they needed, and I'm happy for them. I wouldn't wish my mom on my worst enemy.

"I don't care what you need to do, Slate. But do it. Get your head back in this game, or I'll have to make moves."

His words echo around me like a stampede, but they also give me clarity.

I won't be able to think, let alone play, if I don't get to the bottom of what happened all those years ago.

I need to speak with Cass, but how do I say anything without telling her I went through her stuff?

It's been a bumpy honeymoon period since we officially got together, and this won't help things. I'm in a precarious situation, unsure how to proceed.

I hate to rock the boat because ultimately, Coach is right. If I don't handle my shit, every other aspect of my life will come crashing down.

Heading into the locker room, I dunk my head in ice water, which helps clear my brain, and I resolve to see if I can get any more information from her.

I hardly remember completing my rituals. They were done in record time, and a little over an hour later, I'm home and in bed with Cassidy.

We've been lying here quietly for the past ten minutes. I haven't broached the topic because I've been trying to work out how to do it. I can't even think of what to say. There's no way for me to bring this up that won't allude to my snooping.

Finally, I can't take it anymore, and I break the silence. "How did you end up in Birmingham?"

She turns toward me, peering into the side of my head. My eyes are trained on the ceiling.

"Well, technically, I wasn't in Birmingham for very long. After I graduated, I ran as far as I could from my dad without leaving the state." She shifts onto her back, looking up at the ceiling with me. "I ended up in Detroit. Figured two hours was a safe distance from that man." She laughs, but it lacks humor.

I wonder what she's thinking at this moment. I want to ask, but she continues.

"After college, a friend I met in Detroit got a job at a hotel in Birmingham. She lived in an apartment a few blocks away. That's where I was staying before you."

My head turns to look at her.

"This same friend is how I ended up at your hotel room," she says, smiling at me.

"I still can't believe you stayed in Michigan," I say, remembering our conversations back in the day. We used to say how, when we could, we'd both go as far away as we could manage.

"Not all of us had the luxury of a hockey contract."

There's no trace of malice in her tone, and that settles me a bit.

"True, but if not for that contract, I would've chased a team in any other state," I say, recalling the part of me that needed to get as far away from Michigan as I could.

It was the one thing I really had hoped wouldn't be my lot. I wanted out. Wanted away.

I take a deep breath, hoping this isn't going in a bad direction. I need to refocus the conversation to when she was still living at home with her dad. "Do you ever speak to him?"

"Who?" she responds, sounding truly confused.

"Your father."

"No."

One word, full of so much emotion. Anger. Resolution.

My brow rises. "Not at all?"

"He moved after I graduated," she says, but I already knew this.

Hence why finding her was even harder. The man became a ghost. No records. No forwarding address. And like him, she also disappeared. Her name wasn't what I believed it to be all those years. Her dad, on the other hand, could be dead for all I know.

"Was it bad? Did he get worse?"

I know immediately that question is going to get me nowhere. Her shoulders stiffen and her face transforms into a stone fortress.

"Aiden." She leans up to look at me. "Let's not do this. I left that life behind for a reason. Please don't make me go back there."

Her voice is so soft but decisive, I know I won't get anything from her.

So I drop it, a new plan forming in my head. It's not a plan I necessarily want to enact, but if she's not going to give me the answers I need, I know someone who will.

———•◦•———

I'm up early and in my car. Two hours and forty minutes later, I'm pulling up to a place I had hoped I'd never go to again.

My mother's house.

I throw the car in park and start heading to the door, determination the only fuel pushing me forward.

"Aiden, is that you?"

I turn over my shoulder and see Mrs. Matthews waving at me from her makeshift porch. I'm shocked to see her. Mrs. Matthews was always so much older, and now, after all these years, she must be near ninety.

Apart from Pip, she was one of the only people who cared.

Before Pip arrived, Mrs. Matthews and her husband would make sure I was fed. Would give me shelter if I was kicked out of my house for whatever reason. Or even if I just needed an escape.

"I knew it was you. Henry!" she calls out to her husband. "Look who's here."

Henry, her husband, walks out of the trailer door and toward his wife. "Why if it isn't our famous hockey player."

My lips turn up into a smile.

They always helped me—always tried to, at least. I really should've thought more about them when I left.

Yet more people I deserted to chase my dreams and thrive, while they're here, struggling to make ends meet. The rickety stairs look like a death trap for Mrs. Matthews's frail form. How the hell does she even get down them?

Sadness sweeps through me. I have the means to help, and after everything they did for me, I should've a long time ago. I won't leave this town before making some visits to secure help for them.

"Hey, Mr. and Mrs. Matthews."

"Don't you dare use those formalities with us. Come over and give us hugs," she says, a bright smile spreading across her aged face.

I do just that, embracing the older couple who were better parents to me than my mom.

"What brings you here? Hopefully not to see that woman." Henry points at the trailer my mom owns.

"Unfortunately, that's exactly why I'm here. Need to ask her some questions."

"What's going on, anything I can help with?" Henry asks, likely trying to keep me from having to knock on that door.

"I had a question about Pippa. The girl who lived over there?"

Henry purses his lips before lifting a finger into the air. "Oh, yes. That little thing. Can't say I know what happened to her. One day, she up and left, and no one heard from her again." He narrows his eyes on me. "What's this about?"

I don't know what to say. I'm at a loss on what to even ask.

"What was she like after I left?" I start with, not knowing what to expect.

"We didn't see much of her," Henry says, but Mrs. Matthews shakes her head.

"For a time, we did. She used to play around outside. She loved that lake," Mrs. Matthews smiles sadly, and I wonder what that's about, but she continues. "You'd typically find her hanging out by your place, always staring at the street. As if she was waiting for someone."

Her words hit their mark, tearing at my heart. Pip was waiting for me.

That image is heartbreaking. It feels like daggers are driving through my chest.

"But after the incident…" Mr. Matthews says, and my head snaps to his.

"What incident?"

Mrs. Matthews is about to speak when I hear a door creaking open.

"You come to threaten me some more?"

My mother's shrill voice is like spiders crawling over my body. Shit.

I turn to look over my shoulder to find the cursed woman staring at me. Her hair is a disheveled mess. Probably a late night drinking. She looks like she's been up all night.

"I have to run," I tell the sweet couple, not wanting them to be involved in my drama with my mother.

No one needs to put up with her, least of all them.

"We're real proud of you," Mrs. Matthews says, and it means more to me than she can understand.

"I'll stop by to see you soon."

I shouldn't promise that because I won't. Once I leave here, I have no intentions of returning. But I will ensure to keep in touch with these two another way. I won't abandon them again.

Mrs. Matthews smiles. It's kind and full of pride. It's exactly what I need as I move toward the viper who birthed me. Reminding me that I made it out of here, made something of myself, and nothing this evil woman says can hurt me.

"What are you doing here? Your man already threatened me. I don't need you doing some more bullying."

I lift my hands. "I just want to talk."

"Talk." She grunts. "Since when do you want to talk? This has got to be important." Her lips spread into a sinister smile, and she taps her chin. "That will cost you." She places her shaky hands on her hips. "My time is valuable."

I reach into my wallet and pull out a twenty. She looks down at the bill, her face dropping.

"Is that a joke?"

"Well, *Mom*." I put so much sarcasm into that one word, hoping she recognizes it for the joke it is. "I'm sure someone else in the area would be more than happy to help me, and it won't cost me twenty dollars." I shrug. "Take it or leave it."

"This isn't enough to buy me—"

"I said take it or leave it." My words are harsh. An unspoken threat not to push me.

She goes quiet for a moment and then looks up. I can't place the expression, but if I had to guess, she's coming up with a plan. Not my problem, though. I'll be long gone before she can hurt me. And what more can she do? She already aired my dirty laundry. She doesn't have anything on me anymore, and a sense of relief comes with that. A lightness knowing that there is nothing more this woman can take from me unless I offer it.

"Fine. I'll take it. What do you want to know?"

I think over my thoughts, trying to figure out the best way to ask so it doesn't lead back to Pippa. I don't want to give her any incentive to dig up more dirt to come for us.

"I haven't been here for a while. I'd like to get caught up on where people are."

"Whose fault is that?" she spits. "I'm your mother, and you never come by."

"Cut the shit. Stop pretending you care whether I come around here. The only thing you care about is your next fix and how you're going to pay for it."

"Fine." She huffs. "What do you want to know?" she repeats, getting us back on track.

"I was just talking to the Matthews before you barged out. They said there was an incident here. What happened?"

She laughs haughtily. "Why don't you ask that girlfriend of yours? You know she's Pip, right?"

"How did you know that?"

"You left. I saw her grow up. Saw her after she changed her looks. If you had come back, you'd have known too."

I ignore the jab and continue my course.

"Why would she know? Was it with Pippa's dad?"

Her eyes narrow in on me, seeing right through my motives.

I guess someone like her would easily be able to wade through the bullshit to see down to the truth of things. When someone makes it their life's work to drag dirt up for money, they know the tells.

"Oh, I see. You don't want her to know you're snooping in on her life." She shakes her head, chuckling. "You trying to find out if he hurt her?" She smiles widely, her yellowed, rotting teeth exposed. "Well, that will cost you."

I throw down another twenty-dollar bill. Maybe that will loosen her lips. She narrows her eyes, readying to ask for more, but I shut her down. "That's all you're getting, so get on with it," I tell her through clenched teeth.

"Nope. He didn't. He might've ignored her, but he never hurt her."

"He didn't?" I shake my head, confused.

"Nope." She pops her p.

My hand lifts to my forehead while my other hand rests against my hip. "That doesn't make sense."

"He was harmless," she says, coughing into a fist. "At least from what I remember. Now the Sawyer boy, that's another story."

My head tilts to the side. "The Sawyer boy?"

She nods. "Think his first name was Ace."

At that name, my back goes ramrod straight. I remember him. The first day I met Pip, Ace had gotten in her face. He had threatened her and me as well.

"What does he have to do with her?"

She snickers. "A whole lot, I'd say."

"I don't understand."

"You wouldn't now, would you? You weren't even here," she chides. "You left that poor girl all alone."

Something about those words feels heavy. Ominous.

"Why don't you save us both the time and get to the point," I bite the words out.

"Not sure what it was about that girl, but she always had the older boys following her. First you…"

"You know it wasn't like that with Pip," I snap, unable to keep the anger at bay.

Her unspoken insinuations piss me off. I would've never touched Pip. Not back then.

"Do I? 'Cause the way I see it, you're dating her now."

"It was never like that back then. She was just a little girl."

"If you say so," she says. "But that Sawyer boy didn't look at her like that. Didn't touch her like that either."

My fists clench in my lap. My entire body goes taut.

If he laid a hand on her, I'm going to kill him.

"Where can I find Ace? Does he still live in the trailer?"

She shakes her head. "Hasn't lived here for eight years... give or take."

"So where is he?" I ask, growing tired of her games. Because that's what this is. Give a little, make you beg for more.

"Same place he's always been..."

This woman. She's going to make me work for it. "Spit it out."

"The cemetery."

chapter forty-seven

Cassidy

"EMMA," I CHEER, AS I OPEN THE DOOR TO FIND MY FRIEND ON the other side.

"You gonna let me in or…" She smirks, and I move aside to let her pass.

Aiden said he would be gone and to make myself at home. Being as though it's been too long, I called up Emma and made arrangements for her to come see me. I'm just glad it worked out, and she could slip away for the day.

She pulls me into a hug. "It's so good to see you, Cassidy." She steps back, taking in the place with a whistle. "This is…nice."

I chuckle. "It's perfect. Not too ostentatious. It suits Aiden," I say, glancing around the space that's all him.

She narrows her eyes at me. "Something's changed. You have this whole gooey look to you." She motions toward me. "Are you in love, Cassidy?"

She has a pinched expression, but the way her eyes twinkle tells me she's messing with me. She doesn't find the idea of love to be disgusting, which I know already. Emma is a sap. She loves a good rom-com and has her wedding planned for one day when she finds Prince Charming.

"Things have shifted a bit for Aiden and me."

Emma purses her lips and walks toward a seat, patting the cushion next to her. "Care to explain?"

I do.

I tell her everything, spilling my guts about every last piece she wasn't clued in on.

From the lie about dating him to help with his rituals, and all of that coming to light, to our past and how I knew him before.

"Wow. So...this is like soulmate shit?"

I roll my eyes. "Hardly. We were kids back then. I might've looked at him like he hung the moon, but to him, I was a little kid. Someone who tagged along, and he allowed it to protect me."

"It's so romantic," she croons, and I snort.

"The process of getting there was anything but," I admit. "It's not been easy. He didn't know who I was. I lied to him and that's been hard."

"Sounds like he's forgiven you." She shrugs. "I wouldn't beat myself up over it. Allow him in, Cass. Whatever is going on, it looks good on you. You're literally glowing."

I smile at my friend.

"I'm in love with him," I admit, cheeks heating.

She rolls her eyes. "Obviously. Took you long enough to admit it, though."

I laugh, and she joins me. This feels good. Well overdue.

"What about you? What's been going on in your life?"

She waves a hand. "Nothing this hot. I'm still working at the hotel, but I took another job on weekends at an upscale lounge, bartending. It's something to do, and I make great money."

"That's fun. I'm surprised you'd want to put more on your plate."

She snorts. "This is a lot more play than it is work," she explains.

"The people I meet…" She whistles. "Let's just say, the opportunities that have already been presented to me have been great. I really think I'll be moving up the ranks of hospitality management soon."

"That's great," I say, so happy for my friend. "Sounds like the perfect place to network."

"Don't you know it." She waggles her brows. "So many wealthy men." She sits back on the couch, head tilting toward the ceiling. "So little time."

I chuckle. "Any love interests I'm unaware of with these wealthy men?"

She snorts. "I'm playing the field. Too many options, not enough nights."

That's my girl, always keeping her cards close to her. But I can tell by the way her cheeks turn just a bit pink that maybe there is someone she's interested in. Someone she's not ready to tell me about yet. The girl is superstitious. She likely doesn't want to ruin it before it gets off the ground by spilling her guts.

I won't press. If she wants to talk about it, she will.

"What do you want to do today?" I ask, and she inhales, looking around.

"I'm good with just hanging out. Maybe order in some food? Watch a movie?" She yawns, falling back against the couch. "I worked last night, and I'm actually a bit wiped out."

"I think I have an idea," I say, grabbing my phone and pulling up the number that I saved after getting ready for the gala.

I shoot a quick text, and within ten minutes, we're booked for facials and massages.

"How about a spa day, and we can grab dinner before you head out?"

She grins. "That sounds divine."

"You're in for a treat. This place is magical. You want relaxation, you're gonna get it."

She smiles. "I've missed you."

"Same, Em. Same."

I had the best day yesterday with Emma. I have no clue where Aiden ran off to, but it was fine. A much-needed day with my friend. Now that Aiden and I are dating for real, I feel more comfortable speaking with my friend. I felt like I was lying before, but now Emma knows everything. And since the truth isn't a distant thought, I can speak freely, candidly.

I can talk about Aiden without worrying that I'll leak his story. Everything is out in the open, and it feels good.

Well, maybe not everything, but a lot.

I'll take the win.

I have someone to confide in when things get tough. And they will because that's what relationships are. Hard work. But so worth it.

Tonight, we have a game, and Aiden is off getting ready. I'm just trying to make his life easier by doing the things I did before.

Money may no longer be exchanged, but I still want to help him as much as I can. It was never about the money, anyway.

I have his game day gear on his bed, ready for him to put on before he heads to the arena. The house is clean. Maybe not to his liking, but it will be easier for him to finish it if I've already made an attempt.

I now know that Aiden never really hired me to do these things for him. He hired me because he just wanted me around, so that's what I'll keep doing. Spending time with him and calming him the best I know how.

I have his candy in hand to sort for him. He was out, so I had to go grab it. I'm outside, returning home, when I see that damn man.

The stalker reporter.

"Don't you have anything better to do than harass Aiden?"

He taps his finger to the side of his leg, looking far too haughty for a predator that's been caught snooping once more.

"I'm not here for him," he says, catching me off guard.

There's something so sleazy, so gross about this guy.

"Oh yeah?" I place my hands on my hips. "Then who are you here for? Some other famous athlete lives in the building that I don't know about?"

A leering smile spreads across his face. "I'm here for you, Pippa."

The bag in my hand drops to the ground, and I scramble to pick it up. My hands shake by my side.

How does he know?

"By your reaction, I can tell that Slate's mom wasn't lying. You and Aiden share a past."

"That's none of your business," I snap back. Probably a dumb move because it makes it more obvious that he's struck a nerve.

If I ever get my hands on that woman, I'll end her myself.

"But here's where things get interesting," he says, sounding far too excited for my liking. "I got a phone call from her. Seems your boyfriend paid her a visit yesterday."

My blood runs cold, and my hands shake even more.

He was there.

He went back to that awful place.

"First time in ten years. Now if that doesn't send off red flags, I don't know what does." He taps his chin, but I can hardly concentrate on him.

My mind whirls with all the horrible possibilities of what he uncovered there. What does he know? Will he hate me for it?

"Here's the thing, he wasn't there to deal with his mom. Actually, he was more concerned about you. Your past and if someone hurt you."

My stomach dives, and bile rises up my throat.

"Interesting," he says. "Seems the color has leached from your face, Pippa. Now why would that be?"

"What do you want?" The question comes out in barely a whisper. A dead giveaway that he's onto something big.

"After Aiden went live with his story, I realized there was much more to the player than met the eye. I'll admit, I was wrong about him. He doesn't deserve to be dragged through the mud like I originally planned."

"You're disgusting," I spit the words. "You get off on hurting innocent people. Don't act like you don't."

He shakes his head. "Not true. But…you're not innocent. Are you, Pippa?"

"Stop calling me that," I snap. "It's not my name."

He shrugs. "The thing is, he's not the story anymore. I think what people will want to hear about involves you. The woman he's with. *Her* secrets?" He puckers his lips and tilts his head.

I've never wanted to punch someone in the face more than I do him at this moment.

"The sad part is, he will have to bear the consequences of this story."

I take a step back. "Are you threatening me?"

"Threaten? No. Being real with you? Yes." He moves forward, trying to get under my skin, but I move back. "For Aiden to break a ten-year streak of avoiding that awful woman, there's a story there. I'm telling you now that if I uncover anything, I'll have no choice but to run with it."

"Of course you will. You're moonlighting as a journalist, but you're a scum just like the paparazzi."

His face turns hard. "I am a journalist, and I'll be renowned one of these days."

"So what is this? Your pre-award gloating? Get over yourself, man. You're a subpar snoop who only sees what he wants to see."

He huffs out a humorless laugh, and I know I'm poking the bear. This man's ego knows no bounds, and I'm striking a nerve. Probably not the smartest move.

"This is a warning. If you have anything to hide, anything that will hurt him, the only way to save him from the fallout…"

"Is to leave."

He nods, and for the first time, he doesn't appear cocky or even happy about what he's doing to me.

"You seem like a good girl. Like someone who truly cares for him. If you're hiding something, do you really want to take him down with you?"

With that, he turns and walks off, leaving me alone with my thoughts.

My stomach turns, and I know I'm going to be sick.

I don't even know how I make it up the elevator, but I fall to my knees at the base of the toilet, emptying my stomach contents into the porcelain ring.

Despite my hatred for that damn reporter, he's right. It's only a matter of time before the press catches on. It's only a matter of time before someone finds out what I did. Hell, Aiden might already know.

The question is…what am I going to do to save Aiden from the fallout?

chapter forty-eight

Aiden

SOMETHING IS OFF. I CAN'T PUT MY FINGER ON IT, BUT I CAN tell.

Cassidy has been acting strange. Different.

I shake off the thought and head toward the ice, knowing I can't be distracted tonight.

This game is important.

Coach is trusting me to have my shit together, and I can't let him down. Fuck. I can't let my team down. This is our shot at the Cup. We haven't been this close in years, and I won't be the reason we lose that opportunity.

I kiss my helmet once, like I always do, place it on my head, and once I'm mentally ready, I step onto the ice, kicking off my back skate and heading toward the center of the rink.

The game begins like every other, except the pace is next level from the start. Both teams vying for our spots to play for the Cup.

An hour later, my face burns from a fight that broke out, but it was worth it just to wipe the smug-ass smile off the dickhead's face. These guys are so arrogant. They act like the Stanley is theirs, and they're down. Typical.

The fucker commented on my press conference. Brought up my rituals. Made it sound like something is wrong with me. There's nothing wrong. And I have nothing to prove.

I don't give a fuck what the asshole said, but sometimes it's good to get the juices flowing with a good old-fashioned fight.

It's the beginning of the third period, and the game is closer than I want it to be. Coach is going ballistic, throwing shit and cursing like a sailor. If we lose this, someone might pay with their position.

We're in the lead and we need to hold on.

My compulsive nature wants me to look up into the stands where Cass sits, but I refuse. With the way she was acting today, it could unravel all my progress.

It's not even a second later, when, despite my best attempts, I find myself looking in her direction. Cassidy was right; I need to work through some of these compulsions after the season is over. I'm going to throw myself into trying to find coping mechanisms to help me.

She's beautiful like always, but there's something about her pinched expression that I can see even from here. She's looking at her cell, and she doesn't appear happy.

Her cheeks look sucked in from this angle, but I'm not close enough to be sure. What is she thinking about? What's going on?

Fuck. I shouldn't have looked up. I shake my head, blow out a breath, and focus all of my attention back on the game.

I can't afford to get inside my head. Not now. Too much is at stake.

We just have to hold on to this lead. I skate like my life depends on it, helping to defend. To steal the puck at every opportunity. I have sweat pouring down my back and across my brows. My legs burn and my arms ache, but I won't back down.

The other team has a breakaway, and I pound the ice with

my skates, determined to stop him from scoring. He shoots, but Mason stops it.

Finally, the horn rings, and my body damn near collapses. But to hell with that, we need to celebrate.

We fucking won.

Hudson and Dane skate toward me. The excitement on their faces is priceless. Dane is usually not as visually affected by stuff like this. Not like Hudson, who is more animated. So to see Dane like this makes me realize what a moment this is.

This game was huge.

We are heading into the fifth game. It's not over, but for tonight, we can add one more win to our belt. We're one step closer.

After everyone leaves the ice, I skate off too, then head to the locker room and then to find Cassidy.

She's in the hall waiting for me.

"Congratulations." She gives me a small smile, but her arms are crossed over her chest, and the tightness of her jaw isn't lost on me.

Something is up with her. *She must know.* For now, I won't say anything, but when we get back to my place, I will.

She's quiet the whole walk to the car.

Not one word. And everything feels wrong, almost like a catastrophic event is about to happen.

When we step into the apartment, things haven't gotten better.

It's not until we walk into the bedroom that I finally reach my hand out and stop her from walking into the bathroom.

"What's going on with you?"

"What's going on with me?" she fires back.

"All day you've been acting like something is bothering you. Why don't you just spit it out?"

"Really? You're going to throw attitude at me?" She throws her hands up in the air.

"Yeah. I am. You knew how important this game was."

She narrows her eyes. "And you won."

"Barely."

"What do you want me to say?" She pops her hip out, placing a fist to rest there.

"Just tell me what's going on with you."

She takes a deep breath. "I just don't know—"

Now, it's my turn to narrow my eyes. "Don't know what?"

I take a step toward her, and she holds her ground.

"I don't know if we can be together."

My head jerks back as though she's slapped me. "What the fuck is this bullshit?"

"I just feel like—I just feel like…"

She's breathing heavily, and her fingers twist together in her shirt.

She looks tormented, broken, and something inside me cracks open. I can't stand to see her this way. I don't want to push her over the edge because she looks moments from truly unraveling.

I take a step forward and grab her hand in mine. "Feel like what, Cass?"

Her head lowers, and she whispers, "I'm not a good person."

I place my finger under her chin and lift her head so that she's looking into my eyes.

"That's the biggest pile of bullshit I have ever heard."

Her lips might be set into a thin line, but I don't miss the way her chin trembles. "And true nonetheless."

"Stop this. You're the best person I have ever met."

She laughs, but it lacks all humor. "Yet you barely know me."

I drop my hand and take a step back, eyes never leaving her. "And whose fault is that?"

"Yours…you left." Her voice holds no emotion. It's like she's forcing the words out. They're weak and meaningless.

Why is she doing this?

"I said I'm sorry about that. But now we're together, and you can talk to me, Cass. Tell me what's going on in your head."

"Maybe the time for the truth is too late."

I grab my hair with both hands and pull, growing more agitated by the minute.

"Just talk to me," I practically beg. I'm not sure where this is coming from. She obviously doesn't know I went to Michigan, or she would have said something. So what the hell is going on?

I'm about to come clean, tell her I went snooping in her shit. Screw the consequences.

But I never get to because she throws herself at me. Kissing me fiercely.

Something is different about this kiss. It feels desperate.

It feels final.

But as her tongue swipes inside my mouth, all questions and rational thoughts are gone. My brain has left the building, and the only thing I can think about is being inside her.

With my free hand, I pull my zipper down and free my cock. I barely have time to kick off my pants before she's practically crawling up my body, trying to get closer. Once I'm free of my pants, I grab her leggings, and pull them off her body, taking her thong with it, until she's bare to me. I push her back onto the bed, her legs hanging off the side as I pull her thighs apart and step between them.

"Move back," I command, and she obeys.

I crawl up to join her. She lifts her bottom, opening herself further.

I grab my dick and stroke myself from root to tip, lining myself up with her pussy. I grab her legs, and with one thrust, I sink inside.

God-fucking-damn.

Heaven.

She always feels like heaven wrapped around me. Her tight walls grip me so tight I can only groan out a sound as I fuck her with abandon.

I watch as I slam into her, loving the sight of us joining together.

Loving the view of my dick sliding inside her, disappearing in her heat.

But my favorite sight is when I pull myself out to the crown and her juices cling to my skin, dripping with her desire. There's something so erotic...so intoxicating about that.

I pull out. "Turn around," I demand. "On your knees."

She moves quickly, getting into position.

I slam back in, hand on her ass as I move. She meets me thrust for thrust, my balls slapping against her skin. She moans my name, which only makes me more feral. I'm fucking her like my life depends on it. Chasing our orgasms.

My balls tighten with my impending release.

Reaching down, I place my thumb on her clit and rub her ferociously until her body quivers and quakes.

"I'm coming," she moans, and at her words, electricity shoots down my spine as my own orgasm erupts.

My lids open, and for a moment, I'm confused.

I don't even remember falling asleep. The last thing I remember is collapsing on top of Cassidy.

Lifting my hand up, I rub my eyes, and once I do, the world around me falls back into place.

Today, the team and I fly to New York. Game five is tomorrow.

Looking over at the clock, I notice that, yet again, I've not only overslept, but didn't even set my alarm.

All things that never happened before Cassidy walked back into my life.

My lips part into a smile.

Having her around might not have fixed everything, but at least when she's here, she calms me enough to make me believe with the right help, I can get things under control. I can learn how not to let my compulsions run the show anymore.

Speaking of Cass, I turn to where she typically sleeps beside me and notice the space is empty.

"Cass?" I holler loudly so she can hear me if she's in the kitchen.

Silence.

Not a peep.

Throwing off the covers, I stand from the bed. Quickly, I head to the closet, and throw on a clean pair of gray sweats and head to look for her.

Every room in the apartment is empty.

I begin to panic. Where is she?

My mind is reeling, replaying last night. Remembering the kiss that felt like a goodbye.

How the fuck did I fall asleep? Why didn't I ensure she was all right?

I slam my fists against the counter, needing to rage. To scream. Anything to get these bottled-up emotions loose. But I don't.

I head into the room she used to stay in.

The door is open, and the room is eerily quiet. The second thing I notice is there is not one thread of Cassidy in the room. Nothing. Even from where I'm standing, the closet door is open, and I don't find anything but the clothes I bought her. None of the things she brought with her are in view.

I march to the closet, and my vision swims when I find that her suitcase is gone.

Cassidy is gone.

I'm about to tear this place apart. Call the police. Anything to find her when I see a piece of paper folded on the desk.

Heading across the space, I grab the paper and open it up.

It's her handwriting, and that's when I see it's a letter for me.

My throat feels like I swallowed shards of glass as I read the words in front of me. She's left me. My fists clench, but I keep reading, and what I see next has the note slipping from my grasp.

chapter forty-nine

Aiden

THE PUCK DROPS, AND I PUSH FORWARD, MY SKATES CUTTING into the ice, but it's not enough.

I'm too slow today.

My head is not in the game. *Again.*

We lost game five.

And now it's not looking good for game six.

The center for the Empires darts forward; his stick hits the puck, and then he's off, and I'm left with my dick in my hand.

His lightning-fast reflexes are a sharp contrast to my muddled-down response time.

I try to push away the thoughts wreaking havoc in my brain, but as much as I try, they push their way forward, blinding me to the world around me.

I'm lost in her words.

They replay in my brain over and over.

I can only see them.

Only hear them.

It feels like I'm choking on every single letter.

Aiden,

You were my only safe place. You were my home, and when you left, you took that with you. I don't write this to make you feel bad. I know you regret the past, but unfortunately, the past has a way of resurfacing.

I know you went back there. I know you asked questions. I should say that I'm sorry for coming back to you, but I'm not. Having one more minute with you was worth it. Even if I have to lose you to keep you safe. But as long as you're with me, you're not. I lied to you when I said I wasn't hiding something. I lied to you every time I didn't speak my truths.

I can't lie to you anymore. I did something. Something that eats away at me. I can't have that hurting you.

I killed someone. His blood is on my hands.

The longer you stay with me, the more danger I bring to you. It's only a matter of time before my drama hits you. I'm sorry. I love you. But to save you, to protect you, I need to leave. I can't be responsible for ruining your dream.

I love you now and always.

—Your Pip

"Slate! What the fuck, man," Dane screams, and I shake my head, pulling myself away from the memory.

I push forward, charging toward the puck. But I'm too late. Maverick, the Empires center, is pulling back and shooting. Mason tries to defend the goal, but the puck pushes past him.

As the game continues, I try to rally. Skating with determination, I relentlessly pursue the puck, but it's no use. No matter what I do, I can't move forward. I need to get to the bottom of Cassidy's words. For the first time in my life, something is more important than hockey.

Now back at the airport, ready to head home, I step away from my teammates and grab my phone. I dial the number for Tony, the private investigator Mike had given me.

"Slate. Tough loss, but going into game seven on a tie is more fun. I know—"

I don't hire him to make small talk. "No time for that. I need you for a job."

"I'm listening," he drawls.

"I need you to look into the death of Ace Sawyer. He died around eight or nine years ago."

At some point, I put together a theory. My mother said Ace was dead. That he had touched Pip differently. She said she killed someone. What are the chances that it was Ace?

"Location?"

I sigh. I wish I had more to go on, but I don't, so I give him the only information I have. "That I'm not sure, but he's from East Sanford, Michigan."

"Okay, on it," he says, but I'm not finished with my request.

"I want to know everything. Every detail. I want the coroner's report. You hear me?"

"Loud and clear."

I hang up the phone and head back to where everyone is.

"You okay, man?" It's Hudson who speaks first. He's always the first to get into everyone's business.

"I'm fine," I snap.

He whistles. "Yeah…well…you don't look fine. Spill."

"Give the man a break. He'll talk when he's ready," Dane cuts in.

Not surprising too. Dane is almost as closed off with his life as I am. The only reason I know anything about him, despite him being one of my closest friends, is because of his sister. Molly's the one who lets bits and pieces of his life slip out in conversation. If it were up to Dane, he wouldn't let anyone in. He's harder to crack than Fort Knox.

"What he said," I grunt out even though I'll never be ready. Because whatever I find out isn't my story to tell.

Two hours later, we're landing in Redville.

I didn't utter a single word the entire flight, lost in thoughts of Cassidy and the letter.

It torments me.

I power up my phone and see I have a message from the PI. He's sent me all the info I requested on an encrypted email website. All I have to do is sign in and read what he's sent.

I rush to my car, needing the privacy to go over everything. I don't bother turning it on. Nothing is more important than what's in this file. I need to know now.

It takes me thirty minutes in a parked car to go through everything. To be honest, I feel lighter. Freer somehow. Now I need to find Cass, because we need to talk.

This folder changes nothing.

Cass and I are inevitable.

I can't live without her, and now I need to make her see that.

chapter fifty

Cassidy

'M NOT PREPARED FOR THE BANGING ON THE DOOR. IT'S TOO late or actually too early for anyone to be here.

"Cass, I know you're there."

Aiden.

He's here.

But shouldn't he be back home in Ohio?

The team would have flown back right after the game in New York. But instead, he's found me. He's standing outside Emma's door.

"What the hell is going on?" A very sleepy Emma says as she takes a step into the living room. "It's—what time is it?" She scrubs at her eyes.

I look over at my phone and see it's five in the morning. "Five."

"Fuck," Emma groans. "Are you gonna get that?"

Another knock pounds on the door. "Come on, Cass, please."

"God, he sounds like a sad little dog," Emma says as she continues to rub the sleep from her eyes.

I feel awful that my drama is waking her. "I'm so sorry, Emma."

"Don't be sorry. Just let him in." Emma crosses the space and flings the door open.

The moment Aiden steps inside, it feels like all the oxygen from the room is depleted. "Sorry, I just need to speak to her."

"I get it. And you do. Just give me a minute, and I'll be out of your hair."

"Em…" She looks at me, our eyes locking. "You don't need to leave."

"It's fine. I'll go grab a coffee and then head to the six o'clock hot yoga class." She shrugs. "I've been meaning to try it."

"You're the best, you know?" I tell her.

She smiles. "I do."

Emma heads back into the bedroom to change and a moment later is dashing out the front door.

I turn my attention back to Aiden, who looks very disheveled and obviously exhausted.

He paces the little living room like a caged lion.

"You're sleeping on her couch," he grinds out through clenched teeth.

"I needed a place to stay," I say, not looking him in the eyes.

"And you couldn't take a minute to see that you have a place in my guest room? With a bed."

"No." I shake my head. "I needed to leave."

"You needed to run away, is what you needed."

I lift my brow. "You would know."

His jaw locks. "Oh, so we're back there? I thought we moved past this?"

"We did, but I just needed…"

"Enough," he practically growls. "I don't want to hear another excuse." He levels me with a stare that has my legs quaking underneath me. I hurt him, and my heart squeezes in my chest painfully. "You broke up with me via a Post-it."

I slam my lips together. "It was a letter."

"Semantics."

Aiden runs his fingers through his hair, pulling at the roots. "Just tell me why. Why now? All the shit you're holding inside, you could've told me. Why end it that way? Why not be honest with me?"

I let out a long-drawn-out sigh. "The journalist approached me. Your mom ran right to him after you left her place. He knew there was a story—and warned me."

Aiden's features harden, and I'm afraid that if that man showed up right now, there'd be another death on our hands. I don't want that. Don't need Aiden fighting my battles.

"I realized right then and there that if you stayed with me, my past…my secrets, they could hurt you. I was trying to save you."

"Again, with you putting yourself last." He throws his hands up into the air, frustration oozing from him. "How many times do I have to tell you I don't need you to save me? I should be the one saving you."

I incline my head, as if to say I'll always save you. Love is protecting. Love is putting someone else first. He closes his eyes at the gesture, obviously understanding the meaning of what I'm implying.

"I read your letter," he says.

"So you know why I left."

"I know why you think you left but—"

"You don't know anything." My fingers grip the hem of my shirt, twisting the material.

"So then tell me what happened, Cass. Enough secrets. If you're going to end things, don't you owe me that much? I want to hear the real reason you think you need to protect me."

I close my eyes. He's right. I do. I need to trust him. With my lids slammed shut, I finally talk.

"I still remember the day as if it was yesterday. I remember walking along the path, heading to your tree." I take a deep breath, thinking about that spot. Focusing on the good of that place before diving into the nightmare it became. "I used to go there every day after you left. I'm not sure what I was hoping for. I knew you were gone, and by that point, I knew you weren't coming back. Almost two years had passed by."

"I'm sorry—"

I shake my head. "Don't. Not now. Let me get this out, or I'll never be able to," I respond, opening my eyes but still not looking at him.

If I see him, I might not be able to say these words. Instead, I stand and start to pace, walking around the room, concentrating on the floor.

"It's funny how you can remember something so vividly, even years later. I can still hear the sound of my footsteps on the wet grass. The snow had finally melted, and with each step I took, I could hear the sloshing sound of my feet hitting the puddles. It echoed in the silence of the late afternoon."

Stopping my pacing, I shut my eyes again and take another deep breath in, as my body shudders with the memories that come flooding back. "The sun was starting to set. Only small rays of sunlight pushed through the branches that towered above me. I shouldn't have been walking alone. But in my mind, it wasn't dark yet, and I missed you. I needed to be somewhere that I felt close to you." I open my eyes at that and see Aiden staring at me. His large blue eyes watching me intently. Waiting.

"When I got to the opening by the lake, I didn't see him at first. He must have been off behind a tree." I shake my head.

"I don't know how I didn't see him. Maybe I was lost in my own thoughts, but by the time I was standing beside the water, he was there. Right behind me."

"Ace?" Aiden's voice is thick with emotion when he says his name.

A name I've avoided for years.

"Yeah. I took a step away from him, closer to the lake, and I remember thinking my shoes might get wet. I should have run.

But—the closer he got to me." I shake my head. "I don't know. I guess I just froze. Fear will do that, I guess."

"Fear?" Aiden's voice is hard, with an edge of something I can't quite place.

It borders on menacing.

"His treatment of me might have temporarily stopped when you were there to protect me, but it didn't take long after you left for him to start up again. Only this time, it was worse. Much worse."

"What did he do to you?" Aiden's eyes narrow, and I can see the hate there. The blind rage building with the mention of how bad things were.

I have no doubt that if Ace were alive today, it wouldn't be me who ended his life.

I close my eyes again. It's too much, and when I do, I see it all playing out in front of me. My mouth opens, and words fly out, but in my mind, I'm there…

"Look who's here…all alone," Ace says, making his approach.

"Leave me alone."

"Why would I do that? Now I have you right where I want you. Alone. No one around. I couldn't have planned it better myself." I turn to see him steepling his fingers, looking like a cartoon villain. Except he's no cartoon. He's real, and he's very dangerous.

"I'm going home."

He steps closer, his hand reaching out to hold my arm. "I don't think so."

"What do you want from me?" I snap, trying to stand as tall as possible.

"You can't be that naïve. You know what I want. I want to make you bleed." His words make everything inside me start to shake. Bile rises up my throat. "Can't wait to feel that virgin blood all over my c—"

"Leave me alone!" I say again. This time, my voice cracks as I scream.

"How about this? If you don't fight, I'll take it easy on you. I'll even try not to hurt you. That bad."

His grip tightens, and I fear I'll pass out.

As he holds me steady with his one hand, the other hand fishes in his pocket. He pulls something out. I don't look at him, though. Instead, I search for an exit route. The best way is to cut through the trees and back to the trailer so he won't catch me. I hear a loud sniffling sound and then his hand holding me tightens to the point of pain.

Fear surges through my veins as I struggle to break free from his grasp. It's now or never, as his grip becomes excruciating. I use all of my body weight to pull away. It feels like my encased arm will fall off as his fingers become more rigid, but I pull with all my might, my arm coming dislodged from his death grip, but the momentum I've built up has me falling headfirst toward the ground.

The moment I hit the ground, pain ricochets through my body. My head throbs, and I feel a sharp pain in my wrist.

It's hard to open my eyes, but when I do, they widen in terror. A sharp stick is stabbed into my arm, blood oozing around the wood.

Time seems to slow down as I try to move, and the wood pulls away from my skin. Blood gushes from the wound. The pain is unbearable.

A cry escapes my lips. I grab at my shirt with my good hand and pull it over my head, trying to break free so I can stop the bleeding.

In the midst of my pain, something dawns on me. Where's Ace? I need to run. He'll come for me.

My gaze pulls away from the blood, and I take a few deep breaths to calm my racing heart.

He's nowhere.

I can't see him.

I'm safe.

I take a deep breath and stand, willing myself to head toward help. Someone to take care of this wound.

When I'm fully standing and steady on my feet, I turn my body just slightly, and my breathing hitches.

Oh my God.

Ace is lying face down in the water.

Not moving.

"Ace," I yell. "Get up."

My heart beats rapidly in my chest as I watch him, waiting for him to get up. To move.

But he doesn't.

He never gets up.

As if the sky above can understand my pain, it opens up. Water pouring down from above. It runs over my body, washing away the remnants of blood that cling to the exposed skin of my arm not tied off by my shirt.

"I killed him, and then I ran home. Allowing the rain to wash away the evidence. It was as if I was never there. But it was still my fault," I sob.

He shakes his head, moving toward me like I'm a caged animal.

"It wasn't your fault."

With my head in my hands, I continue to cry. "You don't have to say that to make me feel better."

"You're not listening to me. It is not your fault."

I look up, finally peering at Aiden. "And you know this how?" I stand straight, not liking the way Aiden's staring at me like I might break. "Sorry, Aiden, you weren't there. I know what happened."

"Then you know that it was ruled a drug overdose."

"What?" I shake my head, eyes narrowing to mere slits. "No. He drowned."

Aiden's head shakes back and forth slowly. "He didn't drown."

"I was there. I saw it."

"Did you see him drowning? Or did you see him dead in the water?" he asks, and I raise a hand, palm up.

"What's the difference?"

"There's a big difference, Cass." He takes a large step toward me.

"I saw him in the water. I was bleeding. By the time I looked up, it was too late. But I pushed him."

"And you think you could have pushed a one-hundred-and-fifty-pound teen and kill him?"

"He drowned. Because of me."

He laughs, but he's not laughing at me. He's frustrated that I'm not on the same page as him. "How do you know that?"

My forehead furrows. "It's all anyone would talk about that day. After the police came for the body."

"But what about weeks later, Cass? When the autopsy came back?"

His question catches me off guard. "I don't understand."

"I don't imagine that you do." Aiden reaches for something in his back pocket and hands it to me.

"What is this?" I say as I open it.

"That's the forensic report, Cass. Ace didn't drown."

"What? Of course he did." My eyes scan the document, taking in each word.

"No. He didn't. When you were telling me the story, you said that while you were searching for an escape, you heard a sound, right? A long sniff."

"Yeah." I make a face, not following where he's going with this.

"Cass, Ace died of an overdose. Courtesy of coke with a hot shot of fentanyl."

"But—"

He shakes his head. "There are no buts. You didn't kill him. It is not your fault."

I blink several times, rereading the report. Right there in black and white, it says the cause of death was an overdose. Not drowning.

I swallow, looking up at Aiden. "I didn't kill him?"

"No, Pip, you didn't."

Another sob breaks through my lungs as tears cascade down

my face, but this time, they aren't sadness or guilt. Relief sweeps through me, and I crumple into a mass on Emma's couch.

The cushions depress next to me, and I know it's Aiden.

"Look at me, Cass. Please."

I peek up, hardly able to see him through the river of tears. "I'm such a mess."

He smiles down at me, pushing a piece of hair out of my face. "Yeah." He chuckles, and if I had the energy, I'd whip a pillow at his face. "But you're my mess. And I'm not letting you go."

I sit up, throwing my arms around him, sobbing into his shoulder.

The pain from my past mixes with the reality that I have a future. One that doesn't include being accused of murder.

"It's time to move forward, babe," Aiden says into my ear. "You and me."

"But…my drama. The reporter…"

"I'm not going anywhere. Not now. *Not ever*. It's us. It's always been us." He pulls away, lowering himself down so we're eye to eye. "I'll stand by your side until the end. No matter where the road takes us. Now and forever."

I swallow a lump in my throat. "Now and forever." I repeat his words, a small smile spreading across my face.

"I love you."

My entire heart swells at his words. I've questioned if he could feel the same way about me, and he's just admitted he does. All these years I've felt alone, like nobody could ever care for me. As though I didn't deserve love because of what I'd done.

The truth shall set you free, they say, and it sure the hell does.

I didn't kill Ace. It was a horrible accident. One that could've been prevented if he'd kept his hands off me and hadn't used drugs. I'm free from the binds that have held me in a place of fear all these years.

Aiden loves me, and that's all I'll ever need.

"I love you too."

epilogue

Cassidy

THE PAST THREE MONTHS HAVE BEEN CRAZY.

One of my proudest moments was watching the Saints win the Stanley Cup.

It was amazing to see Aiden shine along with his teammates. They've all worked so hard and to see that result in something so epic was incredible.

To stand by Aiden's side was truly one of the best moments of my life. I can imagine very few things that could top that.

The city went nuts.

There were parades and multiple celebrations in the team's honor. Aiden was presented MVP, an award that brought him to near tears. I wept like a baby.

Honestly, I've never seen anything like it. Truly a moment that will live in my brain and heart for the rest of my life. I've never been so proud of a single person.

As for the drama we had to deal with during the playoffs, that settled too.

The nosy reporter, well, we didn't have to worry about him for long.

When the Saints won the Cup, Billy, who had been transferred to a team in LA, turned back up running his mouth, which alerted the reporter to his scent.

Last we heard, the reporter got the big story he was after. Billy had been sexually harassing one of his new teammate's wife. Apparently, not much had changed. Instead of harassing me, he found another woman, but this time, it finally ruined him.

Now, as the dust has settled in our lives, we're heading back to where it all began.

Shortly after the team won their big game, Aiden's mom passed. It was an overdose.

I can't say I didn't anticipate that happening one day, but the timing was morbidly fitting. She got to watch her son shine, knowing she'd get nothing from it. All those years of her neglect and extortion are done. He gets to live the rest of his life in peace, knowing that he made the best decision of his life the day he walked away from her and that place.

I know that. Always have, but now, I have peace with it too.

Aiden's tried to act like he isn't affected by her death, but I know what it's like to lose the only parent you have. Despite how horrible she was, he needs closure.

My dad's not dead, but in a sense, he died a long time ago. Who knows where he is, or what he's up to? The truth is, I don't care. I know what it's like to be alone. I managed for a long time. I'm not alone anymore. I don't need my dad in my life. Not now, not ever. I made peace with that the day I left.

Aiden never did because his mom was like a cockroach, crawling out of the woodwork to cause problems for him at every turn. He needs closure.

Neither of us will ever be alone again.

We have each other.

And we also have Emma and the family Aiden has found with his teammates.

Found family.

People who love us despite our downfalls. People who support us without wanting a thing from either of us.

Together, with their help, we are healing the internal wounds we've been harboring all these years. Those wounds caused by the people who were supposed to love us. Support and protect us.

Both Aiden and I are in therapy. Not together, but we both want to be the best versions of ourselves. It's helping. Every day, I come to terms with my past.

Knowing I didn't kill Ace has helped, but I still have many demons I need to conquer.

So does Aiden.

The abuse we both endured won't kill us. Instead, we will harness it and grow from it.

"Almost there," he says from beside me. "You ready?"

I look out the window at the passing scenery. So familiar, yet different.

Changed.

Like me.

"I am."

It's not five minutes later, when Aiden's Jeep is pulling up to his old trailer and parking. I sit for a few minutes, working on my breathing. I need to gather all the strength to confront the place that has held so much power over me.

Aiden holds out his hand, and I place mine in his. He lifts it to his mouth and places a kiss on top.

"I've got you, Cass. You aren't alone."

I smile at him, nodding. "And neither are you."

We make our exit, walking around the car to grasp hands. It's support. Comfort. A pact that we do this together.

Turning toward my old trailer, I see a little girl sitting on the step. Her head is turned down, hands covering her eyes. A pang of sadness hits me in the chest. She reminds me of me a long time ago. When I would sit and wait, hoping Aiden would find his way home.

I want to go to her. To tell her everything will be okay. To help her find her strength. But then her head lifts and her hands drop. "Ready or not, here I come," she yells out, followed by a giggle.

She's happy.

Playing.

She's not me.

As she runs off, laughter bubbling through her mouth, my shoulders drop in relief. A smile spreads across my face. Pure joy is all I saw on that little girl's face, and it does something for me. Heals a part of the broken little girl who still lives within me.

"Where's your stuff?" Aiden asks, walking up to me with the urn he pulled from the back seat.

"Shoot. Let me grab it." I turn back toward the car, making my way to the door. I lean down and grab the small box that now holds my past.

Shutting the door behind me a little harder than necessary, I head toward Aiden, who's watching the kids, a smile on his face.

"Let's do this," I say, bumping his hip with mine.

Together, side by side, we walk to the lake. A place he once loved. A place that became my hell.

It looks different from when I was last here.

The trees are full of leaves. The sunlight gleams off the water. It's peaceful and serene.

It's not the stuff of nightmares. Me surrounded by gray as far as the eye can see. A dead body floating in the murky lake.

I see the lake through fresh eyes. It's beautiful.

My sight's no longer burdened by guilt and fear.

Aiden moves toward the lake, standing where the dirt and water meet. He's as close as he can be without getting wet, staring forward, lost in thought. I'm about to ask him what he's thinking when he speaks.

"I forgive you," he practically whispers into the air. To his mother. "I forgive you, and I'm ready to move on."

He removes the lid and tips the urn forward, pouring the contents into the water. "Be free, Mom. Let the things that plagued you here on earth go. I know I will now. Finally."

He puts the lid back on and steps away, glancing at me.

"My turn?"

"Your turn," Aiden agrees. He reaches into his pocket with his free hand and pulls out the lighter. "You sure you want to do this?"

"There are no good memories in these. Everything I need to remember is right here." I tap my head with my finger. "I'm ready to be free too." I smile up at him, his blue eyes softer than they have been for as long as I've known him.

He hands over the lighter, and I take it happily. With the cold metal in my hand, I pull out the letters I wrote Aiden one by one, setting each on fire. I watch them burn, and once the flame licks my fingertips, I drop the remaining remnants onto the ground, allowing them to continue to burn until they're ashes, ready to be swept off with the current.

A final resting place for the past.

Once the last one is gone. I take Aiden's free hand in mine, and we look out across the lake, happy to be free. To be together.

"I love you," I say to the side of Aiden's head as he continues to watch the horizon.

He turns toward me, and for the first time in my life, I see so much love shining back at me. So much adoration. I hope he can see it reflected in me.

"I love you too."

We both look out at the water once more. I take a deep breath, and with the exhale, I feel completely at peace.

"Now, let's go," Aiden says, grabbing my hand and pulling me back to the car. "We've got places to go."

I quirk a brow. "Oh, do we?"

He grins. "Always."

The shackles that have tethered me to this place are gone, and with that, I feel lighter. Happy.

Excited for the future.

Because my future is Aiden.

And I am his.

Fifteen minutes later, we're back in the car, the trailer long behind us, when Aiden pulls the car over in the middle of no-man's-land on the way back to Ohio.

I turn to face him, my brow raised.

"Is everything okay?"

"Yeah." A silly smile lights his face, and my eyes are wide, waiting for him to explain the sudden stop.

When he doesn't appear ready to spill, I ask, "So then…why did we stop?"

I stare at him, eyes narrowed in confusion and amusement. He leans forward, and I think he might kiss me, but then he pops open the glove compartment.

"What's going on?" I ask, as I hear him rummaging, but he doesn't answer.

This is so unlike Aiden. The suspense is killing me.

"Do we have a flat?"

He chuckles, shaking his head and pulling his hand out of the glove compartment, and my heart beats frantically in my chest.

"Pip."

He doesn't call me that often, but when he does, it no longer makes me sad. Instead, I feel safe and loved.

"From the moment I first saw you, I knew you were different. Back then, I saw you as my best friend. A kid who understood me and was there for me when nobody else was." His head drops on a small laugh. When he looks back up our eyes meet, his are shining bright. "Then you came storming into my life, a woman who set me on fire. Someone who made me feel safe. A woman who, when things got hard, I knew I never wanted to lose."

He takes a deep breath before continuing. "When I bought this jeep, it took me three whole months to find the symbol."

"You remembered that they had a symbol?"

He chuckles. "Of course I remembered. I got this car because of you, Pip."

"You did?" Tears well up in the corner of my eyes, and my lip trembles.

"Yep." His one word answer is enough to make my vision fog.

"What did you find?" I whisper.

"An apple. Do you know what an apple means?"

The first drop of wetness falls. "No."

"It means unconditional love." He places one hand on my cheek, wiping away the wetness, and I close my eyes, breathing in deep. "I want you to be my wife."

My lids flutter open and I meet his stare.

All I see is love.

He lifts the lid of the box, and a beautiful oval diamond sparkles up at me. "Now that we are both living in the present, with our pasts behind us, I just want to *live*…with you. Marry me, Pip."

I laugh, unable to stop the burst of emotion bubbling within. "It's not even a question. I'm head over heels in love with you, Aiden Slate." I throw myself forward, crashing my lips to his, but he cuts it off far too short.

"Cass…"

"Of course, I'll marry you."

"Pinky promise?" A grin spreads across his face, and I bite my lip, trying to contain the need I have that's building for this man.

"On your puck." I laugh, and with that, he places the ring on my finger.

A new beginning.

A promise.

An epic ending for two people who were always destined to make each other whole.

acknowledgements

I want to thank my entire family. I love you all so much.

Eric, Blake, and Lexi you are my heart.

Thank you to the amazing professionals that helped with Sweet Collide:

Jenny Sims

Robin Covington

Kelly Allenby

Laura Martínez

Champagne Book Design

Hang Le

Emily Wittig

Jill Glass

Suzi Vanderham

Literally Yours PR

Mikaela Brown

@books_jill_reads

Becca Hensley Mysoor

Thank you to Christian Fox, Angelina Rocca, Kim Gilmour and Lyric for bringing Sweet Collide to life on audio.

Thank you to my fabulous agent Kimberly Whalen.

Thank you to my AMAZING ARC TEAM! You guys rock!

Thank you Stephanie for test reading.

Melissa: Thanks for all your help and for keeping me sane.

Parker: Thanks for always being my sound board and helping me find the sprinkle.

Leigh: Thank you for reading and listening to me bitch.

To the people who would understand this MSUFFL: Thanks for annoying me with your endless texts…in the middle of the night.

To the ladies in the Ava Harrison Support Group, I couldn't have done this without your support!

Please consider joining my Facebook reader group Ava Harrison Support Group

Thank you to all the Booktokers, bookstagramers, and bloggers who helped spread the word. Thanks for your excitement and love of books!

Last but certainly not least...

Thank you to the readers!

Thank you so much for taking this journey with me.

Printed in Great Britain
by Amazon